PIPERS AT THE GATES OF DAWN

. .
.

OTHER BOOKS BY LYNN STEGNER

Undertow

Fata Morgana

Frank X. Gaspar, *Leaving Pico*

Ernest Hebert, *The Dogs of March*

Ernest Hebert, *Live Free or Die*

Ernest Hebert, *The Old American*

Sarah Orne Jewett (Sarah Way Sherman, ed.), *The Country of the Pointed Firs and Other Stories*

Lisa MacFarlane, ed., *This World Is Not Conclusion: Faith in Nineteenth-Century New England Fiction*

Anne Whitney Pierce, *Rain Line*

Kit Reed, *J. Eden*

Rowland E. Robinson (David Budbill, ed.), *Danvis Tales: Selected Stories*

Roxana Robinson, *Summer Light*

Rebecca Rule, *The Best Revenge: Short Stories*

R. D. Skillings, *Where the Time Goes*

Lynn Stegner, *Pipers at the Gates of Dawn: A Triptych*

Theodore Weesner, *Novemberfest*

W. D. Wetherell, *The Wisest Man in America*

Edith Wharton (Barbara A. White, ed.), *Wharton's New England: Seven Stories and* Ethan Frome

Thomas Williams, *The Hair of Harold Roux*

PIPERS
AT THE GATES OF DAWN

A Triptych

. .

Lynn Stegner

University Press of New England

HANOVER AND LONDON

Published by University Press of New England, Hanover, NH 03755

Printed in

5   4   3   2   1

LIBRARY OF CONGRESS CATALOGING-IN-PUBLICATION DATA

Stegner, Lynn.

Pipers at the gates of dawn / Lynn Stegner.

p.   cm. — (Hardscrabble books)

ISBN 1–58465–063–X (alk. paper) — ISBN 1–58465–064–8 (pbk. : alk.
paper)

1. Vermont—Social life and customs—Fiction. I. Title. II. Series.

PS3569.T33938 P56 2000

813'.54—dc21   00–009138

FOR ALLISON

CONTENTS

PIPERS AT THE GATES OF DAWN

. .
.

HIRED MAN

FROM THE VILLAGE ROAD the house could be seen, tall as the maples on either side, and white with a sharp peak at the east and a chimney on the west, and in that smooth ridgeline of woods it was the only break, like a single, jagged tooth. It was not a good place to have built a house, there to catch all the weather, or defy it, and so far from the village road, with a long, steep drive to clear in winter and shore up during the spring thaw. And it was not good land to farm; fine for the cows to climb but not the machines, drawn or powered, at haying, or now in the spring when the manure needed spreading, and then where it was spread at the top the bottom got more or most, thanks to runoff. But the settler who had built it was proud; 150 years ago there were many ways at hand for a man to build himself up, and he would have a house that stood for that. His name was Coulter. He died in the Civil War from a minié ball passing through his heart at the battle of the Wilderness, Virginia, May 5, 1864 — though nearly fifty and not obliged to enlist. He had the house to live up to, and that, people said, was what did him in, not the minié ball.

Afterward, through two generations, the Coulters kept sheep. The sheep liked the slopes and the flock moved amoebically up and over the ridge and down. Day in, day out, wool was easier than milk. When the wool market collapsed the Coulters turned back to dairy farming. They added a piece of bottom land then, down alongside the lake where they grew feed corn, and kept a boathouse on the shore for the big lake trout that came up when the ice went out in the spring. The rest of the shoreline sold off to summer people, but they kept the cornfield and the boathouse where the land was no good, wouldn't percolate, and no one could build a real house. Like the rest of Harrow's dairy farmers they managed all right until a run of five girls shut down the operation. Girls and the bulk tank law, for the big truck would not go up the road to draw off the milk, and the girls, not one of them (on purpose, it was said) married men inclined to the land.

The people who lived in the village saw the house high in its weathery notch on the long ridge to the north, storm clouds fisting about it, or the white cumuli bunching past on their way to somewhere else, or they beheld the house just sitting, drenched in a blue vacancy, the tall windows watching with a stupefied look at all that came and went. It was a fine house with a fine view, and that was the worst and best that could be said of it. After a while the locals had to remind themselves to lift their eyes toward it, though a stranger in town noticed it right off, so white and one-sided in its distant desolate breach.

A dozen years passed since they shut down the operation. The deer and bear, the furtive lovers from Harrow, the real estate man at the end of his tether, paid visits to the house, but they were not many or regular except for the deer who came each fall for the apples. Once a photographer set up on an opposite ridge, and captured the house with thunderheads piling round it; the photo was used for the cover of a mystery magazine.

And then a summer person bought it. Bought it, fixed it up, and before he would bring his wife and children, he paved the infamous road of Coulter's, put back-and-forths in it, gentled it down for the loaded, low-swung station wagon arriving in June for the season. Cost him $25,000 and his reputation with the locals.

They lasted three summers. It was too far from friends on the lake, from their tribe; too far from the chance encounters they looked for at Dugan's general store. On the north end of the lake they found a sandy swath and built a cottage like the neighbors' and left the bumps in the little road down to their camp, just for the annual charm of it.

Now the real estate man had a road to sell. In 1967 farmhouses could be had practically for the promise of being there with lights on and smoke tailing from the chimney and the good sound of a chain saw in the dour November woods. Land could be had if you would keep the forest out of it—that was all—even the government wanted that, to keep the state open for postcards and tourists; the government had even considered subsidies. But a road, switched and paved, with granite blocks upholding the bends, culverts, and ditches and cement berms—that was easy to market, especially to a stone cutter.

Joseph Rinaldi worked the marble quarries in Dorset, as the men of his family had going back a hundred years. They first came from Italy for the adventure and work, men who knew stone. Rinaldi had had enough of cutting, the muscle ache and dust, the dust mostly, and being a bachelor fastened to no woman in particular and not keen on the bunch in general, he fled north into the Kingdom. From the edge of the village of Harrow he saw the old Coulter place, and when he felt the road under the wheels of the real estate man's truck, or rather, did not feel it, for it had been smoothed into near-absence, looping long to and fro as if it led nowhere, or was only a dream in the form of a road that would never end, and then suddenly it did end at a tall white house with the wind blowing clean about it, he signed the paper that same day. A year later Joseph Rinaldi disappeared.

It seemed he did his morning chores, for the milk stood nearly two feet above the agitator when the milk truck came, and the driver emptied the bulk tank and left a carbon of the weight; then he went on his way and did not give thought to Rinaldi's whereabouts, since it was not uncommon for the driver to draw the milk while a farmer was in his house having his first meal. On the kitchen table there was an empty box of donuts, crumbs dotting a plate, so he'd sat down to his breakfast in the daily manner, and everyone thought that especially queer, taking trouble with a plate when you were about to do a brutish thing. Then he walked north, the tracks told. It was mud season, and up to the edge of the woods his direction was plain. Beyond that was anyone's guess.

You could hear the bellows from the bottom of the drive. You could hear them if you had been there, if it had been a Monday and not a Sunday, then the postman would have heard the trouble a day sooner and it wouldn't have gone so bad for the cows—mastitis, infections, one down in the marsh with a breach, another hung up in hog wire. The local farmers did what they could until the brother arrived, but they had their own chores and vet bills, and anyway, the whole thing made a bad taste. It was not that they had feelings for the cows except the kind that come of common need. It was that not one of them would've dared reckon up the number of times he had felt the urge to walk and had had to clench himself against it.

The younger brother, Champ, came with a wife who was as new to him as he was to farming, and as it turned out, she was the better at farming, or managing the farm, at least, and he at marrying. By 1995 they had 7 children, 46 head of cattle for milking and another 40 or so in young stock, 210 acres in hay, 20 in corn down by the lake, and a fine little orchard of Duchess apples for pie making. The infamous Coulter road had heaved and washed out and ground down back to half gravel, though the switches with their granite bases held. Now and then the town grader came up, usually around lunch, so he would have something nice to look out on while he ate.

It was not the best dairy farm in the area but it was not the worst either. The Rinaldis were good with the cows and the land but they weren't much for machines, and that was the third claim of dairy farming that few saw right off. It seemed to trip the Rinaldis again and again—fixing the machines.

From the village road and along it for three miles the house could be seen except if the destination were the house itself. Then, turning off the village road, you lost sight of it cutting round to the other side of the ridge, and approached it blind, for the slope bowed out and the house perched topmost and could neither see nor be seen until face to face with visitors. This meant that the Rinaldis were often surprised, though Ray Rinaldi, the eldest of the children, determined against it, for it seemed to make a fool of him. Ray Rinaldi assumed that there was always someone coming, someone who might see before he had seen.

AT THE HEAD of the kitchen table Ray set a bowl of barley soup and a plate of white bread, then with the toe of his boot he hooked a chair leg and pulled it over and eased himself down. For several minutes his arms lay on either side of the place setting, his hands collapsing into loose fists. He was thinking of his mother's news.

Most of the glass in the windows of the old Coulter place was original, and after 150 years of ultraviolet exposure, it had developed a delicate lavender complexion which seemed to make up for the warping and sundry pocks of time. Through the windows Ray gazed at the pools in the farmyard, muddy where the milk truck had come through and blue where the sky still filled them, and all of them skewed past real and washed in lavender and pretty if you didn't mind the distortion. Ray always had. At the west edge of the farmyard the road began its descent, and it was to this line Ray looked throughout the day as one on an island might glance to the horizon, not really looking, yet still with some vestigial anticipation.

From a liter bottle of cola he chugged without awareness of need. Then he remembered the pills, knocked several into his palm, and chugged again to wash them down. His back hurt; it had hurt for the last six months, but between chores and winter laying on hard and the hired man gone off with the LaPlante cousin from Louisiana, sugaring and calving and fence mending, there hadn't been time to properly tend to it. *Then she says she's pregnant,* he thought, and shoved the bowl away.

He felt another sharp bite, stood to ease it, arching with his palms pressing against the base of his spine, and as he straightened he glanced automatically toward the brink of the barnyard, at the line that was as much the planet curving off into the surrounding darkness. This time a satisfaction—movement. Not the grill of the old man's Ford tilting up round the final bend, but a cap, a brown leather cap and a man growing into it.

Withdrawing into the room's shadow, Ray watched the stranger shift back and forth avoiding the pools and manure slops, his eyes groundward as he mapped a course to the house. There was still plenty of snow about, old packed-down disks in the hollows, small-scale mountain ranges along the road, but the road itself was clear to mud. *And he's clean*, Ray thought. *Must've come along the banks.* The wind was up, a cold ache in the ears, and the visitor hunched inside his collar. Ray could not see his face, just the leather cap and the puffs of breath coming fast, and there was a bag, too.

He slid back into the chair, pulled the bowl into place, tore up a piece of bread, shoved things round a bit. The stranger passed the window and Ray Rinaldi watched and when he heard the knocks he took a spoonful of the barley soup, and another, and then when the stranger had begun to turn away Ray went to the door with bread in his hand.

"I've interrupted your lunch."

Ray looked at the bread in his hand as if just discovering it. At seventeen what he didn't have in height he made up for with muscle, though he'd've rather had the height, especially at moments like this when he found himself looking up to another man in his own house.

"I'll come back," the stranger offered, retreating from the door and down one step, which gave Ray a sudden advantage by an inch or two.

"Well, you're here now," he said, and shoved the bread in his mouth.

"Okay." The stranger set his bag on the porch, but held his position on the first step down. He was still puffing. "It is a long road."

Ray gave a solitary nod.

From the shade of the porch where he had been watching a huge male Bouvier rose and walked over to sniff the stranger's trouser legs, then the bag, and, having dispatched his investigative duties, he returned to his nap on the porch.

"I wondered if you could use a hand up here."

"Who was it said so?"

The stranger looked to the side, as if he'd seen something. "Never learned his name."

"One-eye? One-eye Gottlieb?"

"No."

"He talks, One-eye."

"No, just a guy gave me a ride."

"So."

"He heard your hired man came down with a hard case of spring fever."

Ray Rinaldi made a chopping sound with his breath that was the remains of childhood laughter. Then he remembered her news delivered as she had warmed the soup, and he wanted to get back to work and get shut of this fellow and of the day, too. "You alone, or you got a woman?"

"Alone."

"Trailer's not sizable, is all."

"I see."

"Well, what can you do?"

The stranger considered his bag sitting beside him like a well-trained dog at heel. "Usually I know how to do more than most people need me to know."

Ray Rinaldi stared at him to keep from staring at the bag. Whatever was in there couldn't milk a cow or hay a field. Anyway, there wasn't anything to the guy, thick-wise. He was tall enough . . . well, taller than Ray, and easy on the eyes, the girls would say, but he kept his face to the side, one or t'other, so the look was half of an unseen whole, and Ray had to wonder about the half he wasn't getting. It seemed he was always having to wonder about what he wasn't getting.

"I fix things, just about anything," the stranger added.

"Tractors?"

"Whatever."

Abruptly that settled it for Ray. Still, he didn't want the stranger to know their need, or the softest part of their need—the down machines and broken gadgets; he'd always been ashamed of the family indisposition to devices. "I'm right out straight, I am," he said. There was bitterness in his voice, and he wanted the stranger to hear it; he was sore, with all he had to do and think about—thinking was worse—and this fellow with soft hands and a little brown bag knowing how to do things . . . *and the most he has to trouble with on a day like this is keeping himself clean coming up the road*. "Right out straight," Ray said again.

The stranger examined his shoes. "That's what I heard."

"Ed off chasin' strange. Gawd."

The man gave a smile of knowing meant to include and confirm Ray's own experience, though Ray himself hadn't known anything familiar let alone strange, when it came to women. But he liked the assumption fine, and drew himself up and jerked his chin toward the long pine table at the head of which waited the bowl of soup his mother had made up for him before she had gone off into the Duchess orchard. "Nine chairs. Every one of 'em sat in."

They were both silent, the stranger gazing off toward the apple orchard, which was visible through the end of the porch, blossomed out white, where a woman moved far away as if in a silent movie; and Ray following the stranger's gaze and wondering if he'd dare hire the man without his mother's consent. "Ever worked with cows?"

The stranger cocked his head elaborately and sounded a long pondering note against the back wall of his throat.

Ray squinted past him into the farmyard; he thought he'd seen something. It was just one o'clock, almost warm if not for the wind, and everywhere the light clear and fine-edged like sheets of glass leaning into each other, and it hurt to look through the light, it seemed to shatter in his eyes. Then he saw it was the old man. The old man came into the shattered light of the farmyard, and Ray's eyes teared with the pain of watching. The old man on foot, and Ray knew he'd have to go and fetch the car wherever it and the old man had ended up; and before the old man thought he could have a say in this or any other matter anymore, one second more, and not looking now at the stranger's face but down at the bag, Ray spat out, "I reckon you can find the teat-end," and shouldered past him, meaning for him to follow, and out they went to the barn and to the hired man's trailer without either of them taking public note of the figure walking with slow care toward the house on the top of the ridge.

Two days later Ray's older sister, Luisa, asked the hired man for his name. "Mother needs to know for the books. For paying."

"When would that be?"

"When the milk check comes," she said, looking at him with frank curiosity. He was smiling at her, and she wasn't used to it. Luisa was big and rough-cut like her father, though her skin was nice, and her hair, too, dark and massive. She had grown up without curving, even her face was squared, and now in her twentieth year, owing to a boy who retreated, she was putting on enough weight to settle the matter of boys for good.

"I hear you sewing."

Luisa's face twitched.

"What are you making?"

"Coats. Children's coats."

"Yes?"

"For dress and, well, Christmas."

"Are they red then?"

"Lots times. And the best wool, merino. I sew things on 'em, animals and things. Fairies. Girls like fairies, boys like the animals."

"They sound fine. I'd like to see."

She stared at him. "Dugan's has some. And the store in the village over," she said, gesturing east.

"Well . . ." He seemed to chuckle a little, putting out his hand. "Sam Chase."

As she gripped his hand Luisa thought to say hello, but it seemed late for that. "They'll be there till June," she said. "Likely. 'Cause they are dear. Mostly it's summer people, them who can afford 'em. Take me a month each, they do."

"That's a long time."

Luisa simply looked at him. He was very fine to look at, like a glossy poster of someone you would never meet and who could not really exist.

"I suppose I might see them here, too," Sam Chase said, starting off toward the barn and wearing the same discomfiting smile he had begun with. Then he turned: "When does the milk check come?"

"Every two weeks. S'posed to, leastways."

"Ah."

THERE FOLLOWED ten days of everything from air so balmy that the icicles along the eaves wept themselves down to a fringe; then sleet and a hard freeze; three days of dousing rain; snow flurries, stray memories, throughout; thaws making promises, breaking promises; clouds of hammered pewter, and beneath them, utter stillness; suddenly a sky emptied out, blue and unnerving; and then on the first of May a storm drifted down from the northwest across the Great Lakes, leaving a foot of powder in its wake. The pond ice held, a dirty thin girding. The blush of green that had begun to appear in the fields of old and brown matted grass between the leftover patches of gray snow was covered and gone. The fields with southern exposure where the grass was shin high and nearly good enough for feed were covered. The garden dug up halfway and mulched with strips of the *Times* and rotten hay; the sloppy yard; the rusty machines waiting along the side of the barn like giant bugs—all were neatly erased in the newest cleanest white. If it hadn't been so pretty it would have done more than break hearts.

RAY CAME IN through the mudroom door, stepping down on the counters of his boots and kicking them off in order not to bend, and hanging his barn coat on a peg, his hat on top if it. As he passed through the ell, Luisa looked up from her sewing machine, and he winked and said, "Hey, Lu," gently, because he loved her without complications. In the kitchen he grabbed a dinner roll. The rest of the kids were piled up in the old east parlor, watching a movie, idling on homework. Ray poked his head in, made a face featuring the half-eaten dinner roll, and didn't wait for James to say "gross," which had this month replaced "sick," before which "wicked" had reigned. Showered and changed, Ray loaded a plate in earnest, pork and applesauce and two more rolls with butter, which he set on the long pine table with a glass of lemonade. Carefully, his hands on the chair arms, he lowered himself down. It was then he set his gaze traveling the length of the table until it arrived with unspoken ceremony at his mother.

"Ma." In the way Ray said it there was always a little question snagged up at the end.

"There's pie," she said. "Rhubarb."

"Yeah. Who made it?"

Selda Rinaldi did not look up from the checkbook and bills spread before her. "Pie's for eating, nothing else."

Ray poured a little mound of salt on the edge of his plate. Then he cut off a chunk of pork, touched it to the salt, and pushed it through the applesauce. It was sweet and salty in his mouth, and there was more of it in the kitchen. He decided to let the pie drop.

"Hungry."

Ray lifted his eyebrows, vigorously buttered a roll.

"Because you're late."

"Had five heifers freshen on me."

"Again you're late," Selda said, laying down her pen.

"Five in two days, Ma. Every one of 'em trouble."

"Your man helpin' . . . shore he is, that's for what he's here."

"Well, shore," he shrugged.

For several minutes she resumed the bill paying, licking envelopes, sorting the paid ones into the accordion file she kept in the pantry, opening up the next one. Then she said, "Nice manners." And though Ray knew whom she meant, still he asked, and she replied, "That feller, Chase. Who is helpin' you. He says 'sir.'"

"Did. Doesn't now."

Before coming in, before complete darkness, Ray had walked up above the farmyard to the edge of the ridge that was not the road starting down but fields pitching in dark swells to the marsh at the bottom; the road to the village lay beyond. He took long loose steps and held himself high. For the first time that day he was not noticing his back. He remembered what it had been like, not noticing things, when an act was solid doing and nothing more, not pain or thinking, not words and other decorations. After the barn the air was clean and sharp, and the wind brushed up through the woods that trimmed the fields, smelling of spruce and new snow, and carried the steam from his clothes away, the scent of manure and of milk, the day that was and the thoughts that were tangled up in the day, even what was coming, night and another day, the wind taking it from him. He rubbed the back of his neck, then dropped his hand and let the earth tug gently and steadily at his two arms as if it wanted to pull them down and plant them side by side. He thought maybe he would cry. He didn't wonder about it, just felt it, acute and twisting between his temples, until very soon it untwisted and the feeling seemed to lie out flat and he felt nothing except tired. Below the ridge an island of fog floated above the marsh, and from the marsh where the brook ran out a pale, smudged trace wound along to the village. Then there was the black crescent area of the lake, the black seeming blacker for a gauzy layer of fog drawing off it and over the little village like a veil. The yellow lights were haloed, and Ray liked them that way, not bits of twinkling glass, but soft and touchable, swirling down in. He said "Ray" to the night. Perhaps he had meant to declare himself, or perhaps just to hear his name spoken with authority, but it sounded in his ears as if someone unknown had called him. So much was best not said aloud, even sometimes a name. Until the cold reached inside his barn coat he watched the lights below, the white hand of the fog muffling over the houses, the sharp eyes and voices inside. There was something he did want to think about, something good for turning round in his mind . . . he couldn't remember what. Well, he liked standing there looking down on the scene, while everything just around where he stood—the maples and the dead elm, the tall white house, his own truck at the top of the yard, and he himself at that moment—was clear and wind-etched and indisputable.

"Yes, sir, and no, sir," his mother said.

Ray was trying to remember back the feeling he had had outside. "Yeah, couple times, right off," he said absently.

"And you seventeen and him forty, I'd guess. That's what I'd guess. Forty."

"I said 'Ray.' He don't say it now. And what if he did? He knows who's working this farm, he knew before he come up the road, it was half of why he did, half plus the half that was Ed going off."

Selda Rinaldi's eldest son rose then and went to the kitchen and made himself another plate of food, and this time grabbed a bottle of hard cider from which he took a deep and conspicuous pull as he strode back.

"Ayuh, nice manners," she repeated. "I've yet to see him overstay a visit to the cows. Fer instance."

"Ma."

"Just fer instance."

Ray looked at the pork on his plate. It was cold: the margin of fat had gone white. He'd eat it clear with a crispy black rime, but not white. From the fat and bone he cut the meat in a single piece, and with his fingers picked it up and pressed an edge into the mound of salt, then the applesauce, then he tore at it between his teeth, and did it all again.

It had been over two weeks since Chase had come to work for them and though Ray hadn't had much help with chores—it was true—the man had made a lot of improvements, and once everything was up and running, and most of it better than before, Ray anticipated a big payoff. Nowadays improvements were the thing: you had to stay one turn ahead of the grindstone and take care not to waste blade.

"He fixed the spreader," Ray said. "Rewired the milk room, too. There's switches at both ends now."

"That necessary?"

"S'nice, it is. At five in the morning."

"When he isn't up."

"He's 'round all day, fixing things. That old toaster of your'n works now. Think you'd be happy."

"It's not toast we're needing."

"Well, he's here for evening chores. Was tonight, graining 'em . . ."

"Graining?" she interrupted. "A job for Carrie." Carrie was six years old, the youngest. Her favorite task was luring the cows into their stanchions with the big scooper spilling grain.

"Well, anyhow, he grained 'em. Then he checked the pump, tried to work up the suction on the milkers. That sort of thing."

"Toast."

There had always been something mannish about Selda, even before she married the stone cutter, Champ Rinaldi, when the young men used to make a point of straying by her desk in her father's office. He was the owner of the quarry; she kept the books for him, handing out paychecks to the line of cutters the first Friday of each month. The men felt her not needing them. They did not know what to say to her. They did not know what part of her to look at that was safer than her eyes, which seemed to find the part of them that was naked and cold and ashamed, and not flinch. She had dark, bold, straight eyebrows she did not shape into twin arches, and beneath them those eyes that saw and cared, really cared, it seemed; and perfect lips, like a drawing of lips. The way she laughed was deep and easy . . . and practical, too; it never went on, though it would have disappointed no one if it had. People thought she was taller than she was, which was only average. In her youth she pitched in a women's softball league. The men said "handsome"; the women said "striking." Entering a room they knew her to be there before they saw her, an obscure upright in the center of things.

"What do you want, Ma?"

"I want my boy to have help. I want to see some manure on that feller. Does he scrape the barn and clean up the bedding? Does he wash teats?"

Ray felt it then, it was almost like a drug, her caring and the way she cared, the fierce steadiness of it. He felt it and he wanted it and he hated it too.

"Help?" Ray stood, left the room. When he returned he placed the pie with extreme care in the middle of the long pine table. "Rhubarb pie," he said in the subtlest singsong whisper.

"Raymond," she warned.

He clapped his hands together and held them as if in prayer. "Today he made pie. Rhubarb, truth to tell."

"Enough."

"Not enough. It's not enough of anything, can't you see? You want me to have help, your boy . . . *he's* your boy, Ma. Three years ago *I* was helping *him* and now I'm doing it, all of it, and home schooling, and I get a guy who can sharpen things up around here, put us ahead some, and you're telling me he ought to wear manure, and I ought to choke down another goddamned piece of goddamned good for nothing pie."

She actually looked at it, the pie. "He isn't strong, the way most reckon strong," she said, still gazing, distracted, at the pie her husband had made. "Puts him out of the loop. But not wrong, no son, not bad. Just different, by what 'pears to be. It's that, makes him not well."

"Well enough to drink."

"A symptom, Ray. You know it's a symptom of something much . . ."

"Always his side. How can you defend . . ." He gestured toward the pie, which, to Ray, was looking just then like a disembodied scab; his hand was shaking, he could feel his throat wad up tight. He tried to think back the feeling outside, the wind tracing him against the darkening sky, and the fog below smothering the houses, and in one of those houses, he thought without expecting to think it—though he realized it was the thought he had been looking for outside—in one of those houses lived Heidi Greenfield, and if he had had time, if it hadn't been for her, his mother . . . He eyed her: "He's well enough to breed."

THREE DAYS. Selda was not one for chat, and when she did speak she allowed discernible pauses to enter that tended to frustrate listeners. But it was rare for her to indulge in a virtual lockout silence. To Luisa and the others she gave simple directions. To Ray she said nothing. He was beginning to feel desperate. His meals appeared, his clothes were washed and left folded on his bed, his mail —several notices from colleges—stacked on his bureau. But she would not look at him, and he was determined to make no appeal.

It had been three days and now it was Wednesday, 4:30 A.M., and when he crawled out of bed Ray could hear his mother vomiting in the bathroom down the hall. *So, it is morning and we are both miserable.* Again he heard her retch, and it seemed to him that she was trying to tell him something.

On the floor, on hands and knees, he worked his back, arching and dropping it down into a sway, arching again, dropping, fifteen times; then, gripping the edge of the bed, he stood, thinking *legs* to keep from using his back, and was again impressed by the force of a simple thought. He dressed quickly. In the kitchen he made her a cup of tea and lined a small plate with Common crackers, and took the tray upstairs. The bathroom door was open, the room empty. Uneasily he walked past the bedrooms of his siblings toward the door at the end of the hall, drawn by the smooth brassy knob glowing in the murk, and then as he neared the door, the room, and her behind the door to the room, his eyes traced the wood panels as if to cut and lift them out and see behind. And know.

Had he made it home last night, or was he sleeping it off at the boathouse? *The boathouse*, Ray thought with disgust. Where a week ago the old man had passed out in his own vomit frozen solid round the side of his face like a dinner plate—himself the meal, head first. Ray had had to ease it off with hot water and then, once it was liquefied, he had had to mop it up. And then he had had to take the stinking old man home to mother.

The tea steam rose under his chin, moist and warm and smelling of clove oranges. He was reminded of something . . . *pomander*, the scent of pomander in his mother's clothes. It was a long time since that scent, it was a long time since he had been close enough to smell it.

At the boathouse, he decided, and felt almost cheerful. *Yes, likely as not he's still at the boathouse, serving himself up another hangover.*

Then he heard her laugh, her deep, easy laugh. And not practical the way it was with him and the kids, the *other* kids, he thought with a twist of anger.

Ray heard her say "no." He heard the laugh.

He took the tray back to the kitchen and dismantled it, putting everything away so that she would not know what he had meant to ask; and to forget himself what he had meant to ask; and to never mean to ask it again. Then he went out to find the cows.

THERE WAS A strange warm fog lifting fast to the ridge, and from the ridge rising up all around him. The sky had shrunk to a hole at the top of itself, black and hypnotic, and for Ray it was like looking down, not up, down into a pit that had appeared abruptly at his feet. Ray was already feeling queasy, and now, it seemed, at the deepest level he was beginning to change, a basic rule wobbled; the up-and-down of things was threatened.

He wanted to be with the cows. He wanted to do the work by itself without thinking. Smell the work smells. Hear the Bouvier coming up the pasture behind the herd, cows bellowing back. Feel the taut, soft, swinging udders against the palms of his hands.

Yes, he would do the work. Then he would clean up and go to

school. This was the day he was to go to school. One day each week. They had made allowances, his teachers—because the year was mostly gone, and he was a senior; because he was a good student, self-motivated, they said; and because Ed, the Rinaldi's hired man, had gone off with the LaPlante cousin from Louisiana, and Ray's mother needed him; and because Mrs. LaPlante's sister was Principal Hogan's first and only flame, free and easy, like the cousin from Louisiana. They would review the work Ray had done and assign new work; and in June he would graduate with his class at the top of his class. Despite Ed going off. Despite the old man. Despite the nine chairs at the table, every-one-of-'em-sat-in, and one more that would be needed for sitting in and crying in.

Everyone agreed, Raymond Rinaldi knew how to work. Everyone said "dumb like a fox." Still, he had a funny way of pissing people off, they said. Had a chip the size of block of Barre granite. What if he had cause? Plenty of cause about, didn't do to sport it.

By the time Ray had the cows trickling up toward the barn the hole in the sky was gone, the fog was tearing itself apart, and above him diaphanous white rags dispersed into the predawn, frail rafts across a black sea. Today would be genuinely warm. Today, all of the day, she would not see him. *Well, good.*

The holsteins had gathered at the corner of the high pasture, squirting through the gate Ray had opened, then plodding along the deeply grooved path toward the barn, their black-and-white shapes appearing and disappearing through the mist, like fragments of a bombed dream. The line tightened as they neared the door—number 38 leading, as usual—some lurching down the ramp, others balking at the top, half sliding on their own manure, stumbling when the ones behind bunched and pushed. There was momentum now; the Bouvier could do the rest.

Ray had spread clean bedding the night before, and when he trotted round to the opposite end of the barn he could smell the saw shavings before he entered. At the head of each stanchion he spilled a scooper of grain, and the cows came in and he secured them one by one, moving toward the ramp. He could hear the Boove working the rear, his deep hollow barks delivered singly, sparingly, as though they ought not to be necessary, and were beneath him. Black, block-shaped, shaggy, 140 pounds of herding instinct, his presence was usually enough; but in the dark, in the fog, the cows didn't see so well, and the Boove had to resort to quick, low forays and the occasional bark. Another dog the holsteins would have chased, any other dog.

He was the finest animal Ray had ever known. A name was an insult to an animal like the Bouvier. Ray's grandfather Burton, the quarry king, had given the dog to him four years earlier when it seemed clear that Ray was going to have to grow up faster than most; when it seemed clear that Champ was *about as worthless as teats on a barn door*—was how Grandfather Burton put it; and Ray, who was helping, would need help himself. The dog cost a thousand dollars. People came to see him, the cow dog from Flanders who had cost a thousand dollars. Officially the Boove was Ray's, but really the Boove belonged to no one, he had that kind of dignity and strength. He had been Ray's as a pup, but now he was his own; and Ray was proud to work with him, and glad to see his huge dark shape pushing through the high hay of summer, or crashing and lunging across drifted snow, his beard and belly fur caked white, and his beautiful grave eyes, seldom seen, revealed by the wind of his own passing.

Grandfather Burton was dead now; the Bouvier made up for some of that—the Boove and the truck, which had come from Grandfather too.

Ray turned on the pump. In the milk room he filled a bucket with warm water, took a terry rag from the clean bin, and headed for the cow furthest from the bulk tank. He set the bucket down on the right side of her, and with his left hand grabbed her tail and lowered himself into a squat, thinking *legs*. With the terry rag he washed her. Then he fetched the iodine, and dipped and squeezed each teat, slid the milker up under her and positioned the four suction cups, listening for the fit, the quick inhalation of the pump. The second cow didn't need washing; he started each teat, attached a milker. Above the stanchions the milk flowed through the pipe that ran the length of the barn to the bulk tank, and the soft, rhythmic knocking of the milk machine filled the barn, like the sound of something living, a big, harmless life it would take fifty cows to suckle. Ray moved the bucket of warm water with the rag to the empty center aisle, and hung the iodine dip from a nail on a post. Then he crossed to the west side of the barn and started the first two cows there, each time grabbing her tail to keep it from switching his face, and to help lower himself into a squat. When he needed to free up his hands for attaching the milker, he used his forehead to steady himself, pressing it against her belly, smelling her hide.

The red light on the first milker had gone on. Ray went over and removed the cups and finished off each teat, squeezing at the top, pulling down through the bottom, spraying the bedding or a barn cat if one was about. Then he unhooked the milker from the pipes that ran the length of the building and carried the contraption with its dangling rubber hoses and four-fingered hand to the next cow on the same side. The tendon that held up her udder had stretched and torn, and her teats were green with manure they hung so low, her udder chaffed from the inside action of her legs. Ray grabbed the bucket and iodine, cleaned her up; he would have to tend by her, since the milking claw would sit on the mat, maybe get stepped on, and at two grand apiece, he couldn't afford the damage. Before milking her, he started three others to give him time, and then he milked the old one, letting the device rest on the top of his boot until she was finished. A red light on the other side, and he crossed to finish off another cow, move the milker to the next; then he returned to rub some bag balm into the udder of the damaged cow. Probably have to let her go for beef this year. He glanced up at her annual records framed above her stanchion—volumes, fat percentages, and so on—patted her neck, avoided her big watching eye. *Been a good girl.*

The next cow was young, recently freshened, and didn't take long to empty; she kept swinging her head around to see what Ray was up to, and shying when the milking device came and went. He had another youngster who kicked; had to put a Cow-kick bar on her. When all four milkers were busy, and none of the red lights on, Ray grabbed the hoe and went along behind the holsteins, pulling slops into the gutter.

An hour passed; half done. Some of the young stock were bawling, and Ray shoved a bale into the side barn and hayed them, and then the milk stock too, who had likewise finished their grain, trotting along in front of them and tearing off a square for each. The heifers bawled like babies when they were out of feed, enough to give him a headache; even some of the older girls took to lowing. And since Ray had always found comfort in the knocking of the milk machine, steady as a metronome, but quieter, gentler, as if the whole barn were meant to go to sleep, he tried to keep the cows happy with grain and hay quick after.

Down the line he went—grab the tail, squat, pull the teats, start the flow, attach the milker, move to the next, watch for the red light, go back and remove the milker, finish off each teat, carry the milker to the next. Now and again wash an udder, iodine dip. Time between, hoe out manure, hay the young stock, bottle feed a weanling in the calf pen. *Knock knock knocking* of the pump, buzz of the machine at the distant end of the barn, chewing, chewing, fifty together, rattle of stanchion pipes. Smells of manure, sawdust, cowhide, hay, milk when you fed the calves. Moths leafing about the barn lights. And the barn lights too bright for the lulling dulling *knock knock knocking* of the milk through the pipes to the tank for the truck that would come and take it away.

Between the main barn and the milk room there was a small passageway where Ray kept his milk and pregnancy records, and thumbtacked notices to a two-by-six: inspection certificates, an old, black-and-white aerial photo of their half section of land on which Ray three years ago had made a tiny red dot to indicate himself at fourteen. The switch for the gutter cleaner was there in the passageway, too. Ray flipped it, and as he heard it start up, he paused to stretch his back, leaning against the palms of his hands. The noise of the gutter cleaner bothered him and he decided to wait until the end, shutting it off and listening for the subtle, steady knocking of the milk machine to fill the air.

The Boove had stationed himself just outside the big end door where the hay wagon off-loaded during summer months. He never entered the barn; he lay in the farmyard, waiting. Ray could see his sphinx-like shape against the pale drape of dawn, the mist of his breath hardly visible, and for the second time that morning Ray registered the coming warmth. Today he wanted to be happy. It was possible today.

Closing his eyes, he leaned into another back arch . . . and straightened abruptly. There was someone else in the barn: calves bawling. The Boove rose and walked off, his big square butt sashaying like a bear's. Ray looked at his watch: 6:15. Too early for the hired man.

He swung round from the passageway down the middle of the barn, noting a red light as he passed. Then he heard distant, tuneless whistling, and made a sharp turn back to the red light, squatted, pulled the milker, finished off the teats. Worked.

Only job that's halfways fun, and he homes right down in on it.

Champ Rinaldi emerged from the hay-dusty twilight of the calf pen, smiling. He had two empty milk bottles in his hands. " 'Mornin'," he said.

" 'Lo."

Still smiling, Champ held up the bottles. "Like to suck the bottoms out of 'em."

Ray carried the milker to the next cow. "Remind you of someone?"

Champ went to the milk room and filled the bottles again, then walked the length of the barn to the calf pen to feed another two. Afterward he went back to the milk room with the bottles to wash them out. His hair was combed; he had shaved. It felt okay, being here. She had made it okay for him to be here today, and the boy could not foul it.

"She send you?" Ray asked.

"You got school today, is all. Thought I'd finish up chores."

"Sometimes take a great notion . . ." Ray muttered.

"Give you time to go over your papers and sech."

" . . . to jump in the river and drown," Ray sang softly.

"You spoke?"

"Nothing."

"Thought you spoke."

"Yeah?"

"Thought so."

"I dunno. I'm kinda punchy this morning."

The older man felt relieved. The boy said things. He did not want to have to hear it this morning. This morning he had been home. There was that. In the place where to start from was right. The new man, Sam Chase, had driven him up from town four nights running. So he had gotten home. And it was morning. There was a chance. He was drinking less, it seemed to him, a mite less, had to be less, because he was not in the car or the boathouse or Billy's back room, he was home with her, and she had laughed next to him in the bed, and told him to shave first, and she had made it okay for him to be here in the barn with the boy, too.

"Punchy, you say? Maybe the weather. It's changing, for the dozenth time, and this one'd be for sure, bank on it." Champ stretched largely. "Ayuh, it's enough to make ambition poke right up at your feet for the picking."

"Ambition?"

"Ambition or will."

"Will?"

"Ambition or will, makes but little matter, son."

Ray could not respond. He leaned his forehead against the side of the cow, shut his eyes, felt for the teats.

"The will to do, whatever the doing be. It isn't strong at first, no, it's a tender thing, son, and it don't abide by sense or stick measure. It's a bootstrap move, that's right." He slapped the side of his pants. "No . . . a bootstrap *maneuver*. Just as I say."

"Ambition. Little green sprouts of it," Ray was saying into the side of the cow. "Between toes," he went on, pretending to try to figure it out. "And boots."

"Bootstraps. It's a saying, old saying."

"Bootstraps moving."

The older man smiled tolerantly. "*Maneuver*."

Ray looked over at his father. He noticed then the combed hair, the shaved face. The rheumy brown eyes, too. And his hand shaking as he passed down the iodine dip. He understood what his father was saying, even though he could not bring himself to let the old man know. He understood him when he talked of things like this, and he missed the talk almost as much as he missed believing in the talk.

There *was* a gap between wanting to do a thing and doing it; and something that happened in that gap that made no sense, but that amounted to practically everything. It was where his old man had fallen, between the wanting and the doing. And it was where he himself, Ray Rinaldi, would never fall.

For half a minute Ray felt the old thing between them; it made him sad, and he wanted it back, that heady whole-world feeling, being with his father in the barn in the morning . . . but the feeling was gone now. It was the hair and shave reminded him, the fine word, *maneuver*. It was the tuneless whistling that put him straight.

Ray stood, nodded at the other side of the barn where a red light had gone on, and Champ made a sound, "Whup," like he'd just gotten his orders, and went to tend to the cow, whistling until he remembered how the boy felt about it.

Nothing ever stuck to Champ Rinaldi, not a mood or a task, not even a song. He started whistling one, pure and high and promising, but lost it to another somehow, then there was a general collapse into half-known fragments. Even the name, Champ . . . somewhere, sometime he had been the best, at what no one would say for sure; the story changed from one child to the next, and adults stopped asking. It was the irony that stopped the asking, the corny obvious irony. Maybe he had been a crack shot, maybe it was that —rumor, scattered evidence would have it so—but owing to drink, there was no wage in it now for Champ, or for the sad questions of others.

The thing was, people couldn't help liking Champ Rinaldi, and in more than a tolerating way; they liked him despite or because of his aimlessness. Ask him to help, he'd help—on a saw gang, or sugaring, or to cut open the road to the reservoir so the plow could get up, or put in a troublesome dock, or finish up a shed you started summer before and hadn't finished only for want of company, not skill or muscle. Ask him as he came out of Dugan's with something to crack his own nut—a tool, a fitting, a bag of seed, whatever— and he'd leave off where he was headed and help you, unless someone else tagged him on the way, then he'd leave off helping you for him. He was as good as the last one who snagged his attention, which, by common assent, was not thought to be all that good.

Still, he *was* good. In another time, another story, he might have been a holy wanderer, and none would have expected more of him than what he would lay his hands upon for an hour or a day or a second's thought. As it happened, though, he was a dairy farmer in Harrow, Vermont, and there was never a time when something did not need doing and he was not there reliably to do it. Some of the women, in consideration of Selda, told their men not to ask Rinaldi, not to lead him off any more than he could already be led off.

He was a big man with a boy's face—candy-shop eyes and a soft smile time had eased down some, but not enough for a man his age. At the unlikeliest junctures in his day he developed stories and went on to tell them humorously; even his jokes could be passed along at the church supper, for there was never a cruel side to them. He could be with anyone, and they with him, so little did expectation or judgment distort his company.

The spring Eleanor Colbeth started out for the river to take her own life, the river pounding down the stone gorge, and Eleanor walking through town past the whitewashed houses and the Grange Hall and the United Church of Christ, past the people gathered in Dugan's doorway, toward the bridge, it was Rinaldi they sent to help. It had started to rain, and Rinaldi loped after her with a large striped umbrella. "Mrs. Colbeth," he said, holding the umbrella above her head. "You're getting wet."

Mrs. Colbeth looked down at what she was wearing, a pink wool suit. She had worn it to Easter services. The placket edges were scalloped, and as she walked she let her fingers trace the scallops, top to bottom, bottom to top; they had not been easy to sew. When they came to the bridge they continued on across, and had what looked to be from the doorway of Dugan's general store, a pleasant walk together on a wet spring day, Champ Rinaldi leaning in, chatting, calm and interested, and Mrs. Colbeth keeping dry under his umbrella.

"Innocence is abroad," Clovis McPherson liked to say. Clovis had the camp next to the Rinaldis' boathouse. Whenever he spotted Champ Rinaldi in the cornfield behind his house, in the village, or down at the lake, he'd say aloud in general warning, "Innocence is abroad." Clovis McPherson taught at an Ivy League college downcountry, and was always making such high-flying, stagy announcements, and rewriting or recycling famous lines even if it was only to get the bread passed to him at the supper table. He did not anymore know a lick of common speech; he had been a common man from Iowa and had sloughed off signs of his personal history for the language of leather books, and whatever standing it suggested; and as company, it was said, Clovis McPherson lost out to natural tedium seven days of a week. But he had Rinaldi pegged, so long as you did not count the drinking. Champ Rinaldi drank with malice aforethought.

CHAMP WORKED the west side of the barn and Ray worked the east until the cows were milked, then they opened the stanchions and the cows backed up skittishly over the gutter and filed out. Grabbing the scraper, Champ went along pulling the soiled bedding and manure into the gutter. Ray flipped on the gutter cleaner. He could hear the Boove far off, barking, and he thought to wonder about it, but his father came round the passageway, dropped a big hand on his shoulder, and said, "Ma'll have breakfast. I'll finish up."

Ray glanced sideways at his father's hand. It was soft and heavy and it seemed to put him in mind of Heidi Greenfield, whom he would see that day at school. "About done now, anyway," he shrugged.

"Still."

Ray looked out across the farmyard past the house to the orchard, trying to see the Boove.

Really, he did not want his old man's help. It was too late for help. It had been too late since the day Ray understood that the times he did not have help were *okay*; it was *okay* with his father and with his mother, it was *okay* with the village, it was OKAY with Life, that Ray did most of the work. By default, by silence: there was no one else, and no one had said it was not okay. Maybe it had not been okay with Grandfather Burton, but he was dead now. He had given Ray the Bouvier, he had given Ray the truck before Ray could even drive it, and with these he had said it was not okay, it was not fair. Now there was not a time when Ray encountered the

Boove—in thought or in fact—that some secret corner of himself did not burn the light of hope for someone else at least, another member of this humanity; and in the most extreme moments, hope of total reparation for Raymond Rinaldi.

Champ squeezed his son's shoulder. "I'll finish."

The boy slouched out from under his father's hand, but seemed to have nowhere to go. "Finishing's one. Starting's another."

"Can't argue." Champ tucked his hands in his pockets. "Better get on in."

Ray didn't move. He felt paralyzed. He could hear the Boove, barking, tolling, the sound of distant longing. He could feel his father to the right, behind him, a thickening presence, a great big clot of a man. There was something Ray needed to say, and then there was something he needed to hear after the saying, but he didn't know what it was. Every time he seemed to get near the thing that needed saying, his old man seemed to agree before he had said it, and that was what froze the boy up—the old man agreeing.

"You got school."

"School," Ray said as though galled.

"I started school . . . didn't finish. Had to go to work. A chance to finish school's more'n I got."

"More'n you got, maybe . . ." Ray kicked a chunk of ice out into the yard, "no more than you might've made."

Champ sighed, looked down at the snow, smoothing it round and round with the sole of his boot. "There's an 'if' in there, I can feel it nudging up under a rib or two," he said, and he clapped a hand on his side for effect. "What I got given to me, son, was Rinaldi history, shape of a mallet and a chisel."

In the past Ray might have said, *I'm going to make history, Pa, not get it given to me. I'm going to be great someday.* But now the old man wasn't worth saying that kind of thing to. He had thought about saying it to Heidi, he had thought that maybe she would want to know him better then, or differently . . . *yes, differently* . . . but he wondered how he would feel about her afterward, if he said it out loud to her. He did not need to say it to his mother, because she seemed to know it already. But if he said it to Heidi Greenfield then she would have a piece of it, and maybe it wouldn't look the same there in her hands, and maybe, too, he would have a little less of all he was going to be. And Ray wanted all of everything he was going to be.

Ray moved off toward the farmyard. "I might be late for chores," he said. "Count on you to start 'em?"

"Shore."

"Shore."

The deadpan tone was not lost on Champ. He reached up to his shaved chin, stroking, consoling. It was morning, the sun was haloing over the ridge to the east; it was morning and he was here, and she had said yes, and he was making a start again, and the boy could not hurt him yet. "Better get on in, now, son."

Ray was listening to the Boove, one deep barrel bark after another, and faster, the barks piling into each other. "What's he going off about?"

"Dogs in the orchard field." It was Sam Chase come sauntering across the farmyard from the house, wiping his mouth with the back of his hand, tugging a cigarette from a pack in his breast pocket.

Been up to the big house, Ray thought, annoyed.

"Selda thinks they've got a doe down."

"Selda? My mother?"

"How many dogs?" Champ asked.

"She couldn't tell. She was looking from one of the upstairs windows."

"You been eating breakfast?" Ray said.

"I have," Sam Chase replied with an informative air, keeping his face to one side. "Could not resist."

Ray walked off to the house and fetched his gun. When he came out the other two were still there, talking.

"Finish up, Sam," Ray said, and threw a hand toward the barn.

"What's left?"

"Got eyes."

The hired man dropped and ground his cigarette, then turned into the barn.

Champ found a shovel and followed his son. *So he wasn't the only one the boy said things to.*

THE SUN HAD CLEARED the last high features of the land, and blazed unreservedly at the ridge as the two stamped across the snowy pasture beyond the house. Under the hard light of morning the white pasture looked black, with silver veins of melt water working their way down to the deep courses that reappeared each spring. The men entered the orchard, bearing north and east. The orchard was Selda's place and her concern—she propped up the trees in late summer when the boughs were heavy with fruit, made pies and froze them for the winter, selling the extra bushels to Dugan's, and in the fall she mulched around their bases, fed them manure, wrapped the trunks of the youngest with foil. Even when there was nothing to do, when the grass was high and the leaves broad, she might be found weaving slowly among the trees in the green fractured light, touching them here and there, while traces of an earthly secret played about her countenance.

In the orchard Ray became aware of his own breath, too loud and rough.

Under the apple trees, blossoms lay patterned about on top of the packed and icy snow, the newly fallen blossoms palest pink, and the ones that were days down crinkly and brown-edged, or brown altogether and losing their shape. The air was wet and cool, and faintly sweetly tinged. All about the orchard floor sunlight lay in puzzle pieces with blue shade fitting between, and the footsteps of the Rinaldi men dotting lines across.

They went in silence for five minutes, the younger one leading, hurrying, now and then slipping into a jog with the gun riding seesaw across his hip; and the older one ten paces behind, longer-legged and steadier, keeping up without having to jog, the shovel angling up from his shoulder and ticking the occasional branch. The snow underfoot was white-gray, and the blossoms overhead white-pink and pure, and between the two whites, connecting, were the dark and fluid striations of the tree limbs reaching out from the short, solid trunks. Into the simple morning of the apple orchard the two men brought sound, movement, intent, human complication; so that when they emerged from the trees even they, as different from each other as they were, even they felt their own kind of relief for the place returned to its secret self.

Beyond the grove, flanking the ridge, was a pasture known as the Big Trough, which swept down and up sharply into spruce woods mounting another rise almost as high as the high ridge. Here the wind blew outright, and the snow drifted deep and soft under a thin wind-board of ice, and the skiers who came upon it on a clear winter's day had to race across without falter, holding onto the pace and the weightlessness it gave, or lose the skim and break through into the deeps.

There were three dogs: the Smiths' mop terrier, who kept disappearing in the snow, Jimmy Redmond's duck hound, and a sharp-nosed stray the color of ash. The Bouvier made four.

It was clear that the doe had tried to keep to the woods where the snow was firm and she might outmaneuver them, but they had run her into the pasture where the snow lay deep and she couldn't maintain the distance or the effort or even anymore the advantage of her long, springy legs. They must have smelled her when it began, or smelled her because it had gone on longer than was natural, and she had taken off running with the thing half in, half out, half fetus, half fawn, irrevocably breached, swinging between her back legs, and the dogs crazed by the scent and sight of it.

The terrier and the hound were fighting over the fetus, shredding it as they pulled, and pulling so that it was they who succeeded in freeing it with a sudden *sloosh*, the small triangular face coming last in a rush of dark blood.

The doe was down, alive, panting, stark-eyed.

The ash-colored stray was watching the Bouvier who was lying, sphinx-like, alongside the doe, as if guarding her from the others, except that one of her long legs was bent sideways and stretched across his paws, and he was gnawing on it, idly, when he remembered it was there. The doe did not seem to notice him, or any of the scene anymore.

Ray called the Boove, and the Boove looked over at him, and did not come.

Champ made a lunging motion with the shovel out in front, and let out a harsh "Git"; the terrier and the hound jerked back and almost immediately returned to the torn fixating thing in the snow. The stray seemed to think he had less time, now that the humans had arrived: snarling, he dropped his head and slashed in at the doe's flank, taking some of her away, and it wasn't until a moment or two later that the body of the doe reflexively squirmed. Fully alive, her eyes did not seem connected anymore to the rest of her, did not see the rest of her; she had abandoned to these others all but a private vision, and what she saw, or seemed to be seeing, was a bright field of snow sailing up before her to a high ridge and a high blue sky and around it all a blackening, shimmering halo.

"The doe," Champ called. He and Ray were about ten yards apart, the snow unmarred between them.

Ray lifted the gun to his shoulder, dropped it, moved left, right, lifted the gun again. "Can't get a good shot."

"Better take her," Champ said.

"I know."

"Just take her."

Ray sighted down the rifle again, then let it drop, butt first, along his thigh. "The Boove's too close."

Champ did not think so; he was not a shooter anymore, but he did not think that herd dog was too close. "Shoot up, then."

Twice Ray shot into the air. Jimmy Redmond's duck hound stopped and looked around for something falling to fetch back, but nothing fell and this man was not his master. Having never trained to a gun, the Smiths' dog trusted the hound's investigation and hardly paused in his tiny terrier carnage. But the stray, who'd met up with guns before, skinned it back to the edge of the spruce woods, crumpling in the deep snow as he hurried, clambering on, his hunk of meat trailing gore along the thin crust. Where the shadows began he stopped and crouched down to wait, keeping the whole of the scene in view.

That left only the Boove with the doe.

Again Ray brought the gun to his shoulder, sighted, shook his head. Again he called the Bouvier, but the sound of his voice served only to remind the Boove that there was something lying across his paws he might chew on.

Champ stared at his son. "Time," he said with a look of all-consuming seriousness.

The boy ignored him.

"*Time*," he said again, and his voice now was like a straight black bold line in the snow between them.

"I hear you."

"You got the gun."

"Yeah. I got the gun."

Champ began to feel sick with the urgency to finish the doe. He could not stand suffering—seeing it, feeling it, making it, something came loose inside; it was as if whatever held him in tore open and things began to spill out. For the first time that morning he thought earnestly of a drink. He had already thought of a drink three, four times maybe, but they were not the same as this thought, which was a real thought, and the first step toward having the first drink in a long long run of drinks.

"I'll just have to wait for a clear shot," Ray was saying.

Before his old man had said "time," Ray had felt the urgency to finish the doe; it was not like his old man's urgency, it was the kind a craftsman feels to complete a job correctly. From the age of thirteen he had learned to wait for the good shot, to take the life with respect, to finish clean and quick—why these were important had not much concerned him. Theoretically, it was the suffering. The old man had taught him. But Ray didn't appreciate being pushed now, he wouldn't jeopardize the Boove for a doe already down, the meat likely half ruined. No, he did not like being pushed; it had the effect of setting him in the other direction.

Champ made a coughing sound in the back of his throat, straining for a tone of casual reason. "Idn't gonna be a clear shot, son, by what you're used to, hunting. That dog's fixed."

"That dog works here."

Hiking left, Champ circled halfway round, hoping to gain passage to the open side of the doe, but the dogs came at him when he moved in too close. "They're wilding."

"I'd take 'em," Ray said, pausing, shrugging, feeling almost sluggish now, "but they ain't the problem." Anyway, Jimmy Redmond was a friend, and the Smiths swapped hay labor in the summer months. Wouldn't do to shoot their dogs.

Ray hitched his collar and sucked a tooth. He realized he was hungry and began mentally surveying the remembered contents of the refrigerator.

Champ looked at the doe. He felt close to tears. The one thing about the boy he'd never been able to reckon was how careful he was, the time he took deciding things, calculations fingered over and over . . . before. Before anything. He did it, *shore*, and well enough, too, usually, but Champ wondered if it was really worth all the braining about, all the staring at things; he had to wonder what was lost along the long way getting there. Sometime, it seemed to him, the boy was just gonna be too late. Yes, sir . . . he was gonna be too damned late. "Give me the gun."

Ray gave hardly a snort.

"Now, you don't recall . . ."

"Don't have to."

"My name, why, it means a thing or two, and . . ."

"Did." Ray yawned. "Maybe."

"Damnation."

Shocked, the boy glanced at his father. The old man was slogging toward him, and even through the deep snow he was a big man. There was something else, too, something Ray hadn't seen for a long time—intent, two black beads of intent for eyes.

Ray felt a strange and strangely fierce panic. He did not want to have to give up the gun. And at the same time there was a smaller, younger part of him that wanted to run toward the old man, he looked so gathered together, so solid.

He called the dog. "Come on, boy, come away now. Come. Come on." This time the dog did not even look. The boy knew that the dog knew there were no cows to herd at this hour, and no meal to be had that was not lying across his paws. The boy tried a high sharp whistle, and the sound gored back through him, without effect on the Boove, on the other dogs, on the chill morning air that seemed to be waiting for just this. Obliquely he was watching, he was feeling, the big moving shape of the old man filling in the field of vision, a shadow spreading up the blue of the sky and down the white of the snow.

Lifting the gun, as if bringing it to his shoulder to set in motion the shooting process would prevent the old man from taking it, Ray sought again a clear shot. The dog was thirty paces off his right, along an angle, the doe a tawny layer just behind; the old man was closer, maybe twenty paces, off his left, along another angle; between the dog and the old man there was a short line. Poised above the line was the new sun, a white light tearing through the surface of the air itself, forcing a relentless flash between dog and man, between the boy's two eyes, centered, aching, between the two lines angling away from Ray and angling back to Ray, the old man left, the dog right . . . and for one blown-open moment it seemed there was an actual choice, and the choice was somehow suddenly a free and equal choice, that depended wholly upon practical factors — the dog who helped, the man who didn't; the dog, admired, the man, embarrassing; the dog who slept in the mudroom, the man who slept in the bedroom at the end of the hall lined with children.

The boy noticed his awareness of there being no one else around.

He thought of his mother, pregnant.

In the white snow the black dog lay, calm and sphinx-like, his eyes hidden behind tatters of fur. The doe's eyes were enormous, they were all of her and all of everything now, taking in, vastly and vast, a world that was still hers, more hers now than anyone's. The two animals seemed almost like friends side by side, characters in a living crèche, except there was no baby, no mother, no god above.

The old man was closer and big, still walking, swelling, coming.

The last thing Ray would do was give up the gun; it came down to that.

He fired a single shot. There was a yelp. The Boove scrambled up even as the doe subsided.

"Nicked him, s'all," Champ cried.

The boy looked at his father, surprised by the sound of his voice.

"Spot of blood." Champ pointed. "See, there, along his left leg, wee spot. He's walking fine. He'll be fine."

Ray stared at the dog. The gun had dropped, barrel down, along his leg, digging into the snow. He could not believe what he might have done. He could not believe.

FROM THE BEGINNING Ray had been an easy child, a good boy — not like James . . . *what a corker*, Luisa thought.

James, next in age, escaped the mantle of Eldest Son, and was an impish, passionate troublemaker too easy to forgive. For family photos he was usually found bottom-center, in the thick of things, and mugging, having waited until the last possible split second to transform his face from scrubbed compliance to a mockery that was somehow irresistibly charming. His was a free ride.

In those same family photos Ray stood at the edge with hands awkward, as though some functionary had removed tools from them and would return them immediately following the picture. His feet were parted and parallel with his shoulders, his posture, as usual, perfect—because he was short. His eyes were not innocent, but they were young, a young animal's eyes, dark and cautious, wanting to learn, no doubt learning, but what? His whole bodily attitude seemed to say, to announce, that he held himself in expectation of an event he could not know and that was his alone.

When he was nine years old, Luisa remembered—Luisa could not forget—the fights; not Ray and another boy, but a whole group of boys beating on him, piling on, murderous in their abandon. It was . . . abnormal. She had never seen anything like it, then or since . . . the times she had had to fetch her mother, who came like the engine of a runaway train down the road to pull the other boys off Ray, lying face down at the bottom, not crying, not unhurt, simply utterly clenched against the forces surrounding him.

"You musn't let them get you like that," his mother would say.

"I don't."

This response would perplex her. "I won't always be there."

Silence.

"I'll have a talk with their parents."

Shrug.

What had Ray done? What had he said? They had been reduced to savages, these perfectly ordinary boys, boys from the village and farms whose parents were known and liked, who came to sugaring-off parties, and corn roasts, and caroling. Ray would not say, Ray had never said. He was closed while it was happening, he was closed after, a closed door. And yet it had never seemed to Luisa that Ray knew the answer and was simply not telling, because afterward, after mother had pulled him out from under, he always seemed a little confused himself; she could still see him bringing his crumpled fist to his lips and searching off obliquely, as if something had gone awry in his tireless calculations—an experiment had not quite confirmed its hypothesis . . . or perhaps it had and that was what was confusing.

Other things replaced the fights, subtler things. Once they took his jacket, a Christmas jacket; they took it and one of them wore it right out, to school. At first Luisa thought that the boy had gotten the same exact jacket . . . except that Ray's was gone. When they went to ask about it, Luisa, the oldest, doing the talking, the boy with the jacket, and the ones sitting behind him, stared at Ray, smiled at her, stared back at Ray. So blatant, so cold, a form of indifference . . . no, not indifference, contempt; and it came from a place that had no walls.

With her he was not always gentle, but there was something protective. He was not any more open, though he seemed to relax some.

Still, Luisa could not forget those fights and the uncanny cloud of silence surrounding them . . . those perfectly ordinary boys . . . and Ray, something about Ray . . . sealed, storm-tight . . . and those boys, wide open, coming at him with the rage of the world behind them.

All this rushed back as Luisa watched her brother tramp up from the orchard. She was cleaning out the hen house, carrying chickens two at a time by their feet over to the old duck pen for temporary containment; she saw him start across the yard, that strange half-confused, half-calculating look struggling about his eyes, his fist pressed up along the side of his face, the gun in his left hand, his trousers damp to the knees.

"Hey," she called.

He glanced up, stopped.

"You okay?"

"Where's the hired man?"

The chickens dangling by their feet were trying to peck Luisa's forearms; she gave Ray a funny tired smile, and shook them down.

"They'll get sick if you do that."

"Huh?"

"You can't do it too much, they'll get sick. They got to fight back too, how they can, you know, carrying 'em that way, and if you shake 'em down too many times, why, they'll just chuck on you.

They got a right, you know, it's not funny, they got a right to peck, being moved around that way, upside down. Jesus. There's no dignity in it, none a'tall. Even a chicken's got to have some . . ." Ray gazed off, frowning. "Shake 'em up that way . . ." he muttered.

Luisa felt her breath come all the way in and stay. She flipped the chickens upright and let them bustle back toward the hen house, clucking. "I always move 'em that way," she said very quietly, lidding her eyes.

He jerked his face back at her. "What?"

"Nothing."

"What?"

"The chickens . . . never mind."

"Chickens?" He shook his head. "Jesus." He looked at Luisa as if there were something deeply wrong with her. "Haven't got this kind of time, Lu. Don't you understand, I haven't got time . . . Jesus."

"Sorry, Ray."

"Sorry?"

"What's the matter, Ray? Tell me what's the matter?"

"Jesus."

"Where's Pa?" she said, squinting toward the distant edge of the orchard. "He go with you?"

"Jee-sus-H-Kee-riste. I ask *you* where that hired man hid himself off, and now you've got me looking for Pa. Here," he said abruptly, shoving the gun at her. "I got to go. I've got school. I got no time for . . . chickens . . ." Then he lurched off, and at the edge of the yard he thought to look back over his shoulder. There was Luisa, his big blunt sister with the gun weird in her hand; and then it was as if a load of heavy curtains had suddenly dropped in a heap around him, and he heard a small bodiless voice that seemed to be his, or to have once been his, say, "He's fine, Pa's fine."

IT WAS ALMOST 8:30—no time to shower or change. From the top of the stove Ray scooped a couple of fried donuts out of the grease drainer, a bottle of cola from the fridge, tossed them in his backpack after books and papers, then headed out. He heard his mother upstairs, but he was not prepared to see her yet; he was ready to make it up with her, but he wanted to think how it would be first.

He had to leave, and that—the having to leave and the preparing to leave—excited him beyond the reach of the morning. It did not matter what had or had not happened in the pasture, it was behind, part of a time that was being swiftly discarded.

Ray ate one of the donuts while he waited for the truck to warm up, fished out the second one and started on it. By then he'd forgotten about Sam Chase, and was sorry to see him come around the barn across the yard in that smooth grooved way of his, like a human ball bearing, neither hurrying nor lagging, everything eminently minutely continuously adjusting. For half a minute Ray wanted what his mother wanted—to see some manure flapped on him.

"I thought I'd take a look at the baler," Sam Chase said in a genial manner, and he smiled inclusively, as if many were listening. "That suit you, or do you want me to run more fence line today?"

"The baler?"

"Yes, sir."

Ray peered out over the hood of his red truck. He always felt good, sitting in his truck, looking ahead through the windshield. One hand draped over the steering wheel, his left leg cocked out the side, and the door ajar between him and Sam Chase, Ray felt relaxed, open, and yet protected by the door and the truck encasing him, even by the donut waiting in his hand.

He had heard the *sir*, and decided it was right, and about it said nothing to the hired man. Even though he didn't want to think what might have happened that morning, what might have happened and the things he had had to consider, or had found himself considering, had made him feel older, like a man who's been to a war. It had scared him at first, but now he was beginning to feel just a little proud of his daring, and of the scope of his mind, the practicalities with their cool clean edges that had materialized in his own hands. *This is what it feels like*, he said to himself; and the feeling was immediately embodied by the configuration of the moment: Ray sitting, preparing to leave, places to go, while next to him stood another man who worked for him, who awaited his word, and whose age meant nothing.

"Won't need the baler till there's hay to cut," said Ray, striking an air of boredom. He took a slow bite of his donut. "Won't be any hay to cut till there's hay growing," his mouth full now, "and can't nothing grow with snow laying on."

"Hmmm . . ." Sam responded, as if this were actual news. "So, what is that, in time?"

"Month."

Sam Chase gave a long and thoughtful nod. "That baler's not new."

"Not too."

"I'm concerned that, if the baler does need attention, we might need a part."

"Like as not."

"Some parts can be hard to get."

Now this was smart thinking, to Ray's mind. He regarded Sam Chase pointedly, a private in Ray's army, and felt proud of his handiwork; he had hired Sam Chase, he had told his mother that Sam Chase was going to put them ahead of things—and here he was doing just that. Any half-wit could string fence line.

"Right," he said, slamming the truck door. "Check out the Farmall while you're at it."

Ray had the truck turned around and ready to roll when Sam raised a finger and glided back over. "Say," he began, "you aren't stopping at Dugan's, by any chance."

Ray hadn't planned on it; on the other hand, there was always a thing or two he could need from Dugan's. He nodded.

"Would you mind picking up a pack of Newports for me?"

He indicated that he would not mind.

And as Ray Rinaldi wound down the infamous road of Coulter's, he was already calculating fence line into the weekend's many projects, and feeling nearly smug about having his baler and mower ready to go when the hay was high. *Get in three cuts for shore*, he thought.

HEIDI GREENFIELD had light, clean skin. Even when there was something on it—a crumb, a little smear of raspberry jam, a tag of mud along an elbow—it was somehow charming and impertinent, a tease to perfection. She wore her straight, chocolate-colored hair in a tail high at the back of her head, though it was not the style for girls her age, and when she walked the long tail moved like the arm of a native dancer. To the white clapboard house across from Dugan's many friends came, but none was particularly close; there was something private about Heidi—not dark, but like a thing that was intricately folded, and that would remain so until exact and unique conditions arose; these were the subject of some speculation among the subadult males of Harrow.

At seventeen she possessed the easy, swinging confidence of a child who has been adored from the very beginning, and who is unconscious of both the adoration and the confidence because they exist within the particles of her being and have become something else transformed, not susceptible to the ordinary push and sway of living. Her two brothers were considerably older, her parents were alive, and anyone wanting to meet Heidi, to play with Heidi, to engage Heidi, to look at Heidi, had to run the four-headed gauntlet of her devoted family. They were generous with their treasure. Shrewd enough not to spoil her with words and other decorations. What they thought about her, what they felt for her, was a presence, the air she breathed and, more important, the air they breathed. Heidi was the centering mystery.

It did not seem to matter that Heidi was not a great beauty, though she was as nice to look at as any of the village girls, her blue eyes inquisitive, polite, never critical. Even unkindness did not unduly upset her; she seemed to see it as part of a whole she loved unquestioningly. The pants she wore might be too short, the shirts outsized, her shoes functional, sometimes accidentally attractive. But nothing could really disturb, nothing could undo, the still and waiting identity of Heidi Greenfield. Heidi was Heidi, absolute. It was this more than any of her pleasing attributes—which were, after all, average—that rendered her utterly fetching. It had simply never occurred to her to be anyone else, to attach to herself any of the passing styles, or to find in one, at the exclusion of others, qualities requiring allegiance. The movements of Heidi's life seemed adjusted to the planet itself, impervious to any but the largest and incontestable forces of the universe.

Ray stopped quickly at Dugan's for the Newports, still feeling expanded and expansive, and in control, yes, in control. Dugan hadn't received his cigarette delivery yet, and Ray would have to come back later, after school. He paused in the doorway, shading his eyes. The village street gleamed like an oil slick between the soft piles of slush. Everywhere water dripped, puddled, flowed; passing cars sent up fins of colored spray, steam pumped off the rooftops, and the scene had become a dazzling kaleidoscope of water. Through it, in the middle of it, stood Heidi Greenfield.

He crossed over to her yard without thinking.

Heidi placed a little tub of peanut butter on the windowsill, then she set on the mailbox, on the bird feeder, and on the gatepost three pie tins of crumbs and peas for the migrating birds who had already arrived.

"Hi, Ray." She didn't seem surprised to see him.

Thus the meeting seemed fated.

"Hello, Heidi," he said, trying for an easy formality.

Her skin was impossibly clean.

Ray's tongue was wadding up in his mouth, but he managed to wring out of it the question, "Aren't you going to school?"

"Not till second period."

He didn't know how to ask why, and anyway he didn't care about the answer. It felt good, it felt extravagant, just standing there, half his work done for the day, snow melting, Heidi right in front of him, people coming and going at Dugan's, maybe seeing them together, and this strange new feeling that he had traveled somewhere else, beyond the boundary of the world he and Heidi and everyone in Harrow knew, and had come back changed —a stranger. It was this—being a stranger—that had impelled him to cross over to Heidi's house where he had never before stopped.

"Whose birds you aim to feed?"

"Any that are hungry."

He tried a casual smile. "That's giving of you."

"There's nothing to eat with the snow."

"You'll get crows."

"Yesterday there were towhees and blackbirds, and a dove that came late." She shrugged. "Crow's okay too, if it's hungry enough."

"Or lazy enough."

"A bird can't be lazy, you think?"

Ray looked at her. She was neat to look at—her skin, her pony-tail, her lemon bright sweater too big, probably one of her broth-ers', and unraveling at the hem, he couldn't help noticing, a little tail of teasing yarn wagging in the breeze. Heidi was asking him a question, crossing through the air space to pull something out of him and take it back to her; he liked her taking from him, he could almost feel in his middle a tugging sensation, as if she had a little beak and was pulling a worm from his soil.

"I mean," she went on, "lazy's a human thing. A bird's only got to be . . . efficient. If it works when it doesn't have to . . ."

"Works for what?"

"Food. If it works when it doesn't need to work, or doesn't work when it should, when its body needs food, then it won't sur-vive. Simple." She made a happy, hands-up gesture.

Not one thing suitable for saying materialized in Ray Rinaldi's mind; it felt like a padded cell up there—nothing could get in, and there was nothing in it to get out except bizarre images having to do with Heidi's clean skin. In desperation, he indulged in a long elaborate stretch, giving the back of his neck a vigorous rub, then he began a close study of his fingers, which only brought back to mind her skin.

Long ago he had noticed that there weren't any cars in her drive-way, and now he was feeling the swelling radiating red presence of his truck parked across the road in front of Dugan's.

"Well," he said, "you need a ride to school?"

"I don't have to go till second period," she said again, as if she hadn't said it already.

"Well."

"You don't have first period either?"

"If I feel like it I do."

"Oh."

"I'm pretty much on my own now."

Heidi picked up some snow and used it to clean peanut butter off her hands, her pale tapered fingers moving in adjacent order, like the white bones of fanning wings. "All this snow," she said, squinting pleasantly at him. "Buried the daffodils."

"Yeah?"

She turned and pointed toward the house. "There's a patch under the windows and tulips beside the walkway."

"They yours?" If only he could keep it going . . .

She gave Ray and the territory about him a wide, blue-eyed welcome. "They're anybody's. Anybody who likes looking at them."

"But did you put 'em in, or your ma?"

Heidi lightly cocked her head as if this was not something she would bother to remember. "You can't see them," she said, "but they're there. Perfect green spears. They were just about to open when it snowed."

"Damn snow." The swearing was intentional, because he had just struck on what he could say to Heidi. "Had to shoot a doe this morning. Dogs ran her into the drifts. She was birthing, and the fawn was stuck."

"How sad."

"It was a tricky shot."

"But you got her?"

"Shore."

Now . . . now here he was at the place where he wanted to be able to tell her about the things he had considered, and how it was like some of the things you had to consider during a war or a disaster, laying aside your feelings, and the picture so big that out at its very edges was the beginning of another picture whose existence had never occurred to you but was occurring to you now for the first time; and this other picture at the outermost edge of the Big Picture was itself another country, where the rules weren't exactly changed, just so enormous and so simple that you didn't need many of them; and in this other picture, this other country, he was another and altogether different man. In it he felt himself to be a kind of leader. The trouble was, Heidi was deep inside the first picture. But Ray was convinced that Heidi Greenfield had what it took to see the Big Picture as not all that big, and to go with him beyond it into the other one that had no limits, no frame.

But he couldn't figure out how to say the part about his old man, not the killing part, but the idea behind it, the reason of it. It took time to explain that grand sort of logic and . . . originality; he would have to figure out how it would be, the words and the way the words came, and how she would look when the words came to her—he didn't want to scare her, but he realized now that it was important, somehow it was *of utmost importance* for Heidi Greenfield to understand that Ray Rinaldi was quietly and profoundly different from the ordinary run.

"Will your family use the meat?" she was saying. "I always feel better about it, if the meat is used, like some part of the doe will live in the muscles of the people who eat her."

"Muscles?"

Ray looked at her; he wasn't really listening to her words, he was listening to her voice, it had such a tangible quality, as if he might reach out and grab it and keep it there inside his hands, soft and struggling, a wild bird he could tame. At that moment Heidi's voice was the only real thing in this world to which he had returned; it was real enough, it was *pure* enough, to fly with him into the other world.

About the venison he said nothing: Ray was not one of these losers who would stop for roadkill; he wouldn't shave around a ruptured bladder, he'd as soon not have any of it; and he wouldn't take anything dogs had walked away from.

"Or the brain," Heidi added.

"What if it lives in the liver?" said Ray. "Or toes? Or the wart of someone who eats her?"

"Or a spurt of energy on Saturday afternoon?"

"Saturday?"

"Why not Saturday?"

Why not, why not Saturday, why not anything on any day? A genuine rush of joy overtook Ray, so unlike his usual half rations that it gave him a start, as if someone had run into him from behind, all the way into him, and was now standing inside his body looking through his own used eyes out at Heidi, at newness altogether fair and clear and free of memory. On his face he felt an unfamiliar smile, and reaching up, he touched the pull and shape of the new muscles crowding about his mouth. Because it was so queer, it made him feel so queer, being silly with Heidi Greenfield in her front yard, and late for school, and at the same time, wavering up from behind the silly odd wondrous feeling, like a black tail of smoke rising above a pretty knoll he had just discovered and wanted to walk to and lie upon, was the uneasy sense that at home there was something he had forgotten.

For a moment he thought with anticipation of the literal Saturday, which was three days away, but that seemed to spoil the sense of things, and he heard in his mind the cry, *any day*—a protest, a vow.

"A great dream at 4 A.M.," said Heidi.

"A dream."

"At four?"

"No, I'm up at four." Then he remembered his mother.

"You don't sleep enough."

"I don't have to. I don't have many dreams." He was still smiling.

"You don't?"

"No." He thought about it then. "Not really."

"No?" Heidi cradled her hands and regarded Ray with a simple concern.

"Well, no." Again, in his mind he saw his mother, heard her retching in the distant hallway of the morning. "No, nothing . . . particular."

"Oh."

"But I know that some day . . ." his voice, it was disappearing, it was thinning into thin air, "I still think, that is, I maybe am . . ." Something was happening . . . suddenly something was happening to Ray, it felt catastrophic—the end of his nose tingled, his chest felt funny, squeezed . . . time flowed palpably around him, like a slow heavy liquid, finding the creases and shadows of his being, pulling him down to the bottom of the weight of his years, looking back up through darkening depths . . . He had to cough and look away, cough again; then, fairly whispering, he asked, "Where did you say they were?"

"What?"

"The tulips."

"Along the walk. And the daffodils are over there."

Ray went then, and dropped to his knees, and commenced to pluck, very gently, the snow from all about the buried flowers, feeling blindly for them with fingertips and patting palms; Heidi joined him, and they worked until the stalks were revealed, their spiraling folds of leafage still waiting. They agreed it was going to be warm today. They agreed they might still open if the snow were pulled away and they were given another chance.

Though it was Heidi who seemed to be giving Ray another chance.

HEIDI WENT to school with Ray.

The high school was located in a larger town about twenty minutes east, and driving there nothing happened. They listened to The Point out of Montpelier, a folk/rock station of her choosing; and nothing happened.

The air came up from the south, not a breeze but a wind. It blew over the hills above the high road, and down across the fields to the brook where the willow bushes were putting out a soft, golden haze of new growth. The wind rushed through the willow bushes and left them shimmering in the light, and for the first few miles whenever Ray glanced across the seat to Heidi the gold shimmered behind her like a running halo, but she was not aware of the effect and only smiled at him, singing along with songs she knew, not embarrassed, just there, just Heidi on the seat next to him.

And there was no problem with him missing first period, because he had never before missed it; the secretary made a nice forgiving face and waved him on.

In second period—Civics—Ray sat by the window, which was open, and so nothing happened.

But by third period—Literature and Composition—it was distinctly warm outside. All of the thermometers in the school had been preset to winter standards and no one, naturally enough, had reset them yet to lower levels, since the warmth had only just arrived.

Mrs. Porter—third period Lit/Comp—was always cold; she had low blood pressure and low blood volume, and blamed her susceptibility on these genetic provisos, though her husband thought it had more to do with them moving up from Florida to the place where his family, not hers, had summered for the better part of the century. Mr. Porter had threatened all along to retire in Harrow. Mrs. Porter taught solely to pass the winter, dreaming of orange blossoms and cotton shifts, and keeping the windows closed.

Ray had not had time to shower or to change from his barn clothes. Mrs. Porter's room was warm, the room was baking warm, in fact, owing to the day's natural heat as well as the locked-on thermostats and the closed windows. Ray's clothing, or the scents trapped within the fabric—scents of cows and hay and manure, manure especially—awakened and arose, extending their influence beyond him, and within fifteen minutes, exhilarated to the room's full dimensions, they hung, ripening, over the heads of all present, like very expensive cheese.

Someone said something, a boy Ray did not know well whose father owned a B&B.

Stray words here and there. Hands moving about noses.

"Jeez, Ray," a friend whispered.

Coughing, apparently contagious.

Under low eyes, Ray snuck a look at Heidi. She looked right back at him. It was a strong, strong look, stronger than anything in the room, she seemed to mean to isolate him inside the beam of the look and to obliterate everything else. And it might have worked, except for Mrs. Porter.

Mrs. Porter, still lecturing doggedly about Faulkner's use of symbol, went to the window and with some difficulty wrenched it open. Never before had Mrs. Porter opened a window.

Ray collected his things and managed to walk most of the way to the door, though, passing Heidi, he said under his breath, "what're you lookin' at," and broke into a staggered run.

RAY DROVE TO the Canadian line and back, killing two hours before he stopped again at Dugan's for the hired man's pack of Newports, aiming to smoke one of them himself. Arlen Bell was ahead of him in the checkout line, trying to return a hat. The Lague boys were behind, dirty enough to make Ray like them at that moment more than he ever had, though they smelled not of manure but of balsam, fresh and piney and sweet as burnt sugar.

"She should've called for the numbers," Arlen was saying.

"We don't carry this hat."

"Like to find a way to keep it. Ayuh."

"She didn't buy it here."

"It says on the tag, see, right here, The Ell Bee Jay Hat."

"You vote for him?"

"I hain't sayin' one way or t'other." He tapped the crown of the hat and smiled off, as if recollecting the era of that distant election. "I'm sayin' thisen a fine hat, fine enough for one of our'n presidents, and like it to fool his very self, if he needed a hat in them warm climes, but it don't fit me."

Fleeing politics, Dugan ventured to ask, "Where's your daughter now?"

"She's down ta Hanover since March, thought you'd'a heard."

"Nope."

"Joe done all right by you," Arlen said softly.

"Maybe I did hear."

"Done all right by you."

Dugan did not say anything.

"Hanover's a good piece. We miss her . . ."

"All right."

"If you'd a raised him . . ."

"All right, Arlen."

"Ayuh, she's gone, the kids'r gone, on account a' Joe cotched a job in vegetables at a big grocery outfit, and the whole fam dambly's down there now."

"Hanover. That's probably where she bought it, Arlen. In Hanover."

The register girl was trying to keep busy; she loaded a new spool of tape, tidied up the paper bags, wiped off the counter with window cleaner and a paper towel, careful to use just one sheet, with Dugan standing right there. Having to call her boss from the back room where he enjoyed making up his orders and sorting the day's invoices, just for a customer problem, filled her with dread—especially now. Summer was coming and with it, summer people; Dugan was already gearing up, making room for specialty items it wouldn't do to carry in the winter: puff pastry and Szechwan sauce and fancy cuts of meat, T-shirts with logos and cows, picnic baskets, tennis balls, fishing rods not made to last, expensive wine from California that was made to last but wouldn't, if business kept growing the way it had been. The whole process caused a lot of agitation around Dugan's store.

Arlen leaned forward over the counter, the LBJ hat between them, sadly white and innocent, like something a toddler was meant to sit on but refused to. "The hat and me are here, and Hanover's a fair piece. You got hats back there next to potions. Swap me one."

Dugan fiddled with the money in his pocket. He already knew he wasn't going to win this one. Because of Joe's raise. "So, it's your birthday, Mr. Bell."

"Seventy-eight."

"Seventy-eight."

"I recollect you at half Rinaldi's size here," he said, nodding at Ray.

"Do you."

"Used to filch the wife's raspberries, sell 'em to campers."

Dugan gave a sizable guffaw. "Me or the bears." He glanced at Ray, then at the Lague boys, who were staring down at their submarine sandwiches with great logger longing. "You look at my hats, Arlen?"

Arlen mashed his nose this way and that, and sniffed heartily. "Saw a brown I might would sneak 'bout in."

"What size? Seeing it's your birthday."

"She didn't call for the numbers."

Dugan nodded; he was tired of it all now; he was tired of Arlen because he was tired of summer coming, and he was tired of summer coming because he had to *bet* on the come, make choices, stock up, wait. Any other month he'd've taken the hat, no questions. Right now he didn't have time for Arlen Bell's birthday hat. "But *you* know what size you wear, even if your daughter in Hanover doesn't."

Arlen Bell looked at Dugan as if he'd curdled all the milk in all the milk parlors of Orleans County. "Now how'd I know the numbers without trying the lot on?"

Dugan closed and opened his eyes. He took Arlen by the arm and walked him back to hats and potions.

Ray stepped up and asked for the pack of Newports.

"Have to be eighteen."

"They're not for me."

The register girl gave Ray a beseeching look. She was one of Luisa's chums; she knew Ray wasn't eighteen.

"Our hired man asked me to pick 'em up. He's working on the baler," Ray added to imply that the hired man could not be bothered fetching cigarettes, though this idea in itself was the start of a vague concern, yet another tear in the fabric of Ray's day.

And when she gave in—because she didn't want to have to call Dugan back up front—and told him how much; and Ray, pulling out his wallet, realized that Sam Chase hadn't given him any money for the cigarettes, the vague concern ripped wide open. *Who's working for frigging who*, he thought.

He grabbed the pack and went out, and walked across to the Commons where there was a memorial bench.

Right after came the Lague boys with their short, work-deformed bodies, muscles lumping across shoulders, gathering in calves and buttocks; even their movements were lopsided to injuries and sore spots and obscure aches that would never have time in their lives to heal; everything about them was rounded over and aimed groundward. Skidding logs, hauling logs, sawing logs, loading logs—men who cut spent most of their day looking down, except for the first brief look up to make felling estimations, and then to watch the vertical quiver that preceded the tree's last stand as it reached out and over, sometimes leaping away from the raw pink stump. Ray had to admit they worked harder than he did, two of the best mossbacks in the Kingdom, it was said. They were not talkers; they were used to the woods. They were good men just to be around; had a settling effect.

As the two approached he raised a couple of fingers in salute.

Marcel, the eldest, nodded back.

Martin tried to look up from under the bush of his hair but it required too much of him socially, and he sat himself down without apology, and began carefully to peel the cellophane from his lunch.

The three of them took up all of the bench, their padded arms touching, their legs careful.

For the five minutes it took the brothers to dispatch their subs nobody said anything.

Finally Ray said, "Been busy?"

Marcel nodded. "You?"

"Straight out."

"Heard you got a man."

"Yeah." Ray examined the tip of the cigarette, then shaped the ash against the edge of the bench. "Got somethin'?"

Marcel leaned forward, set his bottle of cola in the slush between his legs, and while he was bent over he snatched a large splinter that was stuck to the side of his sock, and used it to pick his teeth.

"Still cuttin' pulp for Fenton's?"

"Was."

"That mill's always shutting down."

"Well, no."

Then for the first time that year Ray heard the younger Lague actually speak. "We are in disagreement over how we are being paid," he said.

Ray gave Martin's statement a lot of room. When he finally said, "Oh," it was only to give it some more room, to draw it about them, like the scent of something fine and rare. And when by the length of his silence he had acknowledged his sense of being practically honored by Martin Lague's use of his voice and language; and when by the quality of his silence he had indicated his total belief in their gripe with Fenton's mill, whatever it was, he asked them what they were going to do now.

"Got a job over t' Maine. Private contract," said the elder Lague.

"Not enough woods here, you got to go to Maine?"

"It be considerable."

Ray waited; Marcel scratched his ear, and allowed that it was more than a section.

"That'll take a season plus."

"Spell."

"You got a gang?"

"Marty and me, maybe a kid for general fetchin' purposes. A passin' big skid horse, I'd like, I would, it's steep land, and I favor a good solid horse better'n contraptions you got to tinker up and watch out for on the slopes. But we don't have a trailer for a horse if we had one, which we don't."

"Ran on a guy in North Albany, farms with a team of matched Percherons."

"What for?"

"Shore don't know," Ray said. "He's one of these back-to-the-land types. Maybe he'd take the cure and lease one of 'em."

Marcel finished off his cola and sat staring at the empty bottle. "Sounds too fancy for what we got going."

"What'd they want, pulp?"

"Nope."

"Just the hardwood then."

"Nope. Just ash."

Ray made a sound as he exhaled. He offered them one of Sam Chase's cigarettes, trying to use up as many as possible, but the brothers declined. He lit a second one for himself. It didn't taste good, but it gave his hands something to do, and he liked sending smoke out into the clear noon air. He wasn't ready to go home. "Just the ash."

"Ayuh."

Ray shook his head. "Baseball bats."

Marcel smiled. Several important teeth were missing. "Not pulp."

"Not pulp," Ray agreed. He sent some more smoke out into the air. "Never been t' Maine."

The brothers were silent.

"Near the ocean?"

"Naw. North."

Ray gazed across to Dugan's on the corner, then over to Heidi Greenfield's front yard, where he could just make out the green of the tulip and daffodil stalks, surrounded by wells of snow, looking ridiculous, looking fussy and poignant and . . . well, *stupid*.

He had never seen the ocean. An ocean was worth seeing. Some day. *Any day*, he said in his mind, but the words, which earlier sounded a kind of battle cry, had been enfeebled by the sad, though apparently providential coincidence of his clothes and the heat in Mrs. Porter's third-period class. So small, yet it had smashed everything that he and the day and the events of the day had conspired so extraordinarily to make. One minute he was sailing beyond the Big Picture, a stranger to himself, and liking the stranger, impressed by the stranger, Heidi in tow; and the next minute he was cast to the bottom of the canvas, a painted-on shadow of someone not real.

Even the Lagues were going somewhere.

The brothers crumpled their bags, tossed them in the can next to the bench, and stood. Martin unwrapped a Snickers and tore a chunk off with his side teeth. Marcel said, "Could use a kid for the job. Hear of anyone . . ."

"Shore," Ray said, watching them go.

It did not occur to Ray until their truck was narrowing to a point at the bend that they might have had him, Ray Rinaldi, in mind, as a likely kid for general fetching purposes.

HE SAT THERE for a long time. The bench was marble. His back began to bother him, so he removed his jacket, rolled it, and tucked it at the base of his spine for support. Soon he felt chilled, and put the jacket back on; the backache returned, and he tried the rolled jacket again, trading one misery for another, not gaining on either. The day had started with his back . . . and her misery too. Morning sickness. But it was all right.

He tried to puzzle his way through the hours that had led him to this bench—his back, her sickness, the crackers and the orange tea, the door closed on laughter, laughter, he felt sick with the other laughter . . . cows, silent beasts giving milk . . . the Boove lying with the doe, the Boove eyeless and the doe all-eyes, only eyes, and the sun burning between his eyes while the old man kept coming, why did he keep coming . . . Luisa . . . Heidi . . . the smell of his work clothes, just the smell . . . of his work . . . Arlen's stupid hat, he had waited behind Arlen Bell's stupid hat in order to buy with his own money the hired man a lousy pack of cigarettes . . .

When the elementary school let out, Ray saw two of his siblings go in to Dugan's and come out with fists of candy which he figured they bought using the milk money they had not spent at lunch. They were not much fond of milk. It seemed to Ray that they saw him sitting on the memorial bench at the Commons, or maybe they didn't, maybe he was not easy to notice, especially after school when there was candy to eat. They were off to some place, and Ray was apparently not moving from the memorial bench.

None of the younger ones paid him much attention—he was not a parent, he was hardly a brother, he wasn't around, he was up early, he had work. The work was there to do. But it didn't matter. Soon there would be another one who would not pay him much attention. But she did. She cared. She knew the secret thing waiting inside him; it was like the thing inside her, he had got it from her, and someday he would be it.

Suddenly in his brain there was a screaming sensation. He bowed his head, squeezed up his face, but he couldn't make it stop. He thought, *for her*, and felt first a sickening pity, and then right after shame so strong it turned his stomach. Again he noticed his back pain like a spike that came and went without warning, and the cold marble behind and beneath him, and he saw again Heidi's unopened flowers lined up waiting, waiting, everything seemed to be waiting, and he felt with the force of a blow his own solitude, and was glad for it and each discomfort, each and any that could wear away some of the humiliation of caring.

It was always for her, it was always all for her, and the deep silent magnetized love, which was not love so much as forgiveness in advance.

She had standards, fine standards; he could nearly always almost reach them. He could.

The old man never even came close.

Why the frigging fuck did she put up with the old man?

A GOOD MANY of the citizens of the township of Harrow entered and left Dugan's, carrying boxes of groceries, hardware, gardening supplies, gallon cans of whitewash for spring primping. Ray watched as if he were watching a community parade, the sole spectator there on the village memorial bench, spectator and judge. For a while he pretended that they knew he was watching, and were secretly trying to impress him. When Mrs. Langton went in he thought he would get up, it would be nice to help her out with her groceries. He liked Mrs. Langton, she *conversed* with him, and looked in his eyes; she seemed to want to know what was back there, and she wasn't going to look away when she spotted it.

One of Dugan's clerks had her box when she came out; they were conversing in a friendly manner; she seemed relaxed. *Or relieved*, Ray thought. And then for some reason Ray felt less like a spectator, and not at all like a judge, but like the one person who had been excluded from the village parade.

AT THREE O'CLOCK he watched the old man's Ford curl around the Commons, past Dugan's, past the post office and the gas pump, and ease into the gray slush piled in front of Billy's Restaurant and Bar.

Son of a bitch.

The engine choked to a stop. The door opened and the old man hulked upward, and for several moments he stood adjusting his quilted flannel shirt, smoothing back his hair, patting for his wallet in the same place several times.

Even Champ Rinaldi was part of the village parade.

Well, hurry up, if you're gonna do it, do it.

Champ glanced about to check that no one was watching him. He did not see his own son on the bench at the Commons a block away, because he was not checking to see, but checking to check, to indulge in a lingering piece of the lingering dream that it still mattered.

The sight of his father sent a charge through the core of Ray Rinaldi. He sat with an absolute stillness, feeling the electricity, waiting to see if it could act alone, without his participation; wanting it to act alone, without his consent.

Champ ambled into Billy's as if he had never been there, a tourist, a salesman, swiping off his hat with a sad flourish as he entered.

At three-fifteen, because at three-thirty the school bus would drop off Harrow students and Heidi would be among them, Ray Rinaldi quit the memorial bench, crossed to his truck, and went home for chores. When he got to his own drive and started up he found himself thinking about the cows, wondering where in fact they went at night; he shook his head, gave a half laugh—he had never really thought about it. Where do they go? The speculation became so intense, so absorbing, that he actually considered staying awake in order to follow them from a dark distance, and know. The whole question, together with the dulling pace and well-known contours of evening chores, quite suppressed his memory of the day with its strange lurching to-and-fro, its fateful double dealing.

FOR THREE DAYS a restless wind continued up from the south, and the snow shrank back to porous ovals, then shrank back further, revealing specks of introductory color. On the hills around the village the maples stood ready, furled leaves blushing rose-gold as they unfurled, and their limbs seeming more naked now with the knowledge of spring entirely present, and summer coming, and everything late, than they had been against the white virginity of winter where all was line and form. In the lowest places small ponds developed, and about them, marigolds, and among and beyond them, blades of grass straightened by riots to the sun.

And yet there was a more than usual desperate quality to spring that year, the snow so late leaving, and as it left, exposing not only last year's life long gone—the pale tufts of grass, and blackened lumps of half-moldered vegetation, the cinereous vertebra of ferns lying one across another, the raw dirt—but this year's promise so late made, and so far from being fulfilled, foliage and flowers and hidden lives waiting, waiting and straining. Spring's hold seemed unconvincing. Even the voles who had begun and left off their tunneling so many times had retreated to the stone walls to wait and see. The black flies were out, though not in confident numbers; the deer flies hovered about the spruce woods, ventured no further; mosquitoes hatched as they could. And a vague anxiety infected the people of Harrow: knowing that it could not, they were nevertheless afraid that winter would return.

FOR THREE DAYS Champ Rinaldi drank with a terrible rapture. He drank his way so far into drunkenness that he found the clear quiet shining center of it, and from there saw back through the storm that both bound and protected him now, through the storm and past it to the times before. He did not explain to anyone why he drank so, but he knew why; for the first time he knew why, and he knew what he knew in a stated form that made it real and unavoidable and perfect. She was not mad at him.

She had not been mad at him for three, maybe four years. Then, he could feel himself, where she ended and where he began, and the anger plying between them like a little steamer across the river of drink. There she was/there he was; the drinking, the little steamer—everything placed and definite. If he had ventured to reach out and grab hold of himself, or of her, which he did, which he loved to do, he had hands.

Now he did not have hands. He had lost hold of himself.

Riding low in the water, the steamer would come across the river to where he stood, and it came loaded. He had not been able to see what it was exactly, but he had known she was full of something for him. Maybe not love. That was okay. Something wild and out of her hands, down there in the hold beneath the waters.

In the days when she was angry he had something that was his, the heavy cloak of himself worn about his shoulders in the presence of her anger; the cloak that her anger enabled him to find.

CHAMP HAD COME up from the orchard after Ray, and gone directly to the tool shed where he kept a bottle of vermouth, but it was near empty, so he tried several of his old caches in the barn—all long cleared out, probably by the boy. Champ had many times searched them before. Still he looked. Then he angled for the house, where he knew there was some hard cider. Two bottles. He drank one, but it was not right, not what his mouth was tasting for. Selda saw him come in. He knew she saw his aim, because she gave him that direct listening look that was like an empty room with her in the middle of it, waiting for him to do something, he did not know what. He knew she knew, and that she would leave him to it; still, he pretended it was not his aim.

In the parlor they used for occasions he stretched out on the couch and read the newspaper, one leg hanging over the back. Above his head the thin tent of paper quivered lightly as if a fan were on somewhere, and he shook it briskly now and then to conceal the real cause. Selda ranged about the house, picking up this, depositing that—laundry, mail, items strayed from their rightful place—finally he heard her go out to Luisa in the garden. He sat up on an elbow, listened intently.

In the mudroom, stamping feet. The hired man let himself in and took something from the catch-it drawer.

From beneath his quivering tent Champ slipped a hand and waved.

Sam Chase said hello as he was leaving.

Down the hall, Carrie turned on the TV. She was home with a cold. Her deep hacking cough seemed designed for someone older and bigger; the violence of it, the thought of her small body occupied by something unfairly big and possibly staggering . . . tenderness bound up his throat.

It was important to try not to think about her.

Waiting—not too long—he timed his foray for one of Carrie's wrenching episodes: he moved swift and ghostlike to the pantry where Selda kept a bottle of rum for holiday cakes, on the bottom shelf behind the candied ginger. Half an inch left. He poured it into a glass of cola, put the empty bottle back, and returned to the couch. The cola was annoying, taking up so much space, and cold when he didn't want something cold, and muscling back the rum, the clear underdog down there somewhere trying to help him, just trying to help. Throughout the glass of rum and cola he was able to read, but when it was gone he began to feel distracted again.

His hands were still ticking about. There had not been enough rum.

On the edge of the couch cushion he sat now, half crouched as if ready to leap, tapping his fingertips together, thinking, thinking.

Outside Luisa stood up. The motion caught his attention. She knocked the dirt from her knees, and tramped over to the manure pile; when she had filled the barrow, she wheeled it back to the garden. Through the pocked lavender glass Champ watched her. He saw how ugly she was, the fact of it; and then the thing that was waiting to break inside him, broke in earnest, he was wiping tears, he was thinking of Selda with another baby he knew she did not want at her age but would take and take care of; and his eldest son, the things he said; the doe, the gun, Luisa with no prospects, himself with no prospects, no gun and no aim anymore, no caches he did not know were not caches, the empty searches, the emptiness, the empty room and his being in it, his body making it emptier, the way a corpse does, laid out in the room the family never uses.

Carrie coughed.

Selda used a shovel to spread the manure around the garden.

He sat watching her, feeling obscurely sick at the edges of himself, which seemed somehow to be breaking down so that small things were getting in and getting to him—the dark dirt, the manure, the flat, violent sheet-metal light of midmorning, the smell of old donut grease from the kitchen, Carrie's cough. Out there beyond the lavender glass the steady industry of his women droned on. Luisa said something he could not hear, and Selda straightened, stacking her palms atop the shovel handle, and gazed up the slope behind the house, as if considering how to answer. Even while her hands rested and her body stood idle, she looked powerful, storm-tight.

He wished he could hear her answer, whatever it was. Selda never said anything that could be easily thrown away. There was meaning, there was something valuable, even when it was funny it was serious in the middle.

He watched her mouth move, and the soundless words came forth through the beautiful portals of her lips. She had exquisite lips, full and intelligent, like a Greek statue's.

Nodding thoughtfully, Luisa pushed another zucchini seed into the earth.

Suddenly he remembered a possible bottle out in the springhouse, and now he reckoned why she'd gone outside, why she was in the garden with Luisa: he could not get to the springhouse without passing the garden. He could pass the garden and go to the springhouse and get the bottle, and she would not say anything. She would not turn away either. But he could not get past the garden to the springhouse to get the bottle without her seeing him. Seeing him. Seeing him, saying nothing, doing nothing, accepting him, and the bottle in his hand, accepting that too, the clear compactness of it. And its speed, she wouldn't forget the speed; how could anyone forget the splendid and loving speed of a bottle of vodka when you needed it?

He would pay for it. The walk past the garden up the slope halfway along the firepond to the knee-high house, kneeling in the mud before the wee door, and inside the clear water gurgling up from the earth rejected, and the clear slow liquid in the clear bottle left of the door not rejected, embraced; clarity everywhere, surprising and not surprising, secret treasure forgotten in order to be found with a tiny true premonitory thrill of discovery.

Champ Rinaldi looked around the room they used only for special events—even Christmas took place in the shabbier, homier east parlor. Here he was out of the way. The throw cushions in the two big chairs sat cocked and waiting, as if listening to the arrival of phantom guests, the knickknacks kept their exact places, the dried flowers remembered. He looked at the flowers. He had felt alone before. This was different—*a little alarming*—his tongue moved about the words without actually saying them, tasting and feeling without committing to the irrevocable fact of sound. The vague sick sensation he had earlier noticed was changing, becoming active. He felt diffuse. At the edges bits of himself flew off into the dust of the room, too frail to settle, too dim to distinguish from the standard airborne debris of a home. His home. Every time he shifted he felt more of himself disperse: it became critical that he not move at all. He watched the dust in the light of the room for a long while. None of it ever seemed to settle.

Then it occurred to him that if he had a drink the erosion would stop. A good drink. One good drink and he would not lose anymore of himself. He would lose quite a lot on the way to the springhouse, walking, moving, kneeling before the wee door, but it would not have reached his core; and he could stop it, he could maybe even gather some of himself back if it was a full bottle, even half a bottle might be enough.

So Champ Rinaldi rose and went out past the women in the garden who saw and kept working, up the slope of mud and snow to the springhouse before which he knelt. The door had to be dug out with his hands, then shoved open against a wedge of winter debris. Inside to the left, waiting for him in the dark corner like a secret pal, was a fifth of vodka. Full. He gave a whimper; his lower lip began to tremble. *Save me, save me*, he thought, and then he stopped himself from thinking the words because they sounded too dramatic, only felt their echo tolling within. The seal had not even been broken. His thumb stroked the smooth inch-long length of official paper for several seconds before he twisted the cap, brought the bottle tenderly to his mouth, and poured. It slid in with the viscosity of cold oil, for the temperature had slowed it. Pausing, he brought the bottle down and hugged it to his chest so the women below would not see. Then he peered into the springhouse, reaching about, as though engaged in some plumbing adjustment. Again he drank, angling the bottle sharply up so that from the back his head did not appear to move, did not in fact move. He put the bottle back half empty, closed the springhouse door, and hiked down the slope, nodding as he passed the garden, smiling, trying not to beam his guilt. Selda followed him in.

"I'm pregnant," she said, as if he didn't realize. She was removing her boots. He looked at the dirt on her hands. Her back was to him; it seemed he did not have to reply.

"Ray'll be gone in the fall. He'll get a scholarship," she said.

"Shore he will."

"There's two already, here in Vermont."

"Two, you say." Ah, now they were off on something easy, an information exchange.

"They have to keep the shares in order, 20 percent from Vermont, the rest from out of state. He's up there higher than most in grades, and they want him because he's a Vermonter."

Champ took a deep breath and exhaled slowly. He was feeling okay now, the edges of himself were reassembling, like iron filings to a magnet.

Selda went into the kitchen and washed her hands. "He should go," she said.

"Wal, if someone's a mind to pay and he's a mind to learn his keep, why not?"

"James can do some, but he's not like Ray, you can't bridle him. He's never taken much training."

Champ smiled, thinking of James.

"And that hired man's no good."

"No? Seems handy enough."

"Handy," she puffed her lips, "but he's got no feel for cows or farming."

Champ leaned against the kitchen counter, watching Selda put away dishes. He reached out his hand and tried to catch the back of her sweater, but she moved off at just the wrong moment. He was definitely feeling better. He said, "Many don't nowadays," and mentally flipped through his file of stories for a funny one about someone who didn't have a feel for farming.

Selda turned and gazed at him. She was holding a thin white teacup with both hands, as if it were heavy and might slip. "I don't have to be pregnant," she said. "Nowadays a woman doesn't," she added.

He did not know what to say.

Abruptly she began loading the dirty dishes into the now empty dishwasher. "There'll be a new man to train, I'd guess, and James," she tossed a look of helpless amusement over her shoulder, "James'll balk all the way. Luisa's good at everything around here, she likes the farm. And then there's me, if I'm not . . ."

Together they listened to the silence of the end of her sentence.

"What about me?" Champ said finally.

"Yes?"

"Me."

"What do you mean?"

"I can work."

She glanced at him with some kindness. "Shore, you can work too. We'll all of us work." Then she finished loading the dishwasher, jiggling the flatware into the basket, filling the soap tray, lifting and locking the door into place.

"I'll work," he said again.

This time Selda did not bother to respond.

"Gave the boy the evening off, in fact. He said he was feeling punchy."

Crossing to the parlor, Selda folded the newspaper Champ had left draped over the back of the couch, picked up the empty glass of rum and cola, and returned to the kitchen. "I'm too old for babies."

"If I'm working . . ."

"Try to be realistic."

"Realistic."

"You don't do anything." Then with a shrug she added, "Really."

He thought about this while Selda took juice and toast down the hall to Carrie, along with the thermometer. "Small fever," she said, when she came back in.

Champ looked at her face, trying to find an opening. A concept struggled up from the center of him, he couldn't quite grab a hold of it, but he wanted to try. "I care," he said. "I, I care about everything, I still care, I care more . . . it seems, worse . . . how much I care."

"Worse."

"Sometimes I think my heart's been broke."

"I don't know what you're talking about." She made a gesture of vague impatience, turning the back of her hand. "You're just tired."

"No, drunk. Getting drunk. You don't care, Selda, you don't, you see. Not for years."

"I have always loved you."

"Love." He swung his head and looked at the floor. "True, true, you love, a good Christian loves. It's blanked out the soul of me. If you damned me I wouldn't care so much, I'd be happier, I'd have some of myself back to stand up to you with, you and the rest of it, and more to fight the caring too. But this love, loving me and nothing else, well, it's wiped me out, it has. A man can't live on heart, my god, it'll kill him, it does. He needs other things, anger and hate, and disgust, shore, I'll take that s'long as it's said at me."

"Disgust?"

"I don't know who I am."

"You are drunk."

"Not all the way. I still care. When I'm drunk, Selda, I don't care so much, I'm realistic."

She patted his shoulder and he almost flinched. "I really do think you're tired. You know I love you."

"A man has to have something to run against, so he can feel himself and tend his own hurt, have the right to, you see. And feel separate too. Separate, that's important. I'm not separate. The way it is now, why, everything I see, everyone who breathes, I have to care about, it's what I do, Selda, what I do now, what I have left to fight the goddamned love with. And when I can't stand the caring, I drink, I'm gonna drink, I am."

"Well," she said, then again, "well," and she started down the hall, "I'm tired," her figure receding into the interior dusk, "the appointment is next Wednesday."

HE WENT TO BILLY'S and drank. When he couldn't be at Billy's he went to the boathouse. And when he was straight enough to walk out of the boathouse, he went back to Billy's. Wednesday . . . Thursday.

On Thursday night he was seen weaving through the village, barefoot. There was a light snow. Several people tried to give him a ride, but he insisted that he didn't care, and walked the mile and a half to the boathouse.

When the kids were old enough to swim the Rinaldis had converted the boathouse to a one-room summer camp, with a hose that ran up from the lake to a hand pump for cooking and dish-doing, a one-holer in the spruce woods, and a box stove so full of cracks it couldn't heat more than a single room on a day better than brisk. The canoe and the fishing dingy were moved out and chained to a foundation pier, and hung down the bank to the water like a couple of big silver fish. There was a cot for summer naps, three chairs, a Formica table with a bench, some ragged blankets and sheets kept in plastic garbage bags. The place smelled of mice, mothballs, and kerosene, unless the stove was going, then it was smoke. But from the porch the view was fine, just as fine as the view from the many-roomed summer homes belonging to Vermont's absentee landowners.

Friday morning Clovis McPherson, who had the place up from the Rinaldis' boathouse, heard him whistling out on the porch. By then the snow had turned to a cold, spitting rain, and the lake beyond the porch was gray and wind-distressed, and looked like hammered metal. McPherson hollered at him to go inside, "you precious fool," and it seems he must have for the whistling stopped.

Whenever he left Billy's he was too drunk to drive, and whenever he was headed back to Billy's no one with a conscience dared give him a ride, so for three days his car stayed parked in front of the bar like a public notice of intent.

Mrs. Colbeth—forever obliged to Champ—telephoned Mrs. Rinaldi about the barefoot business, and Mrs. Rinaldi thanked her and sent Ray down to the village Friday afternoon with dry clothes and extra socks and boots.

He found the old man in the boathouse, sitting on the edge of the cot, his eyes strange.

"Son."

Ray nodded. "Brung you these."

They tried smiling at each other, but it seemed to say more than they could stand, or were willing to stand, and then they gave up on the tired act of recognition.

The old man was shaking badly—not from the cold, though breath was just visible in the room.

Ray laid the clothes on the cot, and the old man gave them a pat, and then resumed the strange clarity of his gaze. The boy was hoping the old man could dress himself, and figured he couldn't leave unless he had see it done and finished. "Fire's out," he said, and then to give the old man a chance to dress, he added, "I'll make one."

"Shore."

Next to the stove was a bin of kindling, the hatchet there with it. Kneeling on the slate, Ray picked up the hatchet, slid the blade into the cut edge of a board, then tapped the bottom of the board lightly on the slate, once, and it sliced into two neat halves. Then he split the halves, and picked up a new board. When he had enough, he twisted some paper and laid it in the stove, made wickerwork with the kindling, lit the twisted paper, and turned around as the blaze caught.

The old man hadn't moved. Ray followed his gaze outside to the lake. The snow had stopped, the rain had stopped, even the wind had fallen, abruptly, like heavy curtains on the hills circling the lake, so that the water was like a stage cleared for the final act. The clouds were as one, without contours, flat as a flat-bottomed boat; the light was flat too, not a single shadow troubled existence.

Beneath lay the water, gleaming dully, and scarred here and there with jagged ripples that appeared to have no source.

Champ stared into the lake as if into a vast flawed mirror. "She has a piece in this."

Ray did not need to ask whom.

He watched the old man push himself up and move stiffly across the cold floor to the window, placing one hand on the right jamb and the other left; for several minutes he hung there as if on an invisible cross before the window, with the still lake beyond. His trousers lay in a sodden heap by the door, and he was down to a blue plaid flannel shirt the kids had pitched in on for Christmas, and long underwear sagging at the knees and seat. There was no sign of the boots he had worn to the village Wednesday. His hair was pressed randomly in dark tufts against the back of his head, and Ray could make out patches of scalp, and from them, project the curve of his father's skull.

"She has a piece," Champ said again, not to anyone now but as if simply to the Outside.

Ray looked at the pale scalp through the matted hair, the shape of his father's head. He knew then in equal measure three separate emotions:

Disgust.

Love so past, so ancient, that whenever his mind touched upon it, it disintegrated to the dust of a feeling, though if he didn't think about it he seemed to know it was there, to feel it obliquely, taking up actual space.

Camaraderie. A strange, deep, and finally insoluble camaraderie that had to do with being this man's son and this boy's old man together in the House of Selda.

Ray uttered the word, "Yes," to make it official.

After he had helped the old man dress, and had loaded several chunks of wood in the firebox, poking at it to wake up the kindling, he went to the door. "She's not mad, you know," he said, not turning around, telling himself it was easier to deal with the old man at home than fetching back and forth to town when there were chores to do, though there might've been something else, too, another reason, he couldn't say what. He turned to the silence at his back.

The old man looked up at him and began to cry.

With the toe of his boot Ray nudged about a piece of kindling, waiting.

"Well." Champ cleared his throat, dusted the front of his blue flannel shirt. "Catch a ride?"

"Home?"

"T' the Ford."

"Billy's."

"No, to the Ford."

Ray made a sound and kicked the piece of kindling across the room. "Ah, forget it."

WHEN ARLEN BELL went into Billy's at five that afternoon, Rinaldi was already there, at the corner table, with the new man, Chase.

Sam Chase, Arlen said to himself as he sat down, practicing his memory.

He ordered a beer, and when his fishing buddies, Fowler and Pat, arrived he ordered two more for them, and moved his new hat, which had occupied one of the seats, to the empty table next to them, giving it a comforting pat. He then commenced to provide directions to a pond they aimed to fish next morning: "After Bridgeton you head north t' East Paradise, take Route 9 to Dovebury, only you got t' turn in town and run through the new neighborhood out t' the road that goes past the hippie commune, but don't go past it."

"Don't?"

"Nope. When you run outa uphill, why, you wanna take the right fork, and go, say, two good fields' worth and you'll see a road that leans down. There's an old mower settin' there in the hay, that's your sign. Three and a half miles take a bleeder that runs up and around a sugar bush, following the sap line not more'n a hundred yards, and turn then."

"Turn."

"Ayuh."

"Which way?"

"Only can but one. If you don't want t' hit the house."

"House?"

"Ayuh, house belongs to a feller name Miller. It's his pond."

"Miller."

"Then you just keep going down, ever chance you see, head down. Woods're at the bottom, pond's t'other side."

"Well, now, is this hard to find, Arlen?" the one called Fowler asked.

Arlen sipped his beer. "Not for me."

In the corner of the room Rinaldi stood and went to the bar, returning to his table with two drinks, something amber for Sam Chase and a tall clear double for Rinaldi. Chase nodded and made a gesture of salute with his glass toward Rinaldi.

Arlen watched for awhile, then he said, "What kind of human bean would do that, drink with a man bent on sech business?"

The two fishing friends glanced over at the corner table. "What business?" asked Pat.

"Destruction. The business of destruction."

"Rinaldi?"

Arlen gave a somber nod.

"It's Friday night, end of the week. So he's drinkin'. We all 'pear t' be," Fowler argued. He was a small-appliance repairman—blenders, microwaves, toaster ovens—shut down every weekend, no exceptions. He enjoyed his end-of-the-week ritual of excess, particularly in the company of others who enjoyed it more.

Arlen Bell made a sad, fatherly face. "Rinaldi can't start his week for all the endin' he's been at."

SATURDAY MORNING, chores done, Ray sat at the long pine table before a plate of toast with apple butter, beef hash and eggs, and canned peaches in a dish on the side. The coffee was thin as film, and scalding—the only way he drank it. Setting it before him, his mother had smiled, and had even stroked his hair. "My Ray," she said, and he dipped his head to conceal the suddenness of his pleasure.

Modest sounds coming from Luisa's sewing machine—the clack

of the foot treadle, the whirring belt—reached him in a softly contented way, and when he gazed through the window to the edge of the farmyard it was without the ache of vague expectation.

Luisa had already told him about his mother's appointment Wednesday.

Things were settling down.

Selda disappeared to see to the younger ones. It was seventhirty.

Ray forked up some of the hash, slurped at his coffee. His back felt almost okay; if he were careful, maybe the sciatic wouldn't fire up for awhile. He thought about the fence line, a nice project for the day. He'd get Chase to do the bending, wring him out some before he left. Ray had seen the notice Sam Chase had tacked up on the board at Dugan's, offering technical repair services, and, like his mother, he knew this hired man would not be around much longer. So it went. Summer folks'd snatch him up, and at downcountry wages, to be sure. Well, at least he paid attention to Luisa —that was worth something—so long as Luisa didn't think anything of it, make a fool of herself.

The cold bright May sun had cut and edged the scene outside into chunks of colored glass—red, green, blue, barn, field, pond; the weathered silver of the hen house listing slowing earthward, the black pan of the yard and the blacker patch that was the Bouvier asleep in it. Fracturing across the upper view were tree limbs and rose-green maple leaves opening toward summer. It was so bright out, and so dusky inside, that every time Ray looked back at his plate of food he saw for a second or two the lingering photonegative image of the scene beyond the windows. In this way he noticed the shape at the edge of the yard, and jerking his eyes, found its living counterpart—his father. Moving now. Weaving, mounting, sluing abruptly west into the shade of the barn eaves.

Ray put down his fork. Half a minute passed. His lips parted, he could not get enough air. In his ears and at the ends of his fingers his heart raced, as if it had fled to the outskirts of Ray Rinaldi, desperate to leave.

From the edge of the barn out of its penumbra a lesser shade spilled forth, now darting ahead of Champ Rinaldi, who pursued the shadow, which was his own, across the yard toward the house.

Ray picked up his fork, slashed a yolk, filled it with beef hash, and ate it in a single bite. The peaches he sucked in without really chewing them, and he eased down the hot coffee with toast padding his mouth. He had saved the last of the hash and egg for his final bite, pressing the fork across the plate to edge up any remnant yolk.

The old man did not come in the house. It occurred to Ray that he had almost forgotten him, breakfast had been so good.

Finally he carried his dishes into the kitchen and turned into the mud room. *Better start with the lower fields*, he was thinking, *'fore they get too soggy; probably find Chase in the trailer, still scratching himself; be satisfying to roust him* . . . Ray pulled on boots, shrugged into his coat, and went out.

There was a shed roof that angled out over the stairs leading from the mudroom down to the yard. It was a cool place, the ground often holding ice well into May. In the summer Luisa left her garden vegetables under the shed roof until she and her mother were ready to can or freeze; in the fall there were pumpkins and bushels of apples; and now at the end of spring there were still kindling and cord wood, rhubarb stalks, and seedlings and flowers in flats waiting to be planted. And on this day at the bottom of the stairs lay Champ Rinaldi: maybe he slipped on the ice, maybe he'd've slipped already lying down, he was so completely drunk.

"Jesus H. Christ," Ray muttered from the top of the stairs. "I need this."

Behind him Selda appeared with his lunch. "Oh," she said, pausing, then, "well," then another pause and, "bring him in."

Letting his entire weight drop sullenly foot by foot, stair by stair, Ray descended to his fallen father.

Champ was sprawled out flat on his back. The boy nudged him with the toe of his boot, and the old man's lids fluttered and he seemed to murmur a word or two, but there wasn't any sign of useful awareness, least of all muscle control Ray might recruit to help move 215 pounds of slack weight inside. "Jesus Christ on a crutch," he called out to the world.

In the middle of the farmyard the Boove rose from his nap and walked off, swaying lazily side to side; Ray watched him until he rounded the corner of the house. The presence of the Bouvier seemed to humiliate him.

Again he regarded the figure at his feet, not as his father this time but as an unpleasant task.

If he hooked the old man under the arms and hauled him that way he was sure to really strain his back, the sciatic would kick in, guaranteed. But if he pulled him by the heels it wouldn't be so bad.

He had thought about wrapping the old man's head, after it had wobbled so, and thumped on the first two risers; but then Ray figured there were only seven steps, after all, and what difference would it make, he was too drunk to feel it one way or the other, and anyway, the longer this whole thing took the more likely Ray would aggravate his sciatic nerve, and he was determined not to pay for the old man's drunkenness *just once*, just this one day.

The old man's coat bunched up under his arms, and a swath of his belly smiled up at Ray, and his pink palms dangled behind in a ridiculous upside-down gesture of praise and hallelujah. If it had been someone else's back and someone else's father Ray would've laughed.

When he got him inside, he pulled him up and arranged him on the couch in the dress parlor, which was closest. The outside arm would not stay crossed over his father's chest, it kept flopping off. Ray brought over a stool, and let the loose arm rest upon it. Then he went out to the fields, later on to Dugan's for more wire, and at four-thirty, home for evening chores.

"DON'T YOU WANT something 'fore you start?" Luisa hollered from the mudroom door.

He cocked his head. "I guess so. Piece a bread and butter'd do."

"Just made cookies."

"That then," he said, crossing the yard, smiling for Lu.

In the dusky backstage of the parlor the old man was apparently still asleep. Someone had put a blanket over him, and his boots had been removed and were tucked in underneath. The couch backed to an open hall, and across the hall was the kitchen, brightly lit. As Ray passed, the old man blinked and followed him with his eyes.

Leave him be, Ray thought.

Selda and Luisa were tending the bake sheets, one dropping dough, the other sliding off the cooked batch onto a rack for cooling; James and one of the twins were awaiting their allocation, and arguing, as usual.

"Ah, you couldn't hit a decoy with a pink *X* on it," James said.

Bobby gave a derisive snort, and swung his head toward Ray. "Who's the better shot?"

Ray didn't have time to get involved, though he was tempted to say that, long as he was around, neither had skills worth mentioning, *just to bunch their shorts*, he thought. "Ask Pa," he said, "he's awake."

"Hey, Pa, me or James, who's better?"

Champ did not answer.

James swiped a hot cookie and went into the parlor. "C'mon, Pa," he whispered, "you can say. Bobby can take it," he added with volume enough to benefit his younger brother. "He's used to it."

In the kitchen Ray poured himself a glass of lemonade.

James looked more closely at his father. "Pa?"

Champ slid his eyes side to side, three times, stopped, stared purposefully at James, then abruptly he began to blink with counting regularity; then again side to side, stop, stare, blink.

"What're you doing?"

Across the room in the bright kitchen Ray set down his lemonade.

"Okay, I get it," James said, trying to retrieve his humor, "you don't have to say."

The old man was just looking now, his eyes like dark brown full moons, double negative images shining up at James.

James took a step back, his hands limp at his sides. "Ray?"

Crossing the hall, his brother came around the couch and pulled back an edge of the blanket, releasing in the process the sour stench of feces. "Ah, Jesus . . . he's crapped himself."

James stared down at his father.

"Time you got in on some of the action," Ray said, jerking his chin at James. "*You* clean him up." He glanced then at the old man's face from which the eyes looked back with unnerving peace, *seeing* him—that was all—and the seeing shuddered through Ray and left in him a quality of weakness he had never before known. He noticed the footstool, Champ's arm jutting awkwardly out from the couch, exactly where Ray had placed it that morning. Reaching down, he closed his fingers around his father's wrist, elevated the arm not far, several inches, and let it go. It fell like a joint of meat, the hand smacking the hardwood, the stool skidding out and clattering across the floor.

James took another step back.

No one in the kitchen moved. They regarded the stool, not the blank screen that was the couch back, not James whose face had gone from innocent mischief to disbelief, not Ray who was staggering toward the phone.

"You can't move, can you, Pa?" James said, seeking his mother who was rushing to him now. "It's just his eyes can move," he whispered, "his eyes."

MONDAY MORNING Arlen Bell tramped up from the post office to Dugan's. He had sent the wife's package off to Hanover, talked to Saville about grading the road, and now he thought he'd see who he saw up at the store, grab a cup of coffee and a grinder for later.

Second in line at the checkout stood Fowler with a handful of fittings and a bag of chips he'd already torn into.

Arlen waited for him just inside the door. "Heard 'bout Rinaldi, did yer?"

Fowler shook his head.

"Broke his neck outside his own mudroom."

"Gawd," said Fowler with a deep note of awfulness.

"Slipped on the ice, they say. But that's not all of it."

"Ayer?"

"They drug him inside . . . not knowing, you see."

"Not knowing what? That he was drunk? Everyone know'd he was drinking with aim this week."

"Drunk, shore."

A stock clerk rolled up a dolly loaded with motor oil, indicating he needed to stack it about where they stood. Fowler and Arlen moved aside, and lingered in silence for a few minutes, watching customers pass through Dugan's door.

"I mean his neck was already broke on the ice," Arlen finally said with some impatience. "Moving him sawed through the wires. Rinaldi is paralyzed."

"Gawd."

The stock clerk took out his knife and sliced open the boxes, top and front, for display.

Again, Fowler said, "Gawd," and shook his head. "I guess that boy'll do everything now."

"Now's no different than before, truth be told."

"Well, officially."

"He can't be doing nothin' official from Maine," said the stock clerk.

Arlen peered at him. "Maine?"

"Ray took off t' Maine, I heard. With the Lagues. Loggin'."

"Well."

"By gawd."

Arlen slipped back around the meat counter for one of the grinders Mary had just made up, then he drew some coffee from the tall urn, and went up front to pay.

Outside, he worked his new hat about his forehead some, still breaking it in, and gazed across the road where Heidi Greenfield was propping up tulips. A few small clouds drifted above without design, the air was warm and smelled of mowed grass, and here and there sunlight caught in the wings of bugs jittering over the lilac bushes. *Summer*, he thought, stepping off the porch.

PIPERS AT THE GATES

OF DAWN

IT WAS EARLY and the fog crowded down in close. Dru Hammond moved through it like someone wanting to feel for the last time whatever her senses might bring home. Her body felt rested and limber, and for reasons she could not know, unburdened, containing only the eagerness of being first out. She seldom sculled in the morning, though it was best then. Along the path down to the lake the smell of balsam came and went; it was like a good memory she could not hold on to, or a memory that did not belong to her but to someone with a Norman Rockwell childhood. There was another smell, too, faintly mineral, the lake itself, clear and cold and, out in its middle, too deep to plumb—from that place maybe.

Underneath the balsam and spruce, spread in fledgling patches, was moss tipped heavily with dew. She left the path, bent down, and with a sweep of her hand scattered the drops. Once she and Fletcher made love on moss; it was deep and soft, and red squirrels in the maples above had protested loudly, though not so much that they stopped. In those days nothing stopped them.

Ian called it fairy moss, but he was seven and reluctant to give up early beliefs; the replacements were not nearly so attractive. "God and all the other fairies," Ian had said.

She dried her hand against her pile jacket and continued down the path, watching for small branches and other hazards, though last weekend Fletcher had raked it clear, to begin summer properly, he had said—as he always said. Ritual remarks attended ritual deeds throughout their first week in Harrow.

"It exposes the roots more," she had said, tripping on cue. Though it was just as true that she liked him liking anything so much that he would make rituals around it.

The path had been The Path for so long—three generations— that in some places it was half a foot lower than the surrounding forest floor, a brown, winding groove, every feature known by heart: the unnecessary *U* near the top; the tendons of spruce roots flexed across the way at five separate junctures; the broken canoe seat someone had stood on end and dug in like a signpost bearing no message; the fallen maple known as Mr. Good-log to help persuade a distant child who had feared passing the old monster that it was a friend; the jutting rock, a glacial erratic, just beyond the woods on which they spread towels to dry; the final slope of grass to the dock itself. The boys could race down without care, without falling, bare feet drumming. By itself, the dirt did not resonate, but this was a mix of soil and packed vegetation, pine needles, maple leaves, cedar cones, scrolls of birch bark, everything once grown reduced to the dark indistinguishable particles of themselves, echoing not the life of which they had been a part, and not the eternity to which it seemed they now belonged, but something in between . . . perhaps only *possibility*.

Her feet fell to the path, and the path answered back with a series of damped and toneless notes. At least these notes and this hour were hers—neither history nor occupancy had bearing on such matters. In some reflexive way Dru thought often of possession—what was really hers, like the sounds she could make with a violin, or the sound of her footsteps on a wooded path—and of belonging—where or with whom meant less than the feeling of belonging.

She had lost both parents at the age of eight; a house fire. Dru had been sleeping over at a friend's. There was always some interest in the coincidence of her absence that night. The marriage had "problems." Eight is the age of reason, her mother used to say. But nothing could have been more unreasonable than to be driven home the next morning along the tidy suburban street, to a sudden gap in the row of houses, the low consolidated black heaps of the new terrain gently smoking, and her friend's mother not stopping, accelerating past and away, into a future that was suddenly completely unpredictable.

So. She had nothing. None claimed her. A rumored aunt in Alaska, never located. And from someone in Virginia, postmarked Roanoke on the fifteenth of each month, two hundred dollars cash for deposit to the account of Mary Wilcox, Dru's mother. For three months the money came. Meanwhile the authorities did what they could, placed an ad in the Roanoke paper, "Generous friend of Mary Wilcox, regret to inform . . . ," et cetera. But the friend, or relative—it was hoped—never came forward, and the money stopped, and Dru suffered yet another loss, the loss of possibility.

Ten years in institutions. Ten years learning to live in the company of too many, to love solitude, to want the bindings of family; ten years yearning for the weight of history.

When she was twenty-three she and Fletcher Hammond met at a Young Artists concert in Williamstown. She had a gift, it was said; but perhaps not quite enough ambition to push that part of her life out of balance with the rest—too many years in institutions had cultivated a belief in equal measures. And she could not persuade herself that it would not all be lost—the gift, the success, the sudden close friends. Nothing could be taken for granted.

What did Fletcher see, watching her throughout that first concert? What did he need, his wife dead only a few months, the order and perfection cut from his life? He could not bear anyone like Suzie, or anyone who would try that way to please him.

There, third from the end, sat a tall young woman with boyish hair, black and cut short, and mussy as if she had dressed in a hurry or had forgotten to comb it—which somehow struck an even sweeter note—wearing a sea-blue dress with dropped shoulders that more than elaborated a long, pale, painfully elegant neck, bent at the top toward the violin with a broken kind of longing. Her movements were subtly giddy, as if her body wanted restraint, was too much for her; her movements enchanted him. It came time for the encore applause, virtually pro forma in the States. The musicians resumed their seats, the conductor left the stage, the applause swelled for the second time, the conductor strode back out. Then she gazed at the audience with genuine wonder, tipped her head shyly to duck the pleasure, and again gazed out to confirm that she was seeing what she was hearing. To Fletcher Hammond, this was both absurd and astonishing. Maybe she was foreign—he imagined an Eastern Block nation.

In the end, though, what touched him vividly and deeply was the mussed boyish hair, so unlike Suzie, so free of self.

When she was twenty-four Dru married Fletcher Hammond. For the first time since the fire she had something to lose. She had never really *had* anything to lose. And so began an obsession with mortality that would last three months. Wherever she looked people were in the process of dying—she could not gaze at the faces of friends without seeing skin rot and bones rise up; sleep was, of course, dangerous, cousin to death; vague aches reported aggressive tumors; each day she drove her car as if for the first time, sure that an accident was about to happen, and when it did not, sure that she had narrowly missed one; and flying in an airplane was, without any question, a suicide attempt. But she did board a plane with Fletcher because with Fletcher Hammond she now belonged; that conviction transcended all eventualities, even death. Death was acceptable so long as she was where she was supposed to be when it came. If Fletcher was gone, off to ski races, or on business trips, Dru felt homesick, not lonely. He had become a place—his arms, his smell, his voice, his habits, were plantings in a garden that had never before been tilled by the steady presence of another.

Now she was not sure Fletcher had any idea who she was. Sometimes, neither did she. There were things growing in the garden that neither one of them had planted.

They had been together a dozen years; she was thirty-six, he, forty, the boys, Ian and Miles, were seven and twelve—a five-year hesitation between children, and then the quietly desperate second pregnancy, arguing that their troubles were not so bad, certainly no worse than others'.

Maybe they aren't, she thought with some hope, but the thought and the hope were like cut flowers.

If our problems aren't worse than anyone else's, then there's nothing I have to do, absolutely nothing. Settle in, make the best, enjoy the moment. Live it out, this life. She glanced at her hands, as if they held a folded map of *this life*; once you opened it, you could never again fold it quite the same way.

Coming from the woods around the jutting granite she saw that the fog did not oppress the water but lingered about ten feet above, ragged veils trailing down to enlist rising vapors. The surface of the lake was pleasingly flawed, like nineteenth-century glass, bubbles here and there, inexplicable lines, swirls that did not finish themselves. There had been so much snow, so much run-off in the last few weeks, that the water was up to the bottom of the dock, and when she stepped out onto it, she felt a new wobble. Probably the high water had dislodged one of its supports—something for Fletcher to fix while she and the boys swam in the afternoon. He did not like actual swimming, especially this early in the summer when the lake was still genuinely cold. If it was a warm day he kicked about on his back, spouting water, a cartoon ad featuring Himself, Fletcher Hammond III, summer person, natural habitat.

Well, it is lovely, she thought. Privileged. And I'm a stowaway. There are no dues when you don't really belong. Suzie had belonged. At least they've all stopped talking about the wonders of dear old Suzie. *Suzie wasn't perfect but Suzie was perfect for Fletcher* . . . only a mother-in-law could get away with lines like that. And now I'm too old to die young—or that young—no easy beatification for me, no rare sudden Suzie diseases. I will have to perform the requisite three miracles, and collar a few witnesses while I'm at it.

Dru walked about the dock, stopping to waggle above each support until she found the one that was unstable. Later she would choose a good moment for mentioning it to Fletcher; it would please him—camp projects always did.

On the side platform, angled for launching, the canoe and the two shells lined up like eager children, the shells so long that their bows floated out.

"Hello, my darlings," she said, listening to a mysterious quality in her voice, deep and luscious, as if she had only just then waked and had no place to go or be that was not right here. Or as if a lover were near and listening.

The beautiful open wooden shell rocked her bow shyly, *slappety-slap*, against the water, while the trainer sat solidly waiting, white, implacable fiberglass.

Crescent Lake favored the training shell—beamy by comparison, with a closed deck, so that even if she "caught a crab" and flipped, it would not take on water. She had never actually flipped, she had watched the videos, she knew what to do, how to push back in with the oars equally positioned at all times, one straight down into the water and the other straight up, like a flagpole, but she had never had to do it.

The water was so flat today . . .

Dru placed the seat, which she had carried down from the house, onto the dock, then kicked off her Tevas, stretched, and rolled her neck. She performed a yoga sun greeting, extending arms, back, and legs, breathing in or out with each position change, standing loosely at the end, not thinking, just looking at her empty sandals on the dock, poignantly side by side, as if they were waiting for someone who might not come back.

The dock was not visible from the house. They could not see her, Fletcher and the boys, though she wanted both the comfort of being seen and the relief of invisibility. In the fog no one could see Dru Hammond. And if they could see, if the fog rose and burned off against the hot pan of a June sun, and they stepped out on their summer decks and saw Dru standing vertical on the flat gray reach of the Hammond dock, they would see an emergent memory of Dru. For something had ended awhile ago, not far back, Dru could not say when, no event volunteered to score a line between then and now, yet she felt herself to be among frayed ends, waiting, she could not say what for, she was not sure that there was anything coming or anything she ought to walk toward, the matter seemed to be out of her hands. Or something in her rather hoped that it was out of her hands.

At the end of the dock she dipped a foot in the water—too cold for a long swim. On the grassy bank, under a clump of cedar, sat a warped and leaning bin in which they stored life jackets and inflatable toys, extra lines, crayfish traps, the centerboard to a Sunfish that had disintegrated years ago. Rummaging out the best of the preservers, Dru walked back down to the dock and again regarded the shells, the quiet water, the long, lean beauty of the wood racer, color and shape blending with scene. She gave a little shrug and tossed the jacket into the bow of the racer. If there had been a real choice she had made it back at the house, in the middle of their ridiculous fight.

"COLD diffidence."

"I got up to pee."

"Cold diffidence, that's what you give me in the morning."

"I *usually* pee first thing," she said.

"You didn't say anything, not a word."

"Neither did you. And did I get mad?"

"I touched your back, I made a good-morning gesture."

"Look, I wasn't really awake, I wasn't ready to converse. Many people can't right out of the chute. And I frequently get up without saying anything."

"Right. And frequently I don't like it."

"You're being irrational. You didn't say anything either. And when I did try to engage you . . ."

"Half an hour later."

" . . . I got the classic Fletcher minimalist response."

"We can't talk about anything anymore."

"Ah. Another classic." She made coffee, separate funnels over separate cups—because she liked hers strong—dribbling the boiling water down along the surface of the filters, waiting for the puddle to sink, circling the filters again.

Fletcher could have more ground under foot than usual this time, she thought.

Behind her, in his Pendleton bathrobe, he leaned against the counter, not expressionless, but allowing her to see that she had hurt him, that he didn't know why, couldn't see The Thing, but that he was trying, within the limitations of his maleness, to reach her. And that she wasn't helping.

"You just might be too clever for your own good," he said.

"I didn't know that was possible."

He twitched up the corner of a smile. "In rare cases."

From the refrigerator she took a carton of milk, filled a small pitcher, and warmed it in the microwave. She felt Fletcher surveying the back of her, like a land deal that had not panned out.

It would be nice to pan out for people, she thought. For Fletcher. Except I would have to have two lives, one for him, one for me. I could be the great deal he predicted, land that proved under the touch of his hand, the pressure of his mind, the endurance of his vision. And the one for me . . . what would I do with the life that was mine alone, shaped and ruled by the being at the center of me whom I see face to face so seldom? What would I make of the expanse of a single uncorrupted life waiting to be lived?

She handed Fletcher the coffee, avoiding his eyes. There was a lot of that lately—avoidance.

"Well, have fun," he said, turning, climbing the stairs, back to bed presumably, to read until the boys woke. Dru had never known how to do that—linger in bed. Linger anywhere—it seemed . . . unsafe.

The kitchen felt big suddenly, too many cold clean surfaces edging into each other. She wished he had not left and she was glad that he had.

*That ridiculous fight . . . about nothing, **nothing** . . .* she shook her head . . . *about everything then.*

She was a mother, of course; so the claim of solitude at a time when children made few claims.

She was married, of course; so the breezy contact with misery. Singles had to dig for it; it was not readily available—lying about in the sheets, or pushing up through the hard surfaces of unspoken words. Misery had the sort of weed-strength that happiness never would. And neither, strangely enough, had endurance. So what was it that did endure or that was expected to endure between a man and a woman?

Harrow was no Club Med, singles seeking encounters. Dru Hammond desired no encounters. Summer communities were by nature family-oriented. Even the divorced parents of generational broods came to Harrow, the ousted spouse—the one whose family had not been summering in Harrow for generations—renting a cottage, while the descendent spouse occupied the old family house, usually where the grown children fell in, because of the likelihood of many beds, because of the memories. They attended the same cocktail parties and picnics; they chatted with cordial contempt. Or with relief. Or regret. Or perhaps more often than not with head-shaking wonder that he or she had ever been married to her or him for a chunk of years that did not seem anymore connected to the life they were now living, or the person they had become. Marriages that seemed anomalous, excrescent growths on the smooth skin of a shinier reality, fugue states from which they had awakened. Except here were the grown children countering and certifying and loving both. Here were the children. *Ah, Harrow, ah, summer.*

So, she was married, Dru Hammond; she was unhappy, too: there was no connection. She had borne two children, both would grow into men; probably it was best, because she had spent too much of her life with mobs of girls, and knew more about them than a mother ought. Her boys she could love with some of the innocence of mystery. The elder, Miles, had just reached the age of loving insults, which he liked to deliver in public, as a rule, to demonstrate that he no longer needed his mother, that to him, cool and upcoming, she was a little ridiculous, maybe even obsolete. The younger, pale, freckled Ian, basked nervously in his own adoration of her, his mother, worried that something was about to change.

She was practical about romantic yearnings, did not believe in a happiness that was not spotty and unreliable, did not trust impulse, did not want anyone else to, either. She was a musician, after all; there was a score, notes to follow; you all had to play together as best you could.

Lately her husband had traded love for admiration. It was a function of quantities—how much shit she would put up with now, how much before. The years enact their indubitable subtractions. She thought the admiration was important; now she was not sure. She was more lovable, apparently, before.

DRU KEPT THE OARS at the bottom of the path, tucked alongside Mr. Good-log. Fetching them, she noticed the change in the air as she returned to the woods, the softer secret feel under the trees, the brisk heroic quality of the open, the sense that things were expected of her out here. One at a time she carried the oars to the platform. It was always tricky, dropping them in the oarlocks, sliding them out halfway, keeping the shell constantly balanced. She positioned the seat, moving it back and forth in the runners to grease up the little wheels. Finally zipping up her jacket so the oar grips would be less likely to catch in fabric, she freed the line and stepped gingerly back onto the platform. It was critical to drop her weight onto the exact center of the shell, maintain the balance, one foot at a time, lower herself carefully onto the seat, holding her body over an imaginary center line. Now she was in, extending her legs, poking bare feet inside the stiff canvas flaps of the grips. The foot straps were made for shoes, but Dru had always been nervous about flipping with weighted feet in cold water, the life jacket stowed in the bow, not on her. You could not scull wearing a pre-server, it was not even legally required, yet shells were the least stable crafts on the water—tippy. None of it made sense; the lake patrol shrugged.

She slid the oars out simultaneously so that one rested on the dock, the other out across the water, palms up, balanced, before reaching to screw down the keeper bars on the oarlocks. Usually it took several backward body jerks to launch, but the water was so high that a mere shimmy freed her from the slanting platform.

The shell slipped away, uncertain, without aim yet, the twin blades at the ends of endless oars opened out and dipped, closing beneath the surface with a force so smooth it was fated, closing inward toward the stern like outstretched arms, the blade hands coming together in prayer after prayer. The shell arrowed across the cove with the kind of speed she could never quite believe initially, a fantasy of power and grace, the oar blades feathering and meeting no resistance—the shape, the movement, the hour, the fog, the dark sheen of the water, blending to create something very nearly new, and still wild, neither feathered nor amphibious, fibrous, bony, fleshed—a dream of creaturely unanimity. The smooth water seemed to yearn for the blade edge, the blade edge for the taut surface and the deep enveloping water below. Slicing down in, the blades pressed through and along just under the surface, then suddenly up they popped into the fast air, turning flat to the water's flat, and trailing torn water like beaded veils as the oar blades swung back to center, and again turned, and again plunged down.

Three good strokes and she cleared the cove, skimming out across the main reach of the lake where the way was more exposed, the surface of the water more flawed, the wind rising. Here, too, the fog was less stable, had not the slow density of the cove formation, but lurched up as if about to clear, then thickened and swirled right down against the water. Several times she encountered clear spots where the fog was beginning to break—fogdogs, they were called. She angled for the south end of the lake, looking for more sun. There was enough distance between the Hammond dock and the south cove to find a rhythm, and keep it long enough to break a sweat, and then go a little beyond that, to gather and press all of herself into each stroke, so that sweat came with each breath, and breath moved with blade, the right blade always, watched over her right shoulder, eyes glazing. On the forward slide she inhaled, on the pull she released. You were supposed to keep your nose over the imaginary center line—they said that, the coaches at the sculling center—it was supposed to help with balance. But the oar blade had a hypnotic effect, feathered, swinging back to center, palm up, skimming the thin air above the water, and sometimes daring the water itself. It was for Dru almost a religious motion. An inch lower, half an inch . . . or a snagged riffle, the oar blade caught, stopped, diving down deep and the whole thing would go *flip*.

Ten, maybe fifteen minutes she kept it up. Abruptly sun flashed behind her. Twenty yards across the water a yellow arch of light rose from the fog, the fog in layers of torn sheets, and the water between Dru and the fogbow the most heavenly creamy blue. It took her breath away. Then, and completely, it did not feel like Crescent Lake anymore, or Harrow, or Dru Hammond's life—it was like popping into someone else's dream. She let the shell drift into the clearing, oars centered, blades up, pat-patting the blue water. All around the air was yellow and warm, tingling on her skin like the minutiae of something vastly tentacled and alive. Closing her eyes, she felt the warmth finger its way into her dark, cropped hair, to the scalp and down the back of her neck. She opened her eyes, closed them, then again opened and closed, until the moment was simply color, the dark, shimmering chaos of lidded eyes, the pale yellow and the creamy blue, and her knowing color and nothing but color. Around in a ragged circle the fog hung, like watching ghosts.

This is not Crescent Lake, this is a dream, or a lake in a dream, or a memory of a lake from childhood, which is as good as a dream lake.

She threw her head back and gazed up, as if from that spot only, and only at the very moment, it was possible to see through heaven.

I'm glad I'm alone; right now, I would not be anything but alone, she thought.

So, there were moments when Dru did not regret not having a family of her own, or a past that waded into the present the way Fletcher's did. Even his future, the food he ate in his future, was shaped in part by family history, for each summer they came to Harrow, anticipating in ripening turn the strawberries, wild raspberries, garden lettuce, followed by the beefsteak tomatoes, and best of all, the sweetness of August corn; and randomly throughout, maple syrup, Maine lobsters and blueberries, local goat cheese, Vermont lamb, cob-smoked hams from Barton, Ben and Jerry's ice cream from down in Waterbury.

Yes, she thought, sometimes it is good not to know what comes.

Time passed, she could not say how much—enough that she began to feel chilled. Though if it had not been for the music she would have stayed longer. A flute. In the instant that the flute enlarged the spell, it also foreclosed it. A summer person on the shore of the south cove was playing music. Summer people, summer camps, Harrow, Vermont, month of June. The Carlyles and the McPhersons and the Adams and the Hammonds and so on, one and all had arrived for the season.

What am I doing here? And if not here, where?

Sighing, she slid forward, gave a long pull on the oars, and shot back into the fog, pulling and pulling, her mind shut down, her shoulders beginning to ache. The wind came up sharply, flagged, then shoved again across the open reach of the lake. There were brilliant hazy clearings where the water surface riffled and waves formed up, where the shell skittered unsteadily, and her hands on the oar grips went tight. In another place the fog was so thick the ends of the oars vanished. Then she tucked both grips under her knees, placed her hands behind on opposite sides of the shell, and waited. Voices from shore traveled out to find her. Fog did funny things to sound—brought it close when it was far away, or gave false distance to the near. At times she could hear the flute again, solo, maybe Paul Horn, remote and haunting. And then from the north end Harry Young's voice, and his sister who was visiting, the clarity of their displaced voices spooky and unsettling—"Can you pick up the Lobster?"

"Fine."

"I thought you were getting a haircut anyway."

"That's right. Around noon."

"I guess you had better be there when the fish truck arrives. He may not have many with him."

"Well, how many do we need?"

"Oh, a dozen. The children won't touch it, but Winston'll eat two."

"Charge him for the second."

"Why, because he table-talked at bridge?"

"That's right."

As abruptly as they began, they were gone, Harry and his sister, the lobster negotiations, swallowed up in a fog rift or broadcast to some other singular spot on the lake.

Dru had always liked Harry Young. He managed not to notice himself most of the time.

From the another direction she heard a happy commotion, kids on the jetty, poking about for crawfish.

A chain saw, revving, biting into something, the pitch dropping, then *thwunk*, several minutes of silence, again the menacing idle of the chain saw gearing up, whining deep and muffled into heartwood.

"I could make pancakes," a voice offered.

Barking dogs.

Vermont Public Radio, about tomatoes and frost.

What is it, she thought, June 25th? Harrow waking up on June 25th.

In front of her, out of the fog came a woman's voice. She seemed to be speaking directly to Dru: "It's clearing, it'll be splendid."

"Who cares if it clears, I have you . . . a room filled up with you," said a man.

A man and a woman.

All these voices, she thought, these happy happy lives.

After that Dru needed to cry; she shook her head to jar the feeling. She was glad for them, that they were here and had voices—it was like discovering two more members of an endangered species. And at the same time hearing them had the effect of breaking Dru Hammond's heart, just a little, sharply, and without remorse. They were far too alive for remorse, these two. Splendid, splendid—the word flashed about like a fantastic silver fish. When was the last time she had filled the room for Fletcher? When was the last time a day promised to be splendid?

There was something still splendid, still clear, about her time with Ian, but not Miles. Miles was in the world now, swallowed up in the affairs of society, and no longer standing before her, totally present and eager and innocent.

The fog was too close. She wanted to move, but there was almost no visibility. She listened for the flute again, thought to pull toward it, toward the big fogdog near the south cove, then work her way along the shore to the Hammond dock; go home, take a shower, maybe hunt for raspberries with Ian, make a pie. Fletcher liked pies. Slipping the oars out from under her knees, she resettled on the seat, crouched, slid forward, dropped the oar blades down, started the first hard pull.

The oar hit something—a watery *clack*, a man's voice—"Hello?"

"Who's there?" she said.

"Can you help me?"

She came about and, using tiny forward alternating strokes, maneuvered the shell toward his voice. The prospect of an event excited the moment to undue significance, and she felt herself tighten inwardly with anticipation.

From out of the fog the white crescent of a hull appeared down on its side in the water, and there was a man standing on it, wet and barefoot. He was not a tall man. His skin was evenly brown and his eyes in the flat light were black as if the pupils had widened and the color had fallen in. The hair on his head was mostly black with some white weaving along the sides, and fairly thick too, with short waves moving away from the smooth, flawless skin of his face. His beard was a neat mix of black and white—it was beautiful. The black and white made a startling effect in the light. Though something about his expression seemed to be smiling, he was not actually smiling; there was an equal impression of gravity. He might have been East Indian, but she could not decide. His left hand was extended with immense gentility toward her, as if she had just asked for help, while his right hand held several lines, the lines ran to the mast stretching out just under the surface of the water. Part of the sails were billowing above the water, but most were under; as the water gained advantage the small white billows at the surface shrank further. Using his weight, he was trying to pull the boat up off her side, walking up the hull side, slipping, trying again. The boat was a Flying Dutchman. They were not very common anymore. It had been years since Dru had seen one on the lake; there were mostly Sunfish now, which suffered less elegance, and were easier all around—not the sort of vessel you could care a lot about, even if you wanted to. Too functional, too imprecise, anyone could sail one.

"I have not enough weight," he said. "She is sinking."

"Yes."

"Will you help?"

"Oh, yes, I'm sorry, I'm just shocked to find a sailboat . . . in this fog."

Then he did smile; it was a fine thing, small and quiet, and it seemed to have a quality of pureness, as if it belonged to a child. "Where I began there was not any fog."

"Where was that?"

"Not much wind, either."

"Then how did you get here?"

He moved his shoulders in a gesture of helpless puzzlement. "I was only tinkering with the rigging. A new sail. I did not intend . . ."

"No," she volunteered.

"A Flying Dutchman requires two."

"So many things do," she said with cool irony, speaking as much to herself, to her life, to a god in which she could not believe.

She looked at the Dutchman, her mast angling down in the water, her mainsail cleated fast and filling. Then she squinted into the fog. "But how did you capsize in this?"

"Perhaps something in my . . ." He shot a concerned look at the boat. "If she goes turtle . . ."

"I'm coming."

There was really only one way out of the racer and that was to deliberately flip it. She dug the left oar down deep, and the shell rolled simultaneously with a smooth terrible ease. The water closed like a cold hand about her, her lungs contracted, her chest felt caged; she inhaled with a conscious effort, slow full breaths. What a job breathing was when you had to think about it. Tucking the loose oar back inside the shell, she swam up to the bow for the life jacket, fastened it on, then kicked over to the Dutchman. Getting up on the hull was like one of those near-impossible obstacles in a training course; after falling twice and banging her shin, she needed to rest.

"Please," he said finally. He had been holding out his hand all along. She took it, struggling up beside him. They were exactly the same height, she found, with an inexplicable flare of joy.

He fed a couple of lines to her. Immediately, the added weight on the hull began to lift the Dutchman, top mast first, from the water, the two of them reeling in the lines until the critical angle was reached; then Dru leapt backward into the lake, while the accidental sailor curled head-first on deck. The risen mainsail let go a downpour of lake water, and beneath it he sat, this neat brown man looking as though it had all gone exactly as planned.

"Thank you, thank you." He made a gesture with his hand near his face—unusual, indescribably graceful, not a salute, something more personal—that seemed to affirm no more than her alone in the morning fog, helping him, and at the same time nothing less than that, than who she was—which seemed unquestionably to be everything at that moment.

"Any time," she replied. It was a silly thing to say.

"Do you need help boarding your vessel?"

"I can manage."

"Are you certain?"

She had started to swim away. "I saw the movie," she called back.

The shell had drifted a good distance, maybe fifty yards, and it was not until she captured it that Dru realized—remembered actually—that she could not get back in and that no one could have. It was the racer—open-decked, full of lake, it was not made for getting back in, it was meant for racing, sunny days, support boats with outboard engines.

"Hey," she called.

Miraculously, the Flying Dutchman was already moving away, almost gone.

"Where are we?"

He waved once. She could see the brown of his hand through the fog, like the lithe body of a retreating bird. But he did not hear. Fog did funny things to sound.

Oh boy.

She made a guess and started swimming; it was awkward with the life jacket, and towing the shell, but the guess was a good one, and she reached shore in twenty minutes. The young couple renting the Butler's camp let her use the phone, and provided a frayed camp towel until Fletcher came to get her. She hoped it was the same couple she had heard out on the lake, but decided it could not be them—their language with each other had a fractured quality, as if things were being held together with unnatural substances. "Would you mind too much . . .?" And "*Now*, Tom . . ." in a voice leaning toward mockery.

Fletcher came right away, worried and faintly suspicious, it seemed to her. There was a thermos of hot coffee on the car seat, and an old Hudson Bay four-point blanket, smelling of mothballs, which Dru had taken as her own twelve years back during her first enchanted summer in Harrow with Fletcher Hammond, and the Hammond family, and the happiness of sudden history. She wrapped the blanket around her shoulders, sipped the coffee. The jeep bumped along the dirt road, and the tall wild daylilies ducked and nodded as they passed, and she felt full of the novelty of her little adventure.

"I didn't get his name," she said.

"The whole thing'll hit Dugan's by noon."

She looked over at Fletcher, one hand on the wheel, the other resting tentatively on the thick blanket somewhere in the vicinity of her knee. "Why is everyone so interested in everyone else up here?"

"Harrow," he intoned simply.

Of course. Yet there was something pleasant about the answer—so familiar—and hearing him finger the characteristics of Harrow as he did throughout the summer, like beads that would give him perpetual comfort.

He removed his hand from the territory of her knee, as if finding some humiliation in it, and she was sorry to feel its nice weight lift, to sense the small incremental tugs of Fletcher's withdrawal.

Later in the golden afternoon she fetched the shell, sculling back to the Hammond dock tensely, carefully, because the wind had come up as it always did late in the day, and the racer wobbled over the chop, threatening to roll. She looked for the Flying Dutchman, but it was not on the lake, and the shore was either too distant or too cluttered with campers and summer paraphernalia for her to find in the general confusion the man she had helped.

A FEW DAYS LATER Fletcher hired someone to assist with the dock. Half the underpinnings had rotted, and what was not rotten years of winter ice had beaten to shaky remains. The pressure-treated dock wood that would replace the old was too heavy for the efforts of a single man. Plus, there were some electrical idiosyncrasies around the house that had finally, after fifty years, graduated to problems. One of the switches would now respond only to a slap, another required fifteen seconds of reflective silence; the well pump suffered fits of service followed by strange clicking episodes —women and children were warned away at this stage. Fletcher announced that he could not stand another summer among the filigree of extension cords. Improvements were in order, and it was best to dispatch them, and any other unnecessary changes, as they would be viewed, before his parents arrived in August.

He got the name of a general all-around hand from Dugan's clerk in hardware.

"The man only works afternoons," Fletcher reported. It was Monday morning, and he was still trying to get through the rest of the Sunday *New York Times*. Fletcher was dutiful when it came to the Sunday *Times*.

"What's his name?"

"Chase. Sam Chase."

"He's not a local if he won't work mornings," she said.

"That's right. He showed up during mud season, Dugan said. He was the Rinaldis' hired man, but apparently chores weren't his cup of tea. In any case, Rand Spitler gave him their boathouse."

"Their boathouse?"

"Yes, because Chase fixed it up. Rand says he put in electricity, a bunk, even plumbed a sink for them. So he gave it to him for the summer in exchange."

Dru toasted a bagel and brought it to the table with her coffee. "If he's down there in the afternoons I can't swim."

"What do you mean you can't swim?"

"It's awkward."

"Use the beach."

"No, I don't mean that. I just prefer . . ."

He inspected her over the top edge of the Travel section, his impatience with her modesty—a recent development—lending a wolfish dispassion to his yellow eyes. On the cover of the Travel section there was a faded color shot of a Turkish mosque, and a woman wearing shorts talking to a woman shrouded in black. Dru stared at the woman in black with a funny kind of envy.

"For Christ's sake, you're not down there in the buff. Anyway, the guy's a handyman, not Melors the gamekeeper. You're safe enough," Fletcher said, and adding almost to himself, "Gives me a chance to view the goods."

"Maybe it seems as though the goods aren't so good anymore."

"Alas, I wouldn't know."

She ate the bagel in silence, turning to gaze out the window at the lake. It was dry and clear, the wind had rallied up with the dawn, and the water was a hard cold blue she could miss without effort today. Ian was gathering asters along the cedar fence, and behind him, a big Robin poked about the grass among the dewy nets of the tent spiders. The day was only just beginning and already seemed about to trip. She asked if Miles was up, Fletcher shrugged, and she said casually, "I've got a job for him," though she didn't—she was just trying to pack and fill around the wobbling mood.

In the kitchen she collected the second half of her bagel, adding strawberry jam she had picked up at a local farm stand. It was so wholesome—everything in Harrow had a wholesome quality.

There was a heavy work table between the kitchen and dining area, with a slab of worn, hollowed maple on top, and hooks underneath from which a colander, cheese grater, ladle, and other items of cookery hung, most of it dented or stained in ways that were attractive to visitors from the cities downcountry where perfection was a burden not unlike a second job. In Harrow it was the plain flawed thing that charmed, and perfection a tactless error of judgment. Behind the worktable she stood with the warm bagel, alert and protected, and in some secret way already burrowing in for foul weather.

Fletcher stacked the *Times*, excepting the Sports section, saved always for last, which he smoothed out on the dining table and began to read. Without glancing back over his shoulder, he asked, "Are you ever going to get over your period?"

"Is that a male courting ritual?" she said. "Menstrual inquiries?"

He stretched his neck and gave a trifling shrug, as if to imply that interpretation was up for grabs.

"Swoon, swoon," she said in a tone of plodding drudgery.

It seemed he thought to laugh, changed his mind, put on a stupid, hopeful face. "Cavort, cavort?"

She stood her place in silence.

"What, you don't like my come-ons?"

"I don't think I do."

"My luck."

"Luck's got nothing to do with it."

"I wish I knew what did."

"To quote Updike," she said, "'the expected gift isn't worth giving.'"

"I don't expect any gifts. It's beg and barter around here."

"Why don't you try wooing me?"

"Wooing?"

"Yes."

"That still legal? I thought it went out with door-opening and chair-pulling. Or was that hair-pulling?"

"Not exactly."

"Wooing," he said, as if reading from the Sports page.

Dru Hammond made an effort to examine her husband objectively, as if she were inspecting a passport photo—nothing particularly unusual, his physical attributes joined to form an overall impression of straightforward Anglo Saxon good looks that age promised to render increasingly more interesting. His father's craggy features but stronger, larger, the white skin of northern ancestors, his mother's amber eyes with the faint green specks, and just beyond them, something cold and playful that no lens could fix on film. Fletcher knew how to be mean; the meanness had the quick stark quality of a dog bite. Strange that it was this characteristic that converted an affable face to an intriguing one. When Fletcher talked, his eyes became intense, his gaze steadied, as if carefully following a towline to his listener, and just outside the gaze, in a vague, marginal area, was that trace of cruelty twisting about, like a dust devil without bearing.

His hands held the newspaper; beautiful hands—of course, she would never have married a man with stubbed fingers, she could never have stood seeing them move over her body. As a violinist, long fingers assumed importance beyond the norm. There was something sexy about his forearms too—from each elbow to wrist, a single long bone sheathed in human leather, the vivid communication of strength, like a simple declarative sentence.

Once he had been a downhill racer, an alternate in the Olympics at the age of nineteen. He graduated from Harvard with an M.B.A. and a full degree in literature as well, unable to deny what he wanted, or to comply fully with what his parents thought he ought to achieve. His roommate, who had connections, put him onto a high-powered job as a business consultant, but for Fletcher it was the occupational equivalent of idling in traffic. Fletcher, just married, felt he ought to take it; or his mother thought he ought to—it was sometimes hard to separate the two. Companies hired Fletcher to show them how to run their business more efficiently, and he, from the deepest rung of his soul up to the upper crust of his being, could not have cared less about efficiency. The job ignored Fletcher's rampant intemperance.

Then Christmas holiday, skiing the Nose at Stowe, he broke his leg so badly he had to stay in bed for most of a year. When depression finally bored him, he read, he read everything. He was still young enough—twenty-nine—to let a passing circumstance shift the course of his entire life, the way a piece of scrap metal might derail a train.

Maybe Suzie's death—Suzie had been terrifically organized—closed off any willingness to observe the index of model attributes. If life was going to be this contingent, why bother with efficiency? —was the reasoning. The whole thing—the shattered leg, the year of books, Suzie's death—set him up handily for a career in a literary agency.

Since the accident Fletcher had maintained, without much effort, an overall level of fitness, though he'd given up skiing—never looked back, never could bear to look back. He had a faint attractive limp, like John Wayne's. He wore shirts until they frayed at the collars. His hair was brown, without shadings or highlight, without curl—a ten-minute job for the barber whom he visited too often.

She tried to see him objectively, but the passport photo seemed at that moment more like a mug shot; there was too much old stuff crowding in. "Look, Fletcher, it just doesn't feel like an invitation anymore, it feels like a reminder. A past due notice."

"You've said it. It's definitely past due."

Ian came in with the asters squeezed inside a grubby hand, and presented them to his mother. She made a fuss of gratitude, put them in a juice glass and set the glass on the windowsill, then knelt before her youngest son. Somewhere she had read that it was important for children not to always have to look up, that they were more attentive eye to eye. They would benefit from a sense of being honored now and then.

"You must leave more stem," she told him. "Then we can use the tall pretty vase."

"Ian tried but they kept breaking," Ian said.

She smiled at him, trying not to look as uneasy as she felt.

Lately, Ian had been sampling points of view, and had taken to referring to himself in the third person. During the spring she had several times come upon him, whispering frantically to himself, "I'm me, I'm me, I'm me." When she asked him what this meant, he explained that whenever he didn't feel like himself he repeated the sentence to put things right. It was a kind of incantation to ward off a new or strange feeling, she speculated; it was just part of growing up, she decided. But now, this third person point of view . . . His teacher, Ms. Dawn of the Progressive school, advised mellowness and "creative space," among other New Age antidotes, but that was two weeks ago on the doorstep of summer vacation when Ms. Dawn knew she would not have to deal with it.

His discipline impressed her . . . if it was just discipline and a quirky experiment, not something serious.

She looked at the trail of freckles crossing the summit of Ian's small, perfect nose—the footprints of a great explorer, she told him when he was younger. Maybe that's all it is, she thought, an exploration. "We'll find some clippers next time," she said, and kissed him by his pale, delicate ear where the freckles left off.

"There's some in the shed. Ian saw them yesterday."

"Okay."

"Can he use them? He'll be careful."

"Sure. And I know where there's a whole hillside of lupine. We'll go this morning." She got up off her knees and started on the random accumulation of dishes. Beside her Ian fiddled in a cup of blueberries, making a dot-to-dot daisy pattern on the maple work table, then sucking them up one at a time. "Ian's an anteater," he declared, and slurped up another three.

Fletcher appeared at the opposite side of the table, his hands on the edge, his torso leaning over, his voice singsonging threat: "I don't know how much longer I can stand this, Dru."

Ian gazed at his father's equatorial region with the serenity of blue skies; having acclimated to his mother's kneeling, he was apparently not going to look up to the cold face of the north.

"Fletcher . . ."

"I know, I know, but it's creepy, it's getting to me."

"It's a phase."

"Can't *you* get him to stop?"

Dru inspected the ceiling as if there were obvious bare bulb facts dangling down from it, then she touched her son's head apologetically. "Ian's standing right here, darling."

"Well I can't tell where the hell he is, he's in the third person, is where. It's like he has his own personal interpreter. Ian this, Ian that. For god's sake, it's schizoid." Fletcher shoved his face at his son and made a pinching motion in the air, enunciating "I, I, I . . ." with percussive strength.

Ian went AWOL. After all, it seemed to have nothing to do with him.

"Good. You've mastered the first-person singular," Dru told Fletcher with dull enthusiasm.

For several seconds he was quiet. He looked at her, she looked at him; someone sighed as the thin humor drained like water from sand about them.

"We need to talk."

"Yes."

FLETCHER HAMMOND possessed qualities few of his friends were made to notice. He was loyal to Dru, as he had been to Suzie, as he had been to women he had dated in his early youth. At other pretty women he looked with perhaps distant appreciation, as if they were pages viewed over the shoulders of fellow travelers. In some obscure way they merely augmented his valuation of Dru, not by simple comparisons but by supportive uplifting, flying buttresses to his adored wife, Dru. Because he did truly adore her—it was this that inspired the cruelty.

In some way Fletcher felt he had discovered her, had given her things she had never had, things she wanted and needed and had dreamed of during her years in institutions. In the presence of his wife he experienced his own beneficence, and her appreciation—which was for many years like a child's—only magnified it. This was Dru's theory, which Fletcher did not refute; he only wondered why it had the quality of an accusation.

As for his work, Fletcher rarely took on a book he did not admire, or an author whose work was not serious and unpretentious. The others in the agency passed off the literary stuff to Hammond, and it wasn't clear whether they pitied him the lot of his taste, or pitied themselves their lack of courage.

He believed in God. Every Sunday he strode off in a nice tweed jacket, with his grandfather's pocket bible, and a pleasant straight-ahead, matter-of-fact way about him, and a solid snap to his step that was just about more convincing than two thousand years of religious discourse.

"It's the path of least resistance," Dru remarked.

"On the contrary," he replied, "everything argues against it."

"Except heart's desire."

"I do not desire God, my dear. I desire you. I acknowledge God."

But she believed that it took something very like courage to accept the massive randomness of life, the weird fact of it, the continuance of it, and the obvious, rude, and in-your-face end of it.

FLETCHER AND MILES went to the club to play in a father-son golf tournament. Ian was invited to Jake's for the construction of a fort, far more interesting than lupine. And Dru spent two hours in her studio, practicing her part in a Dvořák quintet. She was not with the in-crowd of chamber musicians, who played in the regular summer series, come up from New York and Boston and Washington. She was not so well known, and had never been inclined to work the circuit and make herself desirable that way. But she was good, better than she ought to have been, perhaps. They had invited her to sit in on several concerts during the season, though the invitation had a forced quality, as if they could no longer ignore her presence every summer in Harrow.

That was the other thing about Fletcher—his opinion of her work. He could not have thought more highly of her talent, her discipline, her attitude toward The Thing Itself mingling so just-

rightly (in his opinion) with vague indifference to the rest, the or-
biting overcharged electrons of pomp, circumstance, and title. Perhaps Dru Hammond could have been a soloist, her work recorded;
certainly she could have been first chair. But she was a freelancer in
the Boston area, usually the second chair in the section; there on
the inside it was her job to turn the page.

Perhaps she might have pushed harder, but she simply did not
care quite enough. She had drive, but did not possess that special
component of drive that asked to be uniquely noticed. To be a good
functioning part of something—that was what consistently mattered to her. Part of the music, part of the orchestra, part of the
Hammond family, part of the Harrow summer community, part of
a history growing and gathering momentum beyond The Fire.

And yet, despite all these apparent realities, she felt she did not
belong. She belonged in the fire; everything after did not seem to
count, and something or someone was going to find out that she
was still around and exact payment.

THE WIND HAD settled. At noon she went down to the dock
for a swim, trying to get there before Fletcher and his new helper
started work after lunch. There was a party that evening at the Bettencourts', something to look forward to. The day was fully shaped.
By the time they would get home that night Fletcher would have
had too much to drink, so sex would not be an acute issue. It was a
sad relief.

She slipped from the woods into the open. A blue sky, wan and
desolate. Small diagonal waves lapped against the injured dock.
Fletcher had managed to remove the middle section by himself,
leaving the two close in and the last one out at the end. Dru leapt
from the second to the last section, so that a framed open mote of
lake water separated her from shore. She had brought with her several oranges, and ate two in quick succession, sitting cross-legged
on the dock, the orange slices exploding in her mouth. There was
no one on the lake. In Harrow people gathered for meals, and many
indulged in nap taking before returning to the Think House or
camp project or golf links or the country walk, which made noon
at lake level a reliably quiet hour.

She stretched out in her swimsuit on the warm wood, and placed the last orange on her forehead, its bottom resting over her Third Eye to encourage sleep of another kind. She tried, but she could not see what was making her so unhappy. Maybe it was her age.

The orange felt simple and good. She imagined it passing down its goodness, then regretted taking from an orange, for she had nothing to offer in exchange. "I'm sorry," she said aloud—she was the sort of person who would apologize to an orange. At last after some moments of consideration, it seemed to her okay if the orange simply sat upon her forehead, its round cool weight a benign presence. Coexistence. "I am keeping good company," she announced with pride.

"You are?"

Her hand shot for the towel, the orange bobbled onto the dock. "Yes, I was."

A sleek man with a leather satchel stood on the grass. Behind him the spruce woods rose up, black in the midday glare, and like another dimension through which he had just passed. "I'm looking for Fletcher Hammond," he said.

"My husband."

He made as if to tip a hat, which was charming and somehow not so charming, too.

"Did you try up at the house?"

"There was no answer."

She observed his expression, waiting, asking of her something beyond simple information. It made her nervous and she said, "You're Mr. Chase," to begin the task of social order.

He nodded, and she gave her name, and then he said hello respectfully, setting his leather satchel down on the grass. "I thought I'd take a look at the job. There are things we will need from Dugan's before we can get started." She eyed him as he spoke; he did not smile, which she decided was intelligent, or at least smart of him; and he talked with a quiet, considered manner, seeming to imply that she was being consulted. He was handsome, in an unreal way, like a model. It was funny, how distracting it was, it might just as well have been a deformity.

"I'll see if I can find him," she said, wanting to go.

"I didn't mean . . ."

"It's all right, my orange and I were just leaving."

Sam Chase smiled down at the grass as she headed for the path. With a flirty shrug, she handed him the last orange as she passed, and wondered why in the world she had done it.

Fletcher spent the afternoon working with the new man.

That evening at Don Bettencourt's they saw him again, this time in a white linen shirt and a silk blazer, cornered by Mrs. Williams, her meaty shoulders quivering with rapture.

"Man gets around," Fletcher said, grabbing a bourbon as he bee-lined for two of his golf cronies.

Don Bettencourt swept over and gave Dru a warm appraisal. He was a short man with an ardent whine, married three times, a great fan of women, but with Dru he was especially sweet—adoring Uncle Don. "My dear," he whined lustfully, "what can I make you? A martini-weeni?"

"That sounds fine."

"We heard about your heroism, saving that fellow who capsized from drowning in our lake."

"Hardly."

He kissed her suddenly on the mouth; he was always looking for reasons to kiss.

"I still don't even know who he was."

"Paul Jindal."

"How do you know that?"

"I don't know." He gave a laugh and kissed her again. "Are we having a Zen dialogue?"

She smiled. "Well who is he, what does he do?"

He handed her the martini, and added to his own scotch and soda. There was a tennis-tanned bald spot on the back of his head, flat and roundish, which Dru fixed upon as he bent over the bar as though it were a field upon which the players were about to arrive. "Hasn't been coming long, maybe three summers. He's got some obscure role in the art world, Art capital A."

"Tell me."

"I think he recovers famous pieces. Stolen paintings, descendants of Holocaust victims whose family treasures were confiscated, smuggled relics of the State . . . that sort of thing."

Across the room Sally Bettencourt waved and signaled simultaneously, and her husband, with a last excuse, kissed Dru.

There was Minnie Hartford by the piano, gazing up at Ingram Olmos with a painful optimism; Dru thought not to intrude, and wandered over next to Fletcher. "So on the third I hit a good drive," he was saying, "knocked a six iron to the fringe and then foozled the chip. I was so pissed I three-putted. Then on the fourth I hooked it into the woods and had to hit a provisional, so now I'm lying three and it takes me two to the green. I drained a twelve-footer, but it's still a double bogie."

She decided to take her drink out to the porch and miss the rest of the recap. The wind had dropped. Beneath her the lake was a jade reflection, dark and richly soothing. It was just seven, the time when canoes ventured out, and from the Bettencourt porch, she counted three in the distance, their long thin *V*s making cross-scratches in the jade, and the voices of the passengers carrying across the water, pleasant and untroubled, so that she would have liked at that moment to have been in a canoe with strangers on the darkening lake.

Behind, spread out on patio tables, the food drew takers, and each time someone lingered for Brie and crackers they chatted with her. The conversations had a tinny quality, as if the contents had been emptied out of them. She wanted to care about the new club rules, the Matisse exhibit at the MOMA, Cherie Rollo's skin cancer, but she did not, and found that she could not. It seemed a kind of personal failing, and she would have liked to have taken herself home as one would a moody child.

Harriet Wright spoke passionately of the summer music and her passion only seemed to anesthetize Dru. She had black hair, dyed toward the purple end of the spectrum, teased into a dense and tangled under-curving, and at that moment in the westering light, it brought to mind something painfully swollen and bruised. Years ago Dru had tried to make herself agreeable to Harriet, but Harriet was a friend of Suzie's grieving mother, and it was not easy. "So you're the new wife," she had said, peering over her knitting glasses. "That's me," Dru replied with cheerful hatred, "number two."

Dru glanced longingly toward the lake while Harriet set down her wineglass and sampled the hors d'oeuvres; she was a delicate feeder, like a Persian cat, her lips making dry smacking sounds and her fingers tweezing up bits of food with astonishing rapidity. "You'll be playing that thrilling Dvořák."

"Yes."

"I expect you practice every day?"

"No, four days a week."

"But not with our regular players."

"I do when we are all ready."

"Of course. And then how long do you practice each piece together?"

"Couple of hours usually."

"Fascinating." Harriet picked up her glass by its stem, and Dru noticed then the slightly bent wrist and the quiver. *Parkinson's*, she thought. Or some medication that caused tremors. It changed things somehow, Harriet Wright's trembling hand; so far it was the one thing at the party that Dru cared about, though she could not say how or why. Perhaps only that she herself felt fragile; along some deep-laid course of her life something was trembling like this woman's hand.

Harriet clawed onto the former ambassador as he passed. Others kept filtering by. Twice when Dru needed escape, she used a refill as justification, so that halfway through the party and her third martini she was feeling pretty smoothed out and impervious. When Sam Chase came around the corner and over to the railing beside her she did not move off.

He nodded, and for several minutes peered down through the white columns of the birches to the lake, sipping his drink in silence. She could not help liking him for that. It was the way one got to know a strange dog, in stillness and silence, quiet words, eventually a hand extended.

Below them a green canoe started across the mirrored water, with a single paddler and second person leaning back, trailing one hand and pointing with the other into a nebulous red sun sinking with heavy abandon toward the bottom of the west. They watched for a while. Then Sam Chase said, "Peaceful."

"Yes," she murmured, "it makes it easy to believe in things."

"To believe in what things?"

She swung her head to see him, to see if it was worth it. Through the soft lens of the martinis she saw the face of a possible friend, or of someone who did not care what she said—it seemed oddly not to matter which was true. He moved his hand slowly to the breast pocket of his linen shirt, withdrew a cigarette, and lit it expertly. *He's been here before*, she thought, *he's been around*. "Oh, I don't suppose it matters," she said. "It's mixed up with need, what one needs to believe."

Chase inhaled thoughtfully. He looked immensely at ease.

After a while she asked, "What do you need to believe in, Mr. Chase?"

"Sam." He pinched his chin softly. "Not much."

"Really?"

"Not much to get along."

"You must name something, I insist." Suddenly it was nice, talking. She had thought to avoid this man, but now she was happy for the moment. Because he had no associations here, they knew nothing about each other. It meant that they could talk purely—she could say, *I like poppies*, and he would have no experience of her relationship to poppies, so he would simply receive her statement wholly; it would be an immaculate exchange. Here this man, Sam Chase, was like the Present, and Fletcher was the Past piling hugely into the Present, and in some strange unnamed form the man on the lake in the morning fog, Mr. Paul Jindal, was mixed up with the Future.

"I need to see a pretty thing each day at least once," Sam Chase said with surprising seriousness.

"Doesn't it make a difference what it is?"

He looked at her, seemed about to say something, cleared his face and replied, "No."

"Well, that's handy."

"Something like handy." He offered a smile; it was brief and conservative, as if a smile had gotten him into some kind of trouble long ago. "And you? You've got your family, and this . . ." he made a broad, almost theatrical, perhaps even mocking, gesture that included the party behind them, the lake, all of Harrow, "this scene."

"Oh, I don't belong here. Probably never will, either. I'm a kind of permanent refugee. Yeah," she said, gazing down into the water and now speaking mostly to herself, "burned out and here by special dispensation of the Hammond family."

"Is that good?"

"Sure, it's good, it's what I wanted, I guess. It can be annoying, too. The assumptions, you know, that this is what everyone ought to want."

"I can imagine." Chase turned and looked at her with a certain quiet intimidating intimacy, as a doctor might, or a priest. "So what is it you need to believe in, Mrs. Hammond, here in Harrow, Vermont?"

Before she knew it she had said, "Fletcher."

Sam did not say anything, but she could feel him study her, and she trained her gaze steadily out across the water, imagining herself in a little boat chugging west without thoughts or a plan, going away. Then he touched his fingers to her bare shoulder, and she was snapped back to the porch, out of the little boat. There was a long raw silence, the kind that could go either way between strangers, cobbled into something fine and lasting, or dropped; a silence from which eventually Dru fled. "Speaking of whom . . ." she sputtered with sickening gaiety, and slipped back into the house and the maw of the party.

FLETCHER HAMMOND was a popular fellow. In a manner of speaking it was his job—not to be agreeable exactly, but to be conspicuous in an inconspicuous way. To be, as a social commodity, *au courant*. He had an irritating habit of mumbling things that drew in anyone standing near, and what he did mumble seemed so understated that in the minds of others enhancements quite naturally occurred. This was wildly effective with editors. He might begin by avoiding the subject of the book he represented, talking avidly of other books, reciting famous plots of yore. He drank too much and ate too slowly. He made half-formed references to other publishing houses which he then tried to withdraw, the threads of secrets not meant to have been tugged; he did all this until the editor, driven again and again down side alleys, flung himself on the book for which they had expressly met with enthusiasms beyond the call, and sometimes beyond his budget. Thus, Fletcher made a deal; it didn't always work, but it was his M.O.

The other thing about Fletcher was that he was willing to be outrageous—social service, according to him. *Many are called*, he would say. Especially in Harrow, where it was not uncommon to have lifelong friendships, and to some extent never to have outgrown those early, deeply grooved patterns of youthful commerce. Short Allan Biggs would always suspect he was being left out; Maggie Gould time and again would want what Amy Primack had; Don Bettencourt would forever insist that he was perfectly happy with whatever he was doing, even if it was divorce or the burial of a beloved pet; and likely as not Fletcher Hammond would round off a cocktail conversation with the rude revelatory remark idling in everyone else's mind.

Which, as Dru entered the living room, it seemed he had just delivered.

Harry Young waved her over. "Your husband has been . . ."

"I'm sure he has." She squeezed Harry's arm and lifted her glass to the others.

In a large layered aristocracy there would have been a creditable place for Harry Young, but by American standards Harry had not amounted to much. He was a nice man—which was his byline. In his late fifties he still had yellow curls and the warm cloudless eyes of a golden retriever, and an easy way of holding himself that suggested life had not overburdened him with troubles of any real dimension. In private Fletcher referred to Harry as Dudley Do-Right. His money was inherited, his occupations make-work, and his two children adopted and blindly loved into adulthood. Cocktail parties, light nonbinding encounters at hours of conviviality, seemed Harry's natural habitat, since meaningfulness simply could not anchor down deeply in the man. He was a scratch golfer and a desirable bridge partner, and though not a nimble-footed dancer, someone who was willing, which in a community blessed with more women than men was an especial virtue. In the dust of Fletcher's remark, Harry Young coughed uneasily, and studied the toes of his white bucks, which he seemed to have just discovered with the keenest of interest.

Turning and leveling an expression of disapproval at Fletcher, Dru told him, "I won't ask," though she wanted to know; he could be wickedly funny.

"My too-brilliant wife." Fletcher slipped his arm around her waist. There beside him she knew he was proud of her, his wife, *his* —in her short, sleeveless black dress prickling with the tiniest silver specks, and her skin tan and her eyes Irish blue, and her cropped hair mussy as if she had just been released from a sudden and forceful embrace.

Avery Johns gestured with his glass. "You look like Beluga caviar, Mrs. Hammond, doesn't she look like Beluga caviar?"

"Where's your cracker, Avery?" She dropped her chin on her shoulder, and sent a smoky look back at him, exhaling the words. It was all cocktail party play, but it felt, even to Dru, a little awful just then. Lately she simply wasn't up to things.

Avery laughed nervously. And Fletcher too, with fleeting gusto.

Harry Young stood to her right, then his wife, Bev, who never spoke. Ted Greenwald, a sociologist from Brown. Alberto DePena, a newcomer from Brazil by way of his lady friend, Liz Harrison; the Harrison family had been summering in Harrow for almost a hundred years. So far Alberto had fit in well, owing to his tennis prowess—new blood for the club tournament. And next to Fletcher, Avery Johns, his oldest friend, a Boston journalist, and a hardcore bachelor on the subject of which he was uncommonly amusing; there was something weak and touching about Avery—he spoke often of a book everyone knew he was never going to finish.

"I've been thinking . . ." Fletcher said.

"They've got pills for that, you know," Avery said.

"I've been thinking," Fletcher began again, injecting Avery with a sharp stare, "about the caste system here in our sylvan land."

Alberto frowned and gulped at his drink. "Caste *seestem*?"

"Natives top the list."

"Naturally," Avery said. "Brahmins with chain saws."

John Abbot wandered over. He ran the local gift shop, and his genes, as he put it, had trickled down six generations of Vermonters, which made him distilled excellence, *eau de vie du Vermont.* "Chain saws," he huffed. "Why, we hire up these summer lads for the saw gangs, want a taste of real work."

"Well, after you, John, we find non-native natives . . . that's you," Fletcher jerked his chin at Harry and Harry grinned back, Laurel-and-Hardy style. He enjoyed unique status among natives and summer persons, having bought a big piece on the lake at the age of twenty-two. He was *in* everywhere, and in sentiment, more native than natives. It was Harry Young who had started the local land trust.

"Followed by old-time summer persons," Fletcher snapped invisible suspenders, "like me."

Ridiculously, it hurt Dru to be left out. She leaned in toward Harry and said, not so *sotto voce*, "My husband is pronoun-challenged." But Harry didn't seem to get it; he peered at Fletcher as if somewhere there were a visible handicap he had never before noticed.

"You personally, or the Hammond clan?" Liz asked. She and Fletcher were caste equals, and she resented the word "old" in the presence of her youngish Latin escort.

"Both," Fletcher said. "Let's see now . . . fourth are the permanent summer persons, like the Bettencourts here. Not especially long-time summer people, retired now and here year-round, but in the eyes of Vermont, everlastingly summer people."

Ted Greenwald gave a sage nod, and poked about in his pipe with a matchstick. "This is rich, Hammond. Could cobble up some kind of paper."

"Now we're down to newcomer summer person—five. And bottom rung, the two-week-a-year tourists, the banded leaf-peepers, and always and forever," he turned his head slowly toward Avery, "massholes."

Searching the shallows of his scotch, Avery produced a bored face. "May I quote you?"

"Do please, I so enjoy reading myself."

"What about wives?" Dru ventured.

"Husbands," Liz added. She'd had a lot to drink, and had been mildly defensive about her Latin lover since his arrival.

"Ah, spice," Fletcher said dreamily, giving Dru's bum a pat, which wouldn't have been so annoying if she didn't sense that something was coming she was sure not to like. "Spouses of long-time summer persons enjoy an honorary status equal to his—or hers," he nodded respectfully at Liz, "if and until divorce, after which they go back to Start, collecting as little money as possible."

"Charming," Dru observed, "something to look forward to."

Fletcher flashed a look at her, which had the quality of a warning shot over her bow.

"It's medieval," she shrugged, and added softly, "darling."

They were standing next to the bar, and Fletcher reached down for the bourbon, poured himself a slug, gave the amber liquid a whirl, then sipped with his usual vaguely effeminate manner, the littlest finger curling out from the glass. "Children of summer residents," he drove on, "acquire at birth, and retain regardless, the status of the earliest summer person in their family."

Ted Greenwald lit his pipe and puffed leisurely. "Of course, it's all bottoms up at the club. Summer people are first in, followed by citizens of the township, and thence through an ever widening thicket of Vermonters, otherwise known in the rule book as transients."

"It's funny," Dru said, "the natives are transients and the summer people belong. All we need is the Queen of Hearts."

Fletcher's expression was ominously blank. "Volunteering?"

"Sorry, not qualified." She was still smiling but without conviction.

"I forgot. You don't volunteer, you have to be asked. Invitations only." He rattled the flecks of ice in his glass, the jagged hook of his littlest finger dangling her direction.

The others had dropped into heady silence.

"Here we have a woman so delicate she requires engraved invitations. Fletcher Hammond the Third requests the delights of his wife's bum . . ."

Avery put a firm hand on Fletcher's arm but he jerked it free. "Leave it, Fletch . . ."

"And other tasties . . ."

"Stop." Her face felt red-hot. "He's had too much to drink," she explained to the scattering gallery gods, Harry in the lead.

Abandoned to themselves in a murky corner of the room, she looked at his face, but it was not a face she knew or wanted to know —chilling, indifferent, impenetrable. He sipped his drink at the window. The porch was lit, but there was a black shroud cast out over the lake, and they could see only as far as the railing and *not* see their reflected faces, for which Dru felt a kind of frantic gratitude. There was a lump in her throat the size of a fist, but she managed to say his name, "Fletcher," with hurt in her voice and again, with a deep unmistakable final chord of disgust, "Fletcher."

"Ah, go fuck yourself," he drawled as he turned and left.

FOR MANY YEARS Dru had had a short memory for ugly things, she was so happy to be with Fletcher. But without her knowing it the ugly things had been piling up in shadowy heaps about the House of Hammond, so that now whenever an ugly thing occurred there was no more room left in the shadows, it was pushed out into the center where the light glared, and not only impossible not to see, but now impossible not to see *next to* the murky heaps of uglies that had preceded and that sat now in webbed-over silence like the accoutrements of lamentable ancestors one ought to have dispatched years ago. It made for long fights. If the past informed the present and the present shaped the future then they could never shake the Time of it, it would be with them in some form forever—as memory, as encore, as the ticking of fear against night's window.

Fletcher offered his usual excuses, beginning with the close-at-hand and leaning back over to genetic dispositions. It was the booze; the sexual deprivation of recent times; his mother's over-principled under-affectionate policy of childrearing, his father's imperious distance and spasms of wincing sentiment; the broken leg (which limped out on stage whenever psychology took the mike); and if he was really desperate, the death of Suzie, followed by the brackish end of the gene pool into which Fletcher had apparently dabbled a preconception toe or two.

"Booze," Dru said, starting at the beginning, "that's nothing, that only greases the skids."

He looked genuinely contrite, sitting there on the edge of the bed, his hangover detonating and his eyeballs registering the seismic activity.

"Your hostility was palpable last night," she said.

"I'm not hostile."

"Okay, angry. About sex probably, what else?"

"You were chatting up Chase, and offering Avery crackers for your caviar. Maybe I was wondering why they get it from you and I don't."

"Get what?"

"Provocative behavior. Seduction."

"It's not serious."

"Well, why don't I get it anymore?"

"Because I'm hurt. Because you treat me like shit. Because for years I made a point of not seeing it, I was so stupidly, foolishly grateful to be with you."

"Don't say foolish."

"It was foolish, it was, Fletcher. And it has cost me a lot. Honestly, I can't afford nights like last night, not anymore, I ran out of that kind of currency three years ago."

He swung his head to look at her. "I have changed."

"Yes, you have, it's true, and fighting me every step of the way, I might add. You have changed, but this kind of thing still keeps happening, not so much but still it does. And I don't get it, I don't understand why. Why? What have I done to deserve this?"

"Nothing."

She sighed heavily.

"I guess I was hoping something could happen last night," he said, "we could get together maybe, after the party, for a roll in the hay."

She was lying in bed with her head resting on her arms, and she stared at Fletcher's back, naked and broad, then reached out and drew her fingers across it, and saw the little bumps rise, and she thought of a cold boy or a scared boy, but a boy nonetheless whose skin may be sometimes all he has to speak with. "Then why did you sabotage the possibility?" she asked with a tenderness that was whole and separate from her own hurt feelings.

"I didn't, I mean I didn't mean to, I was mad about having to ask, and . . ."

"So you shot yourself in the foot."

He conjured up a goofy imploring look, sensing that at the very least he might amuse her.

"No," she said, "I'm not going to help you pick the slug out. You humiliated me in front of everyone, your friends . . ."

"They are your friends, too, you know . . ."

"People I like and am trying to get to know, and you made me feel so, so temporary. Wife number two."

"Oh, come on, they all think you're great. I'm the one who looks like a thoroughbred jerk."

"Not in this community. You belong, even in your jerkdom, you will always belong, Fletcher, it doesn't matter what you do, you're a native summer son. And, you know, I can never really belong to Harrow, Vermont, or to the Hammond family, I will always be in some way imported bric-a-brac from the Territories."

"Jesus Christ." Fletcher stood up and went to the closet, pulling a shirt from the hanger and letting the hanger clatter to the pine boards. He turned and studied her as he dressed. "Don't you ever get bored with it?"

She knew but still she asked, "What?"

"What," he said, deadpan. "The wastrel routine, the romance of the outsider."

"Okay," she said, angry now, intensely alert, "forget me, forget my actual past and my possible neurosis, this *is* still demonstrably and historically an insider family in an insider community in an insider region of the country."

"The country? You are kidding."

"The East. The East Coast."

"Spaketh the girl from Independence, California."

"Look at the fellowships, the endowments, the commissions . . ."

"Now, this is unlike you, Dru. Professional jealousy?"

"Well, even I get tired of it sometimes. You should have heard Harriet Wright last evening."

"Forget Harriet Wright, she's an old puff adder."

"I do, I would . . ." she felt like crying, "if things were better between us . . ."

Tentatively, sweetly, he said, "Maybe we can find some hay later on."

"That would be nice," she said, tentatively, sweetly, and utterly without faith.

They did not find any hay later on. The truth was, Dru Hammond felt bruised, and bruised more easily these days, because she kept bumping into those shadowy heaps of the past. The sheer repetition of events annoyed her, bored her, confounded her. Couldn't things at least change? Really, something was going to have to give.

From Fletcher she wanted to feel a serious sustained effort of kindness, and she was aware he hadn't much stamina on that score. A day or two of good behavior, hair combed, teeth brushed, the conspicuous for-credit inquiries adding up on the calling card— "Can I get you something," "How are you?"—tallied and tarried hardly at all before recompense entered the fore. She wanted his kindness, his thoughtfulness, his love, without *any* thought to payment . . . at which point payment would have been swift and ardent.

And they did not find any hay later on because Fletcher had suggested it, and that automatically placed Fletcher in the rank of petitioner, which obliged him inevitably to sabotage it. Real men did not make appeals, they were lured—dumb, brutish, and full of concealed knowledge—into the webby hammocks of their women.

Dru was upstairs in the bedroom in red silk scanties he had given her for Christmas, demonstrating good faith, knowing it was not going to happen.

Fletcher was downstairs on the couch, power-drowsing to the dulcet tones of golf's color commentators.

"I was waiting."

"I fell asleep."

"I see."

"Sorry."

Thus he expunged his petition. And managed simultaneously to insult her, his wife, whose charms were not riveting enough for him to maintain consciousness.

Thus she relieved herself of having to admit that for awhile nothing really could woo Mrs. Fletcher Hammond III.

IT WAS ANOTHER week before they managed to hook up for the next meaningful dialogue, but by then the whole thing had lost its vitality, the newest open wound had sealed over and the chronic aches to which they were accustomed had come droning back on stage like the Greek chorus. Fletcher was into the dock repair, and Dru realized that she really did not want to talk about their foundering sex life, or their threadbare efforts at communication; it all seemed overwhelming and depressing. And if they did intend to talk openly and seriously, she could not imagine how to start, what to grab onto that might wrench open some part of their trouble and expose The Reason. Because the reason seemed to be simply the smallest accumulations of time, detritus from daily friction, dry rot in a foundation that needed partial if not complete replacement, and how did one cleave it all together into something significant and justifiable? How did one cobble it all up into something grandly singular, the Great First Cause, *causa causans*?

The other contraindication was Paul Jindal.

One morning from the flat water of the south cove where she was resting in her shell she saw a figure descend from a white cottage to the water's edge. The morning was already warm, the sun a hot spot on her back, the air still and humming like the atmosphere of a concert hall moments before the music begins. The man was Paul Jindal, though she could not say how she knew; maybe it was the way he held his back, so easy and yet so straight. In full view and watching, she felt paralyzed, guilelessly unashamed of her candor, and happy, happy to have found him—that was all.

He swam smoothly, without show or muscular vigor, for the simple enjoyment of it, it seemed, his brown arms falling into the water with a distant muffled slap, and the commotion of his kicking feet subtle beneath the seamless water. The south cove was shallow a long way out from shore, and when he had finished and began to ascend from the water it was with such gradual intensity that he might have been growing out of the lake itself, like a brown reed. Three times she pulled on the oars, feeling him behind her watching as she approached. The bow nosed up onto the sand beside him, and he waded in to help her out. When she was standing she realized she had said hi two or three times. He seemed to twinkle around the edges of himself; it was like those bright specks that moved across the iris now and then—if you tried to look directly at them they darted away.

He invited her for tea.

From the shore the cottage seemed small and sweet, snugged in against the slope as if the slope had formed around it. Narrow squared pillars framed a verandah, willow furniture, and a paned front door with a lace curtain. The floor of the verandah had been painted red. There were a couple of old canoe paddles crossed beside the door, and a milk can stuffed with cattails. On one side of the cottage a willow trailed long filaments about the corner, and underneath in the sandy soil the grass was pale and delicate, present more as a sample of grass than as convincing fact. An enormous begonia the color of cantaloupe sat on the railing; someone had recently watered it. At the base of the pillars grew several feathery clumps of astilbe. Dru saw how deceptively small the cottage appeared, extending back and up the slope where cedar and birch mingled briefly before giving way to the broad upswing of a hay field. The hay had just been cut and lay in dusty green mounds patterned into crescents stacked inside each other. Along the top edge of the field beside the road that circled the lake stood a row of old maples. The whole effect starting at the maples and dropping down through the neat pattern of the mown hay, the clique of lacy birch, the plumpish cedar, then the cottage, fair and candid like a child's face, the wispy grass, the flat pale blue water, and the morning sun beaming away on it all . . . the whole effect was so utterly perfect that Dru felt she was entering a dream or a picture in a child's storybook. Or at the very least the Disney model of Home.

He left her on the verandah while he went inside to prepare the tea. She hadn't any shoes with her, and thought about this, looking at her sandy feet. Her feet had always embarrassed her, long and thumb-like at the ends, the big toe angling sharply inward from the bone; the two feet placed side by side were like an advanced geometry problem with unsolvable and contradictory angles and planes, a trick question on the last test of the year. Somewhere around the age of thirty she'd given up on concealment and had taken to defensive flaunting. Disowned, they took her places; it was a job. But now looking at her funny feet on the red verandah waiting for a stranger, she felt a kind of wrenching affection for them and regret at her betrayal. The sun was coming on, the smell of new-mown hay sweet on the air, the day starting differently, and beyond the day, a long broad turn had just begun as well, she could sense it; looking down at her feet, Dru was aware of the almost imperceptible *click* of change, a door opening, a gentle waft.

He returned with a tray of orange scones, almond tea, and two white napkins that were old and soft and as clean as they would get. She looked at his light brown hand as he passed a napkin to her; there was so much elegance and quietude in his hand and in the old clean napkins—the two together filled her with an immense and unaccountable longing. It seemed possible then at that moment to achieve the grace and meaning that life had to offer simply within the lived moment. It seemed possible to be grand without history, without family, without money and fame.

"I learned your name from a friend at a party the other night," she said. "Paul Jindal, yes?"

"Yes."

"My name is Dru," she said, leaving off her last name for awhile, wanting to be just Dru.

He smiled with his black eyes and poured the tea. "For Dru."

Their talk wandered, left off, picked up again at another place entirely new and often about some trifle, some silly detail—rhubarb pie, middle names, old live recordings of Sviatoslav Richter. The usual ground, the stuff of résumés and loan applications, they covered with a certain indifference—or perhaps only she was indifferent. Silences came and went like the breezes that passed through, without provocation, without needing to hurry on to some other subject connected to the last. Connections seemed unimportant because they were the connection, they were alive in the same place at the same time. It seemed enough.

If she asked him a question it was often only to hear his voice, which had a soothing quality, and a faint unidentifiable accent. He had a way of using small phrases to say complicated things. "It leaves something behind," he said, describing his experience of a painting that had moved him deeply. And whenever she talked it seemed he listened to her voice and to the words with less care than he listened to something behind them, which was perhaps the authentic Dru. He seemed to want to know her without trappings, the stuff that had gathered over the years, and everything in his manner gave rise to a feeling of being uniquely cherished, like a child, and like a woman. In fact, she felt especially womanly, as though meeting Jindal had aroused a sudden and total ripening from the core of Dru Hammond.

He called her Dru. She called him Jindal. In her mind when she said his name it felt very like a mantra, *Jindal, Jindal . . .*

Many times she went to the cottage, always in the morning, always without consciously planning. Their talk deepened. He spoke of his childhood in Montreal after the second war; his mother was Canadian, his father East Indian, a hydro-engineer on the St. Lawrence. He was close to his father, his mother was unresponsive, a cold realist. She had lost her first child, and there was no point in becoming attached to the second. Dru spoke of the fire, and Fletcher, her music, her sons, Ian entangled with the third person. Together they worried about Ian.

He was kind. Kindness meant something to Dru, perhaps too much; perhaps having been a "charity case" for so much of her life, knowing how little real charity visited the scenes of her youth, she had a special craving for simple kindness. One day when it was cold out on the verandah, he found a blanket and, kneeling before her, swaddled her feet like twin foundlings, an act that would have been totally foreign to her husband.

Your new friend, Fletcher said.

Not all friendships begin and end with the Hammonds, she replied.

Of course. Sensing that there was more involved than he was prepared to deal with, Fletcher's nonchalance was extreme.

On each visit Paul Jindal was wearing the same thing—a white short-sleeved shirt with initials embroidered on the pocket—beautifully pressed—a pair of chestnut colored shorts, leather sandals.

He never invited her into the actual cottage, he never made excuses, or offered explanation, either; calmly he went in and calmly he came out with the tea tray, or a book he wanted to show her, or some object she might find interesting, closing the door so that it clicked into place. Once she heard a sound like a curtain being drawn, and another time while they talked on the verandah music abruptly commenced—she assumed a radio had been set to an alarm. But during the fourth visit someone called out his name with crisp womanly authority.

"Excuse me," he said, disappearing.

She gazed as far away from the verandah as was possible, as if courtesy required at the very least she send her vision away. Across the lake pinkish gray thunderheads mounted; it was not clear in which direction they were headed, and she let herself worry about sculling home in order to use up some of the time. The rest of the sky was a pallid gray veil stretched thin over a distant blue, while beneath the gray the air was tense and humid and difficult to breathe. She wished she were swimming in the cool water, breathing water, a fish, everything soft around her, no sharp surprises and contradictions, everything flowing smoothly together.

The backs of her knees began to sweat. She kept thinking she ought to leave, yet something in her absolutely would not. She told herself it was the thunderheads, she needed to wait to see which way they went, knowing simultaneously that she could reach the Hammond dock in less than ten minutes.

Only when he returned did she stand. "I should be leaving."

"Shall we finish our tea?"

"No . . . that is, yes, except you have company . . ."

He smiled inscrutably, looked at her with a surreal calm, and nodded once. "Yes."

"Me, yes, but I didn't know you were . . . well, why haven't I met your wife?" she blurted out.

"My wife?" He glanced at the lace-covered door with some curiosity, as though considering the possibility, then clasped his hands together and let them hang comfortably across his abdomen. "Christine is not my wife."

Dru stared at him. She had drifted over to the edge of the verandah, where two steps led down to the frail grass, and her head was turned, looking back at him in the dusk of the dimming sky and the shaded verandah. His eyes were black and shining, the whites very white, and his white shirt fluorescent in the gray light. She realized that she wanted him to stop her from leaving, and immediately felt humiliated by the desire.

He made a gesture with his palms facing her. "Christine is my brother's wife. My brother is traveling."

"Traveling?"

"For a while."

"I don't understand." A compressed form of chaos burgeoned inside her head, and she shook it as if shaking would break it up and settle things down into orderly compartments she could pick through at her leisure. "It's none of my business."

"Let's finish our tea, please."

"I don't understand . . . what's going on." The words she had chosen rang oddly in her ears. She went down the two steps, afraid that the woman inside was listening and had been listening all this time, though Dru told herself that there was nothing to hide.

"May I walk with you to your shell then?"

They went to the water's edge, Dru moving slightly ahead of the Canadian East Indian, wondering why she felt sore and betrayed, wondering what right she had to feel this way or any way in relation to this man she did not know anything about.

"My brother's wife," he began, and he touched her back lightly with his fingertips, "had Lyme disease. It was misdiagnosed. Three years without the proper treatment. Heart, nerve damage, crippling arthritis. She was beautiful. Now she is, well, an invalid." He moved his shoulders in a way that implied a somber recognition of fate.

"You mean he just left her?"

"Pain and time together change one's personality." His accent seemed especially noticeable now, almost annoying, as if he were trying for an effect. "She had become someone else. He missed the woman he married. Also it is true that when he was with her he was a man he did not want to know. There are many faces of pain."

"Yes."

"One day without telling her where they were going he took her to the Quakers. They would have cared for her well, but Christine was offended."

"Of course."

Paul examined her thoughtfully. She bent down and picked up one of the sculls and stood it beside her, the blade rising two feet above her head like a flag, and the modest waves of the lake licking up and down her feet as if to console.

"I brought her to my home in Cambridge. There is a woman, Mrs. Porter . . ."

"You don't have to tell me this," said Dru sharply, afraid of Mrs. Porter.

But he proceeded with his calm enunciated speech as if he had not heard her. "Mrs. Porter looks after Christine but Mrs. Porter requires holidays. Then I do what I can for Christine. I bring her to Harrow to change the scene though it seems not to matter."

"Doesn't she want to see anyone or meet new people?"

"No. She harbors anger."

"I guess I would too," Dru said, eyeing the thunderheads, which were swelling with laggard intent toward them.

"No," he shook his head, "you would not. Christine keeps anger as one might a pet. She cares for it, and calls upon it to serve many needs. It is big and bright and it looms greater than any other emotion and so from those emotions she is for a while protected."

Dru did not want to know any more about this woman; what she wanted to know, she knew: that Jindal looked after her, that he would care for his brother's wife because his brother had abandoned her, because she had become, unluckily, a miserable human being; that for Paul Jindal, the field of responsibility was a vast and surrounding domain peopled not with the chosen but with the co-incidences of simple contact. It was an amazing discovery. Not the woman, Christine, fuming from her bed of pain, but the man, quietly taking care of her.

"When we have tea can she hear us?"

"No."

"I'm glad."

"Tell me why."

"I don't know . . . maybe when I'm with you I'm me, I don't know why, some kind of trust, or maybe it's because I hardly know you at all. Really." She gave a laugh. "Anyway, I don't want to share our conversation because they include parts of myself that don't make many appearances."

"I am honored."

Again she gave a laugh, much smaller and full of curiosity, and as much for the formality of his tone as for the embarrassed pleasure it gave her. "What are you thinking?"

"That I think about you a lot."

"Well," she said, happy, nervous, "I wish I were more interesting, to be worthy of all that thought."

A long silence pooled about them. Finally because of the thunderheads she stepped into the shell, and he tipped his head with an air of sublime regret and sublime patience, and let her go.

DRU HAMMOND DECIDED she was falling in love with Paul Jindal. Among other things, the love was possessed of the sudden, fierce, thoroughgoing fascination that is impervious to the outside view. Employing all of the most elaborate reasoning, she still arrived at the same conclusion: love.

Either she was in fact in love with him—the simplicity of this was deeply compelling—or ninety-nine percent of her was in league against the one true percent of her, and this one percent at the core of things was, oddly enough, blind, deaf, and dumb. It was hard to believe.

She reasoned it out: one's own measure is often best found by measuring the might of one's enemy. And so in like manner it was the quality of the reasoning, its brilliance and clarity, its relentless presence, that Dru brought to bear upon the question that ultimately convinced her it was real. Beginning with: *I am susceptible to kindness because my life is hungry for kindness*. Thence to: He is a man who cares not a wit about history or family or situation. And I have no history, my family is someone else's, my situation feels . . . probationary.

And through: He is a man who does not indulge himself; he

doesn't even drink. I am tired of the society of drink, the consequences of drink, the predictability of drink. I am tired of the surround-sound intemperance of Fletcher Hammond—even his temper is a form of self-indulgence.

Jindal is not competitive; he swims for the joy of feeling water touch all of his body at once. How lovely, how childlike. How unlike Fletcher, who likes to win.

He is attentive, interested in me by myself, not in relation to him, or what I might provide him.

And so forth.

It sounded a little corny, she had to admit, listed in the pro/con tablet where some of the biggest decisions often land, but it happened—apparently—to be true.

To defeat the feeling, Dru then advocated all possible explanations that might trivialize it—I am merely ovulating, a hormonal imbalance, I am angry at Fletcher, this is a midlife crisis, I have a taste for adventure, for misadventure, a self-destructive impulse, it's boredom, I have been sexually starved out. But even granting all of these she was still left with the unavoidable brute fact of the feeling, which seemed as overwhelming and flawless and smooth to the mind's touch as a giant egg wobbling onto the stage of her life. The question was what would come out of it?

There was no one she could tell. Everyone in Harrow had been Fletcher's friend first, or if not, their family had known his family, or known his family's friends, or his first wife's family and friends . . . from the tangle of connections there appeared no escape, for no one maintained a discrete entity, no one was sharply edged and pure and uncontaminated by the sepia wash of a century of summers in Harrow. And while she had married into this picture, she was not married to it.

Maybe Sam Chase . . . but there was something about him that was not quite credible. Around him she had the eerie sensation that she was being adapted to with alarming speed, that he was taking up her attitudes and opinions, even her moods, like a human chameleon. He would arrive unadorned, a tabula rasa, she could not detect even a faint disposition except for the thinnest underlining of expectancy . . . and what was it that he expected? After a few minutes of conversation she began to see not only parts of herself in him, but herself on that particular day with appurtenant mood and opinions, a word or phrase she was overusing, a gesture with her hand through her hair. If she was enjoying a peach, he developed a sudden craving; if her mood was dark, spells of solemn gazing overcame him, he stood with tool in hand at the window, he offered his handsome apologics. He seemed to have aligned himself with her, perhaps to comfort, perhaps to invite her to be an outsider with him, and in his presence she felt indeed tempted to rebel, to become a renegade, to exercise freedoms that she may have forgotten she possessed. One day she asked him if he was flirting with her, for it had some of those qualities. Looking not the least surprised, he replied, "What would you like?"

"To know," she replied, "and that's all."

He could talk about Chopin with her, football with Fletcher, toads with the boys. Computers really enkindled him, anything with wires he could fiddle with and rearrange. All around, he was a little scary.

So she did not tell Sam Chase about Paul Jindal. It was funny, these two men about whom she knew so little and who seemed, each in his own radically opposed way, to be filling and composing her summer canvas. Because for all intents and purposes Fletcher had recused himself from their marriage. He had walked off the field, the field was now open, and he was standing on the edge, watching, waiting to see what would happen, or hoping nothing would, or maybe even hoping that something would happen— Dru could not say. It was driving her slightly crazy. In the morning, two or three times a week, she saw Jindal, and in the afternoon, two or three times a week, Chase showed up for work. Once a week Fletcher took the overnight train down to New York, and for a couple of days he lunched with writers and editors, then he caught the Montrealer back to Vermont; the rest of the time he was either on the golf course, or in his study reading manuscripts, on the phone, or immersed in a camp project.

It was a deep cut, this living alone together. She missed him and for that she felt a kind of repugnance. Within the framework of her history, it did not do to miss anyone.

ONE MORNING all three of the Hammond men were on the lawn, setting up the croquet wickets for a garden party. It was hot and humid, the windows along the side of the house facing the lake opened wide to catch the slightly cooler air off the water. Miles was tagging after his father, trying to help, while Ian tinkered with his golf grip on a mallet. From the dark of the living room Dru could see them—my sons, she thought. At that moment they did not seem to belong to her, out there on the lawn, separate and contained in their very own skins, and suddenly so complete, spun off into their own orbits around stars she could not see. It scared her, to see them so. They could, if needed, go on without her.

Ian, his hands working assiduously, his lips rolled inward with absorbing concentration, his scuffed knees . . . the details of Ian's little body almost broke her heart.

There was an old collection of poems in her lap and lemonade on the side table. She fished an ice cube from the lemonade, sucked the juice off it, then held the cube to the nape of her neck, the cool water trickling down the spinal route, unimpeded by a bra, which the heat had discouraged first thing that morning. Fletcher made his standard comments—headlights on, happy to see me—but they had nothing to do with sex: he was not interested in romancing her, but in suppressing the effect of her femaleness. Dru's breasts were small and shapely, and she enjoyed going braless, partly because at age thirty-six she still could . . . and it *was* hot, she told herself; lately it seemed to have been hotter than usual. She considered the possibility that she was only trying to provoke him.

So far the unplanned celibacy was not getting to her. Once they had surmounted the initial hump of anxiety—that it meant the End of Them—Dru and Fletcher (without any actual discussion) seemed to be plodding quietly along, getting a lot more done in the afternoons and practically marching with fife and drum through the stack of summer reading before bed, patting each other's arms with old-couple comfort at chapter ends, and rotating back to back for the long night, each to defeat the demons from his or her own brink of the bed. Fletcher had responded to three of his authors before they began calling him.

How long could sexlessness last? No one, absolutely no one was making any forays, and if anyone wanted to try, more time would only make it harder. Eventually their sex life would be trapped and fossilized in the sedimentary layers of three-hundred-thread-count cotton sheets—*ah yes, the beautiful but rare, and briefly extant sex life of the Hammonds*...

Outside, Fletcher decided to mow the course before he set up the croquet game, and the lawn mower filled the air with the pleasant white noise of male industry. Dru tried to read several poems but at the end could not say what they were about or remember many of the images—there were geraniums in one of them, a yellow dog somewhere else. A vague distraction enveloped her like a transparent cloud; it was there, she could feel it, but she could not see what was causing it, what it was about.

Earlier she had tried listening to Berlioz, but then Chase had thrown the main switch in order to work on the upstairs boxes, and even though it was man-made, the powerless silence had some of the same daunting qualities as a natural disaster. *Now* what do we do? The lack of power had driven Fletcher outside.

"What's wrong with Mom?" she heard Miles ask. It was uncharacteristic of Miles even to notice her these days let alone inquire into her condition, he was so male-focused, so busy jockeying for position on the knee-high rungs with others of his age and sex. Considering all, his attention vaguely flattered her.

Ian straightened; he had a mallet clenched for action, but now he upended it and let the handle drop through the short tunnel of his fingers; addressing the mallet head, he asked, "What do you mean, what's wrong with her?"

"All she does is stare."

"At what?"

"Nothing, s'far as I can see."

"She has a new friend," Fletcher explained, digging a wicket into the grass, "chock full of deep thoughts."

"Thoughts?"

"Deep thoughts."

Ian twisted up his face. "That doesn't mean she's sick or something."

"Something, it means something." Fletcher moved around the lawn, pacing off the fifth and sixth wickets, pushing them in, making adjustments. Ian watched him in silence. He could still summon the fixed and naked straight-ahead gaze of a young child, which never failed to unnerve Fletcher and drive him into a mild state of walking apoplexy. "Now what are *you* staring at?"

"Nothin' much."

"What does that mean?"

"Maybe Ian's having a deep thought." Again with the third person.

Fletcher selected a mallet from the stand and knocked the red ball hard through the first two wickets, and the ball nudged to a stop against the toes of Ian's tennis shoes. Miles was impressed. "Hey, cool," he said, "lemme try."

Without a word Ian started for the path down to the lake.

"Where are you going?"

"Look for crawdads."

Fletcher told him he had better keep his shorts on, the crawdads were biting, which convulsed Miles but prompted a gelid smile from the younger boy as he vanished into the woods.

Fletcher actually looked worried. "Bleatin' Jesus, that kid's sensitive. I've gotta watch what I say."

"Well . . ."

"Honestly, I don't know how to act around him."

Feeling himself to have been consulted in a large and mysterious matter, Miles drew himself up and glanced around as if an audience might be gathering for the occasion. "He's kinda just weird, Dad. Maybe if he hung with some of the cool kids . . ."

"The cool kids."

"Yeah, like Jack Wilkins."

"How do we know Jack is cool?"

"Jeez Dad, it's like obvious."

"Humor me."

"Okay. He's into sports, any sports, he's an animal on the soccer field. Did this." He slapped his shin where a bruise the size of a peony flourished. "Plus he boards everywhere."

"Boards?"

"Skateboards. That's like way cool." Miles flattened his hands on the air and quickly fanned them out to opposite sides, the *way cool* sign.

"I see." The last two wickets stood one in front of the other, a ball's length, and having pushed them into the grass Fletcher pounded in the end stake, unkinked himself, and surveyed the course. He was sweating heavily and seemed to have withdrawn into his own thoughts now, the fatigue registering in and around his eyes as a delicate quality of pleading. Dru felt what was very like a blow of tenderness. Whenever he was building or fixing things he worked with such ardent abandon, and seldom asked for help, and quit long after he should have quit. It made her feel obscurely bad.

What's wrong with Mom?

She has a new friend.

And what about this old friend here?

Yes, what about this one here?

Upstairs Chase thudded softly about as he rewired the bedrooms, a bigger job than anyone had imagined. He had been in their employ going on four weeks, and since he showed up so late in the day he often ate dinner with them now, which provided Mr. and Mrs. Hammond with a timely buffer—they had not fought for a long time. They hadn't done much of anything else together, either.

It was satisfying, gazing around the table at men, young and older; Dru liked men—she and Fletcher had that in common. Lately she had encountered a back door to her affections, a door that opened onto an older form of loneliness from which there was no exit. The peculiar thing was, it seemed Jindal, whether he knew it or not, had led her to that door.

It felt all right, being alive on the planet, but it had never felt all right, being with other people, not since her parents died. After that, everywhere Dru went she knew herself to be a kind of guest.

Outside, Miles had disappeared and Fletcher had taken out his driver and a bucket of old golf balls, and was blasting one after another over the treetops down toward the lake. There was a tournament the next day at the club. He had a smooth, easy swing, all of one movement, with a pause at the top, like a slightly delayed musical beat, that anticipated the releasing action, the club head swinging down with gathering speed and the hips seeming to drive it all forward. There was always a lot of hip in Fletcher's movements, a leftover from his skiing days. When he came in Dru said, "Those all looked good."

"Huh?"

She glanced away, instantly annoyed. "Nothing."

"You said something."

"It wasn't important."

"No, really, what did you say?"

She leaned up from her chair, gathering stray items as she rose, and Fletcher, not wanting to exit, began to help her, removing the beach towels the boys had draped across the back of the couch and tossing them over his shoulder, lifting a vase of withered zinnias from the table, the book of poems. Dru stacked and boxed the cards from the night before—they had had the Youngs over for bridge and dessert. After some minutes, in a breezy, just-making-conversation tone, Fletcher said, "So they all looked good, huh?" In one hand he held the zinnias, their heads wobbling over, in the other the tattered book of poems, and he looked exactly like a suitor who had arrived too late.

She smiled and shook her head as she considered him with the thoroughness of a buyer. "Amazing."

"Really?"

"Alas, not the drives, dear. You. Wanting me to repeat my little praise. You heard it and pretended not to have, and when I didn't you fished it up from oblivion yourself where I was happily letting it sink."

"Well, why not?"

"It's just funny, at your age."

"Hey," he said with a cavalier air, "a good thing is a good thing is a . . ."

"Rose."

"I perseverate."

"In every way apparently."

"Ah, but the real question is," he said, working his brow craftily, "whose ruse was worse?"

From some place deep pure merriment bubbled up. "Say that fast."

"No, really, what do you think?"

Assaying a look of remorse, she confessed, "I suppose my ruse to smoke out your ruse was worse, though awfully clever. I therefore grovel in mortification." And she bowed deeply.

A boyish flush of joy bloomed in Fletcher's face. "Say," he piped, shoving the flowers at her, "how 'bout you and me hook up with some victuals over ta the Lobster Pot?"

"The big city?" Wide-eyed and goofy.

"For you, anything."

Knowing then how much she could love him, what had been and what was still possible, she wanted to cry for the realness of it; and the relief—abruptly and completely it was right, after all, to have married Fletcher Hammond, to have borne his sons, to have stayed. It astonished her . . . it appalled her, too, how easy recovery was—a slip of humor, a little accident of discovery, ground given, however insignificant, on each side, and the tight pressurized feeling in the house, the abbreviated encounters over the business of cohabitation, the closed expressions like closed doors—all had been swept away, banished, a figment of erroneous memory. Now it was as though they were standing in a clearing with a yellow cone of sunlight beaming down about them, and the dark forest retreating concentrically away from them, the center, the place to be. Now nothing could hurt them.

Of course it didn't last. Why didn't it last, why had happiness so little endurance, why had they as a couple so few reserves? Why were they always tripping on the best of their feelings for each other, and allowing the worst to pool about them like shallow brackish water that could not find its outlet, the way clogged, the way lost? He adored her and with intent he hurt her. She loved him, he was everything, too much, too many things to her, and so she needed, or thought she needed, to cut away some of what Fletcher meant. As perhaps Fletcher needed to insinuate that he did not adore her quite so much as he actually did.

JULY PASSED. There had been good summer rains and good sun too, and it looked like by the time August finished out the farmers would get three cuttings of hay after all. Thunder clouds swelled up out of the south and west over Hunger Mountain, Mansfield, Worcester, sooty veils of rain tattered down in the distance until the storm arrived overhead, then for a quarter of an hour or so teams of great drops let loose upon the earth, and right behind here came the sun, the paved roads and the fields steaming as the moisture climbed back up into the air, the air getting fat and heavy with it, and underneath the hay growing, just growing, and the sweet pungent smell prickled your nose as you passed, and conjured not a thought or even a memory but an indescribable feeling of lost contentment.

The Saturday night concerts had begun and Dru was busier with practices. Minnie Hartford, the violist, had been an occasional friend over the years, but this summer Dru found in her the perfect companion. Minnie did not know anyone very well. She was forty years old, plain-faced, plump in a pear way, her teeth were remarkably bad, but she possessed a liveliness that seemed a product of having less to lose, or from not caring what she lost, and this made her comforting to be around. A wake of failed relationships with marginal males was often the object of her attention and wit, and each new loss seemed to augment her dynamism. She got along with everyone and at the same time had no real friends, for no one finally wanted to hold with someone so unlucky.

Minnie and Dru walked together along the dirt roads, observing the farmhouses and the cows, the children haying with their parents, the gardens filling in, and the ponds expanding and contracting with the weather that was always changing. Or they gossiped about musicians. And when they had satisfied those requirements of female dignity, they reverted to the subject of men. Minnie had been introduced to Sam Chase at the Hammonds one night, and later they had encountered him in various Harrow situations. At the Fiddler's Contest they saw him alone, surveying the crowd as if there were someone he needed to find. At the annual antique and crafts fair on the Common there he was, wearing aviator shades, white shirt, and pressed pants, the kind known as matinee slacks, pleated and baggy—one of his many guises. Mrs. Torrance, an elderly widow with a lot of money and heart, had just purchased a spider-legged table, which Sam Chase was carrying to her vehicle.

"I wonder how he does it," Dru said. She had bought a ginger jar, and she and Min were themselves headed for the car.

"How he does what?"

"Gets in with everyone, and so fast. He and Mrs. Torrance look positively chummy."

They watched him ease the table into the back end of a station wagon with a care and calculation that was almost tedious, then he accepted the keys from Mrs. Torrance and the two of them drove off.

Several days later during one of their country walks he drove by in the Leggatts' pickup, Erin Leggatt and Heidi Greenfield on the seat beside him.

Once at the post office where they had stopped to gather mail before their walk he carried a package out to the car. Though his sentences were not especially long, he had a leisurely way of speaking that implied there was much to consider here, that he was taking his listener very seriously. It was a nice feeling, even if it had a staged quality.

Naturally Minnie had trained her eye on Sam Chase, though it was clear even to Minnie, who had a knack for overappraisals and errors of the heart, that something was amiss with Master Chase. "I don't care," she announced energetically, "I like his style."

"You're not alone."

Minnie gawked at her.

"No, no, not me, every other unmoored woman in Harrow though, I'd wager."

Min took comfort in the subtraction of a least one female from the host of enthusiasts. "He looks like Peter Fonda, he's so handsome."

"Too handsome." They were standing by an old farmhouse where the road had turned and was about to rise. The whole family was beyond the house in the field, baling hay, the big wagon trundling along and the rest of the gang, women included, scattered around it. Two barebacked boys rode the load precariously, clung to the sides like brown bugs, and as the bales came they pulled and pushed them up to the top of the blocky hay house, wiped their brows, and hooked up the next one. It was hard work and, thought Dru, shameful hard for a summer person to watch from the cool of the sugar bush. Her own nameless problems shrank to a corner. Maybe if we didn't have so much time, she thought, Fletcher and I wouldn't bother arguing.

What was it about that morning? The house . . . they had rented out the house in Salem, as they had every summer for the last six years. He said they needed the money, though she did not think they did, not at all. It was their home, after all, and renting it to strangers changed things somehow. It hurt her to think of people she didn't know touching her things, the chair in which she had nursed her sons, the room in which she practiced and which had accrued meaning because of all those hours of music. "You don't have to agree with me," she said, "but at least make an effort to understand how I feel about it. It's the first home I've had since the fire."

"I can't afford to think about feelings," he said, but he had seemed edgy. "Houses need to be lived in," he added. Fletcher wanted her to agree with him, his opinions required that kind of support. Oh, he went ahead with his way, whatever it was, but without the cozy comfort of approbation. They had disagreed so much lately he was beginning to wonder who he was.

THE WOMEN crossed over and started up the hill, the road parting a stately grove of maples. Along the right side of the road were calves—all males—and white huts, and they stopped before the first at the bottom of the hill; a dozen more mounted the slope, each chained to a stake, the stake positioned at the entrance to the small white hut of plastic, the huts set beneath the maples, which provided shade. Proceeding up the road, Dru counted four paces between each straining calf, the short chain, the white hut. The calves themselves were beautiful, their black and white hides clean and unmarred, still plush with youth. Each one they passed rolled a desperate eye, lifted his chin and cried out, as if he knew; and when left behind he reverted to the dismal lowing that composed his waiting days.

"Veal," Dru said. "I read somewhere that the ones they use for Provimi veal, the milk-fed ones, are so starved for iron that they lick the nail heads of their pen. These huts don't even have nail heads."

"There's hardly any difference between veal and beef anyway, not enough to do this."

At the top of slope the last calf slept in a soft curled mound at the entrance to his hut, and this one more than the ones who cried out, affected Dru the most; this one who did not seem to know, or who had accepted the misery of his condition enough to sleep through it.

Are we doing this, she wondered, Fletcher and I, the boys? Sleeping before our individual doors? Miles doesn't notice much, but Ian . . . Ian protests. Ian has found a way for a small male creature to protest. The third person. He has become his own advocate. But what is it that he protests, my youngest son?

They walked on in silence. The road turned and broke from the cool leafy light of the sugar bush into hay fields, where the air was warmer and smelled of dried grass and manure, and there was enough breeze to keep the deer flies from landing.

After a while Minnie asked, "What do you mean, too handsome?"

"Min, you are sweet on him," Dru said with a gentle laugh, but something melancholy drifted across it, like a dark tail of smoke.

"He has such lovely manners with women."

In assent Dru replied, "Mannerly," but her thoughts had veered away from Sam Chase. In her mind she was seeing Jindal, and for the first time noticing that there was something she was missing—splendor. She had had it with Fletcher, falling in love and throughout their early years, but it had thinned away somehow, the lavish excitement, the intense color, the importance of small events, the sense that the entire world was present in single moments spent with him, that they needed nothing else. Even Time was unraveled by what they were able to make of the simple accidental fact of Being, she and Fletcher, together.

Then meeting Jindal, the little bits of mornings with him, his voice, his simple language, the images of him, and of his seeing her, hearing her, even when he was not present . . . each was like a tear in the ordinary sheathing of the day, a tear through which it was possible to see beyond to something truly splendid.

From Minnie, she heard the same rustlings. But wasn't it easy splendor, easy and showy and somehow cheap, too, when it was tried for the way Minnie was venturing to love Chase, modeling it up like a lump of clay? Splendor, when it comes, just comes, Dru thought, arrives without invitation. None is ever needed. To whom it comes it comes like rain at the right time and in the right place, the ground parched and given up. It is whole unto itself, an improbable gift. It cannot be asked for, or fabricated, or searched out.

Fletcher and I . . . Fletcher and I have to wake up, because the big easy splendor is gone. There is something we should be doing, some kind of work waiting behind all the trouble . . .

They had made a wide circle, passing five farms, and were ambling along the gravel road where at the bottom waited the Hammonds' old yellow Jeep Wagoneer. Minnie swung her arms and hummed now and then. She had a beautiful voice. "That last one was dead, you know," she said, through the trailing notes of a notturno.

"What are you talking about?"

"The calf. Its eyes were open and clouded over . . ."

"No."

"There were masses of flies." She thought about that for a half a moment. "That's not out of the ordinary, I guess." The gravel washboard of the road caused her to joggle her steps, and when she recovered her pace she added, "I just realized it was probably dead, that's all."

"But it wasn't."

Minnie glanced at her friend and decided to drop the subject.

DURING THE FIRST WEEK of August Fletcher's parents arrived. Dru had hoped that Ian would have abandoned the third person by then, but he was still clinging to it like a life raft from a sinking ship. Lee and Binky Hammond grappled with tact, alarm, denial—"What an inventive little boy." "He does this all the time?" "He's just spoofing us, aren't you, boy? You're just spoofing all us grown-ups. It's a fine game." And in whispers to Dru, "What are you feeding him?"

After it was established that Dru was feeding him food, the senior Hammonds slid comfortably into denial. There was no "situation," the third person did not exist. When he spoke, Lee and Binky Hammond simply scudded from the room.

Ian's friends took it in stride—seven-year-olds were that way, the margin of acceptable weirdness was almost as wide as the world.

Dru was still holding her breath; Fletcher was promoting shock therapy. One morning before he was awake enough to remember that they weren't communicating on any real level, he turned and said to Dru with quiet tenderness and concern, "Maybe it's us, maybe he's upset about his parents."

Together they planned a family outing. For the first time in weeks Dru glimpsed in Fletcher a deep vein of humanity; and for the first time in weeks it seemed she was, after all, in the right place. What was the right place, after all, but the right feeling? Harmony with another makes a home of the entire world, the gutter, the railroad car, the mansion on a hill.

It was the season of the bog orchids, and one in particular, calypso, was the object of great admiration, so finely shaped, so delicately pale purple, and rarest of all. Every summer assemblies of families and friends, nature conservationists, botanists, photographers, and treasure hunters set out through the cedar bogs to see one—if they were lucky—and then to count and report to the state botanists. Never to remove. Each of these wild orchids depended upon a specific and single underground fungus, and the fungus depended upon that specific and single orchid—the relationship was all. The relationship was a kind of tiny intimate community, Dru explained to her sons at breakfast. To take one was to destroy both, and more broadly, to change and diminish the surrounding environment.

Ian sat in awed silence. His pajamas were buttoned askew, his hair pasted up in stiff tufts, and his blue eyes broadcast a softly shocked quality; his mother realized she had caught him in an especially receptive state. The world had not gotten in yet, calypso orchid was first at his door, and the door was flung wide. The outing seemed to be making an impression, and she glanced with concealed excitement across the table at Fletcher.

"I think it's sorta dumb," Miles remarked, "for it to need that one fungus."

Binky Hammond laid down his fork; he had high hopes for young Miles, who resembled him more than any of his grandchildren—the slight, well-proportioned body, the open, friendly face, the perpetually embarrassed smile. "Yes, yes, but why?"

" 'Cause if the fungus dies, the orchid is like doomed. Or what if a deer comes along and chomps the orchid, then the fungus dies. You gotta be able to adapt, like man," he said, deepening his voice. That year at school he had studied evolution, coming home every day with some new recommendation for his own species. In terms of superiority, skull size had settled the matter for him. Several times he had measured his own with satisfactory results; it seemed to make up for what he lacked in height.

Binky gave a nod at Fletcher, as if to imply a good job of rearing was being done, then he gazed at Miles with palpable man-to-man respect. "You're quite right. As a species man is the most adaptable, and therefore the least vulnerable to change."

"I think it's beautiful," Dru said, for some reason not daring to look at anyone, feeling suddenly out of sync. "The specificity of it is . . . well, it's poignant. It's the orchid's version of monogamy."

Fletcher glanced up from his newspaper, cocked his head as if he hadn't heard; a sly quizzical expression crossed his face. "Monotony, you say?"

His mother looked around to check that it was acceptable to laugh, and seeing Dru's face, she said, "All right now, all right," in a schoolmarm's voice, "let's not squabble, Fletcher was being funny, dear, that's all. Humor in the rough," she finished with a suppressed chuckle. Her son's impolite sense of humor had always charmed her—he could get away with it, being a man.

Dru said, "Fletcher was being Fletcher."

"Well, it is rather difficult at times," Lee Hammond observed, folding her hands in meditative grace over the edge of the table, preparing to hold forth. Dru glanced at Ian, who seemed lost in inner space. "I mean by that there are some days that do push out far, don't you agree, Binky," Lee said, patting his leg, "longer days, you see, than others, when you've been together, well, just years, you see. It's rather like Cambridge, isn't it, parts of it I simply don't notice anymore, they haven't gone to ruin, no more than one ought to expect, no, no, but I simply do not need to see them anymore and I suppose if I did I would have a time getting up the proper enthusiasm."

This was one of the more damning descriptions of marriage Dru had heard, particularly from a mother-in-law. It explained Lee Hammond's many social projects that inevitably took her away. Binky rose from the table, his movements deliberate, and stepped out onto the porch, blowing his nose several times with a terrible sort of gentility, and finally locating his pipe, which apparently needed vigorous cleaning, to deliver him from the truth. Binky may have been rather too adaptable.

The family dispersed to its various summer activities; Dru located Fletcher out in the storage shed where he had gone for the chain saw.

"What was the point of that?"

In the moldy gloom of the shed his face possessed a fallow and unpromising quality, as if something altogether unwelcome might drop there and burgeon forth. He made a sound, "Huhnnn," which communicated nothing more than vague incuriosity, turned his back to her, and burrowed further into the shed among the tools and sacks of fertilizer, the broken lawn chairs, abandoned household items, a stuffed white hippo of Ian's that winter mice had eviscerated.

"Just tell me that," she said with more volume.

"What have I done now?"

"Jibes like that at breakfast, what is the point? I mean, here we've barely got a fingerhold on the day, and on a maybe improved mood between us, and our youngest son is in some sort of trouble, and I want to know what the point is of that kind of stinging gratuitous cruelty."

Though it seemed a chore, he managed to shrug.

"You're killing us, Fletcher," she said flatly, "at least have a reason."

"I'm not trying to." He had found the chain saw, opened its case, and was tinkering with the choke.

"If you don't want to be with me . . ."

He jerked his head at her. "You're the one who doesn't want . . ." he seemed confused, "who's got all these fancy requirements," he said, recovering some.

"If you mean I won't sleep with someone who is unkind to me, yes. I regard that as basic. I maybe didn't before, didn't know enough, or wasn't willing to risk, but I know it now."

"Good for you. I mean that too. Trouble is, it's ratcheting up on us, my dear: you've got criteria I'm not inclined to meet, or maybe I can't. I yam who I yam." For an instant he gazed at her with the unwavering resolve of Popeye after his can of spinach. "On the other hand, if we had a little roll, I'd feel a lot nicer about the whole deal. 'Course that'll never happen." He hefted the chain saw from its case and stood ready to leave the shed, but Dru was blocking the doorway, light and freedom at her back. She noticed the strength of his forearm, the shirt sleeve rolled taut at the elbow, the tanned skin, and even in the dimness, in spite of everything, she thought how fine it was, and pictured it reaching across the brown plain of her belly.

"Look," he said, obviously wanting to get this over with, "if it offended you, I'm sorry."

"If?"

"It was supposed to be funny."

"Then why wasn't it?"

"Maybe you don't find me as amusing as you used to. My mother thought it was funny."

"Your mother?"

He dropped his head and stared at the black dirt floor. "Okay, so mother takes a, well, a pragmatic view of marriage. I don't think much of it either. I was just trying to be funny."

"It was a sad thing to say, particularly these days."

"Hey, we could do with a little monotony, my dear. All this arguing . . . I'm beginning to wonder if . . ." He threw his free hand out, palm open, like a sudden white flag in the gloom.

"What? What are you trying to say?"

"If I offend you on principle."

"I don't know what that means," she said, though something about it hooked on and bothered her.

"It just seems to me that when we came up this summer you made a conscious decision to repudiate me. I'm your appointed adversary."

"No."

"Really," said Fletcher, void of inflection. "You still love the Hammond family."

"I was tired when we came up, tired of something. Maybe looking for things in you that don't exist. Maybe just being hurt. I want to feel something different. You offend me on purpose, I don't know why."

There was a long silence. He seemed to agree.

"We're set against each other for some reason, or some accumulation of reasons. Maybe if we designate a day, sit down together, and . . ."

"Talk."

"Yes, talk."

"You like to talk."

A funny nervous sensation crept in about the edges of Dru Hammond. "Well, don't you think it's important to keep communicating? We actually agree about most things, Fletcher. It's true that over the last few years I've asked you to subtract some behaviors, make some changes, so that we as a couple can survive . . ."

"Is it really worth it?"

Her hand was clasped about the edge of the open shed door, and now her thumb worked back and forth across the rough metal of the iron latch as she stared into the dimness at her husband, waiting for the blow.

"Maybe we just don't love each other anymore," Fletcher said with steely calm. "It seems enlightenment might have spoiled it. That has occurred to you, no doubt. Perhaps you've discussed it with your new friend."

"No," she said, not able to say more, staring at the white hippo, suddenly intolerably white in the murk, its guts picked out and piled in little heaps along the bottom edge of the shed wall where the mice had tried to make a home until winter froze them out.

"Ah, skipped that step, have we, *pro forma*, after all," his voice had gone high and British for some bizarre reason, "chatting each other up, best to bee-line for beddy-bye, I say."

"God."

"Monogamy monotony, I've got a big old *mmmmmm* in me," he sang, and flashed a look of challenge at her. "Think I've gone round the twist, do you?"

A minute dragged itself by. She could not see Fletcher now, he was an eddy of obscurity in a dark current flowing around them. Her heart thumped along like the paws of an animal fleeing the scene, and she concerned herself with it because it seemed the thing to do.

Finally he sighed and gestured with the saw, which was hanging against his thigh, "I promised Leo I would help him with a downed maple." Tired, very quiet, his voice a dirge.

"Okay," she replied with courtesy, and stepped aside, and he passed, and she watched him cross the lawn and disappear around the corner of the house, the chain saw unbalancing him, his limp more noticeable, his limp sad and beautiful and immensely human. At that moment she would have been grateful to have loved him purely for his limp, for where and why it was taking him, to help some one of his Harrow fellows, not on principle but because Fletcher was nice that way. You could object, you could even hate on principle, but you could not love someone on principle, that much she knew. Love was what it was, its own rough and splendid beast; it saw only what fed it, and it could consume practically anything, if consuming would make it last.

She would have been grateful to have loved Fletcher Hammond just then, at that moment, nothing before or after the moment, a moment that could not ever be translated into anything else . . . but a dark current was around her now, pulling.

IT SEEMED IMPOSSIBLE to say anything, and so nothing was said outside the daily commerce of the family. Several days passed, muggy and gray, rain in the afternoons, distant thunder, bugs. From a distance the lake bore the look of a spreading slick, the murky hills barely containing it, the sky an open lid of dulled metal. The hours seemed leaden, and had acquired a strange bland quality, as if the Hammonds had entered upon some new form of marital hibernation, a reduction to basic needs and sensory input.

And over the elemental stirrings of the family, the modest to-ing and fro-ing from kitchen to table, from bed to shower, from house to dock, something very like warmth developed between Dru and Fletcher, perhaps because they had come so near the brink of them, or because the brink was just around the corner and they were feeling sad for themselves and for each other, the misery they had visited upon the house, which seemed to have no single identifiable source but which came randomly from all directions in little shocking pieces and refused to fit together, to make a picture they could see.

Yes, it was a peaceable house now, and yet there was more danger in such peace than in all the weeks of contention.

In the kitchen they stood next to each other, their arms touching as if for the very first time, her skin to his skin, the deep veins responding, the mind suppressing. Fletcher prepared the chicken for the barbecue, Dru chopped red peppers for the salad, the boys were set to shucking corn, the first of the season—things were being reduced to consumable sizes and forms. Binky and Lee went out two nights in a row with old friends. The junior Hammonds dined with the TV news pattering in the background; they inquired of their sons, washed up the dishes, read into the open arms of sleep, the inch separating them as cogent as a mile.

Largely unaware, Miles journeyed to the homes of friends— there were more people, it was noisier—returning only to satisfy those basic needs the Hammond family had fallen upon with starved and fearful rapacity.

Ian withdrew further; the third person, though not absent, seldom spoke now. Instead of announcing "Ian's going to bed" in the sunny rebellious voice of a seven-year-old testing territories, he mumbled "Goodnight," his hands hanging at his sides like weights, his blue eyes clouded. This was worse, much worse, even Fletcher saw it. "The kid seems to be giving it up," he observed, but there was no triumph in his tone, no relief, no hope. They wondered if Ian had heard them out in the shed.

A heavy sludge of despair settled to the bottom of Dru. Feelings and practically all thoughts were unbearable; she could stand small actualities—the smell of coffee, the touch of old wood, the look of salad on a plate—but anything that was not physically exact, that could not be fixed and identified seemed to undo her. She avoided Minnie, the Bettencourts, her tennis cronies. During rehearsals she had trouble maintaining the tempo of faster passages, everything lapsed into adagio. Some pieces—Schubert's Sonata in B-flat, the second movement of a Dvořák quintet, three of Chopin's preludes, the final movement of Mahler's Ninth and all of the unfinished Tenth, Prokofiev's Quintet op. 39, an obscure sonata of Becerra's— would swiftly atomize her if she listened to them. In the mornings she awoke tired, at night facing bed she felt sick with anxiety. She would have been grateful for the purity of tears, for the dark rich texture of melancholy and the expansive work that came from the mood, but this, whatever it was, lay beyond tears and melancholy, in fact, had nothing to do with them; they were mere trinkets to a dull and shapeless enormity. This was a cold flat land hunting its own horizon; a shadowy movement in the peripheral sphere that would never come forward and be seen; a dangerous indifference, pitiless Thing; a sustained panic from which there was no escape because there was nowhere to flee, because it was inside and the inside was everywhere now; a slow and soundless explosion that was hurling her body away from all that she knew and all whom she cared about, away from the knowing itself and the love itself, so that her family, one and all, seemed akin to strangers; a dire and limitless tedium that had settled like ash on every side—it was each of these variously throughout the three days, and yet it was all the same thing.

They left her alone, only half aware of something serious, counting on the passage of time, on the healing powers of the mundane plodding relentlessly onward.

She told herself that she was still a living animal, and pressed her attention to the moment, like a face to a window behind which the movements of her life went on. She watched her hands in the dishwater, experienced divers; she noticed her feet, her funny feet—so personal—plying the distances between will and act; she heard her body accept the next breath, and then the next one after that, without credit or praise—it was a little amazing.

When she permitted thought it was about the distant past, before Fletcher; about Independence, California, her father and her mother, her mother especially, and the mysterious friend—a man,

Dru supposed—who had sent once a month two hundred dollars, anonymously. Perhaps an uncle, or a godfather who would find her some day, laden with unconditional love he had saved all the years for her, with tales of her childhood only a mother would pass along, with a special need for her and only her, a particular fondness for funny crooked feet. Because like her, he had lost someone, and with that loss, part of his right to be, to swim freely through the sea of his life.

She thought of the fire, but what was there to think about that? Too many things, nothing. Then had come the institutions. The institutions had both blurred and coalesced into a single image— a long hallway, broad and well-lit, the ceiling is a series of high vaulted sections from which the lights hang down on iron bars at perfect intervals, each one a milky sightless eye, eyes that illuminate but do not see her so that she feels both exposed and misconstrued; part of the door behind her, and through which she remembers entering, is frosted, and behind it there is the green haze of foliage and closer to the glass the running watercolor paints of a crowd milling about, pinkish faces, brown smudges at the eyes and hair, shifting colors below—it is not possible to identify the people; the floor is hardwood and her footsteps sound as she continues down the hallway and punctuate the fact of her solitude; there are pictures on the walls which she never seems to have time to look at properly, nice pictures or interesting pictures, some she can tell from a distance she won't like but wants to inspect to know why; there are doors, too, some of them closed, some slightly ajar, muffled voices beyond, and she feels more hurt by these than the shut ones, because it seems they had thought to invite her in but had changed their minds; the last vaulted section at the end of the hallway is not lit, though the edge of light around her casts forward and she can see the dusky space of the last part ahead; it seems vaguely that there is a turn to the left . . . but maybe not; she heads for this turn that might exist; she hopes it might be a way out.

ON THE FOURTH DAY the clouds passed to the east, trailing drier air and cooler temperatures. Fletcher had taken the boys fishing, and the senior Hammonds wanted to be first at the Bronwen

Deverell auction in Sheffield, where some good antiques were anticipated, so they too had left early. At noon, it was agreed, all would reconvene for lunch, followed by the orchid expedition.

Dru wandered down to the dock and, regarding the mirrored sheen of the water, decided to scull. That was all. The seat was in the mudroom at the house. She came back up the path, then across the little hill, and saw the high trees above outlined in a shimmering morning light, and the blue, the solid blue shimmering as well. She came up the hill past the woodchuck hiding in the goldenrod, and the fiddlehead ferns, and the astilbe, past the spruce that ought to be cut. Breathing came deep and ragged now as it reached in further, and she could feel, too, the muscles down her legs and in her buttocks tighten and release appealingly as she walked. She climbed over the low cedar fence and started across the actual lawn, her shoes wobbling in the places where Rinaldi's heifers, loose the night before, had punched it. Then around the porch through the mudroom door and into the empty house.

Something undone today. A small necessary click that needed clicking.

She stood in the kitchen, looked around, checked the phone machine, went to the bathroom. In the kitchen she poured some lemonade. She thought of sex, but that didn't seem it. Anyway, it was too early in the day and too early in her cycle, and it had been so long, too long, to be feeling that way.

Something was going to happen. No, *something needed to happen.* No, no.

She needed something to happen today.

ACROSS THE LAKE angling to the south cove the shell glided like a bird on outstretched wings. In the shoals she climbed out and towed the shell over the corrugated sand that lay a foot beneath the water's surface, then up onto the beach, tying the bow line to the cleat on the edge of the dock, laying the oars above and perpendicular with a desolate precision. The wheels of the little seat moved in greased runners; the grease seemed to travel at random, and before leaving the beach she squatted at water's edge to rub with a handful of sand the gray slick from her forearms, the backs of her calves, a spot along the inside of her thigh. In every act was a deliberate effort of care, as if the atmosphere itself might shatter about her.

To Jindal's porch she had not come for five days; she did not feel tangled up, or dense with confusion; she felt she was thinning away. She experienced no thoughts beyond the thought that she had nothing to say to him or to anyone, and that somehow she needed to say this much before she lost even the desire to say that she had no desire to speak. Even this would require a difficult exertion. It was what athletes called a *dead lift*.

Up the sand and across the frail grass Dru followed her bare feet. The door was ajar, though the place seemed deserted, so she said his name, Jindal, not to call out but just to say his name in the place that knew him. The lace-covered door opened and a woman in a wheelchair rolled out onto the red porch and sat before her. She was skewed against the right side of the chair, her small torso lumpish and her legs, sheathed in a dark fabric, obviously bone thin. Several magazines were stuffed along the seat beside her, and a pill capsule of some kind had been taped to the front edge of the chair arm. Her hands, her elbows, her shoulders, an ambiguous area at the base of her neck, all were swollen and burled, and Dru realized it was the warping at her neck that gave the skewed impression. Undulations of thick blond hair encircled a face of enameled beauty, like a mask, not pretty and not forbidding either, just coldly admirable, beautiful. The lips were full and bruised-looking, and she held them slightly parted; there was a sensuous, abject quiver to them.

"Mrs. Hammond," said the mask.

Dru looked at her and did not speak.

"You know who I am."

"Yes."

The woman made an open gesture with her hands, turning them in her lap, but they were so knotted-over that the meaning of the gesture was obscured by the deformity.

Dru felt intensely aimless, as if she had no idea where she was.

"What are you looking for, Mrs. Hammond?"

"Mr. Jindal."

"Mister." The narrow almond eyes of the mask stared at her. "He isn't here. Too bad. I am Christine Jindal . . . Jindal by another," she paused, "but you know that already."

"Yes."

"Well, what do you think, Mrs. Hammond, while we wait for Mr. Jindal? What do you think of me?"

"I'll go now."

"No," she said; there was a deep stagger in her voice. "I want to tell you something."

"I have to go."

"Tell me what you think of me, not what he has told you, but what you think." The depthless brown eyes waited, the bruised and lovely lips worked ever so slightly and silently, ever so perpetually.

Dru heard herself say, "Maybe you have forgotten how to be with people."

"Forgotten." She gave a derisive puff of her cheeks and abruptly quit the subject, as if realizing the inanity of querying this woman; or perhaps she was only disappointed that Dru had not mentioned her beauty. "I don't like you, Mrs. Hammond, whoever you are."

"Yes," Dru replied, and what struck her was that at that moment anybody could have said this to her and she would not have been surprised, and she would not have cared either, it would not have changed anything.

"You don't want to know why?"

"No," said Dru quietly, *it doesn't matter.*

"Because you think you already know, you think it's because I know you are in love with him, or you think you are. But I'm not interested in perishables. Love," she spat with disgust. "Don't you see, he needs us. Beautiful wounded women. I was his best worst case. I aroused his intellect, set a fire there in his inmost mind where fires can't be doused, not easily. It was the beauty with the damage, the unnecessary damage . . ." She seemed to wheeze then as if something had started down the wrong pipe; one clawed hand caressed the other. "That is what he does, you know, his profession, recovering art. Of course much of it is badly damaged." A pause, then she finished, "I became his art." In that all had been summed. Gazing out to the water, far away, something almost winsome fluttered across her face, and the face yielded, the expression went sad —just that—for a moment or two before it hardened back to mask. "But even powerful people tire of power, Mrs. Hammond." Here she stopped to inspect Dru with a conspicuous intimacy, like a doctor who finds her patient unsavory.

Looking at the gnarled figure with her knobs and bumps and stick legs, and the flawless face rising like a small oval specter, a child's rendering of a dream balloon floating over a crayon scene of calamity, looking down and feeling in one blow the *Geist* of Christine, Dru became painfully aware of the smooth and flowing extent of her body, perhaps even of her life.

"What do you think you arouse," Christine asked in a mood so black and complicated and weighted down with unfathomable meaning and hatred it seemed the words might actually break her, "and how long do you think that sort of thing lasts?"

"There is nothing, there is nothing so there is nothing to last," Dru said with rising emotion, backing down off the porch. She meant Jindal, she meant Fletcher, she meant the scene of her life. It was the first time in days she had succumbed to a complete feeling, but she did not know what to call it, it was a cold bilious sensation and she wanted only to be rid of it and all sensations, the words that lead to them, the words that clean them up and box them for memory—all of it.

"Love," intoned the mask. "You wait, keep waiting, oh *yes*, Mrs. Hammond, please do wait." The lace-covered door was closing. "Remember to die, too. It's easier that way."

Somehow Dru was back in the shell, pulling away from the cove, from the red painted porch, the hanging begonias, and the willow tree, away from the cottage, the great open hand of the hay field holding it forth like a wrapped gift . . . except that it was empty, it was all emptiness inside.

RIMMING THE LAKE all around were the summer camps of Harrow—dark shingled cottages peering between cedars; clapboard bungalows straddling granite at water's edge, eyeing her as she slid by; modern glass and angles glinting suspiciously through columns of groomed white pines; log cabins, half awake, indifferent; straightforward structures that glanced and glanced away; boathouses; and docks, docks everywhere, empty, waiting, reaching out, not far, not far enough to touch her.

Did they see her?

Again, as in the bright hallway of memory, she felt both exposed and misconstrued. And alone, must not forget that, she thought, I am alone.

The oar blades swung back, down, forward, and the shell moved as though automatic, paring the surface of the water; the movement seemed to cost Dru nothing now.

When she noticed where she was she had already crossed the lake to the point and had started around it, sliding past the Spitler's boathouse where Sam Chase had been living all summer. In an Adirondack chair on the dock he sat, coffee mug in one hand, a manual of some sort in the other, which he used to give a salute. She pulled alongside the dock.

"Well, hi," he said with an elegant calm.

"Hello."

"My first pretty thing of the day."

She could only smile, ridiculously grateful.

"Coffee?"

"Yes."

She pushed herself onto the dock. He drew the oars from their locks while she tied off the shell, then she followed him to the boathouse, which had been built near the dock, a few paces up the bank between granite boulders. It was green with a sagged roof and an open front from which two enormous doors hung ajar. Naturally, there were no windows. A cool breeze swept off the water and Sam Chase brought the doors in until they met, secured the hook, and turned on an overhead light. Now it was quiet. The wood walls were dark and water stained. Spaced pegs supported fishing rods; on the opposite wall hung two oars, one badly cracked. Incongruous smells met and gathered around: mold that would endure, toast, mothballs faintly, ripe bananas from a bowl on a small table, shaving lotion, citronella candle. To the pitched ceiling a bar had been attached where it could be reached, and from this Sam Chase had hung clothes. Inside along the right wall was a platform bed, recently constructed; a red blanket with two black stripes was neatly smoothed and tucked in, and a pillow with a clean white case lay waiting, the press marks visible. The white pillow seemed especially fine. Beyond at the head of the bunk in the right corner was a stove box, and in the opposite corner a miniature counter with a sink and overhead cabinet. Sam Chase took a cup from the cabinet; the funnel was already out. He filled a kettle and set it on a hot plate. There were two places to sit, the edge of his bed and a chair draped with clothes, some of which she recognized from his work visits earlier that summer. Dru chose the bed so that she would not disturb his clothing. She ran her fingers through her cropped hair and waited.

She had stopped thinking about Christine and Jindal, about Fletcher, about Ian and the third person. She was only sitting on the edge of a bed waiting for a cup of coffee. Sweat dried and stretched a thin tightening sheen over her skin; she felt chilled but not unpleasantly, for the coffee would meet the chill with ease. The coffee was real and it would come soon now. Outside a lone crow indolently cawed from the spruce that stood over the boathouse. It was still morning, though years seemed to have passed. It was still morning and it might have been morning just breaking, dawn just then. The soft yellow interior light obliterated both the sense and the memory of sunlight on the other side of the boathouse walls. If she looked back over her left shoulder to where the great doors met, the thinnest white lance of sunshine pierced her, and she would know again that the whole day was still out there, whirling and pressing all its might around, a tempest of illumination. There would always be pipers at the gates of dawn, promising and lovely to hear, to see perhaps, but the day itself would drive them off, the day, the vast brute reality of the day, the day, the day . . . In her mind it came at her like atomic blasts of light, the ancient untamed strobing of the cosmos, the outer reaches of the Big Bang.

But inside the boathouse beneath the pale extinguishable light she felt protected, as in a cave. There was a man in the cave-room, a Mr. Chase—this was how she was thinking of him. Mr. Chase wore a pair of jeans and no shirt. His feet were bare, like hers. It seemed fine—the hour, the look of things, the man.

Mr. Chase pressed a paper filter into the funnel, ground the beans, and measured out two level scoops. He turned and looked at her while the kettle clicked and hissed to the proper pitch, and she looked back at him. Then he poured the water in a thin steady stream around the filter, waited, poured again, the steam rising into his face. He seemed to know that she liked milk, and this small fragment of knowing reached in deeply and gave a terrible gratifying twist. It was enough. He brought the cup to her, holding it between both hands like a chalice. She looked at his fingers encircling the cup. "Tell me that you don't want to make love to me and I'll go now," she said.

"I can't say that," said Mr. Chase. He was standing in front of her, and her face was opposite the flesh of his stomach, and she could feel in her mind the entirety of him gathering for her.

"Then who is going to turn out the light?"

DRU DID NOT REMEMBER preparing lunch. A smokescreen composed of mundane queries and responses surrounded and obliterated the events of the morning. Fletcher passed the tuna salad without noticing that his wife had been with another man less than an hour earlier. It was frightening. A stark cheerfulness infected her, though it bore no relationship to joy, seemed attached to the kind of dread you experience when all the padding is gone from your life, worn from your brakes, and though you can still stop events—herein lay the weird cheerfulness—you know that you are doing real damage each time you try. And if you do not try, it is simply the end of things.

She did not know why she was where she was, she might just as well be somewhere else. It seemed she did not know *how* to know the people around her; or maybe, she thought, looking at her husband, her sons, her mother- and father-in-law poised over plates of food she had served them, you were not supposed to even try. The way it was with Chase that morning, maybe it was supposed to be like that. Maybe you could not know and be close to another— or know very much—they had to be separate, the knowing and the intimacy. The strain was too much. Maybe Fletcher, with his summer-long withdrawal, his cruel quips, his literal words, was saying that he could not love her anymore because they knew each other too well. Enlightenment had spoiled it, as he said. Yet she could not say, if he knew about Chase, whether he would love her more or less. Probably more. It was strange. What was *knowing* except grounds for prediction? And was it good to be predictable, to wear the same set of details day in and day out?

She dug her fork into the tuna salad, eating with blind gusto.

"You seem refreshed," Fletcher remarked, "from your row."

"I feel fine," she said. She forced herself to look at him. His golf tan was beautiful. He had let his hair go longer than usual, and it was thick and a little wild this morning. He was wearing a new red shirt. Even these minor changes in his appearance were somehow upsetting; she wanted everything to be exactly the same as it had been when she awoke.

"There's a good crowd going this afternoon," he said, addressing anyone.

"Yes?"

"Harry's found us a botanist. It'll be jolly, like a field trip."

"Pop quiz the next day?"

He smiled appreciatively. "Of course."

Ironically, Dru's luncheon cheerfulness had a relaxing effect on Fletcher, who seemed less wary, as if he had found an opening in an otherwise smooth wall.

It occurred to Dru that he might want to forget the shed and all that it had summed up or suggested, the madness ricocheting between them. It had been bad since then, bad in a new way. She hated the formality of the warmth between them; they had been addressing each other as if over the coffin of a dear friend who had tactlessly died during a family feud.

After the tuna salad the Hammond family prepared to drive to the village green where they were to meet the other members of the orchid expedition. It was one o'clock. Miles climbed in the back end of the Wagoneer, plugged into his Walkman. Fletcher and his parents took the front seat, Dru and Ian were behind them. In Harrow certain assumptions were always on display.

Ian slipped his hand in Dru's and fiddled with her fingers as if they were his to play with. "Ian's going to be the first one to find calypso," he whispered to her as a promise of sorts, snapping his chin down to seal it.

"You won't pick it, my darling."

Pained incredulity shot through the boy's eyes. "No. He's going to guard it until you and Daddy and everyone *sees*."

"Well, we'll be together, we'll be close," she said, "so you won't have to worry." She was remembering how dense the cedars grew in the bog, how easy it was to lose sight of the others.

"That's right," the boy replied with a shrill, unnatural enthusiasm. "He knows that."

Slowly, tenderly, she worried his hair. "Darling," she ventured.

There was a small responding sound at the back of his throat. He was busy trying to cross all of her fingers simultaneously.

"Can you tell me why you say 'he' when you mean 'I,' when you're talking about yourself?"

The boy shrugged, his eyes forward.

"Because Daddy and I are a little concerned."

"Sorry," he mumbled. She saw his attention flicker out. He dropped her hand and stared out the window. A minute passed. Then as if he'd been set off, he snatched her purse up from the floor and pawed through it until he found what he was looking for—a stick of gum.

She leaned in and whispered to provide privacy in case he required it. "Is it us? Are you scared, or maybe worried . . . ?"

"He don't care."

"Don't? I don't . . . you mean *I* don't?"

The boy's eyes widened as if he were hearing a minor disaster, a glass breaking in another room, or the back of his shirt ripping apart. "Doesn't," he yelped. "He doesn't care."

"Why?" Dru fired the question so that he would not have time to think, so that he would simply answer.

" 'Cause he's a ghost."

"Ghost?" Abruptly there was not a single handhold to be found. "Who's a ghost?"

"Ghosts can't feel anything," Ian said, his voice dropping to covert levels. "They can go places and not be seen. And some-times . . ."

"What?"

The boy smiled broadly. "They can scare people they want to scare, you know, if it's his mission. Make 'em do things. All ghosts have a mission."

"A mission?"

"Sure."

"Are you the ghost, Ian?"

"*He's* the ghost," he told her, as if she were a stupid child.

"Well then who are you, Ian?" she said hoarsely, "if you aren't the ghost, the third person . . . your father has talked to you about the third person . . ." She could see from the trapped look in his eyes that he was agitated. She put her arm around his shoulder and pulled him in, kissing his hair, letting some unencumbered min-utes go by as the car bumped along the lake road toward the vil-lage. In the dusky interior of the Wagoneer the skin about his freck-les seemed especially pale and pure; with age the freckles would darken, change shape, spread, and ones not there would appear with the right or wrong circumstances. The stamp of our inheri-tance deepened, while the conditions of our lives went on to mark us; in the end we were our own murals painted on the walls of time. With luck there might even be a theme, an organizing vision, color, and conceit. Someone could learn something.

Ian ran a finger under his nose, then began to bounce his head side to side, the soundless tune in his mind apparently bringing some cheer.

"It's silly how important it is what we call things," Dru said, striking a jaunty tone. "Let's see, maybe I can come up with an ex-ample. What if I just decided I was miserable, even when I wasn't, even if I was just plain happy but said I was miserable because I just wanted to try it out. Well, if I kept *saying* I was miserable, pretty soon that's what I'd be: miserable."

"He's not miserable."

"He."

"He already told you, ghosts can't feel anything."

Dru wanted to cry. She felt she was reaching into a tangle of sinister games and juvenile neurosis for some tangible part of her son —an ankle, a hand, a single I—but he kept slipping into the morass.

Ian had always been a reasonable child, an orderly thinker. Once in Harrow when he was five he had come home with a poplar leaf in which he had poked the stem of a small red begonia and two long lavender petals picked from something wild. "What is it?" Dru had asked. "It's a dream catcher," he replied with a thin annoyance, as though she ought to have known. He then found a thumbtack and hung the dream catcher from the ceiling where it slanted over his pillow. But something was not quite right . . . a frown, his clear blue eyes probing the space around him. Again he disappeared, returning this time with a toothpick which he used to make a tiny hole in the poplar leaf. "This is so the nightmares can drain out," he explained. Of course, Dru thought, how very thorough little boys are! Later when she came downstairs there were dream catchers everywhere—at each place setting, on the windowsills and chairs, on the mantle at its centering point.

Now if only she could catch him, and catch him in a way that would allow the nightmare to drain out . . .

"So," she began. "He's the ghost."

Beside her the boy sat chewing his gum complacently.

"That means he died. You can't be a ghost unless you're dead."

Slowly Ian turned his gaze upon her, his eyes flat and unrevealing as if he had doused the lights behind them. "No duh."

It was a common-enough expression among the cool and savvy youth of the day, but its place in what Dru thought was a serious conversation floored her. She could not think of anything more to say to her son. In truth, she felt mildly offended.

They parked alongside the village green, and Fletcher leaned out the driver's window to confer with some of the others. It was agreed he would lead, since they had been many times to Mud Pond, and they had the best vehicle for testing unkempt stretches of road. The caravan moved leisurely along Town Road 5, losing Crescent Lake behind the first rise in the landscape, and continuing in a slow curve to the west until the Burnham Road where the first turn was made. With their customary mournful tone Lee and Binky noted changes in the scenery, and Fletcher assented with a grunt or a *hmmm*—it was a ritual summer ceremony, a family call and response. The village of North Burnham was long defunct and moldering down, ever since the train cut its butter freight line past the village. The road held its girth for several miles, the gravel even and the dust settling fast, and no one minding driving close behind another. They took a left fork along a brook, then turned onto the Mud Pond Road. Beyond the last occupied farm the road narrowed, the gravel was gone down to the big base rock that knocked up against the chassis, popped out or wedged against the frame; sometimes there was just dirt, packed down and lifeless, and at other times they hit ledge concealed by a thin drift of sediment. Raspberry bushes, hollowed where the bears had been eating, gave way to spruce woods. Beneath the topmost boughs not a single green needle survived, there was just a lightless cross-hatching of branch and twig by the thousands, the branches reaching straight out from the trunks and the twigs bristling in unison, and the fallen needles forming a rufous mat over the dark forest floor. The road descended to a brook where each car in turn stopped, waddled tire by tire across, and climbed the opposite bank, hissing and steaming. Then they were winding among the lean, tall columns of a young maple grove; there were the sweep and brush of broad leaves overhead, the trifling disport of shadow and light, and a palpable elegance to the bearing of the trees and the mood they cast that brought to silence the members of the procession.

All along the road, wherever the sugar maples and the black spruce and the raspberry patches had not yet overwhelmed them, lay the hay fields abandoned to time, filling up with saplings. Sometimes the farmhouses still stood, though swaybacked from the unrelieved weight of snow, the walls bulged and the structure half collapsed to one side or the other, the paint entirely gone; and sometimes there was nothing left but the outline of the root cellar and the chimney, a green cowl of bramble knitting its way up.

Mud Pond Road joggled up and down over hills, across a second brook, and along the old railroad tracks marked by a solid run of joe-pye weed that burned and stank beneath the Wagoneer, then came a quiet sandy stretch parting acres of red pine that had been planted forty years ago as part of the state's reforestation program.

The red pine descended in ranks, fanning about a clearing loggers had once used as a staging area for skidding out hardwood. At the far edge of the clearing lay Mud Pond—a small lake, really—as still as a painting, milk-blue and surreal as though something shocking had happened here a long time ago. On the east shore resting in the sedges was a wooden rowboat with its bottom stove-in, patches of red paint still visible. And at the bottom edge of the clearing lay the half-sunk Ford pickup stopped where it had stuck hopelessly forty years ago. The red boat and the Ford intensified the eerie feel of the place.

Fletcher shut off the engine and let the dust settle as the caravan poured into the clearing around them. Then he climbed out, snapping his fingers; "Bellhop," he said. Avery Johns had pulled in alongside them. "Having one of your spells, Fletch?" he asked.

"Of regret. I don't believe they have an ice machine."

They were only fifteen miles from Harrow, but it seemed a hundred—and a hundred years. Dru got the boys together—Cutters, water bottles, longsleeved shirts—and chatted with Binky about a bear he had seen years ago; she had heard the story half a dozen times and knew where to ask the right questions.

Small white clouds were scattered uniformly across the sky, marching eastward together as if choreographed for the event. It was not muggy and not as warm as it had been the last four days; a nice breeze toyed by now and then. The air was sweet and peppery with the scent of berry bushes heating up beneath the midday sun. Dru heard several people commenting on the perfection of weather. Of course in Vermont it could change utterly in the space of an hour.

Surveying the group she saw with relief that Sam Chase had declined Minnie's invitation; in fact, Minnie was absent too. If Chase had come the lying would have been more difficult; not the lying to Fletcher and to the world, but to Chase himself, for it was likely he mistook her despair for secret rapture that morning. Maybe he would want more. There would never be more.

When everyone had stuffed their backpacks, tightened bootlaces, flipped through guidebooks, and stood at last arranged and assembled, there were twenty-four adults and six children. The botanist from Montpelier, friend of Harry Young's, would lead; his name was Fred Huppert.

"If you see an actual flowering calypso you'll be lucky. More than likely you'll find the plant. Here's a close-up of the leaf." He passed around a color reproduction of calypso's one tiny ribbed leaf, dark green, feather-shaped, pressed to the ground at the base of the stem. The leaf was almost identical to a common ground cover. It would be the short, twiglike stem that would best distinguish the two plants. They should consider themselves lucky to find calypso, even without its delicate stunning flower.

Sally Bettencourt passed the photo to Dru, who peered at it and leaned in toward Fletcher. "Hardly seems worth it," she whispered, and immediately regretted the words and the scene in the shed they recalled.

A brief shattered look leapt to his face. "I want to find one," he said simply.

"No, I do too." She felt mortally bad. "It's just all these human beings devoting their afternoon to a scrawny stem with a single leaf . . . I mean, it's kind of funny, don't you think?"

"I guess."

Huppert was still educating the group on the biology of bog orchids. Fletcher and Dru stood at the back; Miles was off with the other kids, clambering over some old logs; Ian had pasted himself to Mr. Huppert in order to better absorb data on calypso.

"Did you visit your friend this morning?" Fletcher asked in a low, toneless voice, gazing ahead to Fred Huppert as if listening to his talk.

"No," was all she said. She wanted something more to be said, from him or from her, it didn't matter, but every cog in her mind locked simultaneously; and Fletcher seemed airtight, as if, having surfaced to scope his one question, he had then battened the hatches and dived.

She stared at the long, shadowed grass where the road ended, the moss beside it, and remembered that it was here she and Fletcher had made love ten years earlier. The day was hot, and they had lain down in the soft cool sphagnum moss under the broken branches of a thunderstruck maple, and the squirrels in the trees were upset with them for the quiet commotion of their love. Now here they were in the society of their friends and children, searching for a plant they had never bothered with before. Perhaps they had passed one once, perhaps without ever knowing they had passed many calypsos in those distant summer wanderings.

Fletcher saw where she was looking and gave a nod, a flick of an eyebrow. "Those pesky squirrels."

"Yes," she said shyly, happy that he had remembered and that he would admit it.

From the sunny edge of the clearing they entered the cedars. Ian wanted to stay with Fred Huppert in order to be first to see calypso, if there was one to be seen; and Miles had hooked up with a buddy in the middle of the procession. Dru and Fletcher were close to last. Almost immediately the path vanished beneath blow-down, some of it recent and a lot of it old, so that there might be four or five trunks crossing one over another, and forming a mosaic of soggy brackish triangles. Sedges and tiny duckweed grew in the standing water, while nettles, marigold, mountain holly, ferns, and even forget-me-nots survived in the merely sodden areas. The forget-me-nots were like chips of sky scattered in the glade, blue and cheery.

Dru did not believe they would find the calypso orchid. For one thing, they were all so busy watching their feet, climbing and contorting over logs and thicket traps, checking ahead for the others, that there would never be an opportunity to inspect the flora, let alone detect one ordinary-looking leaf pressed to the very earth. It occurred to her that they ought to be happy with the forget-me-nots, turn back now; the disappointment would only deepen the further they plunged into the bog. The forget-me-nots seemed to try so hard to be perfect, as if to make up for their micro-dimensions.

Within fifteen minutes Binky and Lee, the elder Edwards, and Ina Dunning together with her visitors from Boston, had to turn back. Such a tangle of trees and branches, hummocks, sudden sinking holes, and deceptive greenery, all of it requiring yogic maneuvers and intuitive balance to navigate, was more than they had bargained for. With a throb of jealousy Dru watched them head back.

For a while the path continued to follow roughly the curve of

Mud Pond; they could see the water through the cedars, and once they were close enough to hear a fish break the surface. Now and then sunlight fell across a mossy log, or lit up an assembly of royal ferns, and she and Fletcher paused, blinking, to enjoy the golden contrast and catch their breaths. But after an hour they had angled away from the water, or the open water had simply disappeared as it was meant to in bogs, and there were more and more white cedars standing about, very close together, all of them dead or mostly dead, many of the branches scribbling stiffly across the pale sky, some broken and hanging down in long wooden skirts about the trunks. The occasional laughter or hoot, the conversations that had wandered forward and back through the procession, dwindled as the way thickened. Very little that was green remained. They came upon an enormous bull cedar, six, seven feet in diameter, and around it a cleared radius of space in which nothing could grow— its territory, Dru thought. It was likely this tree had seeded most of the cedars around Mud Pond. Dru stopped to look for the sky, but the dead arms of the trees had crossed it out. She waited to let the others go by. Her heart was pounding.

"You okay?" Fletcher said.

"A little claustrophobic." The inside of her mouth felt pasty.

"Almost there, I think."

"We can't even see the sky," she said, hardly able to listen. "The sky or the water. I'd rather swim back."

"No you wouldn't," he said. "Leeches."

"Leeches?"

"Hey, we're almost there. An hour out, Huppert said." He looked at her, bunched his lips. "Come on."

"I can't stand the dead branches and the deadfall. My legs are cut up. What if we had to hurry, how could we hurry back?"

"We're not going to have to hurry."

"You can't even see the sky," she muttered, then loudly, "I can't see *out*."

He glanced past her to where the others were disappearing. "Don't do this," he said. His voice was strong, not angry. He took her hand and pulled her gently along. "My western girl," he sang, "likes a big piece of sky . . ."

She smiled wanly. "The forget-me-nots were just fine."

"No, no, we are going to find us *ca-leep-so*."

Fletcher had been right, the search area was only another five minutes. The group scattered immediately, bending, squatting, crawling on hands and knees. She looked for Ian and saw him dogging Fred Huppert, who was scrambling up a ragged bank. The woods were less dense, and there was greenery, a lot more than she had first noticed, growing on and about the cedars. After the ordeal of the hike people seemed happy enough simply to be searching for the orchid, though some were not even bothering, they were sitting astride mossy logs, having a snack, talking. Harry Young was one of the few avid hunters, he and the college-aged members of the expedition. Fletcher was another. Though relaxed, he surveyed the ground with an orderly determination.

Dru repeatedly mistook the common ground cover for the orchid's leaf, and eventually the unrequited starts of enthusiasm wore her out. She sat down next to Avery and drank some of his wine. In her mind she turned over pieces of the morning—Chase, Christine, the absent Jindal—each one as shocking as the one next to it, and none seeming to have any play, any relationship to her life. The sum of the morning was a variant reality; it seemed to belong to some other visitor to Harrow, or to a Dru with an entirely different set of historical particulars. And yet it was the sum of her life that had led her to this day. Given total amnesia, she wondered how she, Dru Hammond, would behave. The outlandishness of it all was exciting, scary, and—she decided—intolerable on any long-term basis.

Avery poured her another slosh of wine. "You surprise me, Dru."

"What do you mean?"

"Your lack of interest in the floral treasure."

"I'm interested. I just don't think anyone's going to find it. We've been here, what," she glanced at her watch, "half an hour and no one's even seen its leaf."

"True."

Twenty paces away Fletcher moved with steady silent concentration, dropping now and then to finger a leaf or a stem, to brush aside debris for a clearer view, to lift a fallen branch.

"Anyway, that kind of thing never happens to me," she added, still watching Fletcher. "I don't win lotteries, I won't get the call in the middle of dinner that they want me to solo Paganini at Lincoln Center, and I will never find a rare orchid in a Vermont bog."

Avery nodded thoughtfully. "Does seem unlikely at the moment. We seem to be stationary."

She had to laugh. "Well, there's that."

Fred Huppert was working his way carefully back down the slope he had scaled when they arrived.

If anyone is going to find one it'll be the botanist, she thought, and then Ian. She waited several minutes to see her son appear behind Huppert. But he did not appear. Deliberately she stood and started making her way toward the slope, watching Huppert, watching the crest of the slope. Veering off toward Fletcher, she asked him if he had seen Ian. Fletcher shook his head. Again, she worked her way toward the botanist. Halfway there she called out, "Where's Ian?"

Huppert looked over at her blankly.

"My son, wasn't he with you?"

"He was, I guess, for awhile."

"Where?"

He did not have time to answer. Dru began to cry out her son's name, and the cheerful background chatter of half a dozen conversations abruptly stopped.

No answer, no Ian.

Huppert looked around as if they simply had not noticed him yet. Fletcher was already moving toward him, and when he arrived he said, "Do you remember where you were when you last saw him?" There was a calm urgency underlying his voice like a train moving swiftly through the night.

With the back of a hand enfeebled by the possibility of serious trouble, Huppert gestured up the slope. "The other side . . . I don't know, it's probably been, well, awhile." He gazed around, seeking forgiveness. "I was focused on the orchid."

Though the water could not be seen, the search area was actually near the upper end of the pond where it lapsed into half land, half water. But the other side of the slope led away from the water, through standing dead trees and deadfall into a wall of living cedars and spruce mounting a thick understory; here it was as dark and dense and felt as inescapable as a nightmare. Dru kept hoping someone would wake them all up—it seemed the only way out. And at the same time it seemed just that: a kind of dream. Any minute now Ian would step from behind a tree, puzzled by the look in her eyes; she would be *so happy* . . . then miffed because of the panic, however transient, and he would say he was sorry, the others would be sighing already, smiling, and someone at that moment would discover at his very feet the calypso orchid. They would head home with a story to tell.

The group scrambled chaotically, calling, thrashing here and there. Fletcher soon rounded everyone up. They agreed that every time someone called out the boy's name, the others would listen in silence for a response. So the name of Ian worked its way gradually along an organized search perimeter, *Eeee-Un*, like a foghorn, then there would be the wait, the silence of absence, then again the call went out for the lost boy.

Twenty minutes. It was still not real. Things were not broken; she could still feel, jostling behind her like a big old friend, the life she had known.

"I don't understand," Dru said, "how far could he get in this?"

Worried murmurs. The searchers kept searching.

Forty-five minutes. An hour.

Then it was four-thirty. They reconvened.

Eight adults would stay: the Hammonds, Fred Huppert, John Abbot, who was a fine woodsman, Avery because he would not leave his friends, a young couple from Victory Basin—they said they knew bogs and boreal forests—and a woman named Carol Tebbetts they had all just met, a nurse, it turned out, from Vermont Central. The rest of the group would work its way back with the children, Miles included, and return to Harrow; get help, get flashlights, more water, and some food. A first aid kit, Dru added; she was trying very hard not to break now, to resist the ripping sensation in her mind. Harry Young said he would bring a canoe; that way they could enter the cedar bog from the water and begin to eliminate areas they had already searched. "We need to start eliminating," he said. "It isn't that big an area. It's just too hard to tell from the inside-out where we've already been."

So there were eight people, three flashlights, two compasses. Everyone had brought a water bottle. Two by two they went out from the initial search area, north, south, east, and west following the ragged curve of Mud Pond. The two along the pond—his parents, someone said, *his parents*, she thought—went without compass and flashlight, because the sun would last longest in their direction and the water would orient their progress. When the sun set, it was agreed, they would simply stop and wait for a canoe. Likewise, the others were to make their way back to the water before they could not find it at all.

"Fletcher," she said, when they reached the edge of the pond; she could hear the breathless and pathetic quality in her voice.

"We'll find him."

"Oh, Fletcher."

He squeezed her shoulder.

"Have we done this, have we driven him to this? He said he was a ghost, in the car that's what he said."

"You're dealing with the mind of a seven-year-old."

"I know. But he's been upset, all summer he's been . . . troubled."

"We all have."

"The third person . . ."

"Yeah, well, I'd give my right hand," Fletcher said with a wry disgust, "to have that third person back. I was just getting to know him."

"Maybe that was the point."

"Maybe."

"Well, we did notice him more, we did *see* him."

"Yeah? I think what I saw was my own frustration."

"Maybe he feels responsible, children do that, you know. Think everything is their fault." She had to stop and contemplate that for a solid minute. "Maybe he figured if he didn't have to be himself, his own I, none of it would be his fault. And he wouldn't have to hurt. If he just hid himself behind the third person, like the ghost he talked about, and disappeared . . ." She broke off, unable to finish. "Oh god . . ."

Fletcher pressed her against his chest, and for several minutes she cried. Next to her face she felt him swallow, and swallow again, shoving down his own welling emotions. His eyes were red-rimmed, and there was a small, desperate look in them.

"All right," he said, "now we've got work to do."

They climbed over and through a deep crosshatch of fallen and rotted trees; Fletcher had to pull her from the last of it that rose above her waist. Now and then they sank to their knees in a kind of muck woven through with moss and roots and grasses. Her boots were wet and cold. The slow ponderous wobble of the bog itself was eerie and unnerving, like walking upon the hide of a vast living thing. Whenever they called for Ian they both stopped; if they were close enough they squeezed each other's hand for courage; when the answer didn't come they avoided each other's eyes with an aching sort of courtesy—it was a sad dance, but the only one they could do.

The light around the pond was an intense yellow now, the water brassy and so flat it appeared slightly concave. Despite the beauty it was a dying pond, and this shard of information kept cutting into her heart with the quick, painless foreboding of a fatal wound. Was Ian dying too somewhere in the thick of these things? Somewhere in this wilderness with its stink of evolution, was a blue-eyed human child who had perhaps found his calypso, their calypso, the one they had all been searching for.

The sun slid behind the hills in the west, and the light for a while was a soft gray burnt yellow at its high edges, and tingling throughout in the sun's departure. The yellow withdrew very quickly and the gray deepened to blue, and by seven-thirty the blue had gone black. There were no stars. From the northwest a sheen of clouds had drawn in gradually, and now it was thick and uncompromising; the wind had dropped entirely. The pond and the space over it seemed to generate a kind of light of their own, the light of particles moving freely about; it was a black light but it was still a light. She believed they would find him, she believed that he was somewhere here, and okay. Yes, he was okay.

Dru and Fletcher Hammond found an open patch of moss near the water and prepared to wait.

"Right now," Fletcher said, "there is nothing we can do."

They were both utterly exhausted; her calves were cramping from the sustained tension of climbing on and about slippery logs, and Fletcher had twisted his ankle in a fall and was limping on each side now. They had both, in fact, fallen several times. It was she who had chosen to search the west, by the pond, because she wanted to find her son here, not in the confused impenetrable woods of the bog. Now at water's edge she was grateful simply for the space laid out before her, the open sky.

From a cedar Fletcher tore an armful of branches, piled them against a log, and they propped themselves up against the softened bulk, with several of the branches cast over their legs to keep off the dew. He put his arm around her shoulder and they looked into the black light over the pond. Soon the voices of the other searchers reached them; they, too, had found places along the water to wait for help. About a quarter mile up the shore someone actually managed to get a fire going, probably John Abbot, they decided. Then she and Fletcher turned their faces toward the distant orange flame, so small and hopeful, and even a little ridiculous—in a pleasing way—beneath the encompassing night. Perhaps Ian could see it. Perhaps this fire, to counter the fire of her childhood, would bring a family together.

"I can't stop panicking," she said, grabbing her own hands.

He pulled her in toward him. "It won't help."

"I keep reminding myself of stupid things . . . there are no poisonous snakes in Vermont, no catamounts left in Vermont, bears don't like bogs, do they? No, they don't like them. And Ian won't eat anything green so he can't have poisoned himself . . ."

"He's just lost."

"Why can't he hear us, not any of us, why?"

Fletcher made no answer.

"He must be hurt, that's the only reason." She felt she was going to be sick to her stomach. "I can't stand the thought of him in pain, I can't stand it."

"We've got to stop this. We have to get through this night and be ready to find him in the morning. Okay?" He gazed pointedly at her. "We need to be ready for Ian."

They were silent for a long time.

"Let's talk, let's at least talk," she said finally.

"Yeah."

But neither spoke for another long while.

"What happened," she whispered, her breath against his face, "what happened to us this summer?"

"I don't know, Dru." He wiggled his fingers through her hair.

"Maybe we needed to hate each other," she said aloud.

"Not hate."

"No, not hate," she agreed.

For several minutes they did not speak. Then Dru said, "I need to be able to lose you, you know, do you understand?"

"Yes."

"Because I've lost before." She shifted her weight against him.

"Maybe we were both testing theories."

"We can hardly call it that when no one thought anything out."

"I don't know, honey," he sighed, "but everything went all to smash."

"It did, didn't it?" she said with wonder. She was thinking about the years stacked up behind them, all the complaints, the fights, and how they had cluttered up the view of something very very quiet and very very important. She was thinking about the shapeless growth of ordinariness in the life of a couple, a family; it had to be teased apart, every day, and the parts lifted on high, and songs sung. She was thinking about the big easy splendor of meeting and falling in love, and then about the small quiet hidden things that revealed themselves with time; about the really quite exquisite beauty of the forget-me-nots scattered along the path in the dense woods. They were less consuming, not all-consuming, not like the calypso orchid. But they would likely endure. Yes, they would likely be here next year.

"Jesus, Fletcher," she said suddenly, "tell me he's okay."

"I think Ian is okay. You can't hurt yourself too badly in a soggy old bog."

She nuzzled in against Fletcher, smelling his skin. He brushed the warm paw of his hand down her face, cupped the back of her head, and kissed her eyelids and then her lips with immense tenderness.

She said, "Did we forget we loved each other?"

"Something like that, I guess. It doesn't matter."

"No, it doesn't now." It so thoroughly didn't matter now that even the wild anomalous desperate events of the morning seemed in their own crazy fashion to participate in, even to contribute to, the splendid not-mattering.

A long silence moved in slowly about them.

"He's here," Fletcher said with complete confidence.

"Yes."

THEY SLEPT on and off; there was hardly a difference between the night around them and the night within. At one point, waking, Fletcher said, "I am sorry for my part in derailing our train this summer." And she squeezed in against him and murmured, "Maybe it was time to find a new track."

The clouds scudded off and eventually a sallow light spread from the east over the bog toward Mud Pond. Canoes appeared on the flat water. It was too shallow and too confused with mud and plants for an outboard, so even the state troopers were using canoes. In the weird blued atmosphere of dawn Fletcher and Dru stood watching. The canoes stopped along the shore, people climbed out, then the canoes continued up the shore toward them, at some spots picking up members of the eight who had stayed through the night. Cold, too nervous for hunger, and scared all over again, they waited, *his parents*.

A red canoe led, Harry Young's. She could see the blond halo of his hair. She could hear faintly, then distinctly, the canoe paddle striking the water, and voices, some of them quite clearly, from around Mud Pond and the other canoes. The first light had been slow, but now it came on fast. Across the pond on the opposite hill a yellow band of light started down, then plunged to the shoreline and slid across the mirrored water toward them. The air was cold but when the mysterious warmth of the water encountered it, a yellow milky haze formed at the surface; it was like a scene in a dream, Harry Young in the red canoe coming steadily through the haze toward them. Then suddenly they saw him throw up an arm and cry out, the canoe wobbling and veering off course as he dug in and drove to shore; he was lunging through the water, half falling onto the land. Trees, more damn trees in the way, and for five, ten seconds, they could not see him. But here he was again, with a shape in his arms, and when he remembered—because he must have remembered—the parents watching farther up the shore, it occurred to him to set the boy down, to stand him up as best he could, to show that he was okay.

Harry, good Harry Young, Harry has found our boy . . .

The red canoe was coming now, arrowing right for them, almost here, Ian's small pale hands gripping the bulwarks of the canoe; then she and Fletcher were in the muddy water beside the canoe, hugging him, drinking in his face—his eyes were wild, the pupils . . . Fletcher was up to his knees in the mud, one hand steadied across Dru's shoulder, the other on the back of the boy's head, which was matted with blood and showed evidence of a nasty gash.

Harry said quietly, "He might have a concussion," and Fletcher nodded back.

Then Harry remembered the boat horn and used it to signal the others.

Ian looked from one parent to the other, then back again, as if meeting them not for the first time but for the first time following a long journey, gauging the subtle changes, the penciled-in additions, the funny peripheral sensation of something gone now. He smiled faintly as one at a time they climbed into the canoe, arranging the boy gently between them, never losing contact with him or with each other, or of a future they now seemed once again to possess.

"I didn't find it," Ian said to his parents as if to apologize. "I got lost and I climbed on this high bunch of rocks and ledge so I could see, and then I fell." He touched his head gingerly. "I fell and hit my head and then I couldn't find it."

Really she could not stop crying or smiling or looking at her child's face, the new and the familiar configuration of his presence; she did not even try to stop. "It doesn't matter, darling."

Ian looked up at his father and his mother. He was flopped across both of their laps. "I guess not," he said.

She decided not to mention the disappearance of the third person.

Fletcher took up a paddle, and he and Harry Young paddled them out across the water. All along the shore the searchers appeared; a cheer went up.

Harry Young and the good citizens of Harrow, she thought, *they found us our boy.*

The sky above was as blue as the first blue, innocent and friendly and free. It was so blue it seemed almost to make a sound, a high vibration. Ian gazed up into it with his uneven pupils and his own two little blues. Then he began to move his head side to side. After a while Dru asked, "Why are you shaking your head?"

"I'm not shaking my head," he replied. "I'm shaking the sky."

IN THE TEN DAYS before Labor Day and their return to Salem Dru and Fletcher Hammond enjoyed each other simply, discovering again all the notes of commonality, all the unspoken chemical calls and responses between a man and a woman. Ian embraced the first person with a vigor that surprised even his mother, ordering from his sick bed candy, new paint brushes, even a skateboard. Dru was thrilled by his self-indulgence. Even Fletcher, on his way to the store, exclaimed, "Forgiveness." Miles the Adaptable was only remotely aware of an improvement in the atmosphere, though he did ask his mother what was wrong with his father, why he was being so weird. He was acting *happy*. He was listening to Carlos Santana.

The end of the season cocktail party cohosted by the Lanes and the Tanners fell on the first of September and was well attended by the summer community, which did not normally start to disappear until Labor Day. The party was a tradition that included a large number of locals, and was highlighted by the presentation of the annual Village of Harrow Good Citizen Award and by a fundraising pitch in the form of the yearly activity report by the chairperson of the Harrow Free Library.

"I don't understand why they call it a 'free' library," Dru said to Minnie as they stood waiting their turn at the bar set up in the dining room. "Aren't all libraries free?"

"I used to think so," Minnie said, "until I paid nearly twenty bucks in overdue charges last week. I mean, okay, so I had fourteen books, but good lord, who do we think we are, the Library of Congress?"

"I'm impressed, Minnie."

"Oh, they weren't mine. They were Sam's. Sam Chase's. I assume you're up to speed on our . . . my . . ."

"Well, I heard you were seeing one another. I didn't know you were such chums you were paying his fines."

Minnie took the plastic glass of Chardonnay proffered by the bartender and a cocktail napkin from the stack in front of her. "With Sam one tends to pay for most things. He's not exactly Mr. Fast Draw when it comes to the wallet. Even his groceries are knocked off someone else's debt, work he did or is going to do. Dugan runs a special accounting for him."

"How absolutely charming."

"He doesn't have a checking account. No credit cards. It's all cash or trade with good old Sam."

"Strange," Dru murmured. She could not remember how it had been with Fletcher and the dock rebuilding, the house rewiring, but she hoped there was nothing still owed. She did not want to owe Sam Chase. Thinking back to her morning in the boathouse with him, she couldn't help wondering if what had happened represented a debt established or one dispatched.

They took their drinks outside onto the patio, a broad slate semicircle facing across the mountains toward Canada like the prow of a ship. And standing there it seemed to Dru that they could indeed sail north to another country if they had wanted. But it was too beautiful here, now, it almost hurt it was so beautiful. Early September was unusually warm for the Kingdom. A dry wind blew steadily from the west as if from a crack in the sun itself, which was setting with a final decisive abandon behind a green drift of hills. She was wearing a silk shift, and the wind played it across the backs of her knees, a reminder that the warmth would not be here much longer. Fletcher found her, squeezed her waist, decided to fetch them hors d'oeuvres. She watched him make his way back inside. His hand was open and relaxed as it touched the backs of friends in greeting. She was happy.

Mounting the nearest hill was a hay field where Dru and

Fletcher used to take the boys for picnics in the fall before school made claims; the view was large and arm-opening, and from that hill the world had belonged to them. She saw that the hay had been cut, probably for the last time that season, and as she gazed at the field the late light was discovering it too, so that it flushed a rosy golden hue.

Beyond the patio half a dozen café tables sat about, each with a potted red geranium and three empty chairs. Above them stood maple trees, elegant and old, what was left of the original sugar bush. Some of their limbs had traded foliage for patches of lichen, but in the wells around the trunks, and scattered with almost ornamental precision on the grass, were the leaves that had already turned and fallen—not many, for it was only the old diseased trees who let go so early, but enough to accent, with a poignant rattle and a flash of gold, the end of summer. So much, she thought, has been wasted.

Cliques of guests stood drinking, talking. She would not see Jindal at this party. He had gone back to Boston with his charge, as ephemeral as the sounds she heard through the fog the morning they had met. Indeed, she seemed to associate him with those mysterious voices, human secrets drifting through the mist, and the flute—lovely, without source, everywhere and nowhere, vanishing whenever she sought for it, or for him, for the promise of something better. Yes, he was gone. She would never know what, beyond kindness, he was about, what any of that was about. At least, she thought, it was not bad.

The two women were joined by some of their fellow musicians, then Dugan, sipping apple cider, then Wilkes, a museum director, a nice man, then off she and Minnie went to refresh their wine, snagging Fletcher who had been waylaid several times, the plateful of hors d'oeuvres consumed. He hustled guiltily off, returning with a generous sampler.

A good many guests were still arriving. The locals, of course, had come on time; the summer people trickled fashionably in. Dru noticed the Copes' green convertible Packard, with its fat whitewalls and waxy sheen, glide with a rich heavy grace up the long drive like the opening clip from a forties film, and crunch to a stop in the gravel beside the grass. The top was down and she counted at least six men and women dressed in summer finery, laughing, waving, piling out, even Mrs. Adams, eighty-five years old and as game as her twenty-year-old granddaughter.

"This is right out of Gatsby," Dru said.

They stood there admiring the Packard, and then Dru suddenly realized that one of the men who had disembarked from it was Sam Chase, and he seemed headed straight for them. She hooked Fletcher's arm and led him through the throng, "I have to have more of those shrimp," she said. Away, away, away, she thought.

Later, as the party was nearing its end, and during the award ceremony that was its knell, she found herself alone at one of the café tables. It was dark, even darker under the maple boughs, and she was enjoying the soft enclosure of the night, and the distant comfort of the festivities thriving on across the lawn, far enough that she felt removed but not separate. Dugan and Harry Young, the emcees, were about to begin the award presentation. In the open air even the din had been pleasant, but now it was settling slowly to a murmurous sea of voices, occasional laughter leaping up, subsiding. She recognized Avery's voice, and the woman who ran the library. The trunks of the maple trees stood about like Greek columns, tall and protective. And for the second time that night she was aware of a quiet form of happiness, though this time the word happy seemed flimsy and insufficient. There were over 150 people at the party, most of whom she knew, some well, some by virtue of repeated encounters over successive summers. Many had helped in the search for their son. She was aware of being exactly where she ought to be, and exactly where she wanted to be. Moment, place, people were all one and the same.

Sam Chase emerged from behind the dark column of a maple. "Nice evening," he said.

"Our citizen of the year," Everett Dugan was announcing from the patio, "Mrs. Peggy Farnam."

Chase turned toward the house where the widow Peggy Farnam, *beautician extraordinaire*, as the sign hanging over her front porch had declared for the last fifty years, was accepting her plaque. She had what was called a dowager's hump from bending over the chair, and backlit by the yellow lights of the house, it was especially sad and noticeable. "What is this?" Chase said with a sliver of a smile, "Vermont's variation on radical chic?"

She looked at him. Uninvited, he sat down beside her, his white shirt shocking in the soft black night. "It's a community to which everyone belongs," she replied. "Everyone who cares, that is." His proximity sent a low current of panic through her system, and at the same time she was oddly relieved to have this meeting finally, to get it over with.

"And you do?"

"Yes. I do." I do, she thought with a curious wonder, I care.

"Fancy that."

There was something unsavory in his voice. She joggled her chair back, away from the table, and shifted so that she faced him. "You feel, Mr. Chase, that you have been given license to mock me?"

"My apologies." Slowly, he lit a cigarette, inhaled, exhaled. Then he blew a smoke ring in her direction. "I rather expected you might paddle on over to my place for another . . . cup of coffee," he said. "It's been over a week."

His insolence astounded her. "It" had been over a week? There was clearly only one possible referent for *it*. She leaned forward and looked him full in the face. "Your expectation was preposterous."

"It was engendered by you, Mrs. Hammond," he said with a smooth, cool, informative air. "The original inspiration was yours, as I recall. I was merely the accommodating host." He flicked his cigarette onto the Lanes' lawn, which, having been mowed for the party, was plush and intensely green beneath the outer aura of the patio lights. Held aloft by the short stiff blades of grass the cigarette was still burning insipidly. Like the conquering hero, she thought, *the conqueror worm*. The fact that he had hardly smoked it seemed to intensify the gesture of contempt.

"Yes, you were ever the accommodating host," she said bitterly, unsure for the moment whom she loathed most, herself for having initiated an act of nihilistic self-destruction, or Chase for "accommodating" her. "Now you are being exceedingly offensive."

He lowered his head, letting it roll slightly left then right, bringing it back to center, and his stare seemed to slither into her eyes. "And I think you are getting above your raisin'. *Dru.*" More than the meaning of his words, his use of her first name and the way it was uttered with a familiar cold caress, as if he possessed rights now, let a chill loose down her spine.

Under the maples in the Vermont night his face was gray; his face was as undisturbed, handsome, and lifeless, as carved stone, as a cheap cemetery statue. "Let me explain something to you," Dru said. "I actually think you may understand this, although I hasten to assure you that your understanding is one of the few things I *don't* care about very much at the moment. I came to you in the boathouse that day because you are a human void. You don't belong anywhere, you don't want to belong anywhere, you have no feelings for humanity, you are a cipher, a cosmic goose egg. And I came to you in defeat, do you understand? I came to you because I felt I had lost and I was nothing, everything was nothing, and what better way to celebrate nothingness than to throw yourself into a meaningless liaison with the emperor of zero. I came to you because something in me must have recognized that it would mean nothing to you, and in my despair that was exactly what I wanted — confirmation. I could scream . . . I was screaming," she said vaguely, softly, gazing toward the party where Harry Young was offering an award to Clovis McPherson, "funding the new bookshelves . . ." she could hear Harry announce. "I was screaming and I knew that even if you heard — and you didn't — it would not have bothered you."

Chase sat back in his chair with an ugly laugh.

"You are amused?"

"Used, I think is the word. It seems I was used." His voice revealed none of the essential feelings — hurt, anger, recrimination. He sounded as pleased as if someone had just picked up the tab.

"You were imitated."

Several car engines started up in the parking area behind the house, and Dru saw Fletcher come down the patio steps and start across the lawn toward them, her shawl draped over his arm. The first star of evening was visible in the patch of sky between the maples. *Star light, star bright, first star I see tonight . . .*

"I could tell on you," Sam Chase whispered, his manner excited and furtive, as if they were sharing something deliciously wicked.

She was rising from her chair, her hand outstretched toward Fletcher, but she turned her head back, feeling a kind of languid confidence—a confidence in love, Fletcher and herself, their marriage. "Why would you bother," she said, "why on earth would you bother?"

INDIAN SUMMER

These are the days when skies resume
The old, old sophistries of June, —
A blue and gold mistake.

—from *Indian Summer*
BY EMILY DICKINSON

MY UNCLE JACK—Jack Sayers—would not
have a telephone. In order to reach him, you had to call Norman
and Gladys Courchaine who owned the dairy farm at the bottom
of the hill, and they would pass along your message when Jack
came down for his mail or for his truck, which he parked at the
edge of their barnyard. It was not a very efficient system, but efficiency was one of the few principles, as it turned out, Jack Sayers
had not cared about.

"This is Kimball Dodge," I said with some reluctance into the
receiver. I could hear the milk pump throbbing in the background;
that meant Gladys was in the village and her boys were working the
cows and the old man was in the milk room where the barn phone
hung on the wall beside the sterilizing sink—I knew it well enough.
"Jack's nephew," I explained.

"Kimball . . ." he mused aloud in his thick voice.

"That's right. Kim Dodge," I said, fairly muttering now.

There was a long wordless pause occupied by the sounds of the
milk machine up in Harrow, Vermont, and the echoing hallway
subsonics of other freshmen off-loading their dorm gear for the fall

term at Dartmouth. Against the cold body of the pay phone I stood huddled, for the door to the booth had been removed, probably to prevent long calls or piling-in record attempts, and the exposure to the bustling caverns of the dormitory worsened matters. But in spite of the noise near and distant I could still detect Norman Courchaine's memory working the name *Kim* like a bent key in a lock, and I swear I felt a chill draft as he finally cracked it open, peered in and spied the fifteen-year-old kid who had long ago worked for him, and who had fouled up his new hay mower. At the time my ignorance with regard to farm implements was undiluted by a single drop of common sense. I was a southwestern boy with a summer job in New England. There were not even lawns where I came from, just decomposed red rock or cheat grass or sage, and I didn't know a sickle bar from a silo. The day after I'd broken the mower Mrs. Courchaine had mercifully whisked me into her garden, to save my life, I was convinced.

"I recall," was all Norman said on the phone. It was really kind of him, and so like a Vermonter—quiet, not showy, not asking to be noticed.

"Well, I'm here in Hanover, New Hampshire, Mr. Courchaine, I'm starting college here, on a scholarship actually," I explained, to let him know that I was finally good at something, though at age twenty, a little late. Also, I was aware that Dartmouth was making an effort toward geographic balance in its student body, and that standards had been given a wee shove downward in my favor. "I thought I'd come up and visit Uncle Jack, maybe see the colors. The term doesn't start for a few days."

"I'll pass it on," was all he said.

Another wordless pause lit between us like a hawk on a high wire; I felt nervous and watched. It had been five years since my last summer visit to Harrow—Mother and I had come out for a month, without Dad as usual—and I had forgotten how uncomfortable I always felt trying to engage the locals in conversation, how chatty and foolish and vaguely puppylike a westerner came off sounding in the presence of the grave and observing Vermonter.

Still, I didn't want to leave things on a purely utilitarian note—it seemed impolite; I had eaten his good wife's food, after all, for two months of my life. Plus, my mother had heard from an old summer companion who had heard it from a cousin living in Harrow that Jack wasn't looking too well these days. Of course it was only rumor, cross-country at that, but my mother asked me to pay him a visit anyway so she could dismiss the talk. Her notes to Jack had turned up nothing, since he either ignored or dodged any inquiries about himself—that was the way Jack had always been; he'd rather talk about his neighbor, or the weather, or a book he'd just read. And she couldn't telephone him, so that left me paying a visit.

I ventured to ask Norm Courchaine how Uncle Jack was getting on.

"Fair, you might say. Considering."

"Considering?"

"Well," he coughed.

"He's not sick or anything, is he?"

"He seems fair enough, son."

"My mother would be awful upset if . . ."

"*He's* all right, shore, in his own way. No cause to rile up the cavalry. And accidents can turn a body around. Sometimes." He gave a strange little laugh then, which seemed to cap off any further disclosures. I thanked him for relaying my message to Uncle Jack, and resolved not to call my mother until I had seen Jack and had a chance to determine for myself how he was doing.

How she loved Jack! Everybody did, even if they could not decipher him . . . or maybe *because*. There was no one to compare him to, and he was no threat, in a way. Sure, I had heard some of the stories over the years, they were like folk tales or fables, depending on how Mother employed them or how badly I had screwed up. But whatever people thought about Uncle Jack's choices, past and present, about all the money he had given away, whatever they felt about his *lifestyle*, after one hour with Jack Sayers you walked away feeling you had lost something that Jack had managed somehow to hang on to.

A kid would understand, kids, dogs, teenagers who could think past sex. Certain adults. Maybe revolutionaries, the ones who failed. Holden Caulfield and his kind. And maybe I did . . . I'd like to think so. Maybe I was ready to understand, just out of the nest, and as a crucial part of my ongoing rebellion, maybe I really needed to understand some of the ways sunny, ordinary, even grand things could get all mixed up in the dark underneath.

My mother, Natalie Sayers Dodge, arrived fourteen years after Jackson. A surprise, and, in old Lake Forest society, not exactly one you'd brag on—you were supposed to mature beyond surprises and know everything that was going to happen, because you had, of course, planned it that way. Of course.

Since Jack was Mother's only sibling, and since he entered college at the age of fifteen, they did not know each other as brother and sister but as characters in letters, or cordial inquiries at the tail ends of parental phone calls, and naturally as part of the family summer scene upcountry in Harrow, Vermont. Which meant I knew him even less. Mother grew up and married Dad, a geologist, and we lived in Arizona, Utah, parts of Wyoming, briefly in Winnemucca, Nevada, Santa Fe, New Mexico, the hill country of Texas, and finally back to Flagstaff, and our visits to Harrow numbered only eight, those summers when Mother missed her eastern legacy enough to abandon Dad. Also, she thought I ought to be exposed to her side of history, which she regarded as real history. Dad's history amounted to an untidy shoe box of former addresses, racy postcards from guys he had met on some of his jobs, a commendation from the U.S. Geological Survey, and religious Christmas cards from his parents who had been members of the first tribe of Winnebago R.V. nomads, moving around the West with the good weather until an impatient semi cut them off for good as they climbed out of Death Valley toward Towne Pass, on their way to see Mt. Whitney.

Dad did not like Harrow, thought it was smug and ingrown, thought the mountains were hills, the green unremitting. He had grown up in red rock country, and that was his color, and color enough, too, he would say if you even tried to mention New England's fall foliage. "Real history," Dad said, "is found in rocks, not people." It was hard to argue.

I was thinking about Dad and his red rock the next morning when I left Hanover and drove up Interstate 91 into Vermont. Indian summer in New England. I had an old Ford pickup with cracked leather seats and a bad taillight, but it got me where I was going and was already the envy of a number of Dartmouth freshmen who had never considered actually owning a car. Where I came from, I tried to explain, it was not an option. As soon as I crossed west over the Connecticut River, practically as I was passing the *Welcome to Vermont* sign, I left the smoothed-down landscape of New Hampshire, the impenetrable woods of juvenile birch, every one exactly the same height and diameter—it was a little scary, the sameness—the shallow reed-choked lakes, the big houses with names like *Ryegate* painted on them. In Vermont, steep hills with bulk to them crowded down to the highway, and I could see the Green Mountains beyond, not green but cutout layers of blues that morning, and even though they were not the Rockies, they had a certain dignity, like images of famous old men, solid types in dark suits who were always reserving judgment.

The hay fields had been cut for the last time that year and were velvety with their summer-end exertion, short, intensely green; it almost hurt to look straight at them they were so green. Twice I had to pull over just to walk, my shoes soaked with the heavy dew, and feeling free and powerful and suddenly all lungs, only I couldn't think of anything to shout except "Hey," which made me laugh when I thought about it. Everywhere up the slopes fingering into the dark spruce, lining the dirt roads, bunching together in sugar bushes, the maple trees were burning bright, like great fiery hands. Red, orange, yellow, purple, each leaf seemed to absorb and then concentrate the light as if it was squeezing it in, holding on to it, and the effect on the eye was a beautiful ache. Then you looked away and the afterimage came on, all sadness. It would pass long before Dad's red rock.

God, but it was pretty. *Pretty*, just that. Nothing about it scared you, the way a big western scene could if you thought too long about it. It was like looking at a nice girl in a party dress—you wanted to get to know her and take your time and mind your manners. You had the feeling that it wouldn't let you down, too, the way parts of the West did, and always would, it seemed. It wouldn't let you down because it wasn't making any big grandiose promises.

The day was almost warm, not a fall day and not true summer either, but a day right out of some cobbled-up memory of sweetness and longing, right out of a little kid's dream. Or straight from the heart of memory. Yeah, it was Indian summer all right, which was more than remembering summer, I realized, it was losing it too, like a hand just lifting from your shoulder, letting go, and fall waiting on the other side of the door, and then coming up the walk, not even looking at you, not even caring who you are or what you might think, is old man winter with something heavy in his hand.

You could feel the air, too; I had forgotten that about New England, the tiny weight of air moisture all over your skin, sinuses cleared of their southwestern stucco, hair gone wavy.

I was glad to be alone and driving up the interstate toward an uncle and a place that I knew a little—not a lot, but enough to give the day some shape and purpose. I had been too ready to leave the West to miss it yet, and too eager to get away from my parents to think I needed them at all for a long time. But Uncle Jack . . . he was perfect in a way, just then, for me: he was family, but remote, fabled yet real enough to visit now and then in case I felt, well, out of place; and he was different enough—if that was the word—to satisfy the natural insubordination of a twenty-year-old freshman toting his first beard and a full scholarship to a school called Dartmouth.

THE COURCHAINE FARMHOUSE, a white, two-story Cape with an ell, sat facing the road, its green shutters peeling paint, and the porch littered with a hodgepodge of woven rockers and the folding aluminum chairs you buy at the discount stores in Montpelier, a couple of milking stools, and a picnic table laden with bushel baskets of apples. Gladys always made the trip over to Lake Champlain and the islands in the fall, I remembered, to pick apples that cost practically nothing.

I pulled up the rutted drive, following the broad trail of fresh manure and muddy hoof prints that led from the field across the road where the cows had obviously grazed the night before, to the barn, and parked alongside Norm's old green truck. Except to stop at Dugan's store for some frozen Sara Lee cake, which I had calculated would thaw by the time I reached my uncle's place, I had driven straight through the village to the Courchaines'. Above the barnyard the hay fields fanned out, each field separated lengthwise by an almost invisible strand of electricity. Several wide planks straddled the brook that ran into the fire pond, and I watched as a young cow hurried skittishly across to catch up with the rest of the herd grazing the north field.

Gladys Courchaine moseyed out of her kitchen as if she'd just seen me the day before, and only said, "Well," now and then, as I blathered on about Harrow and the leaf-peepers and Dartmouth. I had passed her maple syrup sign nailed to the mailbox on the road and said I wanted to buy a quart to send to my mother. "Well," she replied. But she never mentioned anything about Uncle Jack. Norman Courchaine was off cutting wood with his gang of French

Canadians, and his boys—one of them acquired twelve years ago from a relative in trouble—were executing some impressive wrestling moves on a wide-eyed heifer in the pen above the barn. I felt sorry for the heifer who seemed to bawl a desperate appeal to me, the stranger, as if to say, see how barbaric these people are.

I left the key to my truck with Gladys, in case someone needed to move it, and started for the path with the Sara Lee cake. Jack Sayers tended a wondrous sweet tooth.

At the bottom of the path sat the storage shed, unchanged in five years, though leaning more intimately against the slope, and thumbtacked to its side was the note pad for those visitors who just wanted to leave a message or a quick hello without having to climb all the way up to the sod house; or for Jack who wanted to leave word for someone coming by. The last note said, "Returning book, Thanks, Eugene," and an arrow pointed down where the book had apparently been left on a bench. Past the shed came the teetering planks over the brook, then the second (not the first) left up the hill along a hedge of cedars, through the tidy apple orchard, and then beside an open field. In the margin where the path bounded the field Uncle Jack had set on posts no fewer than eight birdhouses he had made himself, and I remember thinking of *Heart of Darkness* and those heads drying on stakes, greeting every visitor to the crazy soulless Kurtz. It was a mark of Jack's opposite temperament, those birdhouses, though there were an awful lot of them; one after another they seemed to make the same insistent claim. Funny thing was, I didn't see any birds around them; I think they were too close to the ground or to the path of human observation.

Near the top in the cedar woods, where it was dusky and grass could not grow, the path had been pounded down to a hard, smooth mud that gave up hollow confessions with each step. I began to feel as if I were in some Grimm's fairy tale, *thump thump thumping* in the dark woods with my cake in hand. And with the cedar roots exposed, crossing back and forth, and me high-step staggering along, it was the obstacle course part of the quest. My first glimpse of the house came through tree branches, just the gleam off the tin roof; slipping from the woods, some of the rest of the sod house revealed itself, snugged into the hillside and half furred over with grass and moss and any vegetation that had managed to hang on and make a kind of life over Jack's head. The rest of the house, of course, was the hill itself, or dug in under it, so there was nothing to behold but what you could imagine.

Jack was not to be seen. I did notice that the grass surrounding the sod house had been recently mowed, and next to the steps an old milk can had been stuffed with goldenrod, cattails, and a single slight maple bough looking fairly peaked. Above the house under a stand of white pine were several runs of cord wood, gray, leaning into their squared corners, and staked here and there along the sides.

The picnic table Jack had built sat out on the bluff. At the near end he had placed a metal tractor seat, and instead of legs there was a big rusty spring, ready to wobble some lucky kid about. Past the table the land fell away into black spruce and maples, a few white pine out along the fringe, and at the very bottom I could just see the roof of the Courchaine barn and the fields gathering about it like quilting squares. Above me, above and beyond the midday scene, spread the pale blue of distance, like a long sigh, or a stillness you once knew.

In the center of the picnic table there used to be a handful of wildflowers in a jelly jar. We had had summer dinners at that table, preceded by Jack's famous mint juleps. Of course the kids were always served lemonade—he never forgot the kids. He had a way of inquiring—yeah, he *inquired of* children—that made you really consider what you honestly thought or had been doing—if that was what he had asked—and when you got around to answering it was as the adult you would become and not as the child everyone else, especially your parents, thought you were. It seemed a long time ago. I had to wonder if I had become the man Jack spied in me then.

With adults he had the opposite effect, made them feel like kids, and encouraged goofy or quixotic behavior. Quixotic, that's one of the right words for Jack Sayers.

This time there were no flowers on the table, just a pile of papers . . . mail, actually. I picked up some of the pieces; it was obvious that they had been left out for days, alternately soaked with dew and dried in the thin autumn sunlight. I put them in my pocket and headed over to the house.

Wooden steps descended between planked-up walls of the hillside down to the entry; taking a deep breath, I knocked on the door. The place felt eerie just then, I don't know why. Maybe it was the empty birdhouses I had passed, or maybe it was just the raw smell of the mud surrounding me, like an open grave. Shuffling, a cough, then the door angled open of its own accord—which reminded me that the hill itself had made adjustments to the house over the years, crimping it one way, nudging it another, and the door was permanently off kilter. Jack could whack an overhead beam in the kitchen area and fifteen feet away the front door— which was the only door—would swing open.

"Come in," he hollered from the tiny interior room beyond; he was busy with something at the sink. "Kimball, old man," he added.

"Uncle Jack," I said.

"Jack," he corrected, leaving the distant gloom for the gloom I had just entered. He gave me a stiff but affectionate hug; you can tell when someone is just shy about that sort of thing. "Grown another five feet," he said, leaning back.

"I hope it's the last."

"You better pray, boy."

"Yeah." I was now a lot taller than Uncle Jack, who at the height of his height only touched five foot eleven. A blue-eyed, barrel-chested man, with short muscular legs and a strong rump—that's the word that came to mind—thick, dark brown, almost black hair he kept clipped at the sides and long up top, the brown in retreat and gray coming on strong at age sixty-nine, and a whimsical quality permanently camped somewhere around his eyes, Jack embodied his Welsh genes as no one in our family had for the last five generations. He had never bulked up but he was no weakling. I swear his face was a perfect square. And he had a nice mouth—the lower lip danced about when he talked. Overall, his parts just didn't fit aesthetically together, you might say, and yet I think it was this that gave him a kind of I-don't-care, manly cut about him. It being futile to be vain, he had simply conceded to the physical self that was his, and went about inside it with a matter-of-fact attitude, which I admired to no end.

On the Sunday afternoons of my growing up, when we were in Texas, and a few times in New Mexico I had seen old rodeo riders with a similar way about them. They were busted up and not the best anymore, so the tickets were only fifty cents. They swaggered about, broken knees, dislocated shoulders, scars down their backs from all their surgeries, gouged and sun-creased faces, and usually by then they had a beer pot, but women? they went for it. It was real, I guess; the women knew what they were getting. That seems more important nowadays than it used to be, knowing what you're going to get and not taking much on faith.

Yeah, I always liked the way Jack Sayers wore his body. And Jack was the kind of guy who took almost everything on faith.

"So, you're off to college," he said, trying out a hearty voice, it seemed, and not with much success, I decided.

I smiled. Jack always had a way of making you feel great about whatever you were up to, no matter how long it had taken you to do it. "A school called Dartmouth."

"You don't have to say 'a school called Dartmouth,' Kimball," Uncle Jack said, waving his hand at the edge of his cot for me to sit down. "It brands you as a hick from the provinces." He laughed, saying the words, *heh, heh,* "Dartmouth has a rather wide reputation. But come to think of it, it's good that you say 'a school called Dartmouth,' yeah, say it every chance you get. Wake them up, heh, heh, yeah."

I realized then just how rotten he looked, because he dropped down in a chair next to the window and the light fell upon him like a predator searching out each and every weakness.

The wooden cot was on the right side of the room with a shelf above it where he kept his clothes—that was where I sat, bent forward to spare my head the edge of the shelf. Five feet away on the left side of the room Jack had built a small desk below a window exactly at ground level; outside blades of grass grew from the sill itself.

I stared at the grass, trying to figure out how to ask him what the hell happened to make him look so poorly, and idly withdrawing the mail from my pocket and handing it over. He stood up and shoved the letters, unopened, on top of one of the many overhead beams he used as shelves, then sat back down as if the effort of standing had been nearly too much.

There was something transparent about the skin on his face, like water that suddenly goes clear when you drift into shade, and you can see the bottom with its dull, languorous non-motion. Underneath the weird transparency a grayness lay, but not cold, no, just the opposite, it was like a deeply burning core, like charcoal when it's as hot as it will get, right before it loses its shape altogether. He looked that way, like he was close to losing something altogether. A lurid glow infected his eyes. His lips were cracked and sore at the corners. He had lost weight along his extremities—thin to begin with—but had developed in his middle an unhealthy-looking Biafran bulge across which a pilled brown sweater stretched unwillingly.

I watched him pick up a sheaf of paper lying on the desk and glance with disconsolate tension at a scrawled line or two; he saw me watching him and released it, though his long fingers worked the paper edge for several lingering seconds.

Jack wrote things now and then; I asked him if it was something he was working on. He said *no* like a shot fired, and I abandoned the topic.

At that moment I remember a mysterious sensation, and it was all bollixed up with a scene playing inside my brain: Jack and I were standing in the middle of one of those gag rooms full of gag furniture when suddenly someone we couldn't see, someone behind the scene, pulled a rope and everything dropped, the walls, the table, the chairs, they all collapsed away from us and a light appeared instantly everywhere from no particular source—no shadow-making about it, flat light, like a snow field on a cloudy day—and there we were, sticking up all by ourselves, standing in the weird generic light in the middle of this busted up gag scene, and of course we were looking at each other, with surprise for the first split second, then we were really looking at each other, steady, because it was a lot easier to see Jack now that everything was lying at our feet, and he was looking at me and he knew I was seeing, or could see.

Intense.

Fortunately the Sara Lee cake had thawed by then, and Jack stood up to make us some coffee. I flopped pieces of cake on napkins and we ate with our fingers, taking seconds without having to think about it.

In between, I told him about my profligate two years after high school, how my mother, his sister, Natalie, had taken a Zen attitude, how Dad was relieved to see me go every time I left, which happened to be quite a few times, since I kept having to come home and recuperate from my latest misadventure. Technically, I had not even graduated from high school, was in jail, sobering up, during the ceremony. I spent those two years banging around the West, living on love, buying on time, as the song says. Dad declared I had no conscience, but I did, actually; I was just too busy most of the time to hear it. I was eighteen then, and the day was *loud* with freedom; yeah, stepping out the front door of our place in Flagstaff, the day was loud and buzzing with my freedom. Mine. I needed to feel it like a girl in my arms, all of it, as much as I could get a hold of and then some. A dry, alkaline wind was shoving in from the north, from Monument Valley, picking up red rock dust, the scent of pine, picking up the feel of distance and dangling it right in front of me. I had to go.

Uncle Jack listened, said usual sorts of things just to keep me going, I think; he knew some of the biographical details anyway, thanks to Mother. All filler, it was, my talk, his.

It got to be midafternoon. We took a walk about, hands in our pockets, not saying much. He had a steady, surefooted way of traveling, but it was so slow I had to stop every now and then to let him gain some striding distance. I think he had found a pace that would let him rest even while he moved—an old trick I knew from distance running. During our walk we stopped at the outhouse, up the path beyond the cordwood, to admire its new door and the sliver moon and twin stars he had carved in it—it was that sort of touch Jack never overlooked. When we returned to the sod hut he ducked into the root cellar off the kitchen and brought out a bottle of Scotch, set it on the counter by the sink, and looked at it without releasing his fingers, then he walked away and the bottle seemed to note his rejection.

A silence sat down with us. I realized it was the same one that had been there before, still waiting, like the big man in the dark suit you knew enough to steer clear of even though you had no idea what he was about. In a movie Orson Welles would play him, the big man in the suit. I bet if I had set out three glasses Jack would have known who the third was for. It was that obvious, the secret chatter in the room.

Jack let me look at him again; I could feel especially that part of it, him *letting me*.

"Sorry," I said finally, "but you look like hell."

His body seemed to shake or nod, I couldn't say which. "Heh, heh, Jesus, that's good, Kimball, I appreciate that. And yes I do," he asserted with a queer sort of pride, "I look a helluva lot like hell."

"But what is it? What have you got?"

"Got?"

"Yes, you look sick."

"Well, you're a straightforward sort a' fellow."

"Anyone can see you're sick or something."

"If they were looking. Most of us don't like to look."

"Do you know what's wrong? My mother . . ."

"Ah, Natalie," he interrupted, with a warm smile.

"Please, Uncle Jack."

"Well, I'll tell you, boy, since you press me and since at this point evasion seems unduly coy and without point, I am the victim of some . . . malaise, yes. And there is nothing I plan to do about it. So I ask for your conspiratorial assistance in keeping this from my dear sister, your mother, at least for a time, because she will rush here and try to move me out of my lair into some goddamn hospital where they can insert tubes up my nose (and other unmentionable places) and 'monitor' my 'progress' into the hereafter."

"But . . ."

He waited. "But what?"

"What if it's curable?"

"What if?"

"You're not going to find out?"

"You're assuming, of course, that I haven't, but let's go along with your assumption. Right. I am not going to find out."

I stared at him. He was not smiling, he was looking at me along a straight line, it was like a short jab, and I swear I felt myself quiver from the blow. The next question was so obvious I could hardly bring myself to actually ask it. But I was only twenty, I reminded myself, and I figured I would be excused, I figured if I didn't ask it now I might forget how to. And I have never regretted asking, "Why?"

Several times Uncle Jack repeated the word *why*, each a low murmuring demand, glancing over at me and then out the window, as if he had to make an important, an irrevocable, decision in which I might play a serious part.

"I'm tired," he finally said. "Need a lie down. You come back for supper, Kim, come up before it gets dark. I'll make . . . spaghetti. Right. Maybe by then I'll have figured out something to say about the whys and the wherefores."

I RODE INTO the village with Gladys who had to pick up a part for Norm's baler, along with a few food items from Dugan's. Entering Harrow from the north we passed first through the tapered end of a teardrop, or a jewel in the shape of teardrop, the houses and town buildings increasing in number and bulging out against the lake. The structures were mostly white-washed clapboard with green shutters, and mostly Capes with some modifications here and there, a Greek Revival portico, dec-orative moldings, dormers, a cupola with a weather vane atop a barn. The air was so clear and sharp that the blue of the sky and the white of the clapboards seemed to enter my eyes physically in slices and shards of color, and then the maple leaves piled in, orange, yel-low, red, and the whole scene was impossible to look at, impossibly brilliant and beautiful and pure . . . the purity of the white houses, the white church and steeple, the white posts and pickets, the in-tensity of the violating color. Gladys drove on through her town and parked in front of the general store without seeming to notice, but my eyes were watering.

In Dugan's she made a point of reintroducing me to people who might remember my past visits, and though none of them indi-cated that they did—a nod, a mumbled " 'lo"—I knew from experi-ence that they probably knew more about me than I did, and re-called more than could ever be true. Afterward I helped her carry some secondhand baby items from the trunk of her car to the house across the street, including an old highchair she claimed I had occupied at age two when my mother brought me out from the West. I was headed back to the car when the woman inside opened the door; she was in her fifties probably, with a long single braid of hair, dark eyes, a nice figure. As they chatted she watched me carefully, not unkindly, but with the patient, considering way of people who have the time and are not afraid to get to know you. It seemed at one point that a smile scribbled across her face, quick and pretty, like a fragment from a song you know you will never be able to place.

"Who's she?" I asked Gladys back in the car.

"Well," she began, but a woman from the church bent to Gladys's window, and she was lost in the particulars of the upcoming rummage sale.

I knew I would remember the woman standing in the doorway, her face and the faces of other Vermonters; I would remember something about the quality of the silence, the simple gazing straight out at, that never failed to bring to mind essential questions: What is it, what do you see, what does it mean?

When we arrived back at the farm it was already getting on toward five, and after carrying in the groceries for Gladys I made my way up the path to Jack's and supper.

AND SO IT WAS that in the dusky light of the sod hut on an Indian summer's evening, I was with Jack, as if winds from the horizon had pushed me there for purposes as yet unknown to me, but purposes nonetheless—for Jack that would have been required. We were not old man and young, we were not even Jack and Kimball, we were just two lives, each possessing the secret finishing piece to the puzzle of the other.

And there was hunger, that was a part of it too, I have to admit, though I could not have articulated it back then. Not a simple curiosity, but a kind of hunger that does not care so long as it is satisfied. He knew something, I realized. Jack Sayers knew a great deal then, I mean he *knew*. And it wasn't a thing he had known all along, you could tell that; it was new knowledge, it was still alive, it was still wild and wholly possessed of itself, and of Jack, too, untouched, uncorrupted, untamed yet, and not anything you could ever translate, you had to learn the language in order to hear, you had to let it into your body like a wolf in order to feel the sharpness of its teeth.

Then, I suppose you would have to kill it—some knowledge is like that—before it killed you.

Well, I wanted to know, if I could know, what it was Jack Sayers knew. So I stood up and lit one of the kerosene lamps, for the room had sunk into the deep end of dusk, and then I said as casually as I could manage, "Courchaine implied that . . . well, was there an accident or something?"

"Yeah," Jack murmured, studying his floor, the worn wood planks and the dirt pushing up between them. "An accident, yes, you could call it that, if you had to. Others have had to. Personally, I have not," he added, still gazing at the floor, then jerking his eyes up at me, "Had any accidents, Kimball?" he seemed to accuse.

I shrugged. "Tagged a fence post this summer, thrashed the taillight. And once I creased the fender of Dad's Buick, but that was when I was learning. Anyway, he had already sacrificed the old beater to the cause." This was not what Jack meant, I could tell by the patient slump of his face. "I guess you could say my whole life has been one long string of accidents. Never thought much about what I've done, and I've never been big on planning what *to* do. Even Dartmouth, you know . . . they needed to fatten their quota of kids from the desert, so I dusted myself off and . . ."

"Naw, don't say that, you're there, it's great, it'll be good for the school called Dartmouth, having you. Good for you, too."

From the bottle he had earlier abandoned on the counter he poured himself some Scotch, neat, then granting me my almost age, he poured a second glass. It was old, single-malt Scotch. Jack Sayers was not a big drinker but he knew how to drink, he had that old world training—I really liked that about him, his old world training and the way it mixed in with contrary things and moments. He could make an elegant meal of canned soup and white bread sandwiches. The table would be perfectly set; that is to say, not any category of civilized dining missing—paper towel napkins and one-cent flatware from Dugan's on a piece of old cotton cloth he had picked up at the last church rummage sale; there would be small appropriate gifts for each diner, including the kids, and *always* good red wine which he kept at the proper temperature in his root cellar, the labels eaten soft with mold, and at the end he would bring out a plate of Girl Scout cookies he bought practically by the truckload when it was the season. Then cognac or some eau de vie poured in small clear fat-bellied glasses in the dim light of his sod hut.

Well, when he poured that Scotch—it was a significant drink—and coughed once or twice even though he didn't need to, a cloud crossed the moonglow of his eyes, crossed and departed, and I realized that he might tell me. With a little push he might talk about Jackson Sayers. Which seemed, at that moment, as critical to the next stage of my life as two legs to stand on.

"Is your being sick, does it have anything to do with an accident?"

He just looked at me and said, "Kimball Sayers Dodge, good name. A name with promise."

"What happened, what did you learn, that you won't go to a doctor?"

And then he just started talking.

"Because it was the kind of morning that broke your heart, all at once, like a slap from a lover. A fierce blue sky, it was not one shade off pure, 100 percent blue, all the trees practically giving up trying to stand up to it, it was so high and strong and . . . virginal. Right. Virginal. We were going to cut wood, this man, Chase, and I . . . well," a sudden intake of breath, "we did." He frowned a moment, he looked confused, no, not confused—troubled—then he roused himself and continued.

"Sam Chase. You haven't ever met him, he came up last spring for the first time . . . did a lot of work for summer people, odd jobs, he was keen on computers, wires, technology. I asked him one day where he was from. 'The global village,' he said.

"Did you know I use three cords of wood every winter, Kimball? Probably you didn't know that. Three cords for this place, and it's maybe 275 square feet with the door open, *maybe*. You work three years ahead, so it can dry completely. What I cut this year would've used three years from now. I didn't want to live on principle, you see—that was one of my father's—your grandfather's—favorite aphorisms, about not living on principle."

He had to stop and think about that, for some reason, and it was uncomfortable, how long he had to think about that.

"This year I needed help," he said finally, "for reasons . . . well, we've discussed some of them. Sam Chase . . .

"As I say, it was one of those fall mornings that can bring you to your knees," he shook his head slowly, "down on your hands and knees in your own track. Not to pray, God help us. It's just too much, you know, sometimes it is too damn much, how gorgeous a thing the world is, and there you are with your ratty truck and your chain saw that needs filing, maybe you didn't even brush your teeth, or maybe you weren't pleasant to the old guy pumping your gas, and man, you know you just don't deserve it even if you were nice, and you ought to ooze back in your hole and wait for bad weather, at least wait for bad weather. At least do that.

"It was not bad weather, no, it was beautiful. There I was, in the middle of the world on a beautiful day. With what? Sometimes you ask yourself that, Kimball, or you get asked that by . . . events. And once the question has been posed—*Ah, yes, you, Mr. Sayers, in the back there, what have you got?*—you start noticing that there are things missing. You can't answer the question with anything even close to a complete sentence. Your life is a handful of disconnected nouns and verbs, and maybe if you're lucky an adjective or two. That's all that means finally, not who or what, but how. How it was. The ceremony of it. The thing that makes you not just an animal doing.

"They say, Kimball, *how your life shapes up.* Shapes up . . . sounds promising, doesn't it? But for some of us we discover that our lives have not shaped up, they have shaped down. We started with something big, a vast morsel, rivers in the trees and the lawn full of south, as Emily Dickinson says, and we have stripped it down, worn it to a small orderly thing with edges and right angles, a thing that fits handily in box or a carrying case or a Dopp kit along with the pills we need for the days when it is just too damn obvious. Those beautiful days, Jesus, it was a beautiful day."

"This guy Chase?"

"Yeah, Sam Chase . . . an educated fellow, I confess I liked him for that. He wasn't boring, though he had a deliberate way of getting down to things, usually it was something you could take some interest in. I did that morning, I took interest in what he was saying."

Jack stopped talking then, as if meditating, his elbows resting on the chair arms and his hands folded together.

"So what did he say?" I asked.

Jack looked annoyed. He stood up to shove a log in the stove, jiggle the ash grate, and when he resumed his seat, he leaned back and swiveled at the same time so that the old chair works creaked and whined like the sound-effect props from a radio stage. I felt duly chastised.

"Education is important, Kimball," he announced over the whining chair. "You're headed for Dartmouth, and you'll do well, I know you will, maybe even get to work in your field. Naturally, there are many other things an education provides, naturally. You meet a fellow with an education and already you've credited him with things he may not deserve, and you've forgiven him a lot. You don't even know him, you don't know anything about him really, and you've already forgiven him. Say, for instance, that he swears; if he's educated, why, then he's just making you comfortable, not putting on airs, he's letting you know that he's a regular guy even though you both know he isn't. If he's educated and he never ever swears then he's stuffy and highbrow, arrogant, and slightly effeminate. Someone you may have to contend with some day, but no one you have to like. But if he's not educated, and he swears, then he's plain ignorant and vulgar, and no concern of yours. Then his language is a dumb threat, not a comfort, a mark, not a mask."

"What if he's not educated and he doesn't swear either," I had to ask my Uncle Jack.

"Ah, then, he, most of all, should be feared, avoided, fled. He is the living man."

Just then I noticed something about my Uncle Jack Sayers: he tended to shape his manner of speech to his company—with a child he was straightforward, delighted, curious; with an adolescent male he struck a cool offhand attitude; and, I imagined, with a woman of class he probably played a gentleman of deferential intelligence, speaking of James, Italian art, French cuisine. I don't mean to imply that he was phony, not at all. He was genuinely all of these men, more or less, according to the experience of the other in his presence. He liked to stay in harmony with the company he kept. But at a certain point in his story he seemed to cast off these many half masks, these phantoms we all found so personable and flattering, and to be himself entire, from core out.

"Yes, an education can mislead you down many a path," he was saying. "Illusions . . . education is good for that kind of theater production, too, constructing foolproof illusions.

"Oh sure, I ended up with a college degree finally, after a number of false starts. Ten years of false starts, or ten years of unfinished business, depending upon which end of the day you found yourself occupying.

"The University of Chicago. Hutchins was the chancellor at that time. He thought—and he was right—that the last two years of high school were a waste of time, so I entered college at the age of fifteen as a member of the laboratory school, a heady experiment built on the idea of community. We were a community of scholars; everybody studied the same subjects. In the dorms we actually discussed matters, we took positions—that is so important, Kimball, to take a position. We were Platonists and Aristotelians, without really being sure what that was. What did it matter? because, after all, we were taking positions. There were a lot of bright kids, and weird kids, very weird . . . I did all right, I guess.

"But at some point I decided I needed more experience in the real world. Who knows what I imagined that was? In my third year I dropped out and went to France. I was eighteen at the time, younger than you. The Sorbonne had a course, *Cours de la civilisation française pour les étrangers*, and I thought, Right, that's what I need, a course in civilization. It was cheap, something like twenty-four dollars a semester. You can't buy a decent meal for that today. I started off in a youth hostel, then I moved into an apartment with a French couple. It was . . . it was a formative year for me. They were old and poor. He still taught grammar school, but they had cut him back to *la bibliothèque*. It seems that is the last ignominious stop on your way out the door, helping children to find books in a library. It makes no sense."

For half a minute I stopped listening, wondering where this was all going and what I had gotten myself into.

"The woman spoke English," he was saying, "but they agreed not to speak it with me. We stayed up late at night, speaking French. They liked to talk about the war, about the Germans and how the French treated them. The war was still in everyone's mind. It was hard to imagine, as a young American. And it wasn't just my youth, my country was too young to understand really, the old grudges and hatreds and prejudices of the European nations. They talked about the war and the Jews, the Resistance, and all I seemed to know for sure was that there was a lot I simply could not know. I felt afflicted with my own innocence.

"They were passionately religious; every night from my room I could hear them mumbling, let's see, how did it go . . . *Je vous salue, Marie, pleine de grace*, the Lord is with thee; *vous êtes bénie entre toutes les femmes, et Jésus, le fruit de vos entrailles, est béni. Sainte Marie, Mère de Dieu, prier pour nous, pauvres pêcheurs, maintenant et a l'heure de notre mort. Ainsi soit-il*.

"I had never prayed. My parents were atheists—it was *de rigueur*. You could not say that you were an intellectual if you believed in anything. Science was the god of America then, maybe it still is; or technology. If Sam Chase were here he would say it was technology.

"My father, your grandfather, Kimball, Dr. Sayers, he would not see patients, he did not maintain a 'practice,' though he was attached somehow to Michael Reese Hospital. He spent his time in the laboratory away from humanity, hobnobbing with the microbic deities whom he hoped would deliver the secrets of life. My mother didn't believe in anything; it seemed to embarrass her, philosophies and passions. She was a good mother, just that. A good wife, too. She knew how to love, and it was as quiet and uncomplicated as the clean, folded laundry I found in my drawer every morning. You took it out, put it on, and went about your day within the pressed fabric of her affection. Nowadays children enjoy deconstructing their parents and psychoanalyzing their relationships with them; it has almost become a pastime. But my mother was like a base element, or her love was—you could no more examine its parts, its supposed dark sides and deceptive shine, than you could a chunk of gold. It had no parts, it was, simply, what it was, which made it worth quite a lot, but not very interesting. Of course I loved her, but I did not often think of her.

"No, we didn't believe in anything when I was growing up. Why should we? There was Father's science to explain things, and there was Mother's family money to provide things. I did not know how to pray because there was nothing to pray for.

"Every night in that French apartment through the thin plaster walls I listened to the old couple's Ave Maria. I might have been eavesdropping on two lovers, only it was the mother of God they sought to caress.

"This was the first mystery of a human kind I had ever encountered or had ever realized I was encountering. To me it was pathetic, you see, the prayers in the night—I thought that. But the feeling . . . well, the funny thing was, I felt something that was exactly the opposite of that thought, whatever you want to call it. I felt . . . well, that it was decidedly not pathetic.

"My room was bare by American standards. The woman had painted the iron bed blue, baby blue, and there was a bureau of some kind, a lamp, a chair, and a small table by the bed that stood on three legs, I remember; I remember the three legs because they were like the Matisse painting. There was a square of white linen, tatted and embroidered with someone's initials, draped over the table. A crucifix on the wall over the bed. The window looked out on a narrow damp alley. In the window box she had planted red geraniums; I don't know how they survived, since the sun found that alley rarely, maybe for an hour or two each day. I made a point of reading there during that time. It pleased the woman, my book, the sunlight, her red geraniums. She brought me English tea sometimes. For them it was expensive. She thought I liked it.

"Their apartment was tiny. The church owned the building and allowed them to sublet the extra room. They had nothing, nothing; maybe he made a few hundred francs, working at the school, and he had a very small pension, plus the money I gave them for the room.

"But the most meaningful Christmas I have ever had was with

them, Monsieur and Madame Rondeau. She cooked a light supper for us, and we went to midnight mass, then we came home and exchanged presents, and I never got a better present and probably never will, it was just a pair of slippers. It impressed me so much, because in our family the Christmas presents would heap up two feet high around the tree, like a bulwark, and ah man, it was just like Mammon gone mad, ah man. And of course every year my parents would say this year we're going to have a simple Christmas.

"So I got to thinking, I had a religious crisis while I was there, and I started thinking, these people are so believing, what if there is a god? I had better find out, because this could be bad if there *is* a god and I'm not paying attention: I could pay dearly for this. I resolved to find out. I was only eighteen; it's important to remember that, Kimball.

"I went to a Jesuit priest. We had talks. I suspected he really enjoyed them because he was working from scratch, there was nothing he had to correct or tear down in me, he could design his own tower of faith in the form of a man, and when he had finished, for my internship, so to speak, he found me a job with the Franciscan nuns at Lourdes, as a stretcher bearer."

Jack paused then, excused himself. I could hear his footsteps on the pounded mud path as he climbed up to the outhouse. The sod house was so quiet without him; the solid silence of earth, I thought, feeling safe and warm and awkward too, alone in Jack's burrow. I was used to the vast hardpan of the Southwest, air in perpetual motion, and the kinship of distance, not a tiny space underneath the whirl of things. I checked the fire and contemplated some food, since it was dinnertime, but Jack was gone so long I forgot about my stomach and began to wonder whether he'd fallen asleep on his one-holer. Finally the beam of his flashlight jittered past the window, and I could hear him talking to Maisey, his cat, who liked to hunt late in the day. Then down the stairs and in he tromped, looking refreshed, I imagined. In my mind I was drifting back toward the question of food, and to my relief Jack began fixing dinner, chopping onions and peppers for the spaghetti sauce, and frying ground round in a pan on the hot plate as he talked.

"You may not know this, Kimball, but the Catholic Church is very careful about declaring anything a miracle. They have strict regulations—doctors have to say the illness is incurable and then the cure has to be instantaneous and there have to be witnesses, of course. Maybe once every ten years they declare a miracle. So you don't see people all of a sudden throwing away their crutches. What you see is a lot of very sick people, a lot of people who are dying, whose faith is so strong that you breathe it in, an intoxicating smoke. And their rapture, too, you sense that, maybe you even feel it sometimes, the joy they pull out of the rotten rotting depths of their disease, their pain, their mortality, like something shiny from the mud. Amazing . . . and strange; I probably witnessed more true joy at Lourdes than at any other time or place in my life, the joy that comes of uncomplicated, unquestioning belief. That may very well have been the miracle at Lourdes.

"There's a grotto where Saint Bernadette supposedly saw the Virgin Mary. Every day they hold mass in the grotto; it's the main event. In front of the grotto is an area that looks like a parking lot. The stretcher bearers wheel the sick down there by the hundreds. You know they're in pain, you can see it in their faces, often they are in the last stages of cancer. And what you hear is an eerie, a vast mumbling, it sounds like a colony of insects if you could put a microphone to the ground and listen to that world below. Because they've all got rosaries clutched in their hands, or lying in their laps if their hands don't work, and they are praying. I don't know if they are actually asking for a miracle, maybe that's not kosher, to ask outright, but they say the rosary, and if the Virgin Mary decides to toss out a miracle, to throw her bouquet—that's how I seemed to think of it—they hope that they are there to catch it.

"I worked for awhile in the place they called the *piscine*, where the Virgin Mary told Saint Bernadette to scratch the ground and holy water would emerge. Well, she did, I guess, and a small spring appeared. They built a bathhouse around the spring. It was my job to wheel patients down to the *piscine*, then the priest and his attendants would lift the patient out of the chair and dip them in the holy water. It was frigid water, but they claimed that no one had ever died in the *piscine*.

"Because people die there, that's what you see at Lourdes, people dying, Kimball, people dying."

He paused to combine the peppers, onions, meat, and tomato sauce in a pot, a generous shake or two of chili powder, salt and pepper, chopped garlic. On the second burner he set a larger pot of water, and I watched the coil redden beneath it.

"I'll never forget this woman I had," he said as he found his chair, "her head was swathed in bandages and I was wheeling her out of the *piscine*. It was a cold, gray day, March, I think; we'd had to put out extra blankets for the sick. The army had donated the blankets and they were all blue. I was wheeling my patient up through the crowd to find her a place, everyone mumbling the rosary and everyone with a blue blanket, as if the sky had torn apart and fallen in shredded pieces across their laps . . . Jesus, it was stifling, that droning sound of prayer, it filled the day from beginning to end, it surrounded my world like a new layer of the atmosphere, I seemed to hear it everywhere I went . . . and the gray day, and those blue blankets. Even some of us were draped in them. You couldn't tell one victim from another, no, you couldn't tell them apart to save your life.

"This woman with her head bandaged, my patient, she lifted one hand and said, 'Je vois, je vois la lumière.' My first thought was, *Jesus, I ought to grab someone because I'm witnessing a miracle, and my name is Jack Sayers and I want you to put me on as a witness.*

"Sufferers nearby gasped in unison, dropped their rosaries or clutched them tighter. Tears sprang from their eyes, maybe tears of joy, maybe not—I had the thought that they might be jealous. We were all waiting to see if it would stick, you know. My patient's miracle. The whole thing felt staged, and at the same time I couldn't believe my luck, actually witnessing a miracle at Lourdes. I also remember feeling greatly relieved that it had happened so quickly —I had only been there three months, but I was overwhelmed, I wanted to get out. Every day I felt like a lost lamb at slaughter time —looking for what, I don't know, what was left?—but wandering, wandering among the stretchers and wheelchairs with their overflowing burdens, the monotonous undertone of prayer. And when I did get away, when I'd have a glass of Lillet maybe with another stretcher bearer at the end of a shift, there wasn't anything to say; or maybe if we did talk, it was coarse and out of joint with things, like 'you see the tits on that lady in the *piscine*?' So mostly we'd end up not saying anything at all. Anyway, no matter where you were in Lourdes, it seemed you could hear the steady hum of their pleadings.

" 'La lumière,' my lady cried out again, her hand still up in the air fluttering about like a little warbler about to light.

"A minute later the warbler dropped and she was dead.

"It was the wrong light. The one the brain produces as you're dying. You've probably read about it, Kimball. Chemicals and oxygen, or maybe it's a lack of oxygen, crashing together at the very end. Just chemicals, I guess, just science. It would have pleased my father, that light."

Jack pushed himself up from his chair then, stepped into the kitchen, and brought back a tin of peanuts.

"Bet you're hungry, boy."

I smiled. "Yeah, I guess I am a little."

He left the tin next to me on the cot; he was clearly not interested in peanuts.

"I left Lourdes after that and got a job with Abbé Pierre. He had been a monk but he developed tuberculosis and they told him he had to get out of the monastery. He went to a hospital in Paris. His condition eventually improved and he ran for the Chamber of Deputies, managed to get elected, which I guess was a surprise to him. He was truly a monk at heart. The politics finally disgusted him, and he started an organization called Les Chiffoniers d'Emmaus—Ragpickers of Emmaus—that was when I joined in as a laborer more or less. Abbé Pierre had camps just outside of Paris, and the idea was that people who were homeless would build the camps and then live in them. A lot of these people were really down and out, they were sick or they were serious alcoholics, a number of them had been in the Foreign Legion which was no disgrace at all, except that too many of them returned to France as alcoholics—pretty much unemployable. I remember this one guy, he had a trick of eating glass goblets, like a circus act, and also razor blades, he was attempting razor blades when I met him. It was his own razor blade that finally killed him, not any war. A stupid trick to impress the rest of us.

"I met a guy there, Bernard Gogoloca was his name, a Hungarian portrait painter. Bernard was charming and fearless, he never hesitated with people, even famous people. We'd go to nightclubs, and backstage after the show he would walk right up to the singer and try to get them to agree to a portrait. *And this is my American friend*, he would say, *he's working on his French*—so while he was drawing their portrait I would try to talk with them. Sometimes they would say no, but Bernard would insist, even argue—*you don't have time now? Well, perhaps tomorrow, and ah, so disappointing, we enjoyed your show so much, I've got this portfolio* . . . And usually they'd say all right, I'll give you five or ten minutes. Juliette Greco, she was beautiful, and Eddie Constantine, who was an American actually, a big hit over there, and then there was Margot Rousseau, her eyes . . .

"Bernard Gogoloca, what guts. If it had been me, if I had been rebuffed by Juliette Greco, I would have crawled back in my hole.

"For two months we stayed with the ragpickers. I found it was easier than Lourdes. They were living in the present, they had been reduced to that, but they had a chance to be happy now and then during a day. Maybe the sun would come out and a couple of the Legionnaires would stand up and sing a war song with the lyrics all changed to embarrass the women; there was one guy who recited poems, a franc apiece, and a lady who carried a small log with her everywhere . . . the log lady. She was always excited if you asked to see her log, as if it was her baby.

"In the present they had a chance, you know. In the present we all do, I suppose, and maybe only in the present. But Lourdes . . . there was one thing on everyone's mind there, and it was all in the future. Who would die this afternoon, tomorrow, next week? And the only thing that could happen right now, this minute, any minute now, was a miracle. It's funny how those things take their places in your mind.

"I had a narrow bunk in the back with some of the other volunteer citizens of the camp. There were only a few of us who didn't have to be there; it was a different kind of shame, not having to be there. The cockroaches, for instance. Early in the morning before full light—they don't like light—I used to open my eyes and try not to move, just to see how many were on me, the white sheet exposing each to the count. Once I counted thirty-four. They scurried about atop my belly, like miniature circus performers, and I couldn't help enjoying their busy antics. Eventually I would move, a single muscle, maybe one finger, and they would flee. How little it took to alarm them and yet they were everywhere, scared pervasive creatures. They smell, too, did you know that, Kimball? Get enough cockroaches together and you can smell them, it's a dry peppery scent . . . the shelves in the kitchen, that's where it was the worst.

"You see, Kimball, I could afford to be fascinated, even entertained, by the cockroaches.

"The log lady was young, twenty-five at the most. She had lost her family in the war, they knew that much about her. And they knew that a unit of German soldiers had tied her to a tree and had done things. That was how she was found, still tied to the tree. The log lady kept her head tipped so that her hair fell forward and concealed her face. Her hair was stiff and matted, but you could see that it had been pretty once, straight and gold, like August wheat. I had never actually viewed her entire face at once, just the bottom edge of a cheek, often flushed, and a delicate jaw swinging up to meet an ear I wanted to touch, for some reason.

"Whenever we met in the camp I asked about her log. It pleased her. The last night was no different. I greeted the golden fence of her hair falling down between us, and she responded with a grunt of delight. In her arms she held the log, and together, our heads bowed, we admired its bark, the clean cut of the ends, we let our fingertips marvel the rings moving out, her voice thick and blurred as if it had traveled a great distance to reach me and had lost along the way much of its fineness.

"Suddenly she tipped her head differently, and her hair swung to the side like a heavy curtain, and I saw her eyes—round halves of a hazelnut that had just that second opened, a touch of startle or wonder about them, but not innocence; ruined innocence, that was what I saw. 'It's not a log,' she said with a clarity, that shocked me.

" 'Right,' I said, not knowing what to say.

"A little elfin worry darkened her brow, then disappeared beneath the pale skin. 'What is it?' she whispered. She seemed prepared to trust whatever I told her.

"She was a broken thing and I could not bear to be the author of further damage. 'It's beautiful,' I said, 'like your eyes.'

"The nut closed, the golden hair swung back, but I swear I saw the leading edge of a smile draw up toward her secret ear. I knew then that I had not hurt her but it had been a close call. Too close for me.

"I left the next day with Bernard Gogoloca.

"You see, Kimball, the cockroaches had crept from the circus arena and were entering the stands where I had thought myself high and protected. I did not want to wait for official introductions. I had never had to learn how to live; that is to say, I had never learned how to accept the pain we cause others, having received so little of it myself. Indeed, it was one of my earliest principles—to leave nothing broken along the path I traveled—and if I have succeeded in that . . . though it now seems clear that I have not . . . it sometimes meant that I did not even leave a footprint along the path that was, after all, mine. I was afraid to claim even that, my own path . . . or to make claims . . . yes, that's better. Afraid to make claims."

Uncle Jack poured himself a glass of red wine, declining to contribute any more to my delinquency. He offered me a cola instead as we drained and divvied up the spaghetti, ladled the sauce, and promptly sat down, each taking an edge of his desk. A steamy comfortable silence enveloped us as we ate. Finally when the spaghetti was gone, we boiled another pot of water for the dishes, and he let me wash things up. "What about Bernard," I said over my shoulder, hands deep in the soapy water, "what happened with him?"

"Well, we traveled around together—Epernay, down into Burgundy where we lived on cheap wine and bread, cheese if we were lucky. It was late spring but still too early for fruit and vegetables, especially any that might be surplus, so we did not eat well. We wandered through the village markets, just to look at the chickens, plucked and hanging by their feet like a fringe of yellowy flesh above the meat cutter's table. I would've eaten one raw. Bernard made a few francs, drawing, on market days. He had to be fast or he would lose the interest of passersby. The pressure of time bothered him, for he was a perfectionist, like me.

"Just outside of Chagny, a family hired me to give their teen-aged daughter English lessons. She was going to America for the summer and was interested mainly in American slang expressions, including a few swear words, she told me privately. She had already studied grammar and the proper rest of it so it was just a week's job, providing her with a soupçon of vernacular. She seemed to have a deep fear of not being correct with her American peers, though on several occasions I tried to encourage her to simply be herself. Aimée was her name; very pretty, a breathless way of talking; it was exciting just to be around her when she spoke, as if something splendid was on the verge of happening. Bernard wanted me to fall in love with her—he thought it would do me good—but I thought it might have compromised her trip to America. After all, I was in her parents' employ; it would not have been right. They were letting Bernard and me sleep in a stone shed at the edge of their vineyard with the hoes and grape baskets. The shed, facing southwest, had no door, and at the end of each day, as we ate our bread, we looked out across the tidy vineyard, the twisted black wood and green leaves big with spring, the rows running from our shed across the girth of the hillside, like so many equal choices coming and going with the same force. I thought about Aimée. An orange sun slid slowly down the right-hand edge of the doorway, and the sky flushed when it finally departed, as if ashamed it had done nothing to stop it. I could have stayed there a long time, teaching Aimée.

"After our week in Chagny we decided to hitchhike over to Alsace and the city of Strasbourg to see the Rhine. A dirty cut of water; we left the same day.

"Bernard was getting intense. When he had no one to draw, when there was no one even to persuade or argue with, no challenge, his charm and fearlessness ran the other direction. He was sore at everything, even his own freedom, which seemed a kind of torment to him. There was a cousin in Milan, a banker; he could have had a real job any time he wanted. And I was tired of his insults. As big and unsophisticated as my country seemed to him, it was my country. I had to ask him to shut up and it surprised me when he did. He would not sleep near me that night.

"By the time we were headed back to Paris . . . I guess we had made it back as far as Verdun . . . he kind of cracked up. The town of Verdun is mostly acres and acres of white crosses. One of the worst battles of World War I was fought at Verdun. A million men died, though Verdun did not fall. In World War II it succumbed almost immediately, without notice, but not in World War I, thanks to those million men. Of course you had to ask if it was worth it, or actually, if you found yourself in Verdun you did not need to bother to ask.

"In the cemeteries Bernard began to hear Germans marching. It was the crosses. One hundred or a thousand, or even ten thousand of them, maybe that would have been manageable, but hundreds of thousands of small white crosses with their small white arms reaching straight out . . . I suppose it was too much for him. The cemeteries could not be avoided in Verdun. And if you came through Verdun it was the thing to do, to visit the cemeteries. So we walked among the crosses . . . the terrible neatness of their arrangement, and white, very white, absolutely identical too. Even in death they were like soldiers, marching in place with their little white arms out, but not touching, you know. It wouldn't have been so bad, Kimball, if they had been huddled together, you know, bunched like a crowd of people waiting to hear a speech or to see a show, or to receive a miracle, like the throng at Lourdes, but all evenly separated in perfect even lines, and not touching, that was the hard part . . . for my friend . . . he began to hear the soldiers, to hear them coming, yes . . . I heard people, Bernard and I . . . we did hear them coming, they were, they were . . . coming."

Uncle Jack had to stop then. Maybe it was the wine, or the late hour, maybe it was the whole of that year in France he had brought back for me—the poor old couple, the sick at Lourdes, the rag-pickers, the white crosses at Verdun—well, it might have done me in, too, to go from the poor to the sick to the lost, and wind up with the dead. He was tired, he was mixing up his pronouns, his hand around the wineglass shook. I asked him if I could come back the next day, maybe help him with chores if he had any. And hear the rest of his story.

"Is that what I'm doing?" he said, looking almost surprised, "Jesus, how maudlin, how revolting . . . I'd better stop. But yes, come back, Kim. I'll put a cap on this self-indulgent drivel, and you come back. Right."

I HEADED BACK down the path with one of his flashlights and a quavery sensation in my gut.

I knew Gladys Courchaine would still be up, watching TV; Norm and the boys were long to bed, because they would have to rise at four-thirty for milking. The Courchaines' was a rambling New England farmhouse, full of extra rooms and old quilts and quite often a stray visitor or two. Gladys set a piece of maple fudge cake before me, and I ate it up with a gusto she knew how to appreciate, because here came another piece, and a glass of milk, naturally.

Of course I would not drive back "all the way ta Hanover," and of course I would stay with them so long as my visit with Uncle Jack lasted. And yes, I guessed I would have another, just a tiny sliver of cake. They were solidly nice people, you couldn't knock anything off it, they were the genuine article from front to back.

I watched some TV with Gladys, then found my old room off the ell and tucked in under a pile of quilts. Uncle Jack's voice was still banging around my head, like it wanted out, but I had the feeling that, until I had heard his whole story, it wasn't going to get out. It was a story I was looking forward to with alternating bouts of worry and eagerness.

THE NEXT DAY pulled into Harrow like a load of dubious relatives from the north, gray and windy, an occasional spitting rain, threatening to stay longer than anyone wanted. On the high ridgelines clouds bulked up, glowering and growing as the day advanced. In case there was anybody left who thought summer had not gone for good, flocks of geese flew low over the hills in check mark formation, one side of the *V* shorter than the other, and the geese honking back and forth with their incredibly loud, brassy, comical voices that never failed to throw a shock of happiness my way. They were somehow both magnificent and silly.

Everyone was gone when I got up. It was only seven. Gladys had arranged several boxes of cereal in the middle of the kitchen table, along with a plastic container of homemade applesauce and a teaspoon-full of instant coffee all ready in a mug. It was nice to be back at her homey Formica table. Even if you were alone, you didn't feel alone, sitting there, so many tired hungry people had been there before you and had left the crumbs and smears to prove it.

After breakfast I cleaned up, and decided to stop by the barn to say hello to Norman and his boys.

Norman Courchaine kept the cleanest barn in the Kingdom, it was said. Even on the hottest day of the summer it did not smell bad. He had painted the interior a glossy white, and installed clerestory windows the length of the building, and there were fans generously spaced, so it was always a light airy place you didn't mind hanging out in. Whenever one of his cows made a deposit, he was ready with the manure rake, and he looked elegant, tending it—

that was the amazing thing. At milking time the gutter cleaner ran from start to finish, and the flies followed the manure outside to the cement bin, and the smell seemed always headed downwind. The sixty-six stanchions for the milk herd were nearly filled, a dozen or so calves occupied the calf pen, there was a pig or two somewhere about, a dog in the yard, and plenty of resident cats who dealt with the mice. Every member of the Courchaines' peaceable kingdom looked contented, especially those big, black-and-white holsteins, giving their milk, munching away. And then there was the milk room—the milk room where the holding tank sat was a gleaming marvel of stainless steel and scrupulous sanitation. All in all, a splendid-looking operation.

If a guy didn't know what a bum living it was, having to get up at four-thirty every morning of the entire year, year after year, to milk, and then do it all over again at supper time, every day of every year, and cows getting sick or stuck in a marsh or caught up in one thing or another, and the newborns not always making it, milk prices shooting up, plunging down, machinery quitting on you for no reason (and then there's hay which you have to have, and it's dependent on good summer weather—enough rain, enough growing days, enough helpers) well, it's a hard hell of a living.

The pump was loud, and Norman was halfway across the barn, tending a cow; he nodded as I entered, finished attaching a milker, and came over. In the five years since I had seen him he had not changed much—still visibly fit, with chiseled features, a crooked nose that was handsome in its way, and the distant, amused, and mostly invisible smile of a benevolent patriarch. I put out my hand and he shook it soundly and with his usual grace.

"Grown," he said.

"I guess so."

Nearby a cow let loose a slop of manure. Norman found a rake and pulled the manure neatly into the gutter. "Been to see your uncle?" he said, leaning the rake against a post.

"Yeah, we had a good talk."

Norman didn't say anything; actually, I had the feeling that he wanted me to say more about Uncle Jack. I tried to wait him out, but he had a lot more practice at conversational silences, being a

Vermonter, than I, so finally I said, "He doesn't look so good. I'm going up to give him a hand with jobs around the place."

Again, Norman didn't really respond, except to say that he hadn't seen much of Jack lately. Then he shifted a milker from one cow to the next, and hailed his eldest son, who was down at the far end feeding calves in the calf pen. Albert was three years my junior. We talked for awhile—we had always gotten along. It looked like he would be getting a scholarship to Brown, he told me; planned to study psychology, of all subjects. Far out, I said.

A barn is no place to linger if you aren't working along with the others, unless you haven't a tick of shame. So it wasn't long before I was headed back up the path to my Uncle Jack's.

ABOVE THE SOD HUT and hidden between runs of cedar and spruce were two open fields, as well as a series of connecting paths. Jack and I scythed these areas. He liked to keep them open, even if it wasn't for anything beyond that—keeping the land open. It would be the last time before autumn settled in, then he would not have to worry about growth until the thaw in April or May. All morning we worked; what I lacked in skill I made up for with energy. Jack seemed tired before we started, but he could swing the scythe so that it was just a curving, cutting part of himself. Whenever a flock of geese flew over we both stopped and watched in silence, smiling across the distance. We were lucky it was such a cool, breezy day, I pointed out several times.

Jack made us each a couple of tuna fish sandwiches, chips and a can of cola. When we got to the leftover Sara Lee cake, I said, "So, Jack, what did you do when you came back from France?"

"From France?"

"Yeah, the year you spent in France, Verdun and everything."

"And Lourdes."

"Yeah, Lourdes."

"Well . . . I was shattered," he said, his mouth full of cake. "I didn't know which end was up. When I was a kid we had a cook, a cleaning lady, a gardener, a summer house, et cetera, but the thing is, we pretended . . . it's okay if you have money and you admit it, but we pretended that we were just like everybody else, that we were card-carrying members of the middle class. It was the deception that got to me. I returned to my well-to-do American family and my fine American college . . . after that year in France. It was disturbing."

"I can see that," I offered.

"And I still hadn't decided whether or not God existed," Jack continued. "I suspected that He didn't, but I maintained an attitude, not a very noble attitude, that, if it had words, would have sounded like this: I don't believe there is a god because it just doesn't make sense, but if there is a god I want to get on his good side. Of course I had no real idea how to accomplish this.

"By default I re-enrolled at the University of Chicago. Got a place with a couple of other guys, grad students. Went to classes. Met a girl, Marie was her name, exotic Marie. Brazilian. Maybe she didn't realize that I was different, or maybe she had a high tolerance for, uh, intense guys, but she put up with me. She may have even, well, yes, I believe she genuinely cared for me. It scared the hell out of me.

"This then became my task: to be worthy of Marie. You see, here I had had everything, a good upbringing, a good family, plenty of money, time to enjoy it, a good education, and in France, the requisite rounding-out glimpse of the underside. How could I then have Marie too? So there I was again, crashing into the God question.

"I decided to give everything I owned away, all my things, my books, everything except what would fit in one knapsack, the one I had carried around France. What was the theory? Well, it was a long time ago . . . to simplify, to purify, to render myself honestly poor, nobly poor? to purge myself of my Self by shedding the accoutrements of Jackson Sayers, or to weed away everything but the Self? If there was anything left—and that was a real question, Kimball, would there be anything left and what would he look like, what would Jack Sayers look like without his stuff? Would Marie still like him, maybe love him? I didn't know, I had my doubts, but I didn't finally know. I was confused but I wasn't . . . suicide didn't seem like a viable solution.

"I laid everything out on my bed, it was like my own personal market day. The guys I was living with, they accepted a few books, this and that, but after several minutes they began to realize what I was doing, the extent of it. There were clothes on the bed, a gold watch given to me by my father and engraved with a large cursive *J*, a leather suitcase with my initials. It angered them—it was strange, how angry they became. They tossed the stuff back on the bed and stared at me as if I had just revealed an open sore. They said things, like they didn't want 'to be party to it,' and made me feel that I was engaged in some nefarious activity. I had to shut the door. Then I resumed the task, sorting my things into piles, what would go to the Salvation Army, what Marie might like—she was not well-to-do—what I would keep. This last pile I started jamming into the knapsack, but it wouldn't quite fit, so I thought, well, maybe I . . . I got to have that, so I would pull out something else. In the end there was little satisfaction.

"On the edge of the bed I sat with the knapsack hanging from my shoulders, just to try out the weight of what was left, my worldly possessions; every item in the pack seemed to weigh a great deal more than it used to. After several minutes I decided to go out. There was a coffee shop nearby where Marie and I met often; I walked down there with the knapsack on my back, and the thought I kept having was, 'I could simply keep going, now I could just go.' And even more delicious than that, 'I could simply and irrevocably *wander off.*' I suppose everyone has that fantasy, disappearing into the maw of Life.

"In the coffee shop I ordered a plate of lunch. Beside me the knapsack sprawled in the booth, like a weary companion. It was unnerving, seeing it there. I was responsible for this reduced creature. Afterward, we strolled about, my knapsack and I, waiting for the courage to do something, though it wasn't clear what that might be. Finally I went back to my room, though I refused—to myself, for no one else cared—I refused to unload the knapsack, and in fact lived out of it for several months in my room, as if I were living in the streets.

"Marie's roommate, she told her, 'God, I really feel uncomfortable around Jack, he's just so tense.' She was the one who took the watch, for her brother, she said. She said his name was John, but it turned out his name was Robert. I couldn't imagine why she had lied.

"But the thing about giving away my stuff, you know, it back-fired. It just rendered everything that was left more important than it had ever been and more important than it deserved. I became ob-sessed with the care of those few remaining items; I became their servant.

"Since I had given away most of my books I dropped all my classes. At the time it seemed a reasonable reason—no books? quit school. I got a job as a messenger boy for the University of Chi-cago Press—that was mornings. Afternoons I drove a cab. I guess I was still searching for real-life experiences, the ones I missed grow-ing up privileged, and the ones I would keep missing if I didn't simply throw myself down beneath the wheels of life. I wanted to be counted among the masses, I wanted to feel myself a part of the underground current of society, and I wanted it to be authentic this time, not elective. If I could have I would have joined the throng at Lourdes, praying for a miracle I suspected would never come, a miracle that ironically would have restored me to the life I was rejecting.

"I was so bewildered that I . . . well, I knew that when I dropped out of school I would lose my student deferment, and that any day the draft letter would arrive, summoning me. I was not fond of be-ing summoned. Eventually I recognized that even this was a mark of the unreal life I had known, a life that did not accustom me to imperious demands from above. But then . . . well, I would as soon answer than be called upon. So I enlisted.

"The army is good for people who don't know which end is up. It absolves them of considered thought: all decisions are made by someone else or by the system, and if there is a war, those decisions that are made on a battlefield are, by virtue of the circumstances, impulsive and therefore excusable. To be honest with you, Kim-ball, I was tired of thinking about humanity and my place in it. I needed a rest. I actually thought the army would provide that, and it actually did, which is even more frightening."

Jack paused and gazed out the window, his eyes glowing in the strange dusk of his skin.

The room was growing cold; I got up to stoke the fire, which he had forgotten about, and while I was on my knees with the poker Jack found a sweater for me. "What war was on?" I asked, slightly ashamed of not knowing my history.

"No war."

"Then why did they have a draft?"

"It was just a leftover from the Korean War," he sighed. He looked distracted, as if he didn't know who was asking the questions, he was still back in Chicago in the late fifties. "And the cold war, that was everpresent." Several minutes passed. He ran his hand over his mouth and chin. "Even that's over now," he added, but he seemed to be referring to something else.

"How long were you in the army?"

"Two years. Baumholder, near the town of Idar Oberstein in Germany. It's in the American sector, so it's an American base, the biggest in Germany. We were on maneuvers near the Czech border.

"Some of the guys had German girlfriends. I . . . I wanted one, but it didn't feel right. We were in their country, using it, you know. A certain amount of respect and discretion, Kimball, a certain amount of respect . . . the way you are here in my house. And there was Marie. Plus, most of us would be gone after two years, so we couldn't make any promises, none that we would likely keep. They were nice girls. They thought we all had money.

"Use, Kimball, that was what it was about. Use the country, use the women, use the goodwill of the citizenry . . . it didn't feel right. But they weren't concerned, the girls, you know, I don't think it ever crossed their minds.

"My bunk mate had a girlfriend; her name was Minna. His tour was up and he was headed back to the States, and she just shrugged and said, 'Okay with me.' I guess that bothered him a little, because they had been together for almost a year, so he asked her why. American boys, she said, they are too clean, and they smile too many times in a day, and there is no day that is that good, and no body that should go around that clean. It's arrogant, it's *beleidigung*. An insult. Now, Jesus, what the hell did that mean? I thought about it; I don't think my bunkmate gave it another split second's worth of his clean, smiling attention, but I thought about it, goddamn it. That was one of my problems, I couldn't help thinking about things.

"And let me tell you something else, Kimball, something I think you stumbled into fairly early: thinking will take you only so far, and even then the kind of understanding it offers doesn't have a hell of a lot of staying power, if you know what I mean. Real understanding is the kind that drops in your lap after you've lived through something; most of the time you didn't ask for it and you wish it'd just go away.

"Anyway, I had a job as a supply clerk, which I loathed. College education, any fraction of one, they give you a job that involves paper—I was qualified to handle paper." Jack picked up a piece of paper lying on his desk, waved it about, then as an afterthought, it seemed, crushed it in his fist. "We had weekly sessions with the commanding officer; he would get us all together and say, 'Okay, now is anything bothering you?' And maybe one guy would say, 'Yeah, there aren't enough spoons in the mess hall,' and another Joe would say, 'The shades in the rec room don't work,' and I'd get up and say, 'I think the morale is very low in this unit. And the work doesn't seem that meaningful.'

"The commanding officer, Captain Rowe, he would gaze slowly around, scrutinize every member of the unit, not with anger but with an apparent respectful and genuine concern, the way a parent might who has heard something disturbing about one of his children. He even managed to keep his face blank, like someone preparing to hear bad news he alone would have to deal with. And at the same time there was a definite flavor of . . . indulgence, right, disingenuous indulgence. Finally he would blink slowly, lick his lips and say, 'What do the rest of you think?'

"And not a sound. Nobody would say a damn thing.

"Captain Rowe would depart, and immediately, *immediately* the guys would run him down, and run down the other officers, and run down the unit, the base, the army—you'd think they were in prison. If a guy was gung ho, he pretty much kept it to himself.

"Yeah, I was an all right soldier but I was not a good soldier. In the army you really can't afford to ask too many contrary questions, it's not like a university seminar, they don't want to deal with you on that level. You're not there to think, that's the whole point. If you actually thought about any of it there wouldn't be a goddamn army to start with.

"You'd never make it in the army, Kimball. That's something you can be proud of. But no matter who you are or how you end up in the service, whether you muddle through or march along with a vapid-eyed peace of mind, the last month of your time they always give you a re-up talk. But, you know, they never gave me a re-up talk. I think I was the only guy in my unit who didn't get a re-up talk. Maybe it was some bureaucratic oversight, or maybe they just realized there was no point.

"When I returned to the States I headed as far away from Chicago as I could. California. Marie, you can guess, she didn't wait. I thought Marie and I were . . . that we meant something to each other. But two months after I arrived in Baumholder I got a letter from a friend who told me that she was seeing other guys. He thought I should know, so that I could 'feel free' was how he put it. *Feel free.* The funny thing was, her letters still came, and not one indication that . . . it was over. That just killed me. After a while I didn't even open them. There was a guy who never got any mail. His name was Jack, too. I passed Marie's letters along to him, and he would wait to open them at mess so the other guys would think the letters were his. Jesus, that about broke my heart again.

"At San Francisco State I was able to concentrate enough to get a bachelor's degree. A triple major—economics, government, and foreign relations. It was clear that I still didn't know what I wanted to do, but I felt I should be doing something to help mankind. I took the GREs and scored high enough to get accepted to Harvard Law, University of Chicago Law School and the School of Economics, and places like Michigan and Berkeley.

"It seemed to me at the time that with a degree in law I could get into politics and help save the world. I accepted Harvard, and on a Saturday afternoon in September I moved into my room in Cambridge, and started to meet a few of the other students. I was talking with these guys, they said that you really don't want to go here unless you are truly committed to the law, because this place is like a monastery. 'Yeah?' I said. 'Yeah,' they said, 'it's intense. So if you're just doing it because you think it might be something to do, you won't do very well, or you'll quit.'

"Saturday afternoon, Saturday night, I thought about it, Kimball. Law school. You see, until then it was all in the abstract—a law degree, politics, helping mankind—who could object? Now it was like the wedding night when the groom—or the bride—realizes *Jesus, I made a big mistake, this is never going to work*, and is thrown into a full-throttle panic.

"Sunday morning I went to the dean's office. I hadn't slept but I had managed to drag the razor over my chin and scramble into a clean shirt. Of course, Dean Whatever-his-name-was was sitting in a leather armchair, and behind him was the ubiquitous wall of leather-bound books, and there were the plaques, the desk the size of Rhode Island, the briefs and papers neatly stacked on its corner, there was the ink well and the Waterman pen, the tweed jacket and the stern fatherly face with the half-wilted smile, running out of patience before anything had even begun. If the opening credits had flashed by I wouldn't have been surprised, it bore such a strong resemblance to the first scene of a Perry Mason episode, where I was the distraught but willing victim of my own principles, and he was waiting to help me pick up the pieces of my life.

"In order to cobble up a jot more dignity, I stuffed in my shirt-tails and attempted to lengthen my spine by dropping my chin and my voice. 'I don't think Harvard Law is right for me,' I stammered out.

"And what he did, you know, it was right out of the Perry Mason script: he looked at his watch and he said, 'Well, there'll be two more of you by this afternoon.' That was it. Classes started the next day and I was not there.

"I still had time to get to the School of Economics at the University of Chicago where I managed a full year of course work. Even took a class with Milton Friedman, who won the Nobel Prize. I got a basement room in Chicago's skid row, which is north of the loop, a bad section of town, just cheap rooming houses and greasy spoons, but you could get a meal for a buck. That was where I finally settled the God question."

"How?" I asked.

A broad happy grin appeared on Uncle Jack's face.

"Tell me," I said. "Come on, don't leave me hanging."

"I decided that I was not going to leave my room until I had a revelation. And so I . . . well, I knew that this was not going to happen, but I thought, what the hell, I'll at least . . . maybe this'll appease me, if I go down there and just hang out for a while and nothing happens, maybe I'll finally get it through my head that it isn't going to happen. So I went down to my basement room. Up near the ceiling was a window where I could see the shoes and calves of passersby, but in that part of town there weren't many people who promenaded. I was pretty thoroughly isolated.

"Hour after hour I waited. Then I waited some more. In between praying I thought maybe I would try meditation, empty my mind so He would have room to appear. There was a guru on campus, a guy who had been the object of an assembly earlier that week. A lot of students went, and out of curiosity even I drifted over. The guru was handing out personal mantras, and I thought, what the hell, and got in line. *Ear-ring*, I think that was what he said; there was a good crowd and he whispered it to me, but I swear he said *ear-ring*, long and drawn out as if you were calling a dog who had wandered off. So I tried out my personal mantra— *ear-ring, ear-ring, ear-ring*—in my basement room while I waited for a revelation. It wasn't long before I was thinking about earrings, naturally, and earlobes, and girls I had known, Marie and the log lady, Aimée with her new American swear words, a blind date I had had in San Francisco—she was gorgeous, I mean, devastating, and really nice, and when we got to the dance I went in with her and my roommate who had a date too, and then I left. That's what I did, I left. You understand, Kimball. I feel certain that you understand how a man simply cannot bear it sometimes, how devastatingly wonderful a girl can be.

"Obviously the mantra was not helping me focus. On the contrary, my mind was reaching everywhere at once, now and then skittering into corners I was not eager to inspect.

"I decided that I would write a little. And yet the revelation did not come.

"Finally, I had to pee, so then I made the first of two exceptions, well, three actually, to not leaving the room. Nothing elaborate in terms of self-persuasion. I said, well, I guess it's okay, you can leave the room to use the bathroom, God can't be interested in that sort of cheap suffering. If He wanted you to suffer He'd ask for your first born, or send down a plague of black flies, or make salt pillars of all your friends. He doesn't want to see you wet your pants for Christ's sake, when there's a head down the hall. It's small-time and He's in the Big League, He is Mister Big.

"So I went to the bathroom. When I returned the revelation still had not arrived.

"Several more hours elapsed. I didn't think it proper to read while I waited for God, because books compete in a way with general omnipotence, but I allowed myself pen and paper. Remember, Kimball," he said, raising a finger, "the army had certified me to handle paper. At one point I heard the clack-clack of high-heeled shoes, and stood on my bed in order to view a pair of ankles in dark red stockings float past my lair, like two sugar plums in the dream of a hungry child.

"By that time I was in fact hungry. Food then became my second exception.

"Back from the coffee shop and replete, I dozed, lulling myself to sleep with a mumbling series of Hail Marys that recalled the old couple in Paris. I think I even said them in French, just to vary things. Whenever I awakened it was to make eager investigations of the room and of my person in the event that the revelation had come during slumber. This was preferable to being fully conscious during the revelation for the simple reason that the revelation, as I imagined it, was a frightening occurrence.

"Every so often I would make what I regarded A Concerted Effort. This was when He ought to have spoken or made Himself known to me in some small yet indisputable manner. After all, I addressed him from my knees on a stone floor in a skid row basement—if He wasn't paying attention to *my* sorry soul, He was hardly doing His job. Fiercely concentrating, each word of each prayer fully realized—Our . . . Father . . . Who . . . Art . . . In . . . Heaven . . . Hal-low-wed . . . I made my way through the standard pleadings, adding my personal and increasingly desperate invitation to speak. It was exhausting, frustrating, and finally, after three days, infuriating.

"The third exception? Oh, that was . . . well, that was just to leave the room, nothing more. At one point, after days of silence from Him, it occurred to me that I ought to leave the room simply to leave the room—to assert my ability, my right, my duty, my *choice*, to leave the room. That was all. My choice.

"I finally . . . I think there was a particular moment when I realized the absurdity of it . . . waiting for the revelation. I was lying on my bed, staring up at the ceiling, touching some of the bricks in the wall that ran along the street, and I was literally bored stupid. I mean it, I was frantic to see anything, hear anything. I remember I was attempting to move the muscles of my stomach one at a time in the shape of a circle, and inside the circle I revived the memory of my beloved cockroaches performing in the predawn dusk of the camps outside Paris. Another pair of high heels, dogged by brown wingtips, strode by my window with obvious purpose. They were going somewhere, a party, I imagined.

"There was, there was absolutely nothing there, absolutely nothing, nothing coming into me, not a damn thing, I mean, not a peep. And I sat up and said, *Hey* . . . I finally got to the position— and this is my position now—I sat up on the bed and said, *God, if you exist you can kiss my ass, because you have made no effort whatsoever to reach me, and I have make all kinds of efforts to reach you, and you are a shit, you know, if you exist I don't really want to have anything to do with you, go ahead and send me down there. Because the devil is a hell of a lot more interesting anyway.*

Several moments passed. Jack ran his hand over his face and said, "Right. A hell of a lot more interesting."

IT WAS MIDAFTERNOON and there was a sudden break in the gray canopy. We both knew it would not last. I suggested we go for a walk and Jack agreed.

Outside the light was brilliant; it took me twenty paces and the cedar woods just to recover my eyesight, not to mention my bearings. Between the sagging clouds deep hollows of blue had formed that seemed to draw you skyward headfirst, practically lifting your feet off the ground. Every breath of air was like an original—fresh, cool, untainted. I remember thinking then that it would be impossible for me, Kimball Dodge, ever to have any kind of revelation in a room; the best of me was always somewhere outside, and pretty easy to find if there weren't too many buildings in the way.

We shuffled down his path single file, then turned up along the road that climbed in easy increments to the top of Tufton Hill. In the higher fields beside the road wild apple trees grew. Jack brought along a canvas bag to gather whatever the deer hadn't gotten to yet. He said he was contemplating a pie, which pleased me to no end, not for the pie but for what I hoped it said about his mood. Maybe my visit was doing him some good.

"Have any idea what you want to study at Dartmouth?" he asked me.

"Music," I replied, minus the usual apologetic tone I saved for my father.

Jack only nodded. For me, it was full ratification.

After a while I said, "What about the economics? Did you ever finish?"

"Naw, I couldn't drum up any passion for economics, not like the other students. Besides, they had majored as undergraduates in that one field, they had the thorough basics and I had a mere sampling. As soon as I heard talk of a master's thesis I chickened out. That was '62. Went to New York instead."

"New York?" This was a leap.

"Yeah, it's a big ugly city," he said with satisfaction, and smiling in a sad sort of way.

"So why?"

"Well, I was going to be a writer. If you wanted to be a writer, New York was the place to be, the pulse of the country, the heart of the industry, and so on and so forth. By then I calculated that I had enough experiences to earn me the right to consider them, try to understand what they were about, maybe even offer some sage observations, or what I thought were sage observations."

"I guess I'm a long ways from that."

"Not as far as you think, Kim."

"But I don't think, Jack, I mean, I never have thought too deeply about things. Not like you. And big cities, I don't much like them. Did you even know anyone?"

"No. I got a room in a flophouse in the Bowery, right on Third Avenue. It was run by a guy, his name was Louis the Sheik, which he got out of a book, I think. Louis the Sheik. Jesus. Once he invited me up to his room—he wasn't making a pass or anything, he just wanted me to have a beer with him. He sat on the edge of his bed and I sat in the only chair. I had never seen black sheets."

"Black sheets?"

"I mean sheets that were so dirty they were black. 'What are you doing in New York,' he says, and I told him I was going to write. He glugged his beer and nodded as if I was the sixth guy that day who had told him he was going to be a writer. It kind of unnerved me."

"Maybe he was one himself. Or had tried to be."

"Maybe."

"But you do write."

"Well . . ." Jack and I hiked in silence for awhile. Finally I asked him how long he stayed.

"Well, my room, it was above ground this time, on the third floor, which had the advantage of heat rising from the first and second floors. That was one encouragement to stay on for awhile. There was a bare bulb hanging from the ceiling, and a radiator that every once in a while would slip into a catatonic state, shaking and freezing up, then shaking again—I figured it was going to break loose and come after me one day.

"I bought a little typewriter, a Royal, and a stack of paper, a used dictionary, the works. Then I enrolled in a creative writing course at the New School for Social Research, right in the Village . . . Twelfth Street, maybe. I even took up smoking. It seemed to me at the time that it would be nice to live in a flophouse under a bare bulb and write short stories.

"But, you see, Kimball, what was still bothering me was the idea that I should be doing something to help people, and writing was not helping people, writing was self-indulgent . . . or that's what I thought.

"I found a better apartment in the West Village and took a job with the Welfare Department."

"The Welfare Department?" I said. Another one of Jack's veering turns. "I can't picture you working for the government."

He nodded, looked up the road. "Yup. One year. I was determined to find out once and for all whether I really wanted to help people; also whether you *could* help people, if it was even possible. Seeing the despair and the anger and everything else that occurs in these people who are on welfare, I realized that you really can't legislate it, you can only help people on a one-to-one basis. And I believe very strongly that even if you say you are going to help people, that immediately makes it a kind of self-righteous thing. *I am going to help them.* Well, who the hell are you? Maybe the best way to help people is just to get off their backs."

We had arrived at the first of the wild apple trees. The fruit was yellow, not green; someone decades ago had planted and cultivated and nursed the tree along for whatever unique properties the variety offered. Now, along with the wild green apple trees, it bore riches for anyone who paused on the road up Tufton Hill.

Jack cut left into the high grass and I followed, stooping for apples that at first glance seemed fine but revealed nasty worm holes and bruises, and divots where the birds had dug into them. I tossed them away. Meanwhile, Jack had the right idea, shaking the branches, collecting the fall; the birds had gotten to some but not all, and in fifteen minutes the canvas bag was full.

Behind the tree was an old stone wall wandering along, a remnant of someone's farm. The stones were a clean, scrubbed gray with patches of green and orange lichen, moss around the bottom, and Jack and I each found a place to rest and admire the view.

"Yeah," he said, "helping people is sometimes just a pretty package for self-help. After a year of the Welfare Department I quit; I wasn't finding myself in the misery of others, I was hiding in it. That's not right, not the right way to conduct one's affairs.

"I came up here that summer, to Harrow. My parents were here, and Natalie, your mother, of course—she must have been twelve or thirteen. That was when I met Lara."

Jack Sayers paused then for the longest time yet. Finally, I picked an apple from the canvas bag, and the movement seemed to jog him loose from whatever had snagged him, because he raised an eyebrow and watched as I tried to eat the thing. It was definitely, only, and irrevocably a pie apple, no way around it. I felt my entire face bunch around my mouth, as if to somehow squeeze the tartness back outside where it belonged.

Jack said, "You have to civilize them."

"No kidding," I sputtered.

He smiled.

Recovered, I asked him about Lara, if she was still around Harrow.

"Lara . . . Lara Casey. She was swimming in the lake," he said, "near our dock. Thunderheads were piling in from the south and moving across the water faster than she must have realized. There wasn't time to swim home. I could see her see me on the dock. She changed her course. The way she swam . . . the water hardly seemed to notice her there, ruffling its surface. I leant her a towel and she walked to her camp along the path that circles the lake. The next day she brought back the towel with a basket of lettuce from her garden. She had washed and dried the lettuce; you could eat it plain, it was so delicate, and if you didn't know it couldn't be sweet, you would have thought it was. A lot of things are like that, lot of things. It has to do with belief."

Without a word Jack slid off the wall and started back down the road, keeping ahead of me, as if he needed to be alone.

We commenced on the pie as soon as we got back to the sod house, Jack working the dough, and I peeling as I could. The tree gone wild, the apples were mostly runts now, and it wasn't easy to work the paring knife in and around the funny creases and knots, halve and quarter them, then excise the core which about took up most of the apple anyway. My hand cramped. I began to wonder if it was really worth it. Almost two dozen apples to make one pie. But the story, or myth, of Lara kept me going.

"I was . . . quite . . . taken with her," Jack said, in a whispered tone of mystery. "Dark red hair, and her skin, it was flawless, flawless, and there was her quirky sense of humor. She wove things, shawls, scarves; her fingers were strong and capable, always very clean for the yarn. At the height of feminism she wore skirts that came to the middle of her calves, and sandals dangling over her shoulder, a touch of color on her lips—that was all, no other makeup. Around people, even people she had just met, she was comfortable, it was funny how comfortable she was, but there was something apologetic, too. I think she worried she might offend you with her ease, her way with freedom. Personal freedom, she had that, or knew it the way you know something you have grown up with. That is to say, it was never one of the big questions for Lara. At the same time—and I may be wrong about this—she seemed to need people around her, and of course no one minded that, no, none of us minded that." Uncle Jack stopped speaking, at a loss what not to praise about Lara Casey.

He brought the big board down from its ledge on the kitchen wall. First he wiped it with a wet sponge, then a dry towel, a dusting of flour, moving the white powder about with his palms, then another dusting with a last sprinkle of sugar to give the crust a hint of sweetness. "She saw things most of the rest of us kept missing," he said, his floured hands momentarily twined and quiet, "the not-obvious—that was where she lived, in the not-obvious. And you would be surprised, Kimball, what is not obvious. For instance, perennial questions: Are you happy? Why did you live with the ragpickers? How do you know really when you love someone? How do you know? She would drop that kind of chaos in my lap in the middle of a tennis match or across a cheese sandwich. It kept me on my toes. Because, you see, I thought that that was where I lived, with the big questions. And to a certain extent I did; that is to say, I wore them about, like articles of clothing, when in fact the basic truth, the Naked Thing was underneath, foul and sweating and in need of a little sun probably, heh, heh. Yeah, a little sun.

"Basic truth?" Jack smiled a smile of acute sadness, a *why not?* sort of smile, riding a shrug. "Oh, I don't know . . . then, perhaps, that I did not know how to live. And if you went on, Kimball, as Lara would have, with that charming crease between her eyes, to ask why, why didn't I know how to live? I would have said, if I could have known, 'Because I had never really suffered.' What suffering I had had I had chosen, you see, Kimball. To choose suffering is to rob one of the glory of defeating it. And to defeat suffering is to live.

"Well, what do I mean by 'defeat' anyway? You can't really defeat it, of course, but you can make it work for you. And there's real triumph in that. I had never given myself to the life that was mine, I had given myself to the lives of others, lives I borrowed or attached myself to, because those lives did not repulse me as mine did. Another life was always more interesting, more real, richer in meaning, more fraught with angst . . . angst . . . than mine.

"Again, Lara would ask why? Well, to say that I had had a perfect upbringing would not be right; it was too perfect. I could have accepted perfection—even perfection can occur naturally, like any error—but not a perfection that noticed itself while it attempted to conceal. We Sayers, we were always whispering asides while the real action went forward.

"A man who limps when he doesn't need to—what dignity is there in that? And yet, what dignity can be found in sterling health? Oh, I'm not saying that I was embarrassed or ashamed of my good fortune . . . or maybe I was . . . well, what I'm saying is obvious: ease is shallow and undemanding. It's unhealthy. Your parents, your family name, your wealth, they're all just up the beach, keeping an eye on you from their wide, sandless mats. And there you are, wading about under a big soft yellow sun; no depths threaten you, no sea serpents or storm clouds, no experience is required.

"And no opportunities, Kimball . . . you understand, there were no intrinsic opportunities for me to find . . . to make, I don't know what the word is, for me to develop meaning in my life. There was so little I had to learn beyond my studies, and so few challenges to leave their distinctive and sometimes ugly—that would have been dandy—yes, ugly marks. Even the ragpickers, for them I felt, but I could not feel for myself . . . even my patient at Lourdes with her bandaged eyes, I envied her her life and her sickness, and especially the satisfied weight of her hand falling as she expired. Anyone could see from that that moments before, decades before, from the brilliance of birth to the false light in her blind eyes, anyone could see that she had been *alive*.

"I could not say that of myself."

I WORKED OVER the apples—and what Jack was saying—in silence. He rolled the dough out on the wooden board, folded it in half, then lifted it into the pie tin, poking the bottom and crimping the edges, his hands a little clumsy but tender, very tender. "*La lumière*," he muttered under his breath, "*la lumière*." He seemed to have done with Lara. But I needed him to keep talking, I realized; there was something in what he was saying, in all of it, that I needed to hear.

"You never finished telling me about the day you cut wood, you know, the day with . . . what was his name? Chase?"

Jack threw me a deadpan stare as if I had startled him from a dream. There was flour on the end of his nose and along his brow, and for half a second he looked like a statue of himself, complete with bird droppings. It gave me the fantods to look at him.

"Sam Chase," he said distractedly, "seized his life, other lives . . . rewards of suffering, hah! For pleasure, pleasure, he yielded. An educated man, too. I think I mentioned that." Pausing, Jack gave his chin a vigorous knuckle rub. "Fact, I gave him something of mine, a kind of essay about right living. The way he praised it I knew he detested it.

"We had had three days of rain. Everything glistening, every leaf, every blade of grass, the blue sky, the apples, man, the apples bobbing in the trees killed me. I remember worrying that the wind would come up and knock them off, except that it was too early, they were still tight to the branches. I came down the path around eight, took a fall—there was a lot of rainwater, and I hadn't been feeling well. As you know.

"Norm's electric fence was spitting and crackling, and the back end of the truck gave a slosh when I drove out. Chase was supposed to meet me in front of Dugan's. He didn't have a vehicle, didn't even have a winterized place. The Spitlers gave him their boathouse for the summer. He had fixed it up for them and then they had a debt on their hands—always bad news, that kind of debt from that kind of man. People said . . . well, I *knew* he entertained a lot of women there. Rand Spitler didn't like it. They're old-time summer people, come up from New York every year for the innocence of their grandparents.

"See, there was something . . . sharp about Chase. He knew how to work a crowd, and by crowd I mean the whole damn village of Harrow. He had a slow hand, as they say. You get so used to seeing it there that you fail to notice when it begins to take. Or maybe you don't even mind because the rest of him is straight ahead, or seems to be, or has been to that point. He had established his credentials, in other words. Why, he could fix anything, he was educated, he was soft-spoken when he needed to be, at parties and with the ladies, and he was one of the guys when it was convenient to be one of the guys. He didn't swear much, judiciously, I'd say. And he was a handsome fellow. Looking at him, you had to shake your head. Perfection.

"'Well, hello,' he says, climbing into my truck, like a radio announcer greeting his audience. Then he pulled out the essay I had given him, thanking me excessively, I mean ex-cessively, for *honoring* him, he said—that was when I started to feel queasy—for letting him read the piece, how it had led him to ponder—*ponder*, what a word—social responsibility and self-sacrifice, how he had been inspired to examine some of his own principles, and all this full-throttle gas that I half thought I might punch his mouth just to stop it from blowing out, except for the other half of me that wanted to suck in every last syllable. You know how it is. Anyway, I guess I admired Chase, sort of. For one thing, he had a way with women—not that I couldn't have, maybe, if I had wanted, but for various reasons, for various principles, in fact, I didn't, I ended up as you see me—alone. Because of a lot of what I wrote in that essay, maybe, responsibility, honor, et cetera."

Jack was measuring out the dry ingredients now—sugar, flour, cinnamon, nutmeg, a touch of ginger. I brought over my bowl of hard-won apples, all sliced and browning some on account of how long it had taken me to work my way around the flaws, and with his hands he mixed and coated the fruit.

"Well," I said, "they're not mutually exclusive." A phrase I had recently come across, and having the ring of intelligence, I tended to use it whenever I thought I could. But Uncle Jack looked at me with an exaggerated appreciation, and I felt almost ashamed, because honestly, in those days I hardly ever knew what I was talking about.

"No, they're not," he said, "not at all, Kim." He slid the pie into the little plug-in oven that sat on the shelf over the food cupboard, checked the dials and, weary from his labor, dropped immediately into his desk chair. Ashen and fire-eyed, he looked worse than ever. He had had fits of ragged breathing throughout the day, and at the unlikeliest moments he would pop a sweat, like then. On the edge of the cot, picking at a blister the scything had raised, I considered calling my mother from the Courchaines'. It was time she knew there was something wrong.

"For me . . . and for Chase," Jack muttered, "they were exclusive. Of course we were on opposite ends of that field. And the day we cut wood was the day I understood everything. Heh, heh, you look at me, Kimball, as if you think you're going to learn something you don't know, but don't count on it. Just a story, right? A fiction? You'll have one of your own someday to unravel.

"Chase and I drove out to North Harrow, where, you know, the Sayers family has had a wood lot for almost a century. Two hundred acres would have made a stake, a chance, a means of making it through this life. By God, it would have made a helluva farm and home. For us it was always just a wood lot. Imagine.

"Sam's intuition must have finally kicked in, because he had put a cap on the unbelievable praise. Though I admit his hurting me made me feel better about being in the world on such a nice day. There is nothing like a little pain to give you that necessary edge. I'd had some news . . ." He made a dispelling gesture with his hand, as if to brush something off his desk.

"The rain had gutted the road into the property, so we had to park a good mile from the skid-out clearing and walk, carrying two chain saws, a can of gas, an ax and a splitting maul, and a knapsack with the jug of water, cola, and grub. I noticed that I was somehow carrying more than my share. Normally, that would not bother me, but I said, 'You look too comfortable.'

"He strode along without glancing my direction. 'Do I?'

" 'That may be your problem,' I said, meaning larger things.

" 'I wasn't aware that I had one.'

"To this I made no reply, because when I thought about it I realized he was right, it wasn't his problem, it was mine. It was my problem that I was carrying too much and he wasn't carrying enough, and we both knew that I wasn't going to do a damn thing about it.

For that alone, for that one thing, I might have hated him, but there were considerable hates awaiting us on that day.

"Up till then Sam Chase and I had had amiable commerce. I'd seen him at picnics, parties, I'd hired him, like the rest of Harrow, for this and that. We had a relatively simple relationship on the basic barter plan: he inquired into my writing, which of course I didn't want to discuss in any detail, so we ended up on books. He was a reader. Once we had finished with literature, I would ask about his latest conquest in the department of female pulchritude —that was how I always put it, trying to dress it up, I guess—and we would snort and elbow our way through his exploits up here in the Kingdom. They were all willing victims, the way he told it, and I had no particular reason to doubt it.

"The whole day faced us, Kimball, a truly beautiful day, as I have said. The order was three cords of wood, that's what I use a season, and maybe we'd see our way through half, cutting and splitting, provided things were smooth between us. There would have been another day of work. I needed him. He knew I needed him."

Twisting sideways, Jack gazed out the window above his desk. It had clouded up again, a damp mist forming over the ground itself, as if from something rotten down there, and the dim blurry scene outside was like the opening backdrop to an English mystery flick. "Did I mention that I had heard some gossip that morning? Yes? Well," he shrugged, puckering up his lips, "it was no concern of mine, of course, but in a small town like Harrow things have a way of weaving through people and lives, and the longer you're in a place the tighter the weave gets. So it did bother me, that the Greenfield girl was pregnant. I somehow felt we'd all let her down, all of Harrow, all of history maybe." Speaking through his teeth, he released a bitter snort. "Another fine example of social responsibility."

"Greenfield," I murmured, just to respond, and he looked at me so strangely then I got up to check the pie to duck his lurid eyes. They weren't blue any longer, the fire behind them had shot green flecks through them, and his eyes were almost painful to look at, so sharp and with a kind of wrenching vitality.

The rain began and quickly found a steady clattering rhythm

against the tin section of the roof, while into the sod it disappeared softly, distantly, like matters you did not have to deal with, or people whose voices didn't count. Uncle Jack and I hurried up the stairs and outside to gather tools and other stray items, his laundry, which had not dried. When we had finished clipping the clothes to a wire above the wood stove, the pie was bubbling ready.

It was the best pie I had ever eaten; I had to laugh, the way it transformed the gray wet day and the dour forest we had wandered into . . . just the smell, overpowering the other smells of mold, of the black Vermont earth enclosing the house, of wood smoke and moth balls and mildew, of the past percolating from the very walls of the sod house. Jack made two cuts, a quarter for him and a quarter for me, the second half for another time. Two steam harem girls danced for us until out came the Ben & Jerry's, and the slabs of vanilla melted against the crust like a couple of fat white lovers. Jack and I, we were practically giddy, it was as if we had finally reached the one thing the whole day had been meant for.

After his second or third bite, he raised his fork to eye level and kind of murmured, "The golden apples of the sun, hmmm, right," clearing his throat then and speaking in a strong voice, "Though I am old with wandering, Through hollow lands and hilly lands, I will find out where she has gone, And kiss her lips and take her hands; And walk among long dappled grass, And pluck till time and times are done, The silver apples of the moon, The golden apples of the sun."

Jack was always saying stuff like that, quoting from books, famous people, guys he had known. I had to admit it made me a little jealous, how much he knew and how he could put things together, just eating a piece of pie.

"Yeats," he added.

When we had cleaned our plates I didn't want to stay around for some reason. The idea of heading down to the Courchaines' and hanging out in the middle of their big messy family farm scene struck me as better than fine. The hired man's wife had six-month-old twins and a waitress job at the Inn that took her away around suppertime. Her husband was in the barn with Norm, so Gladys Courchaine was on tap for babysitting. I had in mind holding one of the babes. Or fooling around with their old bird dog, who'd fetch back just about anything.

Maybe I was looking for a little relief; maybe I didn't want to have to ask again what was wrong with Jack because it was beginning to sound as if I was going to find out.

Probably, Jack Sayers, my uncle, was dying. I mean dying *soon*, not like the rest of us, dying someday off in the far future, which floated like a speck, a speck of dust, above the purple band of the horizon. And what was I supposed to do with that?

Sure, my mother had asked me to check on him, but she had not really believed what she had heard; she was convinced that her brother was just fine. He had never ever been sick. So for me it had been a whim mostly, a lark, just something to do, driving up to Harrow; my last shot at pure impulse before Dartmouth and adulthood dug its spurs into me. Now even curiosity had caved in on itself, and I was pretty sure I didn't want to hear any more. But this time at parting Jack actually asked me to help him the next morning take in the dock, which was our dock, the Sayers' dock below the big old shingle-sided family summer house on the lake, and I had to say, "Sure."

At the Courchaines' it wasn't easy to sleep in, but I had somehow managed. Naturally, no one mentioned it when I shuffled into the kitchen and family room area. There were no fewer than a dozen people standing or sitting or leaning about—Norm's cousin come over from Maine for bear season, all the Harrow Courchaines, the hired man's wife, old Mrs. Young who was busy trying to cobble up a land trust that needed a narrow strip of one of Norm's fields, a quiet friend of Albert's named Rufous Tinkler, and Junior Brovarney, son of Big Brovarney, known as Big, so his son became Little Big for awhile, then Junior Big when he got to be as big as his father, or Junior, a man-sized and now man-aged beast-boy I had never liked.

First time I met him I was fourteen, he was seventeen, maybe. My mother and I, and a bunch of family friends, had gone up to Tufton Hill for a picnic. I had run ahead to stake out a good spot. Fog was drifting up from the hollows but no one thought it would linger because it was dry and the sun was still strong on our backs, coming up the road. A shape appeared in the mist, half naked and huge, lumbering along the slope through the goldenrod above me. Junior Big. A long loaf of Wonder bread hung from his left hand, and in his right, hooked by a single thick digit, was a jug of ketchup. Dinner. He jerked one of his paws and the bread swung out; "We're here," he drawled, as if his mouth were already packed with the compressible bread, and meaning, I gathered, that that side of the hill was his territory. I also gathered that there was a female counterpart to Junior somewhere in the primordial mist, though I didn't much want to picture it. Back to my people I fled, angry

with myself for being afraid, and angry with Junior's brute innocence. We're here. Period. Never mind *Je pense, donc je suis*, you still
need a place. That was the trouble with being a summer person,
you always felt that you were crowding into someone else's picnic
spot. Winter had earned it for them.

Gladys made a vague effort to announce my name over the din
—there were several simultaneous conversations, plus the TV was
on—and added "nephew of Jack Sayers," which had the effect of
muffling things down some. (I had learned that Vermonters were
often listening when it most seemed they were not.)

"I do so like Jack," Mrs. Young whinnied, "he's a dear, yes, he's
always been such a dear, dear man." That produced a significant void
in the center of the room apparently, because everyone seemed to
be staring there, like someone had just fallen in and disappeared
without a trace.

Finally the hired man's wife, who was from California and who
had no fear of words like *love*, offered meekly, "Why, everyone loves
Jack."

Everyone loves Jack . . . are we down to the obvious already? I
poured myself a cup of coffee, leaned against the counter, and
wished myself back to the bed in the ell, under still-warm quilts
where I wouldn't have to deal with anything yet.

Next to me Gladys sloshed a can of lemonade into a pitcher and
added water in measured doses. "How was he yesterday?"

"He's sick with something, I don't know what."

"Well," she said.

"You knew, probably the whole town knows."

"Well, I guess," she said quietly, respectful of the irritation in my
voice. Others in the room had resumed their conversations. The
bear hunter flipped to the weather station. "Won't go to a doctor,"
she added.

"I don't get it, why?"

Gladys Courchaine just looked at me as if trying to determine
whether or not I was old enough to understand whatever she might
say. But all she said as she stood there slowly stirring the lemonade
was, "Can't press a man like Jack."

Norm went out with Junior Big, and it wasn't long before

Norm came back with Junior Big, needing a file. Junior was supposed to do some tractoring—he had the biggest bucket loader around—but the points weren't firing right, it seemed, and Norm had gotten rung in, typically, on one of Junior's jobs.

I still had not called my mother, and I didn't want to without having something positive to report, so I asked Norm—his handsome rough-hewn face focused on the kitchen drawer, his hands deep in its tangle of entrails—if maybe he would talk to Jack, "you know, man to man."

"Son," he said, not even glancing up from the drawer operation, "it's everyone's concern, your Uncle Jack, but it's no one's business but his own."

Over by the mudroom door Junior snorted, his big lips wobbled into a smile, then he burped to indicate he was about to speak: "Dead man walking," he said, and snorted in appreciation of the wit he had no doubt borrowed from some other lunkhead possibly one turn of the grindstone sharper than he. "Dead man walking," declared the beast again.

I could only stare my hatred at Junior Brovarney, who seemed as unperturbed as granite beneath the blast of a western sun.

The kid named Rufous didn't smile, though it might have crossed his mind, for he drew his hand back and forth over his mouth as if to wipe out any inclination, and allowed as how he had heard that "oncet," August, or was it July? what people had been saying; then he scratched his head and mumbled, "Helped Pa clean up after the fire, Jack did," and he nodded and gave his head another vigorous scratch as if to convey somehow the bothersome mystery of death dogging a man like Jack Sayers.

Norm found Junior an interim task, outside. I was leaving anyway. They were right, Jack was an independent; probably there wasn't anyone on the planet who had a chance in hell of persuading him to seek help . . . that was what I was thinking as I headed out, but before I had reached the porch I turned back and asked Gladys if she had ever heard of a Lara Casey. Because maybe Lara Casey could persuade him.

"Lara Greenfield, you must mean."

"Greenfield?"

"Well, shore, been married twenty-five, maybe thirty years. Three kids, all grown but one." She looked at me, then gave in to a motherly sort of chuckle. "People grow up, get their selves wed, have kids . . . it do happen, Kim. Only it looks like her last one's about to be grown maybe faster than she'd care to be."

A CLEAR, COLD blue day, still as a picture, seemed to wish me a friendly hey-ho as I hiked cross the field skirting Domm's sugar bush and down to the lake. Jack was already standing on the dock, his hands tight along his sides as if waiting for instructions, his body leaning slightly forward over the water.

I hollered, "What is it, a mermaid?"

"A fish, maybe. Maybe dinner. I'm too old for mermaids," he smiled, and for no reason gave me a hug. If the walk and the weather hadn't made me feel better about coming up to Harrow, that hug did.

God, the lake was so flat and floor-like you thought maybe if you ran out across it and back real fast you could do it before the water realized or remembered, and pulled you down into the chill blur of factuality. It was funny how that worked . . . how your dreams seemed so vivid and it was reality that you couldn't get a fix on, that was like trying to see through water.

Around the lake the maple trees were blazing away, and the tall, lean fir trees stood about like good soldiers tending the fires. Early slants of sunlight traced the ridgeline of the hills, and my cheeks, too, leaving the dales shadowed and the rest of my face feeling cool and alert. Behind us above the dock in the black spruce, chickadees and peabody birds were still practicing their morning scales. And Jack looked practically healthy, there in a pair of green shorts and old tennies, a quilted jacket-shirt up top, definitely strikingly authentic, like one of those arty photographs that captures not just how a man looks and where he is, but where he's been, too. Inside, I mean. He had brought the remains of the pie and a thermos of coffee to reward our labors.

"God bless you," I said, and he tipped his head like the gentleman that he was.

That was when I asked him. I said: "Look, Jack, you have to tell me what's wrong with you. I won't bug you about it, I promise, but you have to tell me, because I *have* to call my mother, who is your sister, after all, and she has a right to know. And she would positively *never* forgive me ever if I didn't at least find out and tell her. At least."

His blue eyes stared at me from the end of the dock, with the blue water behind him and the blue sky above, and for several seconds he was all a kind of blue confusion for me.

"And I'll make *her* promise not to bug you about it, too. As a condition. Okay?"

Jack sat down on the edge of the dock and eased himself into the water, which was about sixty degrees. "Cancer of the prostate," he said. Then he was plunging his hands through the jade surface to wrench loose the pipe fittings. I opened my mouth to say something, but he popped up one of the wooden top sections and tilted it my direction, giving me a long look that said *now you keep your promise, boy*.

"But Jack . . ."

His look reached deeper into me and seemed to grab hold of something vital.

"But it's curable, they have hormones and, and therapies, all kinds of therapies, I've got a friend, his dad . . ."

Now he was pointing at me. "You," he said.

"But God, Jack, this is something they can deal with."

"*You* made a promise, boy."

"Yeah, okay, I made a promise. I made it and I'll keep it and I won't say another word about it, but you've gotta know that I am not happy about it."

"Fair enough."

So I had no choice. And in the end I learned maybe why he wasn't going to do anything about his cancer; it had to do with his own personal sense of justice, I figured, which even I understood was a thing you could not easily alter in another human being. Probably you wouldn't want to anyway, it was so deep inside the pure part of a person that to force it out of whack would be something like a holy crime.

BACK ON SHORE there was a deck built high and cantilevered over the rocks where the winter ice could not reach. In the summers the adults sat watching from chairs and chaise longues while us kids—wet, feral, thoroughly happy—took over the lower dock for diving and other games. One at a time I hauled the dock sections up to the deck, and when all four sections were piled high, and the galvanized fittings deposited in a crate to take over to the boathouse for safe keeping, Jack changed into some dry pants and boots he had brought along in a knapsack, and we flopped onto the deck to divvy up our reward.

It was then I heard the rest of his story, all of it except the last little bit, which I learned the morning I left, as if it were an afterthought. And in a way I guess it was just an afterthought, but a guy wouldn't know that, or he wouldn't appreciate it, unless he had heard everything that came before, or felt, as Jack must have, the weight of the countless moments that bore upon that last single moment of release.

"I STAYED IN HARROW almost a year," he began, "to be near Lara. She was going with someone else at the time so it wasn't, you know, a recognized or real thing, my staying around. We took walks together; just sitting still, Lara couldn't talk. She had to be walking along for the words to joggle out. I liked that about her. I liked that she had personal *requirements*.

"I got a part-time job in a bookstore in Montpelier, and it was there I met a guy, a professor of philosophy, Ira Bloom, who introduced me to Bertrand Russell's work, that whole crowd. Bloom was a local big in New England. Very disorganized, not that I was much better, but it was my job to keep things generally in the right stacks, the right columns of thought, so that when he entered his study each morning he wouldn't have to bother with the old initial search. He made me a kind of apprentice. Naturally, he was working on a book; I think he'd been working on it for about seven or eight years, and I could see why. I mean, I read Russell and some of the others when I worked for Bloom, and I'll tell you, Kimball, while I was actually reading the book, I understood, it made perfect sense, it was all of a piece, and if I was very careful I could hold it in my brain, like holding hundreds of pieces of a puzzle fitted together, and the whole thing balanced on the tips of ten fingers, sagging here, breaking there, but still for the most part together. A picture I could make out. But the minute I had finished, none of it made sense. And not only did it not make any sense, I couldn't remember any of what I had read, nothing. It just went away, poof. I don't think I've ever had that experience since, everything clicking into place, total understanding followed by total amnesia.

"Well, I thought about it. And the only thing I could come up with was that it was all up here," he tapped his skull. "The head does not remember," Jack went on, "the body remembers, the eyes, the nose, the gut, the way the air circles your neck on a cold day, sunlight threading through the butternut fronds to find a reddish curl, the sound of a hermit thrush in midsummer, the smell of boiling sap in the spring . . . yes, the body remembers and the brain is like a secretary or an editor, it records, moves things around, cleans it up, and files it away, tries to make something of one thing or pare down another, maybe so it doesn't hurt so much. Because what I remember about reading those books was where I was sitting on the floor against the wall between file cabinets in Bloom's overstuffed study, and the smell of Earl Grey tea, which he drank until his teeth were the color of stone, the cinnamon sticks I sucked on while I read—I was trying to quit smoking, in case Lara might someday kiss me—that was the sort of thing, the category of things within the event of reading Russell, that I remembered. Right, the body provides the raw material, the natural resources, *the stuff*, Kimball, the stuff of life. Luminous particulars, luminous particulars . . . how many were obscured by the artificial light of thought, of principled considerations? Ah, hell." He shook his head in a sad sort of way.

"So I worked for Bloom and the bookstore, and in the winter Lara came to me. That was what she did. It was as if we had an appointment. She knocked on the door. I was living in the house on the lake. It will be yours someday, Kim, when your mother is through with it, the grand old Sayers camp. I liked to read in the window seats that faced the water, and I was there when she knocked, propped up against pillows, reading Proust, *Remembrance of Things Past*. Now and then I'd look up from the page and out at the lake, frozen to a white empty stage before me. The sun was descending the west sky, slow and smooth as if it followed an invisible wire, and on the icy plane of the lake two skiers made their way silently east to west toward the sun to try to meet it, I imagined, before it disappeared. Behind them in the modest depressions of their tracks thin blue shadows lay down and together ran back to the place where the two had begun, which seemed to be located just below the house. Lara knocked on my door, and I rose from the window seat to let her in. 'Jack,' she said. The way she said it . . . there was nothing I had to say, nothing that had any hope of meaning beyond her arms, and the smell of her skin, like vanilla, and the look of her red hair billowed out on the quilt, and the red shadow of the sun reaching up from the bottom of the sky. 'Don't forget me,' she said. How could I forget her?

"After that we were together. I quit the bookstore; I told Bloom that philosophy was not my cup of tea. He shook his head and told me it was, it was indeed my cup of tea, in-deed, he repeated, breaking up the word, and I seemed to feel it break across my back. A kind of horror, brief but full-fledged, pursued me back to Harrow, to my parents' summer house on the frozen lake, to Lara with her questions and silent testing ways, and her capable hands. And I tried to ignore what Bloom had said. I tried, simply, to not think. Because Lara and I were together, spending our days, spending our desire, using it up. We even spent money."

"Money?" Somehow I never associated Jack with money.

"Yeah, lots of it, just to be spending, to be gulping our lives. Neither one of us cared about it. You see, I had a trust fund. I guess I forgot to mention that. Yeah, I always had that cushion to fall back on. It was a big mistake. Some people can handle it. I don't think it did me any good. I think I would have been better off if I had not had a trust fund, if I had had to keep things on the record, had to have a job, had to commit. It's the have-to's that shape your life, that carry you away. To that point everything could be instantly abandoned . . . or not abandoned. My experiences, what were they but contracted events? How could they carry me away? They were brief, they were optional. I *volunteered*, the way I had volunteered for the army. And where were the storms, Kim?" Jack was practically shouting now, throwing out his hand like a flag, the jacket flapping along his thin arm. "Where were the storms, the failures, the irreparable damage, the jealousies, the lost fortune, the lost leg, the job, Jesus, right, the same miserable job that went on for thirty years, the love you have no choice about, no choice, wonderful words, and you would be dishonorable for it, right? you would be a heel to keep it alive . . . ? Where was that, where was all of that? Where? It's only what has to be, Kim, what *has to be*, that has the power to carry you away. I wanted to be carried away."

He was silent for a good five minutes. We watched an unpredictable wind confuse the surface of the lake.

"In the spring I sugared for old Truesdale. They didn't have sap lines in those days, it was still buckets. Truesdale drove me like a horse. I didn't want Lara to think that I was afraid of work or that I wouldn't work if I didn't have to. And I myself believed in the value of hard work.

"We were together in the winter, and in the spring, too, when I sugared for Truesdale, and helped around as I could, doing this or that—mending fences, putting in gardens for people, generally lending a hand where a hand might be needed. I believe I read quite a lot. In the summer we were not together. Exactly why I can't remember, I may never have really known. She had requirements, as I said, and part of them, vital to them, was that they had to be found and met. Both, but the first especially. She seemed to believe or to feel, though she never actually stated this, that to discover the needs of another human being was to love that human being. It was like a confession, both parts, finding and letting them be found.

"In the summer we were not together. Lara just didn't say anything. Maybe I hadn't found out her needs, or maybe I didn't let her find mine. Probably that, now that I think about it.

"Then my mother died . . . I went back to New York. I got a job as a bag man for an air freight company, Bor-Air, up on Eleventh Avenue and Thirty-ninth. What we did was, well, basically, we broke down all the freight that came into our warehouse, put it in trucks, and sent it out to different airlines at different airports. Clothing, refrigerators, whatever was being shipped out of New York City. I was the bag man. They had these little onion bags, the kind you put suet in for birds after you use up the red onions; I wrote down what was going into what truck, then I would put the tags or invoices for each truck in an onion bag and give it to the driver. There again," he raised an unsteady finger, "I was qualified to handle paper.

"Occasionally I was down on the floor, moving freight around. It wasn't just a desk job. I would ride out to the airports with the drivers, mostly it was Newark, Kennedy once in a while. It was a low entry job; there were some pretty rough characters. One guy, I remember, he had a knife and he cut somebody, and I had driven out to Newark with him just that morning. He was one angry man, and not very stable, but we got along all right; it was funny, how protective he was, like I was his kid brother.

"The boss was a wonderful guy, Bernie Shapiro, a rugged, hands-on type, very decent. And Archie Green, another decent guy. I'll never forget what Archie Green said to me, he would come up with stuff like, 'When I die I want to be buried face down.' And I said, 'Well, why is that?' And he said, 'So the world can kiss my ass.' He was just full of aphorisms like that. Then there was a black guy we worked with, Justice Smith, a kind of Zen character who did the work and floated by on another level, minding his business but with a distant sense of humor about the whole scene. He'd lost his father in the streets; that was all we seemed to know about him. Whenever Justice had something he wanted to say, we all stopped to listen, even if it didn't make a helluva lot of sense.

"So, there was a real cross-section. I can remember going to work with a feeling of great, sometimes tremendous freedom and anticipation and joy, going to my menial job—there was no stress, it was an easy job, I was working mostly at night, and it was not a full-time job for me, maybe thirty hours a week. Leaving my apartment at five, going through the crowds and taking the subway, going to work with my work clothes on, I felt that no one was going to mess with me, no one could mess with me, I had nothing to lose. Because at the same time I felt that I was right there in the current; that was why no one could mess with me, you see, because it was the great current, and I was drifting in the middle of it with Bernie and Justice and Archie and that big crazy brother with the knife. And we were just doing the work.

"Say, you have probably already figured this one out, boy, but let me tell you anyway, the most terrible thing is not to do anything. It's an insight that not everyone has, like these freight guys I was working with. I never told them that I had a trust fund, but if I . . . well, sometimes I'd kid them . . . 'What do you want to buy lottery tickets for?' or maybe they played the horses, and I would say, 'Well, what the hell are you going to do if you win?' And they said, 'What are you talking about?' And I said, 'Well, what if you win a million, what are you going to do with it? You know, it's just going to mess you up.' And they said, 'Hell, you kiddin', I'd love to get messed up, you call that messed up? You need a psychiatrist, man.'

"Yeah, they were incredulous . . . *if I could just get rid of my job, this terrible job* . . . but that's what gives their life meaning, and *hating* their job gives their life meaning. And then this fantasy of not having to do the job also gives their life meaning.

"That was when I decided to give away my trust fund, all of it except a little cushion, I don't know, maybe ten grand. Since my mother's death it had grown considerably; it had become, well, a burden. In my head . . . it kept talking, *you don't have to do this, you don't have to do that*, and especially, *especially*, you don't have to make any commitments, no sir, not one.

"Natalie, I told her I was getting rid of it. She was a teenager, it was the sixties, and giving things away was the *shtick* then. 'Groovy,' she said, except she hoped I had a job at least. My sensible little sister. I didn't tell my father, because he would have been puzzled by it. He was missing mother—it hadn't even been a year—and I just didn't want to bring that up, the money and all. I was missing her too, but there isn't a lot to think about when you're missing someone, it's just a blank sheet of paper and nothing to say that'll make a difference.

"There was a buddy I had worked with at the Welfare Department, I mentioned it to him in a letter. I remember the phone rang and I picked it up and he said, 'Hello, shit-for-brains. You don't want to do this, this is a mistake.'

" 'Well, I'm gonna do it,' I said.

"The next day I walked into the American Friends Service Committee in New York, and I said, 'I don't want this money,' and I wrote out a check. 'There's only one condition and that is that this is a one-shot deal—I don't want to get letters and appeals or anything like that.' And they said, 'Yeah, sure, we understand. And we'll hold it for ten days, in case you change your mind.' So the deal was, I was supposed to call them in ten days and give them the go-ahead.

"They thought I was nuts, of course. I mean, there I was in my freight yard clothes. They bid me a warm farewell, 'Thank you, Mr. Sayers,' and all that, but they thought I was certifiable. Someone in the office, probably just idly, called the bank, and they found out that the check was real. But then what happened, the funny thing was, I *forgot*, I forgot to call them. So on the tenth day the phone rang, 'Uh, Mr. Sayers, sorry to bother you, Mr. Sayers, sir,' this poor guy stammered, 'about your contribution . . .' 'Oh, yeah, right,' I said, 'cash it.' I reminded them about my condition, and they stuck right to it . . . the only time they got back to me was a couple of months later they invited me to a banquet. They would send a car around, and there would be speeches and toasts and a six-course dinner for a hundred of New York's finest, in order to thank Jackson Sayers, said the engraved invitation. I did not attend. And they never contacted me again. I really was very appreciative of that. It kind of changed things for me at the freight yard."

JACK STOOD UP, stretched, and walked off into the spruce woods—"business," he said; I had some business of my own. When we returned to the dock, he suggested we take the canoe out for a last paddle before hauling it up for the season. It seemed a good idea to me. The lake was calm, the sky empty, far away, detached, as if it really didn't care what happened down here today. Or as if we weren't exactly in the world this morning—it seemed a little like that to me—that we were outside of time, Jack and I, moving along some private tangent with business of our own, and immune somehow to the comments and the criticisms of others.

I knew that whatever he told me, whatever, it would be all right with me.

The canoe was an old Old Town, painted green, with wicker seats, mismatched paddles, and a marginal repair job along the port side. I threw a couple of life jackets in the bottom, just in case, and took the bow because it forgave inexperience and favored crude muscle of which I seemed to be largely constructed . . . when you stopped to think about it. Up to that point, I mean, that September visit with my Uncle Jack Sayers, I hadn't thought to think about much of anything, while Jack had spent his whole life thinking, every step of it. He had a personal code, and I had little more than the free and easy moment.

Neither of us spoke until we cleared the point. The cove was half a small circle, like a gallery, the bank climbing darkly green and serious, the water answering with solid jade, or the depthless green of a dream, and above the water, a twinkling yellowy fairy light flitted around like a secret you couldn't quite catch, but which you suspected was thrilling, maybe a girl you were about to meet, a girl who was going to love everything about you. Or maybe nothing except the secret, the mystery. You could tolerate a lot, it seemed to me, if there was mystery in your life. I had felt it in the West now and then, like a wisp of smoke, and then I had cared less about that day's discontents.

Our paddles punctured the water in relative unison, mine left and Jack's right, feathering, swinging forward, plunging; feathering, swinging forward, and along the way dropping strings of clear beads that did not immediately vanish in the water, but resisted an uncountable beat before joining the greater body. More often than it seemed necessary, I felt Jack dig and angle the blade straight off the stern in order to change our course slightly. The air was cool and dry, without scent, which seemed a scent itself, the scent of newness or promise, the scent of the future very near. I tried to think of Dartmouth, but it was Jack Sayers in his twenties my mind returned to with a strange fascination. Jack had been true to form. His empathy for the freight yard guys . . . true to form. The principles, the discipline, the money, the considered action . . . true to form. But what was wrong? Something. Something was elusively wrong.

Until the age of ten I had a birthmark. It was about the size of a small maple leaf and roughly shaped like one, stretching up the right side of my neck; the dark brown tips actually breached the jaw line and implicated the face. I had been a particularly pretty child, with milky skin any Welsh man would be proud of, and curious squinty blue eyes, lips that painters like to paint, bowing up at the top and pouting out below, the color of a Valentine's Day rose. Mother said that even the pure selfism of a child, usually trained out as quickly as possible, was beguiling in me, so that my training was late and half-hearted, and I grew up more self-indulgent than most. People seemed to enjoy watching me about my greedy youthful enterprises. But there was this birthmark. My fingers used to visit it with an automatic regularity. It was rough in one place, smooth as lip skin in another, the color not a nice brown, and I was fascinated, or my fingers were. To my mother it was an anomaly, something to be excised at the right time; my father went along with her in such matters. But to me, there was something splendid, something even admirable about it, rambling along under my fingertips, so boldly what it was and so disregarding of the rest of me. It seems an odd thing to say, but Uncle Jack reminded me of that birthmark. And while we paddled away from the dock I felt my hand reach up along my neck for the place where it used to be and encounter not the past but the future in the form of a scraggly, half-hearted beard.

Along the broad mouth of the cove and rounding the point the soft *plink* of surfacing trout acted as natural accompaniment to the long subtle note of the canoe stealing through the water, like a bow drawn across low strings, the cello moody or tragic. I felt suddenly and inexplicably excited, and yet very calm, as if I had just stepped into a great and irresistible thing that was carrying me away, a river, or the downward slope of a hill, or a girl I would have to love. There was nothing to do except be there and drift along with the momentum.

Past the point Jack gave a deep pull and laid his paddle across his knees as the canoe slid out across the pale, sky-dyed expanse. I did the same, squinting the sun down to sharp slits, waiting . . . waiting for him to speak. But he didn't say anything. We just sat there in the middle of the lake, not saying anything. The occasional burble of the water around the hull of the Old Town intensified the silence. Jack sat behind me. I didn't turn around. A sensation, a kind of weird amnesia crept up on me: I forgot what I looked like, and more than that, my body seemed to take a back seat, way back in the back row somewhere, and I felt whatever I was to be just eyes seeing out, or just the seeing out. I was also afraid that if I turned about to look for Jack, he would be gone. So I forced myself to wait, gazing at the green ring of land far away and small-seeming, and at the bright spots of the autumn maples that, even as we sat absolutely still in the still canoe, were not lasting. None of it was lasting.

Finally, in a voice of quiet consequence, he said, "There is a lot to forget."

I made a responding sound.

"Not forget after, but *while*, while you're working or dancing or helping a friend, while you're paddling a canoe across a lake, in order to really live each moment. Sure, there are things from the past that count and things coming up in the future that you might want to consider, there's your integrity and good ideas. But there are things that shouldn't count, old business, discriminations, even fine old philosophies can smother you, can tangle like the strangler fig around your seed of a chance to live. It is just a chance, that's the rub. And the responsibility of time never lets up.

"A man has got to clear that stuff away, Kimball, he's got to hack it off and forget about it. Life is not a given, not guaranteed just because you are born into this world. In one sense, yes, the air is rushing in and rushing out, but in other ways, no. Even your own dreams can be toxic. Perhaps especially your own dreams."

I was afraid to turn around and look at Jack. I wanted to hear what happened the day Jack "understood everything," I wanted to get there. To that day with Sam Chase. And I thought, if we don't look at each other, if there aren't any distractions like eyes and gestures, the *otherness* of each other, the story might escape quickly as if it came from both of us, impelled by the force of our conjunction. So I said, "You quit the freight yard."

"I quit."

"Then what? More jobs?"

"Half dozen."

"Which you quit."

"Sure, I quit them. They were just more experiences, just another experience. I was still laboring under the delusion that the more experience you have . . ." He didn't finish the sentence.

"What?"

"You know, I don't know, I don't know what that was all about."

"Notches on a belt?" I offered.

"Naw, I didn't feel that way about it. I just wanted real experiences, I guess, I just wanted to live at the center of things. And I wanted to work with my fellow man. To participate at a palpable level. Even time, I wanted to feel the push and shove of time, to dip the measure stick into the purity of common acts, pull it out, and know exactly where I had been: two runs to Newark, one transfer and a four-block walk to the woman with the dying child, a neck ache and three beers, one pronouncement from Justice Smith, one page on the old Royal . . . I wanted to be down in the engine room, not up on the promenade deck, to be where what was happening everywhere was actually made to happen. Not only did I *not* want a free ride, I wanted to be the ride itself. If that makes any sense.

"But there were too many choices. When there are too many choices cluttering up the scene, and most of them you don't really want, you end up taking them, you know, maybe just to clear it out so you can see what you really do want. And the funny thing is, it's even harder to walk away from something you don't care about. Think about it, Kimball, when you can take it or leave it, you usually end up taking it. Funny, huh?"

I said, "What about women? Lara?"

"Lara," he intoned.

"Did you ever see her again?"

"Oh, sure. Came up to Vermont now and then, summers, Christmas or two. We were still good friends. Still are. By then we had a, well, we had developed a level-eyed affection for each other. And I dated a couple of women with some serious involvement. But there again, they must have sensed that . . ."

"What?"

"Well, I didn't have a career exactly. I suppose I could have thrown one together, but since I hadn't so far, they probably figured I wasn't going to the mat for much of anything. It wouldn't have been right, marrying someone, having a family, when I had no steady job and no promise of one. I guess they quit me the same way I quit the jobs. Maybe they liked me, but maybe they thought I didn't have a life of my own. Maybe they saw something appealing in me, something they thought was authentic, a forced simplicity, the way I saw something honest and straight-ahead and raw in the jobs, a proximity to the real thing. Which I guess is just exposed necessity. Right? The real thing is when you can actually see what you need, when it's naked and obvious and inescapable. When it isn't dressed up to look like something else, or tucked away in the gleaming recesses of the palace. What does a rich man need? Well, first of all, he needs to need *something*. It's how we define ourselves, Kimball, one person needs to sing, another needs to eat, but the needing tells the tale and shapes who we are becoming.

"But why did I quit the jobs? That's what you want to ask. And, Kim, there were five more years of jobs. Why? Well, maybe I lost interest, maybe I thought I had figured it out, the world of the freight yard worker, the world of the dance instructor—I did that for awhile—the starving artist, Lourdes and all of that, the welfare worker, the roustabout . . . oh yeah, I forgot to tell you about Louisiana. I worked as a roustabout in the oil fields. Man, it was hot. *Then* I wished I was handling paper."

We were both quiet for another long while. Jack picked up his paddle, and by his second stroke I had mine in the water too, and we were moseying vaguely south, southwest toward the town beach, which was a pale gray scar in the green circumference. I remember realizing then that some of what Jack Sayers was telling me could not be trusted. He implied that he was dabbling in occupations, and for phony, highfalutin reasons, but I knew, everyone knew, that Jack had a broad and deep feeling for humanity, a huge tenderness that simply could not quit because there was nothing contrived about it, he was born with it, born trying to give himself away, his things and his deeds, to the world, as if he might actually satisfy its unquenchable needs. Maybe he figured it was all he was good for—good for giving away.

"My father," he said, "your grandfather . . . when he died in November of 1975 there was more money. Which I gave away. In case there was anyone left who didn't believe it the first time. Of course, you know, I know now, that it was I who didn't believe it the first time . . . or the second.

"Yeah, I sold the old place in Lake Forest, gave my half of the proceeds away. The summer house I deeded to Natalie. I gave everything away, the stocks and bonds, the cash, everything except enough to buy twenty acres of hill country in Harrow, Vermont, and in May I moved onto that land with a chain saw and a tent. About a week after I arrived a mongrel with a savage eye wandered out of the woods. I gave her some bologna and she never left. Franny. Most dependent dog I have ever known. It got so I had to lift her into the truck even, and there was nothing, absolutely nothing wrong with her legs.

"It took me several months, part of the summer and into the fall, to build the sod house. Ralph Tinkler's barn had burned half down, and he let me have some of the charred beams and planks that were still okay, since his insurance was paying for new. Out past the bend where the old butter line used to run there was a stack of posts soaked in creosote, been there forever; I got some of them too. It was just some kind of shack I was going to build, what I calculated I could achieve with zero experience and practically no money. I wanted to have a garden, so I cut up a bunch of sod and stacked it, and pretty soon I noticed that I had a wall of sod. So I kept stacking it until I had a square, and I thought, well, that'll be my icehouse, because I knew I wasn't going to have any electricity. That'll be a fine icehouse, I thought. But it got later and later in summer, and closer to fall, and I realized I didn't have a place to live in yet. The mongrel and I were still in the tent. So I thought, this may be it, this may be my house, this sod, which became the area where the cot and desk are. I dug down three feet and I added on the kitchen and the root cellar. A buddy of mine knew where there was a big pile of tin, so I got a load of free tin. I put in on the inside walls and on the roof. Then it was November . . . I didn't even have a floor, I just had duckboards, the kind they have all over Venice for the high tides. I'll never forget the day Franny and I moved in. I still hadn't put tarpaper on the roof, it was just boards I could see through, and it was raining, and I remember going to bed with a raincoat over my head. But it was one of those great moments, just to spend that first night in a house that was my house, and which I had built with next to nothing.

"And I have been there ever since," he announced with a whimsical and yet strangely challenging pride. It made me think that maybe Jack had had something he needed to prove, which I guess was a pretty obvious thought to have.

"And Lara?" I ventured to ask again.

"Well, I saw Lara more often then. She knew about the second lot of money, and she clearly did not think much of what I had done. Because, as I mentioned yesterday, she could see what was not obvious about it, what I was avoiding. Even my sod house, Lara used to say, let's see . . . she called it the *architecture of escape*. Anyway, what did it matter? She was married by then, had one boy and another one on the way. Her husband, Tom Greenfield, he's a builder, a good one. And a real decent guy, I think, I've always thought that, just the kind of guy Lara deserved. Right." Jack nodded as if he needed to agree with what he had just said, scratched his chin, and gazed out across the water. He seemed to be having trouble breathing, or at least he was having to work some at it.

"I had an opportunity to give her a hand once several years later, five years. I was glad for that, for that opportunity. Tom and the boys—there were two by then—had gone off on a special fishing expedition to Florida. His folks were paying for it. It was some big deal, with a guide and all, down in the Keys. While they were gone we had a terrible ice storm, really horrendous. The ice was three inches thick on the power lines and the weight of it finally snapped them. They ended up rewiring the whole area, and it was two weeks before the power was restored. The maple trees, the ones on the common, and in the yards and lining the drives, the sugar bushes—the ice had cocooned them as well, down to the littlest twig, and it was an awful sad sound, the shattering crack of the branches giving up and rattling down like a tangle of old bones.

Then came the sound of the chain saws, day after day the whine of the chain saws dropping to a moan as the bar sunk in deep, and then when it cut all the way through, rising just a little to idle, to whimper like a man not used to whimpering, then the revving, the crying out . . . Jesus, the sound of the chain saws drove me crazy.

"Lara and her family were living out the Sibley Road then, not in the village, but the Sibley Road bridge had lost a couple of struts from a truck that had slid out of control on the ice. The town hung a Closed sign at the bridge, until they could get back to fix it, which left Lara fairly isolated. I snowshoed over to her place to give a hand with things."

Several loaded minutes of silence, dense and inscrutable, trudged by. Then Jack murmured, "Yes . . . I was glad for that opportunity," and he began digging his fists into his eyes, the way a kid does, and kind of coughing or clearing his throat.

"You okay?" I said.

"Yeah, right, yeah, I'm fine. Pollen."

Naturally, nothing bloomed at that time of year.

The canoe nosed toward the town beach, which seemed to await Jack and me, as if we were explorers with a mere hundred yards of water to cross before discovering some place entirely new. But there was contrary evidence. From a grassy terrace where picnic tables sat the sand sloped, not gradually, for there was not a lot of genuine sand, it was a kind of gritty, muddy hybrid, but it sufficed as more than token and swung hastily down to the water where small wind-made waves dropped like toy replicas, sized for the children who were not there that Indian summer's day. An empty ocean beach is wild and primordial and uplifting, but a deserted village beach on a lake is a sad place, full of memories and echoes—the voices of children, radios, Marco Polo, smells of lotion and roasting wieners, warm beer, sun-soaked skin, the towels and suits and blankets patched about in a burst of rag-tag colors, the different bodies belonging to the rest of humanity, the luscious one belonging to Her. Her of the summer. And now of summer's memory.

I thought back over what Jack had just told me. I said, "The girl you mentioned yesterday, the one who is pregnant, she's Lara's daughter?"

"Heidi," he said, but it was almost a whisper.

Abruptly Jack turned the canoe. We paddled at a strong pace until we reached the cove, and this time Jack made no adjustments in direction, the initial aim and the force of momentum brought us there in less than twenty minutes. There was a fierce, smooth intensity to his paddling that prevented conversation or community; we were a two-part machine moving full tilt with a purpose that, beyond reaching the dock, was indeterminate. We were just the line connecting two points.

Jack was out first, hauling up his end of the Old Town, his face closed. Ten paces south of the dock the boathouse leaned into the bank; we carried the canoe filled with nautical miscellany along the narrow path, muscled the whole thing up on our shoulders and suspended it from ceiling hooks, like a hammock, because the rest of the room was already jammed with an old Dutchman, an aluminum dingy, parts of a pontoon I had destroyed at age twelve, the flotsam and jetsam of generations of Sayers and relations. A heavy rusted padlock hung from the boathouse door; Jack snapped it and started up the path, his boots pounding, and I had to jog a little to catch up. I could hear his breathing, raspy and uneven.

"You are going to tell me," I said, "you are going to finish." I knew then what I had known all along—darting off in the oblique space, like the motion of a bat at twilight—I knew that Jack Sayers was avoiding something.

"Yes," he snarled, and when he turned, I saw that it was less anger than confusion, a baffling conundrum of private making, that had infected his voice, because looking at me behind him on the path he said "yes" again, this time with gentle defeat, as if an insistent child had pestered him. Or as if I were some messenger of Fate, and he had no choice in the matter.

Crossing the road, we tramped through Domm's sugar bush, which spread above us like a vault of yellow-tiled mosaic fitted directly into the sky itself, the green gone from every leaf and every single one wholly yellow, with the blue-sky borders around each, and then the branches black against the yellowness, the ground yellow too with the fallen pieces. It was breathtaking, and it was no place to converse. A breeze followed us into the woods, and the light, the light, the pure and dazzling flickering light . . . I turned my face about, blinking, gave a happy "hey, *la lumière*," I shouted, and Jack swung around with a startled, almost boyish smile, and nodded and replied, "*la lumière*."

Then we reached the upper edge and the sun reappeared, a dull, distant throb over a cornfield harvested long ago. Jack dropped into the stubble. For half a second I thought he had fallen, and I remember a pang of worry—*I will never know*. But he was propping himself up on one elbow, his barrel chest seeming oddly bigger than I remembered, like someone who has just taken a very deep breath, his eyes disenchanted and hungry, facing into the sun, I assumed, for the niggardly warmth it might offer. Behind and above him a little, I sat myself down, to make it easier, or to give him privacy, or to engage in some brand of my own avoidance. There were the woods, the lake, the village houses and church steeple off to the left, nestled like white eggs in among the fiery colors, and in the distance, the long, green line of the mountains. An autumn postcard from Harrow, Vermont.

"You are what, twenty years old?"

"Yeah."

"I have known you all of your life, Kimball Sayers Dodge, and all of your life I have been here. No moves, no so-called improvements or advancements, no trips even. Here. I could list off the jobs but why bother? Odd jobs, jobs that made me a few bucks here and there. Because a few bucks here and there was all I needed. In fact, about three hundred a month. I wanted to be the self-possessed man. By giving everything away, cutting down to the essential, I had hoped to possess just that, only that, at least that—myself.

"I thought I could feel the push and shove of time, the irresistible current surrounding me. But I was the one pushing. My principles . . . principle this, principle that. And I the willing victim, the sacrificial lamb, the first and last timber on the bonfire of my principles." He picked up a stone, rubbed the dirt off with his thumb, to see if it was anything special, I thought, then he tossed it away.

"At each juncture, each job, each turn in the road, I adopted new principles. They were my children. By the time I came to settle in Harrow, I had them all assembled, hair combed, teeth brushed, shirts tucked in, what I would and would not do, what I believed and did not believe. And I took care of them, I was faithful to them, I adhered to them with a fatal purity of vision. They were made of me and I was made of them. I did not adjust well. It is the nature of principles precisely not to adjust well. They are not soft, like flesh; they are hard and abstract with many edges, some of them so sharp that you don't really notice when they are cutting deep into a part of you that you might have cared about. A part of you that was alive.

"But life . . . matters of life, they pass—hunger, desire, joy, curiosity, shame, health, wealth, friends, even love, the dust and detritus of dailiness blowing in and out open windows, and the open windows just a quaint way of giving shape to the time blowing by, and there you are in the middle, Kimball, in the gust of your life passing. Because they don't close, those windows. You can't keep any of it in.

"But a well-made principle rises above the fray like a flag, like a new sun, like the face of someone dead and dearly loved, forever fixed in that final state of loved-ness, mythicized away, away, away into the land of real permanence. That is the only kind of love that lasts, Kim. It is death that preserves love, that hardens around her face like an enamel mask. The face you loved to see, and to see seeing you . . . especially that.

"If there was a great current surrounding me it was the result of selection. My life was my choice, whether or not I really lived it or lived it fully, it was still a life lived. You see, I speak in the past tense now . . . I notice that now, how often I speak in the past tense.

"No," he said, shaking his head, though I had not asked him a question, "I'm not sorry that I did what I did, but I am sorry that I had to do it. And there is a difference. A man does what he has to do. But I wish," he said poignantly, like a boy at Christmas, not sure he should reveal himself, "I wish I could have figured out how to solve the problem . . . the problem of how to live, you know, through a more normal life, had a career, a wife, and a child. It was my choice not to. And neither devouring passions nor the guidebook of practicalities corrupted my life; indeed, my life has been pure of these.

"But one more thing you should know, Kim . . . I have been happy, in the way that we mean *happy* when we have to say it, when someone asks us, or we are thinking pointedly about it. The people I met in my life, and my life, however I lived it, offered me a kind of joy. Sure, it was random, since I was never in a position to expect happiness, to count on it, but oh, it was sweet, when it came knocking, it was as sweet and pure as a girl.

"Well, so it was my choice to live alone, to have no career that I was passionate about. It was my choice to be poor, to let bare necessities determine the direction of my day. And yet any one of those days," he raised a single finger into the cool air, "I could have picked up the telephone, someone else's telephone because I would not allow myself a telephone, and I could have called the bank. Yes. There was a bank. And there was a cushion in the bank, not a big, soft, sink-in cushion, but a cushion, yes, that prevented me from ever being carried away even by the narrow choices that were mine."

Jack picked up another stone and this time tossed it away without polishing it.

I waited, then I said, "Jack."

Then I waited some more.

I heard him sigh.

"CHASE HAD THE chain saw," he began, his voice flattened out, his back huddled against me, the one who was listening, as if against an approaching storm. "Chase had it but I had had it first. Things would have been different with that simple reversal . . . if he had had it first and I had had it later, after lunch.

"We walked into the clearing and I went to work, making a way through the brush so I could get at the base of a medium-sized maple. Sam dragged off the brush. Then I was ready to drop the tree, and the fell was clean, the base jumped a foot or so, but the direction was right. I limbed it up, then cut the trunk into sections. Chase did all the dragging, and he kicked the big sections loose and rolled them into the clearing where we were going to cut them down to sixteen inches and split them. I began on a spruce. I usually throw in a certain percentage of softwood, spruce or pine, for starting up a fire, and for late in the season when it isn't so cold. The spruce was monstrous, what they call a bull spruce, knobby with burls, a good load of wood, but it pinched the bar and we had to use the wedges, persuade it this way and that, give it a shove, and still it twisted off at the end and took out a couple of young white birches.

"We decided to eat lunch and think about it.

"It wasn't so warm that the sawdust stuck to your face, and there weren't any bugs to speak of, that late in the summer, and as I mentioned, it was a beautiful day. Sam Chase had been working hard and steady. And despite the news that morning . . . well, I was trying to feel better about things. It is in my nature, to try.

"We were hungry; we were eating our sandwiches. He handed me a can of cola, the bag of chips. He had a respectful way of passing things, and you couldn't tell if it was real or not. There were five sandwiches and we had each eaten two when Sam took out his pocketknife and laid the fifth sandwich on the sawed face of a log, and made an incision as neat as a surgeon's. One half was noticeably larger than the other, an intentional error, I assumed, and it was this half he passed to me without a word.

"We had talked, a phrase here, a word there, having to do with the work. But since the earlier subject of my essay we had not, well, we had not chatted. I looked at the big half of the sandwich in my hand. And I said in a jocular, manly voice, *har har* and all that, 'How're you making out with the ladies these days, Sam?'

" 'Not bad,' he replied.

" 'Any keepers?'

" 'Hardly.'

" 'You mean you're never going to settle down?'

" 'I don't believe so.'

" 'Well, now, why is that?'

"He paused to think. He had a showy way of thinking, head cocked, brow crinkled, a faint *humming* sound in the back of his throat. 'It seems I'm not fond of compromise,' he said at last, and wearing a wispy smile that was appealing for its delicacy, for the understatement it implied.

"I thought about that for a while. It made some sense to me, of course—I myself had not been one to compromise, though for different reasons. I finished my sandwich, took a glug of cola, and was reaching for the baggie of cookies when Sam Chase added, 'I had to impress that upon a young lady last month.'

" 'What, that you don't like to compromise?'

" 'That's right.' He made a gesture in the air with his hand, lax and indiscriminate.

"I thought about that while I ate the cookies. Sam peeled an orange. There was something in the way he had said, 'that's right,' a clipped satisfaction . . . and the gesture, like the half-lazy swipe of a bear's paw when the prey is already down and dying . . . *that's right*; I did not understand it then.

"I sat in the shade and I watched Sam Chase. He wiped his mouth with a white napkin, made two folds, and slid the napkin into his shirt pocket. I noticed how sleek and clean his features were, the modeled planes of his face, how composed his expression, as if nothing could ever really bother him. I watched him pack up our lunch remains with a deft and methodical efficiency, rolling the plastic wrap into a single thin tube, crushing the cola cans so that they were as flat as coasters, placing the orange peels in a small Ziplock and sealing it with a run of fingertips. After he had folded down the top of the chip bag, he used the leather punch blade on his knife to poke two holes through the pleats of the bag about three inches apart, then he found a long pliant twig and wove it through the holes so that the bag would not open. It was clever in the way that Sam Chase was clever, making do with whatever was available, but making it work regardless.

"I was still thinking about what he said, but it was not real thought, there were no words lining up in my head, making meaning, there was only a sound like the hollow sound of knocking on a door at the end of a hall, and the knocking would not quit, and you did not really want to walk all the way down that cold hall with the leaden walls and the menacing gleam in the floor, you did not want to see who it was or find out what they wanted because something in the knocking told you that you were not going to like it, that they were going to ask something of you that would be very very hard.

"Finally Chase rose and dusted off his pants. Behind him, I too rose. I saw my hand reach forward, the fingers curl around his shoulder, to stop him. 'Chase,' I said. I seemed to be listening to my own voice, as if it belonged to someone else, a third man.

"He flicked his eyes my direction. We were still in the shade, but I could see the gleam.

" 'Are you saying that you forced this young lady?'

"He didn't answer me. Or he did. He looked at me—we were about the same height—and the skin around his eyes gave a twitch, an almost imperceptible leaping-up, as though he were sharing with me a secret he thought I would enjoy knowing.

"I said, 'You forced her to have sex with you?'

" 'Forced?' Again, there was the lax gesture. 'Well . . . that would involve liberal interpretation. You know how these, uh, rustics are, they might need a guiding hand. Of course, things sometimes go smoother if the hand is adorned with brass knuckles. Helps them to understand just how badly they want it.'

"But the knocking did not stop, Kim. Ah man . . . it should have stopped then, but it did not. And the hall was now on the basement floor, the basement floor of an enormous building, a hospital maybe, and the door was the door to the outside, and the knocking was louder but not angry, it was pathetic and steadfast, the knock of someone who needs help and who is going to keep asking until they get it. And I heard the smothered voice that was mine say, 'Who was the girl?'

"He was walking away. I could not see his face. I watched him shrug, a quick, slight, effortless motion, twitching up, down, a shrug of no account, really. He said, 'Just one of the local yokels,' and gave his head a vague yank to the side, as if he was looking for something he had very little interest in finding. 'Her name is Heidi,' he said, 'yeah, Heidi.'

" 'Greenfield?'

" 'Green as the fields of the Lord. And a hot little slut, too,' he added. Then he picked up the chain saw and strolled back into the woods where the bull spruce was waiting.

"I don't remember what happened next; nothing, everything. My mind seemed to lug down and stall, flooded with rage. He was cutting and I was dragging. Heidi, Lara's Heidi . . . with this thing who called himself a human being . . . he had the chain saw and I was pulling at the slash . . . I knew one thing, one small, sharp, pure piece of fact: that Sam Chase would have to pay, somehow he would pay. But I was still having trouble thinking past the fury wadding up inside my head like a big fist.

"Chase was cutting and I was dragging, and the air was close around me as the chain saw filled it with a whine and cry. The obliterating sound, the prolonged scream it spiked through my head . . . there was no room for anything else, so I did not have to think even if I could have.

"The dragging was more arduous and I began to feel dizzy. Chase nicked off the branches with the rounded end of the bar, and I grabbed them by their tip twigs and pulled them clear of the trunk, so that he could keep nicking them off, one after another, without interruption. Shorn of its green and lofty outreaching arms, the spruce was hideous: the bulbous growths of the burls, some of them a foot in diameter, distorted its girth, there were patches of a gray, scabrous lichen, and the sap oozed like running sores. The trunk was still attached to its base by a few stubborn splinters, but it gave Chase an angled prop; he would be able to bring the saw bar all the way through into air. Toward the crown of the spruce, for about the last third of its length, the two young birches that had been bent over and brought to their knees, held the weight of the tree. It was both blessing and curse: to top it Chase would not have to cut over and under, he would have clearance to rip straight down through without dropping the bar into the dirt, but he would have to examine the birch before each cut, searching for trapped branches that might spring free without the weight of the spruce.

"When he had cut the lower sections and I had freed them and rolled them down into the clearing, he began working up along the taper, the chain saw whining high, then muffling down to a low, strangled moan as the teeth of the chain dug deep into the wood. It was then I seemed to hear the other chain saws, the ones that were filling the air so many . . . no, not that many, it wasn't that many years ago, when the maples, entombed in ice, broke with the weight, and I strapped on my snowshoes and crossed over to Lara's house to give her a hand, and from the top of Tufton Hill I could hear the chain saws in the village and around the lake, cutting into what were healthy maples, cutting into principle. Out Sibley Road, in the dale, you could not hear the saws. It was another world, whole and separate, in Lara's house. The bridge was down, and we were apart from the world, and yet there in her eyes it *was* the world, and for a few days nothing else had meaning, we did not need it to mean, we did not care if it meant anything, where we were. We were living in the house together, that was all. For three days. I could not hear the chain saws beyond Tufton Hill, and it was as if none of it was really happening, none of it."

Shifting his position, Uncle Jack stretched out his left leg and brought up the right, resting an arm on the knee, and then he picked up a piece of cornstalk and began poking at the black dirt with it for something he hoped yet to find, it seemed, a small lost item. Time went on.

"So, Sam Chase . . ." I gently urged.

"Yeah. Chase. He had the chain saw. And I saw the branch of the young birch, white and so supple that it had not snapped, it had only bent in half right under the spruce. From where he stood Chase could not see it. But I saw it. It seemed to register automatically the way people you have known all of your life greet you without really greeting you, without really seeing you. For much of my life I had been cutting wood, and I knew the suppressed authority of the bent branch.

"I saw the branch beneath the heavy spruce that Sam Chase was just then cutting into, just running the bar across, and all of my sympathies washed over the thin, white, bowed branch. And there was a suppressed person behind the one who was seeing this who wanted to see something else, to see the branch leap up unexpectedly, triumphantly. This suppressed person, he was with the old French couple on their knees in the late night, *Sainte Marie, Mère de Dieu, prier pour nous, pauvres pêcheurs* . . . He was at Lourdes with the bandaged woman, and he saw her see the light, and with her hand he slipped as she slipped into the darkness . . . He hid with the log lady behind the downfall of her hair, he was brother to the ragpickers . . . son to the dead men of Verdun. In Baumholder he was faithful to Marie of Brazil, and he was with her when she was not, when she lay with other men . . . and he, the suppressed person, was the revelation that Jack Sayers waited for in the room half-buried beneath Chicago's skid row, yes, *he* was the revelation, who needed to urinate, to eat, to choose before his own god; he was there on the edge of Louis the Sheik's black sheets, saying that he wanted to write, and in Louis the Sheik's sad flamboyant ridiculous glorious name of self-celebration, for *the crow doth sing as sweetly as the lark when neither is attended.* And he, this suppressed person, he came to Harrow, Vermont, to marry Lara Casey, to make children with her, and to use up, to bust up, time . . . but he was . . . not worthy . . . afraid . . . too late . . . He came to Harrow with desire in his hands, and around that desire he, the other Jack, spun a net of responsibilities that the desire itself had triggered, like a fly ticking a spider's web, until the desire, the love, it was love, the love was wrapped up tightly, encased and preserved but never consumed, no, never."

Jack was crying then.

I touched the flat of my hand to his back. My throat was dry and knotted up.

"Because this suppressed person, Kim, it was also he who saw the bent branch waiting, its final authority; who shouted above the moaning chain saw, 'The girl.' *Ah, the girl, the girl* . . .

"Chase yanked the saw out of the spruce, turned it to the side and let it idle like a dangerous dog. I noticed that he was less than two inches from cutting through the trunk.

" 'What?' he hollered back.

" 'The girl,' I repeated, 'Heidi,' I said, saying her name, which was probably what settled the matter for me. 'Why? Why did you have to do that?' Why *did* he? When he had had so many and could have so many more, when he didn't care, when he could take it or leave it, why didn't he leave it? I had left it, I had spent my life leaving it, why didn't he just leave that one . . .

"But Chase cut me off with a laugh. 'Jack,' he grinned, 'you're such a romantic. How touching.' Then he dropped the bar back into the slot, a raw deep wound by now, and I watched him finish cutting through into the savage air. A mere second. The birch branch leapt up and kicked the chain saw into his face. He was still grinning, and the grin, intact, slid off with the flesh.

"Jesus Christ, Jesus Christ," Jack kept saying, shaking his head, "Jesus Christ, *pauvres pêcheurs*."

All around us a casual wind wove through the corn stubble, and the dry leaves still clinging to the short, naked stalks raised a papery rattle in protest.

"Jesus," said Jack again, and again I listened to the wind rattling faintly among the dead leaves. Because by now my eyes were closed to the present.

"There wasn't time," he said, "there just wasn't time to leave him and go for help, he would have bled to death before I could get back. He had to walk, I made him walk the mile out to the truck, holding half his face on with his hand, the one eye squirting out now and then between his fingers and dangling by a couple of threads of living matter, and the blood flowing, just flowing from him. We got to the truck and he fell across the seat, and I closed his door, and when I climbed in he put his head on my lap, ah man, Jesus, he put his head on my lap and looked up at me with his ravaged face and his one eye loose, and the other one just watching me with a kind of bleak wonder.

"Thirty-seven miles to the hospital on winding, two-lane roads. He was still alive when I got him there. And he was alive the next day when I went down. And the day after he was dead. They had called in a plastic surgeon, and the guy was disappointed; he had done a neat job of it, sewing the face back on, though it wouldn't have ever been good-looking again.

"The other doctor, the G.P., he told me that I couldn't have done anymore than I had done. He said that Mr. Chase was just not very strong. The trauma, he said. Then he told me that they hadn't been able to locate any family, did I know of any?

" 'No,' I said, and left."

DOWN BELOW US in the corn stubble three crows lighted, flapping up in a sudden chaos and dropping again, like pieces of torn black paper caught in a fugitive wind. They were arguing over something, whatever crows eat probably, and their *caw-cawing* seemed to shred the air itself. A milk tanker gleamed along the road, its air brakes blustering through the village, then easing off on the long straight climb to the next farm. Jack stood. The crows scattered to treetops, wobbling and waiting for our departure. We hiked back to the Courchaines' in silence.

It made some sense to me, what had happened, because of Jack's great feeling for the rest of us, and because of his principles, the right and wrong of it. At the same time, it didn't make *enough* sense to me: he knew Sam Chase was a player, he knew that going into the day; and the girl was okay, except for being pregnant. And it couldn't have been the essay; it couldn't have even been just the rape . . . if that was what it was. But something about that day or that moment had invoked his whole life, as he said, something had called up the suppressed person, but I could not see what it was exactly. And I felt again that blurry submerged sensation of trying to see through water what was real.

When we reached the Courchaines' he started up the hill to his place, waving me off. I called him, and he stopped. I thought I had to say something; I guess I wanted to say something. So I said, "It was mostly an accident, it was okay, what happened, you know, in a way it was definitely okay, I think, in the big picture. An accident."

He turned on me, and there was something wild around his eyes. "No, it was not an accident. Don't ever think it was an accident, boy, don't ever call it that. I claim that moment . . . and a few other moments in my life, too. But you are right about one thing, it was okay, it *is* okay."

There wasn't any despair in Jack's voice. What I heard was strong and unambiguous, a bell ringing across a clear night.

"So is this why you won't do anything about the cancer?"

We stood looking at each other for the longest minute.

Finally, Jack offered an equivocal shrug.

I had wanted to find out what Jack knew, what he had learned. I realized then that Jack Sayers knew himself. That was what he had found out, what he knew. Just that, all of that. Himself. It struck me as both simple and monumental.

My whole body felt supercharged; I couldn't think what to call what I was feeling, but it was a hell of a lot bigger than love even. It was like what Jack had said about feeling the gust of your life; I could feel the gust of our lives, and it was full of smells and memories; it had distance, and a big, quiet mystery that was somehow intimate too, like a scarf in the gust swirling round my face, and I could almost hear a singing in my ears, *it's okay, it's all okay.*

"Uncle Jack, I leave tomorrow. Classes are starting."

"Right."

"I thought I would take a drive this afternoon to look at the colors."

"Good idea."

"Will you come with me?"

"No."

I paused, pushing dirt around with the toe of my shoe. "And I've absolutely got to call my mother tonight, I thought after supper. Do you want to come down and talk to her?"

"Give her my love," he said, disappearing up the path.

I DIDN'T SLEEP WELL, and I guess I didn't expect to. But even though I was up by six-thirty, I still hadn't beat Gladys, who was already in the kitchen with her sister-in-law, Vivian, making apple pies to freeze for the winter. They had the TV on, and there was a cigarette in a dish near Vivian, and Gladys sipped from a cup of Postum every third or fourth apple she peeled. I asked them how many pies they would make and Vivian said around fifty, which cramped my hands just thinking about it. After sloshing down a cup of coffee and one of Gladys' home-fried donuts, I offered to carry a load of the winter rations out for them. The pies weren't big and bulging with apples like the one Jack and I had put together, not lavish, one-shot deals, but they had a modest sufficiency, their tops uniform and fairly level so that they stacked up nice and tidy in the freezer, like promises that were easy to keep and could be counted on. There might be a lesson in it, I thought, which was a new sort of thought for me to be having; of course, I attributed all new thoughts about the art of living to Jack.

A morning news-talk program came on and we listened to an interview with a young actress who could not stop dithering about how early in the day it was to do an interview. I remember thinking, *because you don't have anything to say, early or late.*

By then I had my hands in the bushel basket with Gladys and Vivian, and it made a nice, funny picture in my head, the three of us. I wished I could have snapped it and sent a copy to my mother and father in the West, who would not have believed it.

The picture was still in my head when a young woman came through the door, evidently to help with the pie making, and Gladys introduced me to Heidi Greenfield. I was stooped over the bowl, an apple in my left hand and a paring knife in my right, and when she came through the door I did a cartoon double take and sat up directly, as if my spine was made of rope and someone had just jerked it straight. The left hand with the apple and the right hand with the knife dangled loose and seemed to go numb at my side, refusing to work. Because Heidi Greenfield was Jack Sayers, or she was Jack's girl ghost, or his sequel. For a moment I was stupefied, and then slowly it came clear. Without any doubt about it, Heidi Greenfield was Jack Sayers' daughter.

Which, in terms of explanations, went the limit.

I watched her in the kitchen, putting on an apron, picking up a paring knife, selecting a half dozen wormless apples. The thick, dark, chocolate brown hair, the squarish face, the Welsh blue eyes, and around them the same curious whimsical play of tiny muscles that seemed to imply that already, *already*, she had interesting humorous comments to make—about us, about the stacks of apple pies, about something she had seen walking up to the farmhouse. And maybe, like her father, about principles and how to conduct one's life.

I was aware that Gladys Courchaine was watching me. And I knew that she knew what I saw. And we both knew that she would never say or confirm anything ever. She had a talent for being quiet.

Heidi (my cousin, I thought) set to work, her ponytail swaying like the arm of a native dancer. My cousin, I thought again, my cousin is carrying Jack's grandchild and Sam Chase's child—which makes us all family to a stranger.

EVENTUALLY I WENT out to the barn to say goodbye to Norm and the boys. Jack's truck was gone, I noticed.

They were still milking the cows, but each stopped to shake my hand with that simple elegance of theirs, and to wish me luck at the school called Dartmouth. I took a last long look around the Cour-chaines' peaceable kingdom, the beautiful holsteins with their quiet eyes, and a deep sniff of sawdust and milk, old hay, fresh manure, the skunk (faintly) who lived under the west wall. Then I crossed the farmyard to the bottom of Jack's path and left a note on the pad tacked to his storage shed. Why he didn't hang around to say goodbye I guessed I understood. After all that had been said . . . well, maybe we had found the center of the current where goodbye and things like that didn't mean much. There, it was all hello and goodbye which meant it wasn't either one. And I didn't say thank you either. That would have made him sad, if I had thanked him, because we had each contributed in our way to what had been said and what had been heard just by being who we were, the right notes struck at the right time, and needing each other to make the harmony. So I just wrote, *Jack*, and a line, and then, *Kim. Jack—Kim*, like the double note of a heartbeat. And so that he would see the names together. Me too, so I could see them together; it seemed very important to me to see them together. After that I wanted to get in the truck and drive, for I was crying like a damned baby. I figured Jack was out driving somewhere too. There is nothing like a long drive to smooth things out.

Gladys did not follow me out the way Westerners usually do, to see you off with hands lifting into a big night sky that is itself lifting like an enormous wave; she stayed in the house with Vivian and Heidi surrounded by bowls of sliced apples and the murmuring TV. The farmhouse receded in the wake of my pickup truck like a white ship on that big, black wave—a wave that might have seemed, if you stopped to think about it, to be carrying us all away.

AUTHOR'S NOTE

When I first conceived of *Pipers at the Gates of Dawn*, I saw it as a short story cycle, along the lines of Sherwood Anderson's *Winesburg, Ohio* or Steinbeck's *The Pastures of Heaven*. I was interested in community—in particular, the insular communities of Vermont where the fact and the idea still coexist—and I thought that by working through a mosaic of characters, I could get at both the social and personal import of community. Eventually, three of the stories elbowed out the rest, which seemed less alive, less thematically substantive. At which point I realized that what I had was a triptych: three narrative panels containing several unifying elements including a single setting, and a character (the hired man) who catalyzes events but is not central to them; three novellas that advance and enrich each other. Together, they seek to examine, among other things, the conflict between the traditional values belonging to communities with established identities, and the increasing pressure of what I call in-migrants from the global village—outsiders whose beliefs tend to be more homogenized yet, ironically, less stable. But of course, the novellas are concerned with intimate community as well: the community between a father and son; husband and wife; even between a man and himself, his past, his principles. If the village (a village not unlike the one in which I live) and its way of life represent the known, then the hired man is the unknown, the man from Nowhere, a stranger whose identity seems as mutable as the weather, who has no commitments, who pursues nothing more than the requital of transient desires.